O'Ceagan's Legacy

O'Ceagan Saga Book 1

Lillian I. Wolfe

This print edition is published by:

Pynhavyn Press

http://www.pynhavynpress.com

Cover Design: GetCovers.com

Digital heart image custom design combining elements from Graphics Factory, used with permission, and hand drawn design by Rene Averett.

FROM THE AUTHOR

FROM LILLIAN I. WOLFE:

I wrote *O'Ceagan's Legacy* ten years ago and published it in 2016. Since then, I have grown as a writer and feel the quality of my writing has greatly improved. Going back and reading the original of this book confirms my thoughts. So, I've reedited the book, enhanced and improved much of the writing, improved scenes and added a few more.

Edition 2 is essentially the same story I told in 2016 but enhanced by my growth as a writer. If you read it back then and buy the book now, I hope you appreciate the changes. If you're new to the book, I hope you love this space fantasy tale as much as I loved writing it. It is the first of a series and the third book is not complete, although two other books in the same series are out. I hope to write the third book in Grania's story in 2026.

Lily Wolfe

ACKNOWLEDGEMENTS

Many thanks to my friends and fellow writers who have offered suggestions and encouragement. Special thanks to my beta readers Patricia Kelly, Judy Glaser, Peggy Hancock, Nancy and Steve Sorbets, Michelle Lüke, and Margaret McGaffey Fisk for taking the time to read and comment. Thank you to the writers at High Sierra Writers who have helped me improve my writing skills over the ten years since this book was originally published. Never underestimate the value of a great critique group and wonderful beta readers. Your input helped fine-tune this story and is very much appreciated.

Thank you to the artist at Get Covers, who created the wonderful book cover that captures the spirit of this novel so well.

CONTENTS

JUMP GATES FROM EARTH TO ERINNUA

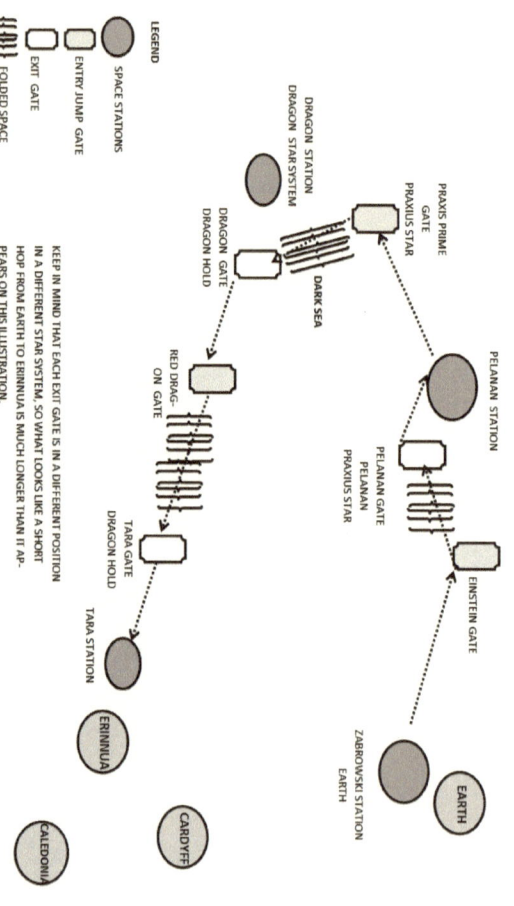

LEGEND

- SPACE STATIONS
- ENTRY JUMP GATE
- EXIT GATE
- FOLDED SPACE

DRAGON STATION
DRAGON STAR SYSTEM

DRAGON GATE
DRAGON HOLD

DARK SEA

PRAXIS PRIME
GATE
PRAXILUS STAR

RED DRAG-
ON GATE

PELANAN STATION

PELANAN GATE
PELANAN
PRAXILUS STAR

EINSTEIN GATE

TARA GATE
DRAGON HOLD

TARA STATION

ZABROWSKI STATION
EARTH

EARTH

ERINNUA

CARDYFF

CALEDONIA

KEEP IN MIND THAT EACH EXIT GATE IS IN A DIFFERENT POSITION IN A DIFFERENT STAR SYSTEM, SO WHAT LOOKS LIKE A SHORT HOP FROM EARTH TO ERINNUA IS MUCH LONGER THAN IT AP-PEARS ON THIS ILLUSTRATION.

PROLOGUE

A WAILING SHRIEK ERUPTED from an ancient-looking stone cottage squatting in a well of land between gentle green hills. Once, the farm next to the cottage might have been a thriving family parcel, but now it wore the run-down look of long unused land. Wooden fences, collapsed and broken, rotted in the grass while bare hints of furrows remained in the land. Only the waft of smoke that rose from the stone chimney sticking out of the perma-thatched roof indicated that anyone lived there.

A short distance from the house, a sturdy white horse paced restlessly from one scraggly tree to another not more than fifty feet from the first. First a bit of a trot, then slowing to a walk, followed by anxious glances toward the cottage as if the animal waited for something to happen. As the sun began to creep below the hill, the eyes visible through an unkempt mane were a deep reddish brown with telltale red rims, a sign of an albino animal. The horse snorted, a cloud of warm breath rising in the cool air like a plume of smoke from his nostrils. He turned his head again toward the cottage, a wild aspect in the eerie-looking eyes.

Front legs lifting from the ground, the pale beast rose in a salute toward the cottage before its hooves fell to the ground again and it resumed pacing.

Inside, the cottage appeared as timeless as the land outside. A mere three rooms, the kitchen shared the end of the main room with a small bedroom off to the left and the bathroom about half the size next to it. Very little seemed modern except for the food dispenser squatting next to the counter to provide meals. They came out hot and fresh so long as the supplies were maintained in the refrigerator portion. Next to it, an ancient-looking hearth blazed with fire fed, not by wood, but by perma-logs that held a month's supply of fuel. The open fireplace shared its warmth with the bedroom on the other side of the common wall.

Within that room, a worn old woman lay in a big four-poster double bed, her deteriorating body barely making a bump in the bed dressings. Moira O'Ceagan Sheehan looked as frail as the years she bore as she teetered on the brink of her mortality. Still, she fought against it with the spirit that had driven her for the past one hundred seventeen years of her life. Despite her faith in God and the Promise, Death was the enemy she'd held off all these decades, and though she faced it, she would never yield willingly.

Even though her eyes were closed, Moira's fingers clutched her rosary, the one her mother's mother had given her as a babe at her baptismal in Wicklow. It had belonged to her grandmother's mother, a family heirloom handed down. Alas, Moira had no immediate family in Ireland to pass it on, and she had dire need of it now, so she clung to it as if it were the key to her life.

A rustle in the room, a sound so subtle that it might have been the whisper of a breeze against a curtain, caught Moira's attention. She cast an intent gaze toward the old oak dresser and a wooden chair facing the bed. Something in the shadows, just a faint outline against the darkened wall, seemed to shift, and Moira sucked in a determined breath.

"So, you're coming for me, are you, Old Hag?" she spat out, her voice barely strong enough to be heard. "Well, I'll not be going with you, so just take your devil spirit away from here."

She gripped the cross on the rosary even tighter, her knuckles turning whiter with the pressure, and she turned her gaze to something beyond the cottage walls. A strained smile stretched her lips as she mouthed a silent prayer asking for protection.

"Ah, Moira O'Ceagan, I am not your enemy," a pleasing feminine voice sighed from the shadows. "I have come for you, 'tis true, but not as the coachman. I am here to bring you affirmation and peace. You know that in your heart. My name is peace itself."

"You do not speak the truth, White Witch. You are the harbinger of Death." The words tumbled out in spurts as the old woman gasped, straining for breath.

"'Tis truth, dear lady. You have heard me keen twice for you thus far, and this is the third, and last time I visit with you. In the language of my kind, I am Bean Sheilan, the bearer of peace. It is your people who made it *bean sidhe* and gave it new meaning. I am here now to sing you to your rest and to mourn your passing. Peace comes. Embrace it."

With that, the high shrill keen of an unearthly creature began as Moira's fingers twitched in spasms against the cross. She drew one last gasp as the piercing sounds that assaulted her ears morphed into sweet, impossibly beautiful music while somewhere in the distance, a horse's whinny echoed around the hills. The keening changed to a low wail of sorrow that continued for several minutes before dying out into a soft sob.

Out of the darkness, fine-boned hands reached to open the first dresser drawer and sift through the contents. They paused to feel the delicate silk of a scarf then let it drop back in the drawer, reaching instead for a drab blue-green woolen shawl and pulling it out. As the hands rose to swing the shawl around her shoulders, the face of an incredibly beautiful, fair woman came into the thin beam of light stealing through the mostly shuttered window. Long, almost pure white hair tumbled below her shoulders, and she lifted it up to rest on the back of the shawl.

She reached into the dresser again, searching through items until she found a passport with a photo of Moira in it. This, she put in a pouch at her waist, then turned to the body on the bed and gently pulled the rosary from the lifeless fingers.

"You have no more need of this. I will ensure it is delivered to your heir." As she added the beads to the pouch, she turned to survey the rest of the room, her eyes taking in each detail of the old cottage.

Turning back to the bed, she laid her hands across the now empty ones of the spent human shell. In a language older than Gaelic, and event hat of the fair people of Ireland before them, she whispered, "Travel safe, dear charge of mine."

She spun away, waved her arms in a circular motion around her head, and chanted, "*Necare', necare', wyth haldah.*" In response, the air began to move, swirling around the room while her arms continued to circle.

The air became gusts of wind gathering the items in the room and pulling them toward the middle. From the fireplace, flames rose to catch the silk of the scarf she had touched earlier. As the fire and destruction began, the white lady bowed her head for a moment and then left the cottage. The cleansing had begun.

She made her way up the gentle slope to the white horse, which had calmed now, and together they began walking away from the burning cottage. Even the perma-thatch wouldn't stand against this fire.

Shouts behind her drew her attention, and she turned to look back again as two men raced across the empty fields of the farm toward the burning house. With the flicker of the flames reflecting in her dark eyes, she gazed up at the darkening sky and the first lights of distant stars. A shudder shook her shoulders, and she knelt to pick up a handful of rich earth and rubbed it against her right cheek, inhaling the scent of peat and new grass.

"My future waits out there, puca. Will you still travel with me?"

Nickering softly, the horse nudged her shoulder.

She stroked his mane with affection, and they resumed trudging toward the highway that would lead them to Dublin.

CHAPTER ONE

Grania

WHILE SHE RAN DOWN the narrow corridor, Grania O'Ceagan tugged her over-tunic into place, slowing enough to step through the sliding door onto the bridge of her ship. *Her ship.* At least for this trip to Earth, she served as the captain, and she glowed with the pride she felt at this moment.

"There she is," her brother, Rory, who manned the communications station, said in welcome.

Not the most glorious announcement of her arrival. But the family owned and operated the *Mo Chroidhe,* and her brothers didn't hesitate to let her know she would get no undue consideration from them.

She slid into her seat in the captain's chair and gazed out the forward window. Just ahead, Zabrowski Station orbited the planet halfway between the inviting blue marble-hued ball and the moon. After over three hundred years in orbit, ultra-steel patches, dents, and scrapes emphasized the station's age. Yet it still passed muster as solid and stable. Built in the wagon wheel design deemed most practical for ship docking, it afforded enough space for up to thirty vessels, from small passenger liners to giant freighters, to dock at one time. Not that the station saw that much activity at once. Most often utilized at half-capacity, a dozen more ships than usual nestled at the docks, leaving only a few open slots.

A small freighter, the Mo Chroidhe, came in at half speed. Grania watched the monitor, showing the dorsal solar sail as it shifted away from the sun to prepare for docking. The ship's automatic thrusters fired, driving it forward a little quicker. Tucking a stray strand of her long auburn hair back into the practical bun at her neck, Grania locked her eyes on the read-outs as they flashed across the monitors, checking their docking speed. Her fingers danced across the control panel, making minor adjustments to the speed and angle.

Behind her, Rory spoke into the comlink to the station, getting final clearance for their docking. His easy-going, cheerful nature reflected on his freckle-sprinkled face and contrasted with the captain's intense, all-business one. "Mo Chroidhe is standing by for docking, Zabrowski," he said, leaning toward the computer's microphone. "Do ya' have a berth for us?"

"Copy that, Mo Chroidhe," a stern woman's voice on the station replied. "You're cleared for gate seventeen, that's one-seven. Estimated docking time is ten mites."

Rory glanced at his sister to see her acknowledgment with a thumb-up signal. "Copy that, Zabrowski. We're cutting engines and retracting sails now." Even as he said it, he made a chopping motion to his brother Brendan, who keyed in the sequence to fold down all the sails except the dorsal one.

Despite his dark, intense looks, Brendan looked younger than his siblings. Nonetheless, he knew his job, and the sails dropped as he adjusted the engine power to slow the ship for docking. "We're at quarter, Grania," he called, a smile slipping onto his lips. "Smooth as butter from here, right?" His voice, like Rory's, carried the undertone of an Irish brogue.

"Aye, that it is," Grania replied, giving him a brief glance before her eyes returned to the screen to watch the live image as the ship aligned with the docking gate. Automated process or not, her granda had drummed into her to never leave these things to chance, so she double-checked his work. A system could fail, and a person had to be ready for anything.

When they were almost on it, Brendan began the countdown to docking, calling out meters rather than seconds. At thirty, he lowered the dorsal sail, which folded neatly on top of the ship. At ten, he cut the engine power, allowing just the momentum to carry them the rest of the way. "Three ... two ... one."

The ship rocked from a slight bump as the nose cone of the ship eased into the docking receptor. Locks caught it and secured it to the station. "That's it! We're in," Brendan announced. Grania heard the pride and happiness in his voice.

"*Biochas la Dia*," Grania said, the old Irish thanks to God rolling off her tongue. "Congratulations on your first Earth station dock, little brother." She grinned at him, sharing his joy. Only eight years earlier, she'd made her own first trip. And this trip ... This trip, she was the captain.

"It wasn't hard." Brendan made light of it. "It's not so different from docking the shuttle at Mac Lir Station."

"Who are you kidding?" Rory challenged the remark, springing from his console to throw an arm around his brother's neck and rough him up a little. "You were nervous, and you know it. And, you had help from Nia. She double-checked everything, all your calcs."

For a few moments, Grania studied the station-transmitted image that showed the ship tucked into the docking cone. They provided it to allow the crew to have a valuable visual of the exterior to check for any damage before going out again. For now, she just took pleasure in seeing the old girl safely here.

Mismatched metal patches covered several spots along the body, a few dents bounced sunlight at angles, and it looked like it had traveled hundreds of light years in the space lanes. Near the docking nose of the ship, almost hidden under the cone, a design of intertwined birds within a heart—painted in bold colors—accented the ship's name, *Mo Chroidhe*, My Heart in Gaelic. Beneath that, smaller letters declared the name of its home world,

Erinnua, also known as New Ireland, a mid-sized planet in the Dragon Hold Federation.

Satisfied with the ship's status, Grania switched on the audio from the station, listening to the reports and news being broadcast. Then she crossed the small bridge to stand behind Brendan. "Actually, not so much checking, Rory. The lad had the whole thing pretty much under control. He'll make a decent spacer yet. Good job, little brother."

Giving him an affectionate hug, she winked at Rory and added, "But you'd better get back to that console and get the off-loading details. We want to get this cargo unloaded as soon as possible and get the new crates onboard. We're about three-quarters filled, so we can take some extra if shippers have anything for Dragon Hold."

"On it," Rory replied, resuming his seat, and starting to check the dock schedules to see how long before they could offload.

The control deck door hissed as it slid open and Grania turned to see Nansi, the ship's second engineer, stride onto the deck, a broad grin on her face. "That's it, then, Brendan. Another O'Ceagan logs his first trip to Earth. Your granda will be proud."

Eyes alight with pleasure and hope, Brendan laughed. "Will you be keeping your promise, Nansi?"

Older by many years than the siblings on the deck, Nansi had traveled the space lanes on the Mo Chroidhe longer than half this young group of snappers had been alive. She'd been part of the crew when Brendan and Rory had been born. In fact, Grania was just a small child when Nansi first came onto the ship. Only a little shorter than Grania, Nansi Nic Collene carried her sturdy, fit body in a defiant stance. A wide streak of silver cut through the thick, black hair she'd pulled back into a tight roll at the nape of her neck.

Face serious and eyebrows pulled together, she peered at the youngster as if to say, did I say that? When it came, her hearty laugh rocked the deck with its merriment. "That I will, lad. Drinks at Murphy's Bar are on me tonight. Dinners are on Liam, though."

While the two boys laughed at this assertion, knowing their older brother's stinginess with a coin, Grania just smiled and turned her attention back to the manifest. "Well, let's get the ship locked down and ready for unloading before we start the celebrating."

Still grinning, Brendan sprang to his feet and headed toward the door to follow Nansi. "Aye, Captain. I'll just be giving Nansi a hand in the cargo bay if that's all right?"

Grania nodded, barely glancing at him. "There's a half dozen crates bound for *Cardyff* that we can contract, Rory. They look to be medium-sized, with canned foods and winter clothes, it says. I'm sending a bid on them. Not too much else heading our way."

"How long d'ya think we'll be staying here? Long enough to take a shuttle down?"

"To visit the old homeland? It's possible, but I'm not wanting to stay any longer than it takes to unload and fill up again with new cargo. Docks cost money, boy-o, and Granda expects a profitable return from his ship."

She finished dumping the ship's log onto a data pod for storage and started toward the records vault tucked at the back of the deck, just as Rory muttered, "Well, feck ..."

"What?" Grania deposited the pod in the vault and turned toward Rory.

"They're having a software problem with the dock 'bots and currently they are not working. An engineer is looking at them now, but they say they expect a six to ten Earth-hour delay before they can get them back in service. 'Apologies to all ships, extra credits for docking due to the delay.'"

The station robots were the main dockworkers to get the ships loaded and unloaded, so until they were back in action, the ship couldn't get the cargo off or new cargo on. Grania leaned over Rory's shoulder and read the message for herself, noting the time delays and other details. Although their ship slotted in as the eighth one in line for unloading, they were twenty-third for reloading. That translated to several more hours tacked onto the time once the 'bots were working.

"Feck, indeed," she said, her face tightening in a frown. More of a delay than she hoped for, but nothing to be done about it. "You go ahead with the others for those drinks. I'll log us in with the station and check out the board postings. I'll meet you at Murphy's."

Grania

EVEN THOUGH SHE DIDN'T need to check in with the stationmaster in person, Grania followed the established custom, one that her father and granda adhered to as they traveled, and they taught her to do the same. Besides, she liked this contact with people in the Earth sector of space. They always shared entertaining stories, bits of news, and dropped a tip or two on cargo opportunities.

Not to mention the stationmaster had a handsome assistant by the name of Vilnius, about Grania's age, with whom she enjoyed spending a bit of time. Her step grew a little lighter in anticipation as she approached the station office.

Disappointed, she found only Stationmaster Hartman behind his desk. He looked up and a smile spread across his aged face. "Grania O'Ceagan! Welcome back to Zabrowski. How is your grandfather?" He rose to give her a hug.

"Ah, he hasn't been feeling too well these past few weeks—a bug of some kind that he picked up in Alonzo. It's been the devil to get rid of, but we're hoping he'll be doing better by the time we get back to Erinnua." Grania made light of the severe illness plaguing her granda and hoped that her words were true. Although he'd rallied some before they'd left on this trip, he was still too ill to do any traveling.

Hartman clucked a bit in sympathy. "Well, he's a tough fellow and a fighter, so it will take more than a little germ to keep him down for too long. Give him my regards and tell him I'll have a bottle of Paddy's Black to share with him on the next trip. And," he paused and reached behind his desk to pull out a small bottle, "a smaller version of it to help him get better."

He handed her the pint bottle of blended whiskey, a real treat for her granda to have. One of the best reasons the old man said he had for making the trip to Earth.

"He'll be appreciating that, for sure," she said as she tucked the bottle into her shoulder bag. "We've brought our youngest brother on the trip this time, and I've been thinking that with the unloading delays—"

"Oh, yeah. Sorry about that. The 'bots are an upgraded new version and supposed to be better, but this is the third time this month that the darn program has glitched. Vilnius is down with the programmer now, trying to figure out what happened this time."

Well, that explained Vilnius missing, Grania concluded and hoped she might have a chance to see him later. "Right. That sounds typical. Upgrade problems... Anyway, I thought that since we're delayed, I might take my little brother down to Ireland. So, how is the weather downside, and are there any Earth delays or other things I should be aware of?"

"I haven't received any notifications," he replied as he opened a screen on his computer and reviewed the latest reports from the London station. "Looks like London is clear, and a shuttle will be going down at oh-nine-fifteen station time. There's a connecting one to Dublin about an hour after the shuttle arrives. Looks like decent weather in Ireland; a few clouds, but no rain expected." He rubbed at the beard on his chin. "Makes me wish I could make the trip down with you. Some of the best fishing in the world down there."

"That's what my granda always says," Grania replied, a smile on her face. "He likes the western side for the stream fishing; says his granda taught him there."

"It's a great area," Hartman agreed. "I don't suppose you or your brothers do much of it?"

She shook her head. "Naw, not much. The lakes and streams of Erinnua don't have fish in them. Thanks for the information. I think I'll be seeing about a couple of shuttle tickets."

Grania

BY THE TIME GRANIA joined her crew over an hour later, they were well into celebrating. No matter who or what job, a crewman's first docking at Earth always called for a party. Not that any of her crew needed much of an excuse to head to the nearest bar. For this crew, Murphy's Pub rated as the only place on Zabrowski Station to celebrate. Besides the authentic Irish drinks, it also served honest-to-goodness Earth-style pub food, which made it something of a rarity on any station outside Dragon Hold.

Stepping into the place felt like stepping back in time, or so Grania's granda had told her several times over the years. Finished with wooden walls and illuminated with elegant sconces that were reproductions of antique ones, they provided enough light to see your food, yet make everyone look appealing. Tall stools, all of which were filled with spacers downing a drink and, in some cases, a plate of fish and chips or a steak pie, faced a long, heavy wooden bar off to the right of the entrance. The delectable scents of vinegar, onion, garlic, and herbs from the kitchen wafted through the place, enticing appetites. Recorded Irish music provided the background sound and to someone from Erinnua, it looked, smelled, and tasted like home.

Grania paused just inside and looked around the crowded space, her eyes seeking the group that she knew would be at one of the larger tables at the back. Sure enough, she spotted Rory's red-blond hair just beyond a rowdy group of Arcano cadets.

Of course, Brendan being just a teenager and limited to the one percent alcohol drinks on this station—and only two of those—meant that the honoree had been demoted to non-alcoholic drinks while the rest of the crew grew rowdier. Still, the lad appeared to be having a great time, Grania noted as she located a nearby empty chair and dragged it over to the table the others had commandeered.

"Any word on the loading status, Grania?" Rory asked after she'd ordered a pint of ale. "Have they fixed the problem yet?"

She shrugged. "Not that I heard. I'm guessing we're stuck here for at least twenty-four hours. Possibly longer, depending on how long it takes to get the 'bots working again. Hartman said that Vilnius is giving the programmer a hand so maybe he can figure it out soon."

"Or could be he already has," Liam said, winking and tilting his head to one side, indicating she should look.

Grania twisted a bit to see the bar entrance as a tall, dark-haired, ruggedly handsome man made his way through the crowd of bodies toward their table. Vilnius always knew where to find the crew of the Mo Chroidhe. Spirits lifting along with her body, Grania sprang to his warm, almost crushing, hug.

As he planted a big kiss on her lips, she pressed closer, savoring the moment. Her inner voice muttered, Damn, I shouldn't have rushed to get those tickets. Ah, well, Liam can take Brendan down to the planet.

"I thought you were tied up with this 'bot problem. Is it fixed then?" she asked when she caught her breath after he broke that kiss.

Vilnius scowled a moment, then shrugged. "We'll see. We found a coding line that appeared to be corrupted, so that might be it. Guernsey is correcting it and he'll reboot the system. Then we'll see what happens. So in the meantime, I thought I'd come down here and see my favorite crew. I saw the Mo Chroidhe dock and wanted to get here as soon as I could. It's been a long time, my girl." His smile dazzled, and his deep blue eyes twinkled as he squeezed her again. Then he let go and looked around for another chair. He captured one from a nearby table and pulled it in next to Grania, forcing everyone to squeeze over a little.

"It's really crowded in here tonight," Nansi shouted over the noise.

"All the bars and pubs are packed," Vilnius yelled back. "We've already missed a half dozen departures, so all of those crews are still here and what else is there to do while you wait?"

"Well, there are vid-theaters, aren't there?" Brendan ventured an answer.

Vilnius gave him a look. "There are, but they aren't so exciting. And you are the little brother, yes? I'm Vilnius Majeck." He offered a hand.

"Sorry! This is my brother, Brendan. Bren, meet Vilnius." Grania hastened to make the late introductions as the two men shook hands.

Brendan shot her a tolerant look. "I know who it is, Grania. You've all jabbered about him often enough. But 'tis good to meet you in person, at last."

Vilnius raised an eyebrow. "Jabbered about me? Do tell."

"There's nothing to tell you don't already know," Grania said quickly. "Do you have much time now?"

"I hope enough for one drink if I can get a server. If Guernsey tags me, I'll have to head back to assist with the restart and that will take a while."

"Cold start, huh? I could offer a hand if you'd like. I'm pretty aces with computers," Liam volunteered, a slight slur in his voice.

"Oh, that's all I need. A half-sotted Irishman messing with the machines."

"Hey, I have a way with 'em, ya know. Just like I can sweet-talk the lasses." Liam raised his glass and chugged more beer.

"I just bet you can." Vilnius signaled a server to place an order and just about everyone ordered another round, including Liam. "And that settles that. You don't venture near my computers, Liam O'Ceagan."

They all laughed at the firm proclamation, but Grania knew the problem must be serious and confidential if Vilnius didn't want Liam to lend a hand. Even half-sotted, her brother had a real knack with coding and machines.

After that, the conversation moved away from the station's current problem to the general round of catching up on what Vilnius had been doing since they had last seen him and filling him in on the latest in the O'Ceagan clan. It would have been about six months Earth-time, but just under two rotations around Erinnua's sun. Before they'd gotten through the whole family, Vilnius' comlink chirped an alert from Guernsey and he rose to head back to the station's control center.

Before he left her, he pulled Grania into an enveloping hug and said he hoped to see her before she launched, but it looked like he would be tied up with getting schedules and 'bots straightened around for at least the next twenty hours.

So much for a romantic interlude on this trip. Grania sighed in regret as she watched him saunter away, her heart twitching a bit and relishing the sight of her desirable, sexy man.

CHAPTER TWO

Grania

"SO, THIS IS WHERE Gramps was born?" Brendan asked, standing next to Grania on a hillside overlooking the Wicklow hills south of Dublin. The various shadings of grass, farm fields, and hedges made a patchwork blend of green that seemed to never end.

"Look at all that green, would ya?" he added as he made a three-sixty turn to gaze in every direction. Behind him, the green unfolded all the way to the sea. He and his sister had crossed it about two hours earlier as they took the shuttle from the London spaceport to Dún Laoghaire, the Dublin city harbor and shuttle port.

"Yep, this is it. If you look about five hundred meters to the west, you can just see the framework of a house where he says he came into being." She pointed to a ruined stone cottage to the southwest as she spoke. "And later, the family built that bigger farmhouse off to the right. Another family owns it now. Once Gramps left for the stars, there was no one left to inherit, so he sold it." Like most of their family, they referred to their great-grandfather as Gramps.

"Do we have no relatives left on Earth? I thought Granda talked about an older sister of Gramps that sort of raised him. Did she not have any family?"

Grania shrugged, inhaling the fresh scent from the grass surrounding her. "He spoke about Great Aunt Mo. She was Gramps' older sister, almost sixteen years older if I remember it correctly. Although she took care of him and raised him, she moved away from the farmhouse before Gramps left. Then, she married a barrister in Wicklow City, and they lived there. As near as I know, they had no children. She must be long dead by now. Granda hasn't heard from her for several years."

As she spoke, she gazed at the land again and an odd feeling tugged at her whole body, a strange pull, almost like recognition, within her, as if she could sense every stream and rock in this land. She'd experienced that sensation of being a part of this country—this land—from the first time she'd seen it. Genetic recognition, her father called it. Something about their family being able to connect with the soil that had been their home for many generations before they'd left for the stars. He'd sensed it the first time he came here, just as she'd felt it when her granda had brought her to this spot just after her fifteenth birthday on her first Earth trip.

"We're a unique people, Grania," he'd said. "We are fey, my girl, and we have ties to this land that cannot be broken. No matter where you find Irish people, you'll find they feel a longing and a link to this island. I've heard it said that other Celtic people have similar ties, a deep connection to the homeland. The people of Wales have a word for it. They call it hiraeth and there is no real way to explain it. You just feel it."

Perhaps, she mused, it explained this odd longing to see a land that drew you to it as if to your home. Her father, her brothers, and she, herself, had been born on Erinnua in a star system situated a long distance from this small island in the Atlantic Ocean of Earth. Even her mother, a third generation born on Erinnua, had been so excited to see Ireland the first time she came and had felt the call as soon as she'd first arrived on the land. Grania knew that both Rory and Liam had experienced it also, but she wondered about Brendan. As the most grounded of the family, the serious one, he looked for explanations for everything.

As she looked at him now, Brendan squinted off into the mist in the distance, a puzzled expression on his face. "Something troubling you, Brendan?" she asked.

"'Tis odd," he said, the soft lilt in his deep voice sounding almost reverent. "It's like I've been here before. Like I know it. Fated fairies, I think I have dreamed about this place. Isn't that peculiar?"

Her lips curved into an amused smile at the childish expression they'd all used as kids. While their father had used it instead of stronger language around them, he also applied it when odd things happened, things that defied logical explanation. "Genetic memory, Da calls it. Something within us recognizes this place."

Brendan raised an eyebrow at that as an amused smile touched his mouth. "What about Mum's side of the family? Are they from around here also?"

She shook her head. "No, the Nicmara family came from the western side of the island, a town called Kinvara, up toward a plateau of stone called the Burren. It's a barren-looking area if ever there was one, although several little towns were built around it. It reminds me of the Bergen Plates back home."

"Could we go see it?"

"Not this trip. It's across the country and while 'tis a small island, that's still several hours away. Liam just messaged that the reboot worked, so we're on the schedule to depart in ten hours. So, we have time to see a few more places around here and eat lunch. Then we'll head back to London Port in time to catch the evening shuttle up."

As Brendan turned to follow her back to their vehicle, he asked, "Wasn't there a mad pirate woman around where Mum came from that she named you after?"

Grania slid behind the controls as he climbed into the passenger side. A hint of a smile curled her lips as she recalled those wild stories their mum had told them when they were children. "Grania O'Malley, sometimes referred to as the Pirate Queen. She was a sea captain, had her own ship at a time when it wasn't common for women to go to sea. Aye, she was tough and fierce and went up against England's queen. Mum said I'd be a space captain, just like my namesake who commanded a ship."

"You'll get the Mo Chroidhe one day," Brendan said matter-of-factly, as if that were a given.

"When Granda gives it up, possibly," she replied. "Nothing is certain, lad. He could give it to Liam or Rory... or even you."

He grinned at her. Jeez, that smile lights up his eyes and one day it will bring a sassy young woman to her knees, she thought. Brendan had been blessed with their Da's looks and brains.

"Naw, you're the eldest, and you'll inherit it, for sure. Besides, you're already a grand captain. Didn't Granda let you take the helm this trip? He wouldn't have done that if he didn't think you were the best. You were always destined for it, Nia."

"Maybe," she mused, turning the vehicle back toward Dublin. "You know, destiny doesn't always unfold the way you think it will."

"Now, don't go looking for the pixie in the oatmeal," he admonished, even the tone of it sounding like their father. "Some things do work out. Look at Gramps. Bet he never dreamed when he grew up in that valley that he'd one day leave for the stars and have his own merchant ship. I'd bet fate began working on him from the day he was born."

"And they say you're not a dreamer," Grania laughed. "Fate or circumstances. They could be one and the same. For certain, there was, as there has often been on this island, very little or no work for a young man with no land of his own. So, like many before him, he set sail for a new land. It just happened to be on a distant planet at a time when the space program was putting together a new colony and promised the Irish, Scots, and Welsh they could have their own star system with at least three habitable planets. Quite a huge undertaking, but it held out hope, which was something he didn't have a whole lot of back then."

Brendan stared at the rich-looking green fields where spring crops were already beginning to bear fruit. "It seems like a wonderful, fertile place now. I suppose when Gramps left, Ireland had gotten over-crowded like most of Earth did, huh?"

"Too many people, not enough resources. That's what spurred the first colonies off the planet," Grania said. They were the first of the immigrants, heading to other planets to build a new life. By the time Gramps left Earth, the jump gate technology had developed to a safe level and the gates, 'folded' space to travel through it. Now, we're whizzing across it at rates Gramps can't believe."

"I suppose it's hard for someone his age to grasp wormhole theory." Brendan cast one last look at the peacefully-looking valley and turned back to follow Grania.

Rory

ZABROWSKI STATION EXEMPLIFIED **A** typical, high-profile spaceport, crowded at most times, but exciting with the bustle of spacers from different worlds, different stars. Only a few looked alien since humans had only encountered five other planets with life on them and the natives that had developed there were suited to their own planet. Two races, both from the same planet, weren't air breathers and didn't frequent human spaceports, rarely traveling at all.

On his fifth trip to this station, Rory O'Ceagan still found it exciting and new. Although he liked to explore when he had the chance, he had too much piled on his plate today. Since the reboot of the cargo system had delayed off-load and re-load, and likewise, departures, it meant that more spacers than usual were crowding the narrow corridors and filling the few pubs and recreation rooms on the station. Bored people, hoping to kill a little time, even packed the cinema while waiting until their ships received clearances to unload or load. Even the station ventilators had trouble keeping the mix of odors from food to sweaty bodies from the air.

Amid the crowded venues, Rory pursued the task Grania had set him, finding more cargo bound for the Dragon Hold system or even their next planned trip to Winthrop's Star. So far, he'd checked out six of the eight people who'd posted on the shipping board on the station to find passage for their cargo.

Often the space stations were like swap meets where one ship might bring in a load of cargo that needed transport beyond the station, but the ship itself didn't continue on or went a different direction. Under most circumstances, they found another ship to pick up the cargo to the next destination or final point. With the delays and the number of waiting ships, all but one person he'd contacted had already placed their cargo or weren't willing to pay the transport price he'd set. The one he'd just spoken with had a small shipment, and they had reached an agreement on the price, so that added a little more.

With almost twelve cubic meters remaining in the hold, he hunted for another small load or two to take. As he made his way down the corridor, he updated the ship's available space on the board listing and sent the details on to Nansi, so she could plan for it.

"I've got one empty block down here, boy-o." She sent a verbal back to him, her husky-lilted voice barely audible in the noise.

"I'm working on it. It's a ragin' zoo out here right now. Never saw so many people all in one place. Is everything unloaded now?"

"Aye, it is. Just got the Bergen system one off ten mites ago and the robots are bringing in the new cargo now. Have you heard from Grania?"

"She sent a message that she and Brendan were heading back to London's port ... expected to arrive here by twenty-hundred station time." That gave him about five more hours to fill the spot Nansi mentioned.

"Good. These 'bots need watching, so I'm off."

He grinned at the mental image of Nansi overseeing the worker robots. She disliked and distrusted the mechanicals for all that she earned her living as an engineer. Ship's engines were one thing, however, the mobile 'bots annoyed her. If she didn't program them, she didn't trust them; she'd declared it more than once.

A moment later, his mobile communications unit, or Mobi-com, as almost everyone called it, pinged again with a response to his recent update. "Possible bargain if you can transport me with my cargo," the message informed him.

He considered it for a moment or two. Although the Mo Chroid-he had two passenger cabins, one had become more of a storage unit. The other cabin needed a quick refresh to use. Grania had said she didn't want any travelers on this trip, but it would bring a extra amount of currency to take the cargo and the customer. He replied, "Meet to discuss? Murphy's Pub in ten mites?"

The affirmative answer set Rory's path to a turnaround and back the way he'd come toward the pub. If this worked out, he just might have a full hold for them, plus a passenger. That would be better than they would have had if they hadn't had the delay at the station.

Grania

ALTHOUGH LONDON'S SHUTTLE PORT status showed only moderate delays, the check-in at the gate still snaked around several roped stanchions when Grania and Brendan arrived. They didn't have much time before they needed to board their shuttle, so they scrambled to find the quickest check-in counter they could. Brendan motioned to Grania when he spotted a shorter line near the end of the counters. Even with automated ticketing, it still moved slower than a range tortoise with a bum leg.

As she stepped into the line behind Brendan, Grania noticed an elderly woman standing near the line. Her pale blue eyes looked alert as she scanned the passengers, appearing to seek a specific person. Around one and a half meters in height, the woman somehow stood out, despite her petite stature. Flighty white hair formed a halo around her face as it tucked into a thick bun at the back of her head. She wore a faded blue and green shawl wrapped around her bent, old shoulders. Beside her, a large trunk, about two meters long by one and a quarter meters wide, rested on a lev-dolly. Her eyes met Grania's and held. For a moment or two, something about her gave Grania a chill, as if she recognized this person, although surely, she could not have.

The sensation grew, then changed to unease as the woman made her way, with slow, uneven steps, the short distance to where Grania waited in line. When she spoke, her low voice carried with the lilt of the land they'd just left and with a sense of familiarity that Grania recognized as being like her father's sister, Aunt Catherine.

"Excuse me, lass," the woman said politely. "Might you be the captain of a ship bound for Erinnua?"

Surprised, Grania gaped at her. "I am. How would you know that?"

The woman returned a kind-looking smile. "I messaged up to the space station to inquire if there might be a ship leaving soon for the Dragon Hold system. The stationmaster replied that there was and described you. He said you were downside, and I might find you here. I very much need passage, you see."

"Passage?" Grania repeated, still trying to calculate the likelihood of this woman finding her in the crowd of people here. "You want to book a cabin for yourself?"

Nodding, the woman pointed to her chest, "Aye. 'Tis just me and me travel chest. All I have in the world is in it, and I will not be returning. Just a one-way, lass. I must get there; it is a family thing, you see."

Grania took a few moments to consider the space on the ship. They had one free cabin in satisfactory shape that could be used for a passenger. Unless Rory struck pay dirt on the station, they had room in the hold for the box. "It's fifteen hundred credits for the passage, plus an extra two hundred for your cargo."

"Oh, no," the woman protested, her face falling in sadness. "I have only thirteen hundred credits to me name after the shuttle ticket and I would be wanting the box in my room with me, not in the cargo. It has all me things in it, you see. Please, Captain, I truly must get to Erinnua. Can you not help an old woman out?"

Startled, she almost jumped when Brendan tapped his finger on her arm. She jerked her head to glance at him. He dipped his head toward the counter, indicating the line was moving and they needed to keep up.

"Go ahead," Grania said, snapping her head toward the line. "Keep our place. I'll be along shortly." She had it in her mind to say no, it was a set price; however, the bonus of the extra credits earned for a passenger made her hesitate.

"What is your name, ma'am? Are there no relatives here to help you?" She glanced around, looking for someone who might be with this woman.

"I'm called Moira O'Cairn. And, no, there's no one now. Just distant relatives on Erinnua. That is why I must get there." Even as her eyes pleaded with watery sadness, the woman's name stopped Grania cold.

"Moira ... the same as my twice-great aunt's name," Grania mumbled aloud. Her granda would not forgive her if she left this old lady stranded here.

"Thirteen hundred credits, you say? Well, I'll not take all your money for you'll need some when you get to Erinnua. I'll take you and your chest aboard for twelve hundred." Fated fairies, indeed. What were the odds of an old woman with her gramps' sister's name finding her in a spaceport? Surely, the fates must be at work, and despite everything, Grania still believed in serendipity.

"Bless you, my dear," Moira O'Cairn cried. "I trust your great-great-aunt would approve."

"I never met her, but I expect that she would. Do you have you a passport ready to go?" Grania had already pulled out her mobi-com to transmit the passage information to the Mo Chroidhe and the Port Authority to allow Moira O'Cairn to board for the station with the destination of Erinnua.

"Get checked in for the shuttle flight. The Mo Chroidhe will launch at 23:45 station time, so get on board the ship as soon as you can after we arrive." She glanced over her shoulder to where Brendan stood almost to the front of the line now and scast an anxious stare at her. "If you need a guide on the station, I'll have my brother Brendan escort you to the ship. I'll talk to you more on the shuttle. I have to go."

As the old woman nodded and thanked her again, Grania turned and pushed her way back to where Brendan now stepped to the counter and placed his passport on the scanner pad. As she passed people, she glimpsed the glares as they assumed she cut the line and heard a few unhappy mumbles. Ignoring them, she slapped her passport next to her brother's. In less than a minute, it validated the electronic tickets and popped out two boarding passes.

Grabbing them, Grania led the way to the boarding gate. They still had 20 minutes until the shuttle departed. Already the lounge teemed with passengers. Grania wondered if the old woman would make it onto the shuttle, let alone to the gate on time.

"What was all that about?" Brendan asked after they'd found a pair of seats facing the shuttle pad.

"We have a passenger on the way home."

"Are you kidding me? That old woman?" Eyes wide and mouth dropping open, his expression conveyed his disbelief.

Pulling out her mobi-com, Grania checked the message that said that twelve hundred credits had been transferred to the Mo Chroidhe's account. "No, 'tis not a joke. She just sent the credits."

"But we weren't going to take passengers," Brendan objected. "You said, not this trip."

"What can I say? Something about her struck my heart and she needed to go so desperately. To be with her family, she said. There's no one left here for her, Brendan. How could I tell her no?" She shrugged her shoulders.

Rory

MURPHY'S PUB OVERFLOWED WITH spacers, yet it only took Rory a few minutes to locate his potential client. A dark-blond, bearded man of medium height and a somewhat stout build, he stood alone at the bar rather than seated with any of the small clusters of people who chatted and played card games to pass the time. As Rory strode over to the bar, the man held out a welcoming hand. "From the Mo Chroidhe, I presume?"

"Aye, I am. Rory O'Ceaghan, at your service. And you are Mister Harhiman?" He ignored the offered hand. It wasn't common to shake before a deal and this wasn't one yet.

The hand dropped as easily as Harhiman had extended it. "Right. Ansel Harhiman. I have a load of cargo and myself to be moved to Winthrop's Star. Can your ship do it?"

"Well, that would depend on just how much cargo you have," Rory said with candor. "I have some space still available, so show me what you've got."

Harhiman opened a file on his mobi-com displaying the cargo space requirements, weight, and number of units to move. In moments, Rory calculated the space they would take. "Now, would there be any problem with stacking those crates?" he asked as a precaution. Sometimes the weight could be an issue when stacked, even though most of the standard crates supported multiple levels.

"None at all," Harhiman answered. "They carry trinkets and some luxury goods. Big market for them on the outer planets."

"Well, we have space in the hold to take your shipment, Mr. Harhiman. The problem is the Mo Chroidhe wasn't designed as a passenger ship, so our cabins are all crew cabins, that being they are on the smallish side. We happen to have a free one on this trip, so if you don't mind—"

"The small cabin isn't a problem," Harhiman replied before he could get the words out. "And I'll pay you well for the transport of both my cargo and myself. Would three thousand credits be adequate?"

"Perfectly adequate, sir," he replied, hiding his excitement. Almost double the going rate. Grania will be pleased. He keyed the acceptance into his mobi-com, heard the ping as it went to Harhiman's, and within a minute or two, the credits transferred to the Mo Chroidhe's account. Now, he could shake on it and offered his hand.

"Just out of curiosity, I am wondering why you didn't have a ship pre-arranged here instead of leaving it to chance?"

Harhiman shook on the deal and put on an engaging smile. "To be perfectly honest, when I shipped out to Zabrowski station, I wasn't sure which direction I was going to go once I got here. I had three potential buyers and didn't lock it down until just before we docked. I hoped there would be a ship going out soon to Winthrop's Star or Dragon Hold or even Batterforce from here. Guess I got lucky."

"I'd say we both have a bit of the luck today." Rory grinned back. He'd brought the cargo to almost capacity for the trip home, and he just added a healthy bonus with a passenger. He signaled the bartender for drinks, ready to celebrate. Pulling out his mobi-com, he sent a quick message to Grania to give her the news.

Grania

"OH, FOR CRYING OUT LOUD! Hellfire!" Grania swore as she read the message from Rory.

"What?" Brendan asked, alarmed by her tone.

"Aw, Rory has taken on a passenger from the station," she answered. Her brow wrinkled as her nose wiggled up in irritation. "So now we have two passengers and one cabin."

"What about the second cabin?"

"It's not presentable, Brendan. It's become a fecking storeroom. We'll have to see what we can do when we get back to the ship. Ah well, on the plus side, the off-loading is completed and the 'bots are starting to load the new cargo on. The deck's almost filled, and we are on schedule for departure. Rory's done a fine thing there." She admitted that much, and she couldn't blame the lad for doing his job.

Delayed for fifteen mites already, the shuttle pilot announced they would launch in a few more mites. Grania glanced around the cabin, scanning the faces. "I don't see our passenger here. Do you spot her?"

Shaking his head, he said, "No, I've been keeping an eye out and I didn't see her in the waiting area either. Maybe she couldn't get on this shuttle?"

Just then, a bit of a commotion occurred at the boarding door and the old woman appeared, shuffling onto the shuttle with small, nervous steps. Her eyes darted around in awe as she made her way down the aisle to an available seat a few rows ahead of them. The shuttle attendant followed on her heels and helped her get settled in her seat, pulling the padded seatbelt restraint into place and locking it as Moira's hands fidgeted at her shawl.

"Probably the first time she's ever been on one of these," he mumbled, settling back.

"You're likely right," Grania agreed, still gazing at the old woman. Although she looked so familiar to her, she couldn't place it. One thing was for sure: she didn't peg the woman as a frail flower when they talked at the station. She seemed more than capable after getting herself to the London spaceport and locating her in the place. She may not know how to lock in a seatbelt, but she knew how to survive.

CHAPTER THREE

Grania

"**I WISH YOU'D HAVE** checked with me before taking a passenger, Rory," Grania groused as she stacked boxes and shoved them into a corner of the spare room.

Her brother picked up odds and ends and tossed them into another box to go to the hold. "Well, I wish you'd have told me that you'd booked a passenger," he snapped back. "You'd said you weren't going to take on anyone this trip. I thought you'd be pleased with the extra money and cargo my passenger is bringing."

She straightened and turned to face him, her expression softening. "Don't get me wrong. I am glad for it, and you did a smashing job getting extra cargo. It's just that we don't have time to get this cabin in proper shape for a passenger." She waved her arm at the electronic equipment stuck in one corner, the data server in the other corner, and collections of mismatched items scattered throughout the room. "I'm not sure the sleep capsule is charged or even prepped for a gate jump."

She should have alerted the crew to begin work on the cabin before the shuttle launched from London, but she didn't think of it until they were on the way and the mobi-com link couldn't connect. They wouldn't have had much time for it anyway with getting the cargo swapped out. Still, it presented more of a problem now as she gazed at the clutter in the cabin.

"So, what do you want me to do? Break the agreement with my passenger? Give up my room?" Rory caught the suggestive expression on her face as he said the last. "Oh, that's it, isn't it? Are you wanting to give your granny-lady my cabin?"

"You could bunk in with Liam. Since you two often sleep at different times anyway. Besides he has the extra sleep capsule in engineering since he prefers to be there for jumps."

Rory's normally cheery face twisted into an unhappy scowl. "Fine! I'll do it. Some reward for my valuable work." He wiped his hands on his pants after he dropped the latest load of items in the box. "I'll go move my things, but you can tell Liam."

Grania nodded and watched as he turned to the doorway. "Rory? Thank you. You did a smashing job, and I appreciate this. I know it doesn't seem fair. I just don't see another way around it."

He hesitated, gave an exasperated sigh, and dipped his head in acknowledgment. "I know. You're right."

She finished moving the filled boxes after he left, then closed the door and coded it shut. That cabin would have to be cleared out when they got home, she decided. With a pang, she recalled it had once been her mother's cabin. Not that anything still in it belonged to her mum. Back when Alais O'Ceagan lived, there had been a homey touch to it—lace runners on the vanity, framed images of the house in Galanwy on Erinnua, and of her family. Even the scent of her mother's perfume lingered in her memory, although the cabin smelled of musty, stale air now. She pressed a button on the door controls to clean to and refresh the oxygen.

Many times, she and her mother had shared an afternoon tea in the little cabin, sitting on the narrow bench and just chatting about anything that popped into their heads. She treasured those wonderful memories. Not like the nightmare that came later.

Grania shook herself out of her dark contemplation. They were in the past, and that's where they belonged. She turned away from the cabin and started up the narrow corridor toward the ship's bridge. As she passed the other passenger cabin, she noticed the half-opened door and assumed their guest had boarded to his room. He was talking on a mobi-com, but she caught the words. "... just after the jump. I'll be in touch."

The man's voice sounded pleasant and unaccented. She wondered if she should introduce herself and raised her hand to knock when his face filled the opening. She pulled back in surprise.

"Hello. Was there something you wanted?" he asked, not unfriendly, just a bit brusque.

"Sorry. I was passing by, heading to the bridge, and was about to knock. I'm Grania O'Ceagan, the captain of this ship. Welcome onboard the Mo Chroidhe." She rushed the words to get them out before he got the wrong idea.

The door slid open a little wider, recessing into the wall panel. "Ah, Captain. Your brother speaks high praise about you. It's a pleasure. And thanks for taking on my cargo and myself. I wouldn't have wanted to wait for the next ship out to Winthrop's Star. Sometimes it's several days before you can find passage."

"Aye, that it is," she agreed. "Fortunate for both of us, since we also had room to fill in the cargo bay." Now that she had a better view, she saw Harhiman was an above average handsome man, older than she, and in somewhat fit shape, although a little pudgy at the waist. His long golden-brown hair pulled away from his face into a wrapped short tail that was very much the fashion of Altarus. "We'll be getting underway in about fifty mites. Let Rory know if there's anything you need."

Now smiling, he nodded. "I will, but I'm sure everything is fine."

"Good. I will be talking to you later, no doubt. Breakfast is available from the service unit in the cabin, although you're more than welcome to join the crew for supper tomorrow."

"Dinner at the Captain's table. Quaint custom." His eyes crinkled in amusement as the edges of his mouth tugged upward.

"Not so fancy as that, I'm afraid. Nevertheless, it is a family custom to invite guests to dinner. Until later, sir." She gave a polite nod and turned away to go to the nose of the ship. Yet, she caught the appraising gaze in Harhiman's gray-green eyes and a hint of something less amiable before he pressed the close button on the door.

"IS SHE ON BOARD yet?" Grania asked Rory, stepping onto the bridge.

"Not yet."

"Brendan, where did you leave her?" She pivoted toward her navigator.

"Near the shops, since she wanted to walk around the station a little," he answered, his tone a tad defensive as his eyes widened with concern. "This is her first time on one, Grania, and it's likely a fascinating place to her."

Grania rolled her eyes. "Let's hope we don't have to go hunting for her in the twenty mites before we launch. What about her chest? Is she towing it around, too?"

Brendan shook his head. "No, I brought it aboard myself. It's in her cabin. Whatever she's got in it, that trunk is heavy."

Grania raised an eyebrow. "I thought it would be mostly clothing. Perhaps she has a few household items adding to the weight. You know, packing up what's left of her life on Earth and moving to a new planet must be difficult at her age."

"Difficult at any age, Grania," Nansi said, just catching the end of the conversation as she came onto the bridge. "Liam says there's one last load to board and lock in and we'll be set. We've had to wait for it until it transferred from a ship on the other side of the station. We should be done in about thirty mites. Everything in the engine room is set, double-checked, and ready."

"Sails?"

"Checked them while you were gallivanting on the planet. All fine. No rips or pulls in them. No kinks in the lines. They're set. Have you seen the other passenger yet?"

"Harhiman? Just talked to him a few mites ago." Grania turned her attention back to the pre-launch check.

"And?" Nansi prodded.

"And what? He seems all right. But ... Oh, I don't know. He's fine."

"But what?" Nansi took the seat next to her.

"It's nothing really. Just a feeling. Something seems a little off with him."

Rory turned to stare at her. "What? He's a trader. Nothing odd about that, is there?"

Grania shook her head. "I said it's nothing."

"So what about the old woman?" Nansi asked, changing the subject. "What prompted that?"

"I guess I felt sorry for her," Grania replied, her eyes running down the list of the new cargo they'd loaded. "She seemed so desperate to get to Erinnua, and it's the last of her family there. I felt that Granda would not leave her behind and I couldn't do it either."

"Since when are you a soft touch?" Rory asked.

"Just shut it, Rory," she warned, her eyes narrowing. "Or you'll be the one I'll be sending out to search for her."

He just grinned at her and turned back to his console.

"She'll be an easy one to find," Brendan quipped, an amused twinkle in his eye. "She's the only little old lady with a blue-green shawl on the station."

Sheilan

AT THAT MOMENT, THE crew of the Mo Chroidhe would have been hard-pressed to find Moira O'Cairn, as her passport read. After leaving her travel trunk with Brendan to load, she'd made her way to a station bathroom and shifted into the young woman form she wore most often. After tying the shawl around her slim waist, she took a leisurely stroll around the station, studying everyone and everything she saw.

For Sheilan, this enterprise meant more than an adventure, and the risk was huge. If it went wrong, she could be stuck on a far world forever, never to return to the land of her soul again. Worse, she could be condemned by the tribal council for her actions, which were pushing every rule repeatedly impressed on her. She risked banishment. She could still turn back, reclaim her trunk, and return to Earth on the next shuttle.

But return to what? A purposeless existence with no family to warn or grieve with? An endless wandering across a land that had been lush and sweet when she had first seen life, but now had become worn and over-worked after centuries? Is this what her existence would become if she didn't pursue her plan? That possibility frightened her more than the unknown of space and a new planet.

So, she shook off the worries that tried to reason with her and concentrated on learning as much about this strange new place and what might lie beyond as she could while she explored on the station. Humans were the same, no matter where they were; however, some beings on this space platform weren't quite human. While some were similar, others looked very different. Not that the difference troubled her; she often interacted with odd forms of life. Still, she did wonder about them, where they came from, and why they traveled. What was their home world like? Did they think at all in the same way as humans?

She stood for several minutes, staring out a full window at the docking ports with the backdrop of the stars behind it.

It looks like constant night out here, she thought. For all those dots in space being stars, precious little light showed in the blackness except for the reflection of the moon on the ships. While dark didn't bother her, she'd seen many humans go mad in too much of it with the fears they had of what they couldn't see.

Mulling her ideas over, she strolled along the large curve of the station. It looked like an Earth shopping mall with a theater, clothing stores, foods for sale, and all the other things that humans craved. She came to a bookstore and entered to browse around. A display on one wall showed various maps of different star systems in the Milky Way Galaxy and she read the markings on them as best she could, but most of it made little sense to her. She motioned to a young man who appeared to work in the shop to assist over.

"Excuse me, but can you help me? Is one of these maps of the Dragon Hold system?"

The lad gazed at her with the glossy-eyed stare that young men often got around her, then flashed a smile, and peered at the display. "Let me see." He studied the various maps and shook his head. "No, we don't seem to have one up here."

He bent to thumb through the rack display of dozens of folded maps, but he came up empty-handed. "I'm sorry, miss. We appear to be out of that one. Is there anything else I can help you with?"

"No, that is all I sought. Unless you have a book about it? One with photographs if possible."

He blinked and held up a flat data stick. "Our books are all digital, you know. Do you have a reader?"

"Oh, no, I do not. I did not think ..." She had not shopped for reading material in a long time and as she scanned the store again, she realized that all the displayed books were, in fact, book-sized data screens with the book covers displayed. Below them were dispensers with the data sticks loaded for customers to purchase. "Ah, never mind then. I should have realized."

With a beguiling smile, she swept out of the store and into the hub again. She had hoped to see what Erinnua looked like and if it resembled Eire at all, but she would know soon enough.

She stood for a while outside a place called Moonspin Ink, where she watched a man being tattooed with a serpentine design. After all these millennia, it appeared tattoos remained in vogue. She recalled handsome young warriors who decorated their skin with clan marks and fantastic creatures, real or imagined. Even young women would sometimes mark their skin with them like permanent necklaces and bracelets. She shifted her gaze to her left wrist and pictured a knotted bracelet marked around it. With the thought, the image appeared on her fair skin, a dark blue and blood red twist of lines. She left it for now and moved on, eager to see more.

By the time she needed to shift forms again and go to the ship, Sheilan had seen and absorbed as much as she could of this construct in the sky. She deemed it interesting, but not as enlightening as she had hoped.

Grania

""**THERE'S OUR OTHER PASSENGER,**" Brendan called out as he spotted Moira on the monitor displaying the ramp to their ship. "And in time enough to get her settled in. I'll be seeing to that, Grania." He sprang to his feet as he spoke.

She looked up from her station and caught his eye. "You'd best show her the basics in the cabin. She may not know how the food machine works, and she's probably never seen a jump pod. And be sure to invite her to dinner tomorrow."

"Aye, captain," Brendan acknowledged, a bit formally, as he dashed out before she could add any more.

Grania rolled her eyes. Her youngest brother wasn't that intimidated by her. Sure, he knew to tell a passenger about the basics, but she didn't trust he would remember.

"He's doing fine," Nansi said, as if she'd read her mind.

"I know. Maybe I worry too much."

"Naw, you're just cautious like your granda. He taught you how to run the ship the way he did, and he would remind you whether it was your first or twentieth trip."

Just then the ship's exterior com buzzed and Grania pressed the communication button.

"Permission to come aboard, Captain," the familiar voice asked, and a grin spread across Grania's face as she keyed the door open.

"It's Vilnius."

"That it is. You'd best go see him. There's a little time yet, girl. And it will be a long spell before you're back this way again." She saw the hesitation on Grania's face. "The ship is ready. Go see your man."

With that assurance, Grania hopped out of the chair and out the door as soon as it slid open, her slim frame slipping through the narrow space and into the corridor. She ran down the passage and took the stairs two at a time to meet Vilnius, who paused at only a few steps up when he saw her. "I didn't think you'd have time," she cried as she flung herself into his open arms.

"I made time," he said before he kissed her, pulling her closer to him. "How could I not see you before you left again?"

"But the station..." she started.

"Is under control. Nothing that can't wait..." He paused, lifting his arm to look at his chronometer. "...at least thirty mites. Your cabin?"

"'Tis a narrow bed," she replied with a sheepish grin.

"Won't be the first time, love," he responded as he took her hand and led the way back up the stairs.

Neither of them craved the sex so much as they did the intimacy, the closeness with another person. Both had work that allowed little time to build genuine relationships with a partner. For Grania, only her brothers and Nansi manned the ship, and she fancied no one back home, especially for the short time she spent planet-side.

While she knew Vilnius had more opportunity, few women who passed through the station seemed to interest him. Male crewmembers on ships still outnumbered the women, and most were already in a relationship with one of their mates. Not that Grania gained his attention exclusively; he still proclaimed other women didn't attract him as much. She had known him for several years since she had first arrived as a not-quite-legal teenager at his station, and her grandfather had introduced her.

As they snuggled on Grania's small bed, she wedged against the cabin wall with her body almost spread on top of him. They savored these precious moments that would carry them through the next long separation. Vilnius traced his finger along her collarbone, then up her neck to her chin where he paused, then leaned in and kissed her again. "It's never enough time, Nia. These brief periods are just tiny drops of joy in the deep wells of our lives."

"I know," she answered, her voice a little husky with the emotion overwhelming her feelings. The problem didn't have a workable solution. His life, his work, centered here on Zabrowski Station or maybe someday on another station, where he would be stationmaster. And damn if she didn't want to be a spacer all her life. She'd dreamed about it ever since she could remember. She loved it, just as the sea captains in her family had craved the feel of the ocean. As the grandchild most likely to inherit the Mo Chroidhe one day, she had done everything since she came of age at thirteen to prepare for that task, her desired career.

Not for the first time, she told him, "You could find a woman on Earth and marry, Vilnius. You could have a family on the station. It would be all right."

"That I could. But it wouldn't be with you. You are my light, my joy. When we're together I feel complete and yet, we can't be together all the time. Would you give up this traveler life of yours for life on a station?"

"You know I can't." They'd had this conversation several times. "Nor would you give up your future for life on a ship."

He sighed. "It's a dilemma, isn't it? Two people who love each other but love their work more and seemingly no middle ground."

She laced her fingers through his and laid her head against his chest. "That it is, my dearest. We need a space station that travels, don't we? That would solve it."

He held her closer, his chin on the top of her head. The low-toned alarm on his chrono chimed. "Time to go, Nia. You have a ship to launch, and I have code to analyze."

She pulled herself up, reaching for her shirt. "Something wrong? I thought everything came up fine."

"Oh, it did. The corrupted code looks odd. Not like something that would have just mutated; it's more complex. It seems off. I want to run it through some analysis to see if anything comes from it." He pulled on his uniform jacket before reaching to enfold her in his arms for the last time of this trip. His passionate, bittersweet kiss lingered. "Travel safely, my darling Nia."

"And you stay safe, my love." Her voice dipped on the last words.

Vilnius spun, stepping out the cabin door as Grania pulled her long hair into a twist, pinned it, and headed to the bridge.

CHAPTER FOUR

Grania

"MO CHROIDHE, YOU ARE cleared for departure."

The crisp, feminine voice of Zabrowski station's scheduling computer gave the final advisement, prompting Rory to fire the reverse thruster engines to ease the ship away from the dock. At the navigation station to the rear of the bridge, Brendan made minor adjustments to their course, easing the back end of the ship farther away from the cone.

Grania watched the live view on the screen, seeing the sides of the ship from starboard and port cameras as her vessel made a clear, unhurried exit. Smooth, very smooth.

Her brothers knew what they were doing and how to handle the ship. Even Brendan on his first run to this station had it down. Granda would be proud. No orders necessary now, she observed in silence as the ship began the swing around the end of the docking cone and turned toward Earth for a breath-taking, head-on view of the planet. Even though darkness concealed the landscape down below, tiny dots of light gave shape to the continents where cities lined the coasts and flourished within valleys. Granda told her the nightglow of light had been like that since the 20th century, except for a period of almost twenty years when there had been a shortage of power at the end of the 21st century and night lighting had been discontinued.

At his station, Rory looked up at the view on the screen. "It always gets to me. Every time... every time, we leave." His voice choked, rough, and raw sounding as emotion overwhelmed him. Grania understood. So many family stories connected to this world, so much of their heritage. How could any of them explain the emotion they felt each time they came and left this planet? Even though they'd never lived here, Earth claimed a part of their souls.

The ship completed the rotation, her nose now pointed toward the open space ahead. Rory swung back to his console and brought the running engines online.

"Our course to Einstein's Gate is locked in," Brendan advised. "'Tis looking clear ahead and we have an estimated thirty-two standard hours to arrival. Time to sail deployment is ten mites."

"Sails are cleared, locks are now released," Rory replied as he pressed the buttons to unlock the exterior compartment covers to allow the sails to move into position. "On your mark, Grania."

The captain didn't observe the time so much as the distance from the station. Once they cleared the edge of the moon, they would catch the sun's light, which would give them a boost of power, propelling them to the first jump gate. Grania wanted the sails raised to take full advantage. Mindful of the countdown, she watched as the station diminished in the readings until the green light came on, then glanced at the time and gave the order. "Deploy sails now. You're right on it, Brendan."

Within minutes, the sail poles and spines had snapped into position, pulling the silvery sails into full swirls. The dorsal sail along the top of the ship rotated a few degrees toward the sun's glow emerging around the edge of the moon. Soon, more of the sails caught the light, and energy kicked into the ship's engines.

"We're ready for full power, Grania," Liam's deep baritone sang through the com. "Sails are at fifty percent and climbing."

"Copy that," she replied. "Let's do it, Rory."

With that command, the small freighter, resembling an inflated blowfish in a black sea, darted into the vast darkness of space.

Sheilan

IN HER CABIN, MOIRA, or more properly Sheilan, gazed through the small porthole to watch while Earth grew farther away until the ship began the quick acceleration, leaving her home planet behind. More than those on the bridge, her attachment gripped her very being. For centuries, her world had evolved with this planet. While not precisely born there, she'd come into being through the soil of that island she now left behind.

Although she wore her young woman form now rather than the old lady, neither represented her true form. Sheilan could change back and forth between the two, and she preferred the young woman. A scratching noise emitted from the chest in her room and a hint of a smile curved her lips. The imp wanted out.

Unlocking the chest, she threw the lid back, raised the top drawer within it, and exposed the bottom section that contained dirt. Not just any dirt,

this was the fine, rich soil of County Wicklow.

From within the dirt, an urgent, muffled whinny drifted out.

"We are just underway, puca. Be patient a little longer until I am certain we are secure here."

Again, a sharp whinny. No longer Moira, Sheilan cracked a bit of a smile at her companion's complaint. Like her, the puca had never left their homeland before, but unlike her, council rules didn't bind him. Pucas were chaotic, free spirits in the world, and presumably, the Universe. Nothing bound them; nothing controlled them. That he seemed willing to listen to her could be a miracle in itself.

Sheilan checked the cabin door, opening it a bit to glance into the hallway, looking both directions. Everything seemed clear; no one in the passage. Closing the door, she found the button that locked it, then turned back to her trunk.

"It appears to be safe enough now, puca. You may come out."

Wisps of white and sparkling gold energy rose from the dirt, swirling and gaining color as it coalesced into the form of a youth, rather than the horse form the puca often used. In this guise, he stood a little shorter than Sheilan, pale skinned, with his light brownish-blond hair worn short on the sides and a longer mane through the center of his head. But the first word out of his mouth sounded like the indignant whinny of the horse.

"How long did ya fancy keeping me locked in that trunk?" His complaint segued into a string of curses in the old language. His speaking voice resonated with a musical-sounding tenor and carried a heavy touch of a brogue.

"Behave yourself," she answered, "or you will be spending the whole trip in it."

"Will I now, witch?" he retorted, and fire blazed in the pale blue eyes.

Sheilan cracked a smile. "Ah, Dari, what would you have me do? Let you run loose on the ship, disturbing everyone? Would that get us to Erinnua? Or maybe you would just like to return to old Erin?"

Dari settled down, reaching for a pair of breeches that Sheilan had packed. As he pulled them on, he continued, "Where are we? Have we left the Earth station yet?"

"We have. Can you not feel it in the motion of the ship?"

"It feels no different than it did from the time we first left Earth. Always in motion. Gentler than river waters, though." Dari related everything to his prime element of water.

Sheilan studied her companion's human aspect for a few moments, then asked, "I have often wondered, Dari, how did you choose that particular human form?"

He appeared to be a lad of about fourteen, with long legs and a skinny body. His large, round eyes showed the peculiar reddish lids that were more obvious on his horse form. Below a button nose, his mouth curved up in a cheery arc, giving him a very young, impish appearance.

"This particular one? As I recall, a cocky young fellow ventured into my bog one day and I took a fancy to him."

"You lured him in."

"No, not at all. You always assume the worst of me. In fact, the lad fell in quite by accident and had not even seen me. Now, I do not deny that I have, now and again, used the water horse form to lure some obnoxious stranger to the bog, but 'twas not the case this time. I rather liked the youngster, and he was a genial lad, so I helped him back to shore. I kept his look because I liked it, and I have used it all these years since."

She shook her head in disbelief. "It sounds an unlikely tale to me. Could be you are a helpful spirit now and then, though. Would you like tea and cakes?"

While not required for their well-being, their kind did sometimes consume food while in the corporeal form. "They have provided a food machine in the cabin so we may eat here."

With a nod to her, Dari began inspecting the small cabin. "Not very big, is it? Not even as large as that cottage bedroom. I think my pony form would not fit very well."

"Like as not," she agreed, setting the teapot on the small pullout table with a bench seat on each side.

With a bouncy step, Dari took a seat and snatched a jelly-filled cake. "You seem worried, Sheilan."

Sitting, she nodded. "I am. Have I done the right thing? A bean sidhe following her family to a new land is not unprecedented, but leaving the planet? I do not know if the Council will approve or if I will be banned when they learn of this. In spite of that, what else could I have done?"

"Indeed, what else?" Dari answered as his young face took on a knowing look before he took a big bite of the cake, then attempted to speak with his mouth full.

Are there any ... of your family ... line still on Earth?"

"No, none. I would have felt the tug if there had been. The only new connections I've sensed these last few years have been from the stars." She broke off a piece of cake, nibbling on it to find it better than she had expected, very moist and with just enough spice.

"Then your path appears clear, it seems. You have done what you must do. Do you reckon that these new Irish still remember us? Do they still tell the stories about us? Will they know what we are?"

She shrugged. "I cannot say, puca. One would hope." She poured the tea and sipped, savoring the taste as she wondered what would be different about this world ahead.

They sat in companionable silence for a few minutes, each sipping the tea and eating cakes they didn't require. Long years of interacting with humans had imparted some strange habits, as well as an unusual companionship. Sheilan often wondered why the puca bothered with her company. Companionship wasn't in the creature's nature any more than it existed in hers, yet here they were, two ancient beings traveling to a new world. Nay, a new solar system, when a small island on Earth had been the only place they had ever known.

She responded to a clear, compelling motivation. Charged with the clarion duty to a specific ancient clan of Celts, she had no choice except to follow the order to fulfill her obligation. With no such constraints, the puca had no ties of any kind to bind him. His race, like hers, existed long before any human ever set foot on the soil of Ireland. Older even than the De Dannan, the Fair Folk, who preceded the humans. So why did Dari choose to come on this journey?

He snorted, sounding very horse-like. "I know what you are thinking, Sheilan. You think that I have some nefarious purpose in taking this voyage with you." He licked at a jam-sticky finger before continuing. "But you are mistaken. I came because I wanted an adventure. Something new. 'Tis too many centuries we have lived on the planet, and that island, beautiful though it is. Even a puca can get bored. Especially when no one much notices us anymore."

She cocked her head, a small smile playing on her lips. She'd heard this before, and it added no more than he'd said at the start of this plan. "At least, you speak the truth there. Few venture to the countryside anymore and those that do are rarely in tune with the greater world around them. They do not know us for what we are."

"Most cannot even see me," Dari's complaint took on the tones of a whinny.

"No fun to be had in that," Sheilan agreed. For a puca, the lack of anyone to torment with his own brand of humor stole the joy from his life. What more could he do?

"These people," he gestured to the world outside the room, "the travelers, they see you."

"They do. But it takes a lot of energy to maintain a solid form visible to all of them. The girl-captain invited me to dine with them all tomorrow's eve before we make the first jump, whatever that is. It will be difficult to continue to maintain. I almost did not make it up from the planet to the station."

"Then why hold it now?" Dari asked and just as easily as he'd materialized from the trunk, he vanished into a cloud-like wisp of energy.

A reasonable question, she reflected, then released her own energy to its base form and a transparent shimmer replaced the once solid-looking body.

Perhaps a tour of this vessel? Dari's thought touched her mind.

"Why not?" The whisper of her voice spoke like a rustle of a breeze through the forest. Together, their non-corporeal forms shifted without constraint through the cabin wall and into the hallway beyond.

CHAPTER FIVE

Grania

"WELCOME TO THE HOSPITALITY of our table."

Grania greeted her guests with stilted formality after they took their seats and the rest of the crew joined them, excepting Nansi, who manned the bridge this dinner time. "It's a tradition on this ship to gather everyone for a dinner and a toast to a fair journey as we are approaching the first jump gate. So, let us begin with the toast." She lifted her glass of wine to her guests and said, "Enjoy the hospitality of the Mo Chroidhe on this journey to our home world of Erinnua. We expect to arrive there in another fifty-two Earth hours. May your time on this ship be pleasant."

As she took a sip, she sized up her passengers. Harhiman took a deep draw of the wine. As a man who, no doubt, often transacted business over dinner and a drink or two in many star systems, his pleased expression suggested he quite enjoyed this rangeberry wine. However, the old woman, Moira, sipped tentatively and the expression on her face stayed unchanged and pleasant as if she didn't taste anything unique in the wine, which she should have. The rangeberries differed from any fruit found on Earth, or so her granda had told her. A spacer such as Harhiman would be used to the unusual flavors of other world drinks, but to someone who'd never left Earth, the flavor would be very different.

"How do you like this wine from the south of Dunderry?" Grania asked. She reached for the bowl of beef and bacon stew that the auto-chef had just delivered in its ready-slot and passed it to Moira, as her only woman guest, to be first served.

"It is quite good, a nice bouquet although a bit on the acidic side," Harhiman replied and lifted the glass to study the clear, dark rose-colored liquid for a moment. "It's made from a native berry, isn't it? Not quite a fruit taste, just a little bitter."

"Yes, the rangeberries tend to bitterness, although they usually give the wine a tart flavor."

As the next stew popped out, she handed it to Harhiman, then distributed the rest to her brothers before taking the last serving for herself.

Loaves of bread were already on the mess-room table, a large model that rose up from the floor when needed to provide dining space for a dozen people with adequate comfort. The backless stools folded flat for storage, so the room provided a conference room, dining room, and recreation room, as they needed it.

In a few moments, another ding heralded the arrival of a platter of Earth-raised vegetables, a special treat for the evening's dinner. Grania motioned to the bread and vegetables. "Please, help yourselves. While it is not the most elegant table, the food is excellent. And you, Miz O'Cairn, did you find the wine enjoyable?"

The old woman glanced at the still almost full glass in front of her. "'Twas fine, I suppose. To be truthful, I do not drink much, so I cannot say if it is a good wine or not. I must confess that I am a bit of a teetotaler."

"Ah, forgive me, then. I didn't know. Something else, perhaps? A cup of tea?"

The woman waved her off. "No, no, 'tis fine. Water will do nicely." To emphasize the remark, she picked up her water glass and took a drink, then reached for the bread and snatched up a slice.

Conversation slowed to nothing more than polite requests for food or butter to be passed as everyone settled into eating. They stocked good quality food, even the replicated food that used base proteins, powdered vegetables, and other food products when fresh wasn't available, were quite flavorful unlike some that tasted more like sawdust and paste.

As Liam offered refills on the wine, Grania leaned back and gazed at Ansel Harhiman. Tonight, his long hair was pulled back into a knot at the base of his neck in the Arcano style and he wore a black shirt with a deep blue silk jacket that hid the bulge at his belly. "Mister Harhiman, Rory tells me that you're on your way to Winthrop's Star. I might know a ship at Dragon Station that can take you if they're docked when we get there."

"That would be quite excellent," he replied, as he wiped his lips with a napkin. "I am, of course, eager to get my cargo moved on, but I can afford to wait a day or two if the ship is close unless there is another one going. For that matter, I may have a few trinkets to sell on Erinnua or even on the station there."

"Like what?" Liam asked, settling back with his wine. As second born, Grania's brother was just two years younger than she, but he didn't start in the space trade until after he'd gotten his engineering degree. His bright hazel eyes sparkled when he was amused, like now. He pushed a long strand of reddish-blond hair back from his right temple.

Harhiman reached into his pocket and pulled out a small pouch from which he withdrew a necklace with a rounded jewel shimmering in the center. "Like this beauty. Rare and quite elegant, don't you think?"

"Hardly a trinket," Grania said, leaning forward a little to see the extraordinary gem a little closer. Called a Luna jewel, if she was not mistaken, the stone glowed like the moon, even in darkness. The light's source came from a mineral that absorbed light and reflected it back.

Harhiman handed it to her to view better. "Yes, a bit more. They're only found on Partha, and I have several to sell."

"Gorgeous," Grania said as she turned the jewel over in her hand. "This must be worth a fortune."

As she glanced at Brendan's face, she guessed her brother was likely calculating the value of just this part of Harhiman's cargo. She passed the necklace back to Harhiman and asked, "What else might you have in your cargo? The manifest said general merchandise."

He grinned. "Well, I didn't want to go into too much detail. It is mostly household goods, linens, and tableware from Rigel, and a few odd collectibles from there, as well. More jewelry from Partha, but this little beauty and her companions represent the cream of the crop." He tucked it back into his pocket, securing the seal-zip on it.

"It looks like trading is a profitable business," Rory said. "Maybe I should consider it."

"It can be, but I've been at it for many years now. I've built up a good trade route and that takes time. Even then, the profit on the jewels won't be as much as you might think. By the time I subtract all my expenses, the margin won't be more than maybe ten or fifteen percent."

Grania nodded an acknowledgment as she wondered about the truth of that statement. It seemed like a small profit for the amount of money and effort spent to obtain the merchandise. Perhaps in quantity, it might be worthwhile. She turned her attention to Moira O'Cairn, who had been mostly silent throughout the evening. She hadn't eaten much of the food either, she noticed. "What about you, Miz O'Cairn? This is your first trip in space, I believe you said."

The old woman sat up a bit and cleared her throat. "Yes, indeed, 'tis the truth. I have not done much traveling, even on Earth, although I have been all over Ireland. But this whole experience is all new to me. If you do not mind my asking, you spoke of a 'jump gate' ahead. Perhaps you can explain what will happen there. Forgive my ignorance."

"Certainly. It's not ignorance so nothing to forgive. Liam, will you kindly explain how the gates work?"

Her brother shot her a glance through narrowed eyes that clearly said she had caught him off guard. Most often, Grania carried the conversation, but this time, she wanted to observe her passengers. Besides, wasn't he the engineering whiz who understood all the details of the gates whereas she just had the basics? Although younger, Grania knew he still resented her advancement to first officer and in line to inherit the ship.

Clearing his throat, Liam started the attempt to explain the gates to someone who, Grania was sure, had never heard of folded space. "Well, the first gate we're coming to is called Einstein's Gate, named after Albert Einstein, a scientist who first proposed bending or folding space to shorten travel between two points. You can think of it like a pleated accordion with the bellows expanded. When you enter it, the box is squeezed and the distance shortened from the entry to the exit." He held up his hands to try to demonstrate the concept, pulling them closer to each other as he talked.

Dropping his hands, Liam continued, "When this gate, the first one ever built, was created, it was possible because of a natural flux, a wormhole, in space. In simple terms, these were the folds needed to make the gates work, and they already existed. After almost four decades of research and trial, a team of physicists finally created a gate generator that measures and helps to control the stability of the wormhole. This allows a spaceship to safely travel through it to the gate at the other end. That's the simplest explanation of what they are."

As he talked, Grania noticed the old woman seemed to be following the explanation quite well, her eyes watching Liam's hand gestures as he described the process. Harhiman, on the other hand, leaned back in his chair and studied the room. His eyes drifted from one area to another as if he was cataloging everything in it. In response, she cast her eyes to follow his and wondered why he showed this interest.

"I see," Moira said when Liam completed his explanation. "So, this folded space will take us to Erinnua?"

"Not exactly, ma'am. We use a series of gates to go from Earth to Erinnua. We start with Einstein Gate which will take us to Pelanan's Gate and the station there. Then there's a second wormhole gate at Pelanan, which is in a star system called Praxius. We cross a part of that star system in about twenty-seven Earth hours and go through the Praxius Prime Gate, which will bring us out through the Dragon Gate into the Dragon Hold star system. From there we'll go through the Red Dragon Gate to the Tara Gate, which is about eight Earth hours from Tara Station."

"I believe I understand it. Thank you for explaining." Moira smiled and gave him a courteous nod.

"Having said that," Grania cut into the conversation. "There are some procedures to follow prior to the gate jump. Each cabin bed is also a jump pod. When I give the order to prepare for the jump, you—all of us—will lie down on our respective beds and activate the pods. This will prepare your body and sedate you for the jump. Distorted space, which is what you encounter when you go through a wormhole, can be quite disorienting and disturbing for people, so it is easiest to be asleep while it occurs.

"The pod also monitors health and keep your body stable during transit. It is perfectly safe, so you needn't be worrying about it." She hoped she sounded reassuring as she wondered what a woman who had never traveled in space might be thinking or feeling about the upcoming jump. At least, she'd seemed to have grasped the concept of the gates.

Grania omitted a bit of information in this orientation, not mentioning that once the ship entered the gate, it began adapting the environment for jump travel, which meant lower temperatures, minimal oxygen, and low lighting to conserve energy and resources. While the ship could withstand the pressure of jump travel, humans could not tolerate it for more than a short time. Without the jump pods, a human wouldn't survive the jump.

"Well, that most certainly does sound exciting," Moira replied with a cheery smile. "I thank you again for finding the space for me on this ship, Captain. I am most grateful for it."

"You mentioned you had family on Erinnua. Will they be meeting you at the station or on the planet?"

"I do not expect them at either location. My departure from Earth did not allow time to notify anyone."

Grania blinked, finding the response odd but none of her business. "Ah well, in that case, you'll find shuttles from the station to three main cities, Cnoc óir, which is also identified as Gold Hill, Abhainn Mhór or Big River and Derrybeag, which is Little Derry. From there, you can find transport to any of the other towns."

"I thank you for the information, captain. I have some arrangements to make when I arrive, it would seem. Now, if you will excuse me, an old lady grows weary easily, and I still need to be studying this jump pod to learn what I must push." Moira pushed back from the table, ready to stand.

"'Tis not hard," Rory said, rising to his feet. "I'll be coming by shortly before the jump to show you exactly what needs to be done." He offered his hand to help the woman stand.

"Ah, that is very kind of you, young sir. I do appreciate all your hospitality. A true Irish family, you are. 'Tis been a pleasure."

As she left, a spreading warmth of gratification rolled though Grania's soul at the compliment. To be considered Irish by the Irish conveyed an honor for one not born on the island. However, she had learned nothing more about Moira O'Cairn as the woman had evaded talking about herself or her family.

Soon after Moira left, Harhiman followed, thanking them for the dinner and their company, before heading back to his cabin. He was, Grania decided, a sales merchant of the smoothest kind; one who liked to impress you with his talk and show you a few nice jewels before slipping in the not-so-valuable trinkets. Still, something about him just didn't feel right to her, and she couldn't put her finger on it. She said as much to Rory.

"No, I don't think anything's odd. He's just a trader, Sis. They all seem a bit smarmy, as Grams would say. You're just nervous about taking on passengers. At least, the old lady seems a safe bet."

"If you're asking my opinion, I'm with Rory on this," Liam said as he moved toward the door. "I'm heading back to the engines to relieve Nansi. And thanks for calling on me like a kid in school." His tone oozed with sarcasm, and he lowered his eyebrows to frown at her.

"Ah, you did fine, Liam. I just thought the explanation coming from you would be easier for Miz O'Cairn to follow. Thanks for that." She grinned at the childish pout on his face, then spoke to Rory. "And what was with you volunteering to help her with the jump pod?"

He shrugged, "I dunno. She just seemed so uncertain of it all and she's an old lady. I thought, what if it was Grams?"

"'Tis a fine gesture, anyway. And Grams would approve, I'm sure."

She began picking up the used dishes to put into the cleaner. "Go notify the gate we're on the way and see if there's any news."

Not that she expected any. The gates kept the wormholes remarkably stable, although there was always the possibility of a worm wiggle, an uncommon incident like a storm in the hole that could alter the trajectory and make for a longer jump or throw off the planned course of the ship through it, which could leave them in a different place than they expected to end up.

"Right," Rory said, turning to return to the bridge.

Brendan fell in behind him. "I'm just going to double check the jump course."

"I thought you were going to help clean up!" Grania objected, turning in time to see the door shut behind him. With a sigh, she began picking up the rest of the dishes. Captain of the bloody ship and she ended up with mess-duty, again. A woman's chuckle brought her head up when Nansi came in.

"The boys took off on you again, eh?" Nansi went over to the auto-chef and pulled out the waiting dinner. "Did all go well tonight?"

"As well as possible, I guess. Harhiman is a braggart and a bit shady, I think, although he seems perfectly charming. The old woman is not very talkative and evaded any questions about the family she's on her way to see. That's a bit odd, don't you think? It seems she would be willing and maybe a little eager to talk about them."

"Maybe not," Nansi poured a glass of wine for herself. "It's possible that she hasn't seen them in a long time and just doesn't have much to say. This is all new to her, Grania. The space station, the ship, space flight, leaving Earth... it's a lot for anyone to assimilate."

Grania sat and refilled her wine glass. "Yeah, I suppose it is. You know, I don't think they even know she is coming. I asked if they would meet her at the station or on the planet and she didn't seem to know." She paused to clink her glass against Nansi's. "Here's to an uneventful trip home"

"Aye," Nansi agreed. "And it looks like it will be very profitable, Captain. A full load in the cargo hold plus passenger fees."

It was all to the good. They'd done well so far on this trip. Better than she had expected, in fact. Her brow furrowed with a pair of worry lines. While the passengers were a bonus, she wished she didn't feel so uneasy about them.

Reading her expression, Nansi said, "It concerns you to have taken passengers, doesn't it?"

She nodded.

"There is something that doesn't feel quite right about either of them. I can't say what it is. Maybe it's just both of us nervous after what happened with your mother. We can keep a wary eye on these two. Err on the side of caution, as it were."

"Agreed." Grania finished her glass and stuck it in the cleaner. "Start this when you're done, please, Nansi. I'll be in my cabin for a while."

CHAPTER SIX

Sheilan

IN THE SMALL CABIN borrowed from Rory, Sheilan reverted to the transparent version of her young aspect as she floated above the jump pod/bunk in a half-reclining position. Dari, now in the wispy form of a small pony, sprawled with hooves on the soil in the chest and listened with as much attention as a puca could while the bean sidhe related the dinner conversation.

"They expect that I will use this pod-bed thing during these gate jumps coming up. One of the lads, the one they call Rory, will be coming around to show me how to work it. I hope he does not plan to tuck me into it." She chuckled at that possibility, and Dari responded with a whinny-ish snort. "No, I doubt it could hold me even if that were to happen."

Is there anything to concern us about these gate-jumps? Dari's thought-voice asked her, making a nickering sound of concern.

"Of course not. We're energy creatures, not those fragile flesh bodies that humans have. But I think—" She broke off, then changed to thought communication. *Did you hear something, Dari?*

A noise outside the door, I think.

In an instant, Sheilan changed into a wisp of energy, almost invisible. Wait, she commanded and shifted through the wall.

On the other side, in the hallway, Brendan hesitated at the door, a puzzled expression on his face. His brow wrinkled as he strained to hear something, and Sheilan could guess what had gotten the lad's attention. Dari's horse-voice carried well, and the lad had likely heard the sound through the walls.

After a minute longer, Brendan shook his head and continued down the passage toward the cargo bay. Sheilan watched him as he went, seeing another young man in her memory, who looked very much like young Brendan did. That had been a long time ago, at least two centuries. In an instant, she returned to the cabin.

"All is well," she told Dari in a soft voice. "'Twas only the young lad, who probably heard your horsey-voice. The four young people on this ship are all siblings. The eldest is the woman, Grania, and she is the captain for this trip, but from what I have heard, the usual captain is her grandfather. I am pretty sure this is the destined path for me, Dari."

Before she'd even finished talking, Dari vanished back into the trunk. Perhaps the horsey rebuke offended him, she surmised.

Grania

"MESSAGE COMING THROUGH FOR you, Grania. It's from Zabrowski Station." Rory glanced over at his sister. "Maybe it's your boyfriend."

Shooting a feigned glare at him, she keyed in the message to her terminal. "Hello, Zabrowski. This is Captain O'Ceagan."

A crackle of interference emanated before the signal cleared.

Vilnius' voice came through, although without an image. "Good evening, Captain. Glad I caught you before the jump."

"We're about thirty mites away from the gate. To what do I owe the pleasure of this call?" While thrilled to hear his voice, she knew a station-to-ship call often meant an unusual event or something important the captain needed to know.

His voice was muted and less official sounding as he replied, "I have bad news for your family. A message came in through the Dublin feed a short time ago to be relayed to you. It seems your great aunt Moira may be dead in a fire at her Wicklow cottage. The neighbors reported that the whole place went up in flames. They found no sign of the old woman, except for a few burnt bones. The authorities are still testing those. She'd been ill and if a fire broke out, it wasn't likely she would have been able to get out. I'm so sorry, Grania. I'm relaying the full message to you now."

"Aunt Moira ... That would have been Gramps' oldest sister. He hasn't seen her in about thirty years, but this will still be a blow to him. Thank you for the news, sad though it is."

"If there's anything I can do from here, let me know. If something more conclusive comes through, I'll relay it on to you." Vilnius paused a moment.

"One more thing that isn't related – simply for your information – it looks like our automated robot program was sabotaged. The code we had to remove and re-program isn't any part of the original. The support programmers say someone attempted to load a virus and almost succeeded. Make sure your safeguards are in place. We're not sure how it was transmitted but take precautions. Safe journey, dearest."

With that, he ended the signal, leaving Grania with a lump of emotions in her throat. She'd never known her great aunt, and her great grandfather had seen little of her since their lives had gone such different directions. Odd that she and Brendan had been discussing the old woman jua mere two days earlier while they had been there in Wicklow. If they'd gone to the family farm, would they have found the burnt cottage?

As she'd told Brendan, Gramps had been about eight when Moira had married and moved to Dublin City. After he grew up and left for the new opportunity on Erinnua, there'd only been a few occasions when he'd been back to Earth and connected with her. Still, he spoke of her once in a while with deep affection. As she mulled it over, she found it even more of a strange coincidence that their passenger bore the same given name as her aunt.

"Was she the batty one or the hoity-toity one?" Rory asked, reminding Grania he'd also heard the message.

"Hoity-toity. She married well into a prominent family in Dublin, according to Gramps. Not that she was too highfaluting, but she did kind of look down on the spacers in the family. I think she told Gramps that we were nothing more than space gypsies, gallivanting across the stars."

"As if there is anything wrong with that," Rory replied. "It certainly beats being stuck on a farm. I hated it when Grams made me work in the fields."

"You always hated hard work."

"Did not! I didn't like having to dig in that thick clay they call dirt to pull up a few vegetables."

"We work with what we have, boy-o. Lots of places back home won't grow anything, so we're lucky to have land that actually produces a decent crop." Grania replied with a laugh.

"Yeah, I know."

She turned her attention to logging the relayed message from Earth to send on to her granda. Let him break the news to his father. Next, she sent a message to Liam with Vilnius' advisory.

Rory checked the readings and reports from the gate again. "It's looking solid, Nia. We're scheduled for jump in 25 mites. I'll just go show the old lady how the jump pod works and make sure she can handle it."

As he rose to his feet, Brendan stepped onto the bridge. "Everything is secure and ready, Grania." He bumped fists with Rory then added, "Now, I'm not saying this is bad, but I think your old lady talks to herself. I overheard her chattering as I walked past your cabin."

"Aw, it probably helps her organize her thoughts. Grams does it often enough," Grania said. "Probably, it comes with old age. Check all the coordinates for the jump again, Brendan."

"I've been over them three times already. They're fine." Brendan snapped the words at her as he slid into his seat and jerked the keyboard to him.

Grania read it as a clear indication he found it annoying that she had asked again. She rotated her seat toward him. "I'm aware. But make sure. I had word from Vilnius that the station 'bots might have a virus. Since the ship interfaced with their program, I need to be sure our data is correct before we jump. I've relayed the message to Liam to run a Macfee-Bios test on the computers."

Brendan nodded and called up the program, his deft fingers keying in the codes. "I get it. Sorry that I snapped."

While he worked out the course with his tablet to double check the ship's computer, Grania worked through her own pre-jump check. Fifteen minutes out, the view of the gate grew on the forward monitor. It literally resembled an open gate. Two elongated power generators provided for the station and stabilized the wormhole entrance. They were each fifty meters tall and over three hundred meters apart; a blue-white thread of power connected them at the top and bottom.

Beyond the gate, Grania could barely make out the blurred, weaving pattern of the dark space beyond. Even though nothing appeared solid, she realized the wormhole effect created distorted-looking space. Beyond that twisting tunnel waited the other gate and the next star system. In the far distance, on the ship's starboard side, the reddish halo of Mars provided a beacon in the sea of celestial objects outside the gate.

"The course is solid. The numbers all remain solid."

Brendan's voice brought her attention back, and she acknowledged the check with a quick word of thanks. He opened his mouth to speak, but hesitated, lips still parted. "Something troubling you, Brendan?" she asked.

He shrugged, his shoulders lifting a bit while a sheepish expression on his face hinted at embarrassment. "Aw, it's going to sound silly, but when I passed by Rory's cabin, I heard a sound like an animal of some sort coming from it. And I swear that old lady was talking to it." A nervous chuckle punctuated his comment.

"What?" Grania said, her voice tinged with amusement. "An animal? What kind? She couldn't have brought anything on board, surely."

"I don't know. It made a funny noise, like it was blowing air and then, it whined or something like–" He attempted to mimic the sound.

Grania laughed, which made him frown. "That sounds a bit like a horse. It's an animal you can ride on Earth. Next time we have a chance to visit, I'll introduce you to one. 'Tis a big beastie, and I'm pretty sure there isn't one in that cabin. More likely Miz O'Cairn is watching a vid or listening to something."

Brendan nodded, the frown still wrinkling his forehead. "You're probably right, but I'm simply saying there's something odd about that woman."

"What woman?" Rory asked as the door swooshed open and he came back onto the bridge.

"Miz O'Cairn," Grania replied. "Is she set for the gate?"

"Aye, she is, Captain. She caught right on to how it works." He sat at his station and checked for any new messages. "Looks like we're all clear for the gate in seven mites. The wormhole is stable."

"Go ahead with the prep warning so our guests have a few extra mites to prepare."

As Rory made the jump announcement, Brendan locked in the course and set the autopilot. From here until the end of the jump, the ship had the com. "The ship's set. I'm heading to my cabin."

"Go," Grania acknowledged, then addressed Rory. "You, too. A quick question first. Did you notice anything odd in your cabin?"

He stared at her, surprised by the query. "You mean besides the huge trunk in the middle of the floor? No, that was all. Only the old woman and that trunk. Thinking on it though, there was a musty smell in the room, like something old, you know. Kind of an earthy odor. Why?"

"Nothing, really. Just something Brendan said. Go on to your pod. I'll be right behind you."

She turned to transfer the ship's full control to her cabin before she locked the bridge controls down. She didn't do it often; however, with passengers aboard and Vilnius' warning, she didn't want to take any chances.

Then she was out the door and hurrying down the corridor. As she sprinted, the autopilot announced, "Gate jump in two mites."

CHAPTER SEVEN

Sheilan

"SO, THIS IS A gate-jump, is it?" Dari asked.

His nose wrinkled as he stared at the large main screen embedded into the wall of the bridge that showed a real-time image of the view in front of the ship. At the moment, the black background showed dotted streaks of color that twisted and spun like a seasick kaleidoscope as the ship hurtled through the wormhole.

"I think I must say that I prefer dirt travel. 'Tis not so disturbing."

Sheilan gazed at the screen for a few more moments before looking away. "'Aye, you do speak the truth, Dari. 'Tis much simpler and quicker. Dirt takes only a blink of an eye to travel, but you can't be carrying anything with you that way."

"True enough. On the other hand, I have everything I need." He gave a horsey chortle in amusement. He currently wore his human youth aspect, although not the corporeal version. A full manifestation required more energy, so, like Sheilan, he only generated the illusion. If anyone else had been awake to see them, they would have appeared solid, unless they touched them.

For the moment, the pair preferred these human forms and spoke aloud rather than using telepathy. Although unnecessary, it helped them to identify with the people around them and to see the ship from the human perspective.

The only things they required were being on the ship and the trunk of so-called Irish soil back in the cabin. Though taken from Wicklow, the actual dirt originated beyond the veil.

As they had entered the jump, Sheilan, in the form of the young woman, had reclined above the jump pod in her cabin. She did not need to utilize the pod, as the change in the ship's life-support system during the jump wouldn't affect her or her companion. Although Dari had returned to the dirt in the trunk when Rory had arrived to instruct her, she let the puca out after they'd made the transition. While the humans slept, they could explore more freely.

"Is there truly nothing else you need, puca?"

"What more should there be? I have no need of material things, as you do not either, yet you insist on collecting these human objects now and then. My purpose is what I choose it to be. Whether I am a monster in the lake or a willing horse companion is my choice. I amuse myself however I wish."

"Amusement is all, is it? What about others of your kind? Do you not miss companionship?"

"I have you for that, do I not? Are we not companions? Am I not here with you when I could be in a cozy bog in the countryside?" He snorted a laugh of merriment.

"That we are. Sometimes though, I like to be with me own kind, others of the sidhe. This voyage—" She paused to wave an arm around the ship and point toward the image of space warping around them. "This may mark the end of that if the Council banishes me."

Dari grew serious. "Then is it worth it, Sheilan?"

"It is my purpose. I must do this if I am to have a reason for being. For centuries, this family has been my sole charge. I cannot recall a time when I haven't been bound to the O'Ceagan family."

"Why? I do not kin why your kind became bound to this duty in the first place. How did it come about that a b'ean sheilan would be given such a strange duty?"

She turned to leave the bridge, moving without hindrance through the wall into the hallway. A moment later, Dari popped in next to her.

"'Tis a fair question. The Gaiatian Council has existed as long as the spirits of the Earth have, Dari; you know that. While you may not be pledged to them, they grant the pucas the freedom you enjoy. When the first beings came, they were benign folk, who were one with the land. They were caretakers who took only what they needed from the land and the seas.

"With the arrival of the Celtic tribes, the land suddenly had a warrior race living on it. Many battles and too much bloodshed amongst the tribes occurred regularly. While it was a violent period, the Council did not interfere. Spirits worse than you, puca, were allowed to interact for good or evil. Eventually, the humans sued for peace. They wanted the Council to control the spirits of the land.

"Their spokesman, a man called Druid, made contact with the Council and proposed a bargain with them. In exchange for controlling the spirits, the humans would honor the spirits and care for the land. The Council then chose to give them a gift, the b'ean Sheilan, a death spirit for each of the clans represented. I was called forth for that purpose."

"I still don't understand why they bound your kind to these people?"

"From the way they fought each other, I think the Council figured they'd kill each other off, but they persisted. Then, there were more invasions and a reason for the tribes to unite to protect the land. I was created for the O'Ceagan clan, and I have been true to them for these many centuries. Alas, Moira O'Ceagan was the last one on Earth."

"So, you have roved out into the Universe to search for more of the clan rather than just take your freedom. Foolish."

"What else would I do? Wander around like a lost soul with no purpose?"

They made their way down the corridor as they talked, passing the vertical stair hatch to the next level as they went. Back beyond the bridge, a hallway extended the length of the ship and ended in two more closed doors. The one on the port side appeared to be just beyond the back wall of the bridge. Sheilan popped in long enough to see Grania in her pod and confirm it was the first officer's quarters. The second door was centered in the back, in the curved aft section, and a brief inspection led her to conclude it was the captain's cabin and was unused on this trip.

The remaining cabins were on the next deck down, which she and Dari had explored on their last excursion on the ship. She pointed downward and allowed herself to drift through the floor.

Dari arrived at almost the same time, appearing beside her rather than floating down. She started toward the end of the corridor. While her cabin was near the front, the other passenger was in the last cabin on the right, and that was where she wanted to go now. She picked up the thread of the conversation as they walked.

"For my clan ... I still detect the pull, and it is here, Dari. On this ship."

"These people?"

"Aye. I have found my family. 'Tis this O'Ceagan family. The tie pulls me like a cord around my soul. First, It touched me at London spaceport, then again in the tug to the captain and her brother. They are the direct line; these four young people are taking me to my new home. Pure luck or fate that the ship I needed to get to the new world held my clan."

"And is the old one forgotten then?" Dari stepped in front of her, a serious expression on his normally cheery face. "Is it that easy, b'ean sidhe?"

"Of course not, puca. 'Tis my birth soil. Like every soul and spirit from it, I am tied to it. Besides, it is only a jump away."

"It had best be a better delivery system than that trunk of dirt!" His eyes narrowed and grew redder in a countenance that hinted at the duality of his nature.

"Indeed, that is a truth. T'was was necessary this time." She halted at the last door. "Look, we are here. Let us see what the famous trader might have in his cabin."

Harhiman reclined in his jump-pod, deep in the trance-like sleep that every person on the ship endured in order to travel through folded space. Sheilan looked him over, noted the relaxed appearance of his features. Nonetheless, she had sensed dishonesty about him when they had dined with Grania. More than that, she had noticed the uneasiness, distrust even, in the girl. She believed the young captain had good instincts.

So, what secrets did this trader have? She glanced around and noticed that Dari hadn't come into the cabin with her. His usual curiosity would have no regard for others' places or property, but this time, he didn't follow. Peculiar. She peeked around the small cabin. Not much room here to hide anything. It was a bit smaller than the cabin she used, which, she understood, belonged to Rory O'Ceagan.

A standard travel bag sat in one corner, still part way unsealed, showing it to be empty except for a few grooming items. The arm's-length wide closet held three tunic-style shirts, two pairs of pants and another pair of shoes. A light traveler was Mr. Harhiman.

She moved on to the open door of the accommodation. A night kit with the edge of a razor poking out sat on the small sink. Otherwise, it was the standard on the ship—an H20-sonic shower and the toilet. Barely enough room for a big man to turn around in the space, she mused as she recalled the size of the great Brian Bóruma, now called Boru, although it proved adequate for most humans.

On the desktop, next to the food server, a personal tablet lay flat and opened. Although dark, it appeared to be connected to a power port and charging.

Satisfied there was nothing more to see, Sheilan slipped through the wall into the empty corridor outside the cabin. No Dari. She spun around to gaze back up the corridor toward their room. There he was; his image projection appearing as little more than a wisp. She jumped to his side.

"What has happened? You're fading."

The puca's thoughts reached her mind. I do not know. My energy is draining.

He poofed out altogether, just the sparkles of his energy form hanging in the air.

I am going back to the dirt for now. Dari's voice whispered in her mind.

She followed him into the cabin and lifted the lid on the trunk. As soon as she moved the inner cover from over the dirt, Dari zipped into the rich soil.

"Is it the wormhole draining your power, do you think? Rory O'Ceagan told me that organics cannot travel through them without being in a jump pod. I did not think it would affect us."

Is it bothering you?

"No, it does not seem to be. Is there anything you need?"

Just give me some time to recharge. It will not be long. A little moisture would be most appreciated.

While both spirits were energy beings, the puca was a water elemental more than an Earth one. Sheilan located a container of water and splashed some into the dirt. If they were going to rest while he energized, she might as well conserve energy as well, she decided, and blinked out.

MUCH LATER, SHEILAN MATERIALIZED on the bottom deck of the ship, where engineering and the cargo hold filled the entire area. To the starboard side, the control room occupied a quarter of the space while the actual engines occupied an enclosed space below this deck. A steady hum from the generators provided a white noise in the room, although the vibrations from them made Sheilan tingle. Stacks of cargo, three levels of it in some places, filled the remainder of the deck.

As she peered into the control room, it seemed cramped with all the equipment that filled it. Several computer screens covered one wall and the dizzying blur that was the wormhole flashed across three of them, covering the forward view, the starboard, and port sides. The aft view displayed only a black screen. Dozens of controls on the consoles were raised buttons and levers, some displaying lights and words while others were just metal-looking squares with symbols on them. Behind them, big machines drove it all.

Scarcely enough room for the jump pod within it, Sheilan thought.

Now, her interest centered on Harhiman's cargo. The so-called Luna jewel had been interesting. Even though she hadn't touched it, she'd detected a tingle of power emanating from it. She counted on that sense of energy to guide her to the man's cargo. If he indeed possessed many of those jewels, they would be like a beacon she could sense when she came near enough.

Across from the engine room, an open space and ceiling-high air lock marked the docking bay for ship access. Next to it, a walled alcove gave access to the human-sized external air lock. The cargo crates were arranged in three long aisles down the ship's interior from just behind the engineering bulkhead, continuing almost to the back wall. Two smaller lines of crates were at the rear of the ship, with a narrower aisle that ran between them. She started there.

Some crates were well marked with their contents: farm produce, clothing, machinery, glassware, tablets. She noted quite a few of those. Many others were only bore code numbers to identify them. The ship's cargo manifest would provide the details to the crew.

Curious about the contents, Sheilan chose a random unmarked crate and shifted into it. In her transparent state, she could see the contents in fractal patterns based on the structure of the elements in it. If she had seen the Luna jewel in this state, she might have known how it generated power. As for this crate, nothing in it indicated that kind of energy. The items here were inert matter, yielding no discernible power.

She continued down the aisle, popping into a crate now and then to check it out. One was filled with a pattern she recognized at once, sheep's wool. Another held a cold crate inside with cheese filling every inch of the space within.

Deciding that the crates she sought were not in this section, she spun around and retraced her steps. As she reached the engineering room, Dari popped in just ahead.

"Refreshed now?"

"I am. Have ya found anything yet?"

"No. I think they must be in that section ahead." She pointed a transparent finger vaguely toward the large hold beyond the room.

Dari stared at the long rows of crates and frowned. "That's a lot of crates to search."

"Aye." Doggedly, she started forward, peering at every container.

Certain that she would detect the energy vibration she'd experienced before, Sheilan didn't linger long in an area and only rarely popped into a crate to investigate. Although she detected a somewhat active energy source, the frequency didn't bother her. By the time they'd covered two aisles, she'd begun to think Harhiman's jewel may be the only real one and whatever else he'd brought could be something far different.

Until she started down the last aisle and mid-way slammed into a strong vibration that was like the jewel, but more than the bauble Harhiman had dangled. And the second energy tone was stronger, more powerful. Enough to make her unsteady.

"Oiff!" Dari called out; his voice alarmed. "What in Gaia's name is that?"

"I do not know. There are two pulsing together. I feel a bit queer. What about you?"

"Worse than before." His words were weaker, muttered more.

She turned to see he was struggling to hold his form again. "Get yourself back to the cabin. Whatever this is, it affects us. You more than I, it appears."

He disappeared before she'd finished speaking.

Shifting to pure energy, Sheilan the power affected her a little less acutely, but still she experienced a drain. Determined, she moved forward and darted into the crate, giving off the strongest pulse. Half materializing to see the actual items, she blinked in the lights from the top level of Luna jewels, which nestled in egg cartons. As Sheilan drifted down, she found that beneath them, under a false bottom, were rough-cut crystalline rocks giving off the power that seemed to drain them. Almost exhausted from the effort, she jumped back to the opposite end of the cargo bay, then shot to her cabin.

Pale glitters materialized in the cabin, swirling in a spiral as the energy form struggled to pull herself together before diving into the soil at the bottom of the trunk. Dari's touch brushed against her as she entered, confirming he had returned to the soil for strength.

CHAPTER EIGHT

Sheilan

ROSARY BEADS PASSED THROUGH fingers that were neither human nor solid, moved instead by the b'ean sidhe's energy field. She didn't caress them in the same sense a human would touch the cool Connemara stones. Instead, she detected the energy components of each stone, no two exactly alike. In them rested the power of the elements of Earth that linked everything created within the sphere together. In this manner, Sheilan knew the stones, recognized their pattern and their origin. She realized they held a power, albeit not the kind the humans ascribed to the marble. To them, the nuggets in this relic with the worn-looking silver cross dangling at the end were a holy object, a way to commune with their God.

This particular rosary, the one last clutched by Moira O'Ceagan Sheehan, had been in Sheilan's own non-human hands once before. That had been many, many years in the past when it had first been crafted in the time of a great woman sea captain. Her name was Grania, just like the captain of this ship. And no accident, that naming, for a family link connected the two.

"What is that ya keep fiddling with?" Dari's voice asked as he materialized beside her.

"'Tis called a rosary. This one belonged to Moira O'Ceagan most recently, although it has had many owners over the centuries."

"A rosary? Is that not a religious object? Since when do ya fool around with religious things?"

"To humans, it is something they value with their faith in the One God. True, 'tis naught but a series of good old stones from the western land and a piece of silver worked into a cross." Using her power, she raised it up to float in mid-air, the stones holding a round shape as the cross dipped to the bottom of the circle.

Dari peered at it, eyes alight with his curiosity. "True, they are fine stones. From around the Galliv area, are they not? I recognize the pattern. Once, a companion of mine carried a knife hilted with the same marble. Now, that is a practical purpose."

"You would think so. But these beads were carefully cut and shaped for this trinket. Once, a small quarry existed just south of Galliv, which is now Galway, where the stonemason shaped pieces of the marble for jewelry and weapons. Perhaps he made the one for your friend. At any rate, the Aodhagáin ordered the stones for this rosary and a skilled silver craftsman set the stones in cages and linked them together, along with the little cross, as a Christening gift for his granddaughter, Sorcha ni' Aodhagáin. This was the clan I was bound to, which eventually became O'Ceagan."

"Sorcha's mother had been an O'Malley, the first link between the O'Ceagan and the O'Malley clans and it was when this rosary was given to the babe that I first was introduced to the O'Malley bloodline that has woven in and out of the clan for centuries."

"O'Malley," he repeated. "There was a so-called pirate queen by that name once, in the time of the first Elizabeth of England."

"There was. Grania O'Malley, as time came to identify her. The daughter of an Irish merchant in Connaught. She was a cousin of Sorcha's grandfather. And 'tis a far distant relative of that Grania who, much like her ancestor, commands this ship. She, too, was a merchant shipper and even though the vessels sail far different seas, there is much that is the same."

The vision of the child on that day was locked in Sheilan's memory. It had been a happy day, and her ethereal form had witnessed the celebration of the child's baptism as a burst of colorful energy and pulsing emotions. "I recall the old priest baptized the wee child. I believe she was scarcely a year old, and he blessed both her and the rosary in Holy Water."

"All water is holy!" Dari proclaimed. Sheilan knew his perspective of the element lived on a different level from humans. As he spoke, his expression reflected a sudden alarm. "There is water on this new world we are going to, is there not?"

Sheilan cocked her head to the side and considered. "I am sure there must be. Surely, humans would not set up hearthstones in a place with no water."

"Have you never seen the Great Desert on Earth? Scarcely a drop to be found and yet there are people living there." The puca shuddered at the thought.

Sheilan lowered the rosary, once again admiring the blue-green stones worn smooth with so many years of people touching them, caressing them as they prayed. Close to two hundred million years old, they were, before they were plucked from the ground, cut and shaped, and then painstakingly polished by human fingers. Ancient. With the primal power of a young planet within them.

"What will you do with those?" Dari asked, interrupting her contemplation.

"They are an inheritance, to be passed from the hands of the dying to the youngest girl of the clan. Or so Sorcha decreed when she handed them to her granddaughter Meave, and so it has been. Until Moira O'Ceagan, that is. She held on to them to the last and now I will deliver them to the youngest."

Dari gnawed at his lip. "And might that person be the young Grania?"

"It might. Or there may be younger lasses in the clan. I have not enough information about the whole family yet."

"And here you sit, playing with them, mulling over them. Something troubles you."

"It does, my friend. You know me well. The crystals in the crate down in the hold are something powerful. Something I have not encountered before. The pattern is completely unknown to me."

"They are not from Earth ..."

"Yes. I perceived that. Apart from their effect on us, I sense they are dangerous to this crew, these people. I would warn them, but how? What can I say? Would they believe me if I told them? And how could I tell them how I know? More than that, would I be violating the code of my obligation to the clan if I told Grania?"

"Have you not already done that with this whole trip? What is one more violation of your code in the grand scheme of what you have done?"

"Ah, Dari ... You are a bad influence."

"Me?" He feigned surprise in his wide-eyed expression of shock. "'Twas you who dragged us onto this ship across the expanse of space on this quest of yours. You are the wrong influence. I am merely your stalwart companion."

In spite of her concerns and worries, Sheilan smiled at the indignant display of the impish creature. "Truer words you have never spoken. I am the guilty party. And perhaps you are right that my transgression will be none the greater for taking it another step."

"How human you've become," Dari said as he reached for a cup of water, absorbing every drop simply by immersing a finger in it. "Long ago, you would not have worried about the people or what became of them. There is a dishonest man on the ship. There is nothing unusual about that, yet you feel the need to warn the captain. I admit, it does concern me that the man's cargo has a negative effect on our kind, but if we stay clear of it, there is no harm. Tell me now, why do you believe you need to warn them?"

"Are you telling me now that I should not?"

"I am just asking you why you want to interfere in this. It does not concern the sidhe."

She folded the rosary in half and sent it floating back to the shallow jewelry compartment in the trunk's top tray where she'd kept it since she'd packed. As it dropped precisely into place, she considered her answer for a few moments. "He is an odd man, that Harhiman. While he appears to be human, he is not from Earth. I would guess he is the offspring of settlers who colonized another planet. 'Tis what I sense about him that disturbs me. Not just dishonesty, but an aura of ruthlessness and possibly violence. If anything happens to this ship, it is the end of our transportation. No way back to Earth except by drifting, assuming our energy forms can survive and navigate in space. Beyond that, I do not feel a death warning for any of the O'Ceagan's on this vessel. It is not their time, or I would be sensing the call. Yet, I do feel there is danger. Possibly from that cargo, maybe not."

"Well, then, do what you must. There are many ways to warn her." Dari's mood lightened, and he popped back into the comfort of the soil.

Indeed, she knew more ways, but only one she could do right now while the ship's crew slept. It might prove effective enough. Decision made, Sheilan vanished from the cabin, materializing almost instantly inside Grania's cabin.

CHAPTER NINE

Grania

AUTOMATIC SYSTEMS CUT IN when the Mo Chroidhe approached the terminus gate of the wormhole. The computer started a countdown for the sleeping crew to hear, even though they could not yet respond, while the jump pods began the cycle to awaken them. As a safety precaution, the passengers would not be pulled out of sleep until the ship passed through the gate and everyone resumed their positions.

In her cabin, Grania's pod started the warming and awakening sequence fifteen mites ahead of the rest of the crew, timed to allow the ship's captain to have a first check of the ship's status and abort the awakening sequence if any problems registered. A mask and small belt-hook canister of oxygen hung on the side of the pod in case of a problem with the ship's life support system. It supplied enough oxygen to get the captain to engineering to determine the problem and either repair it or abort the awakening. Additional oxygen tanks were available there to allow her more time to fix the problem.

As Grania came out of deep sleep and the pod's cover lifted, her first thoughts went to the ship's status. A bit of grogginess held her, a moment or two of disorientation, before she took a deep breath, tasting the air as her hand reached for the oxygen mask, as a precaution. Good, she decided. Nothing stale about it and a moment later, the ship's computer confirmed life support had returned to normal levels.

"Proceed with wake up," she ordered. She sat up, stretched, dropped her feet to the floor, found her boots, and headed to the accommodation. Within five minutes, she started toward the bridge. The rest of the family would wake within minutes, and they would run a full check of all systems, standard procedure.

This jump marked the fifth time Grania had captained the ship through the wormholes, yet waking to a completely sleeping ship still seemed peculiar to her. The silence in the corridor made her jumpy, as did the slowing streaks of space in the monitor screens and the distinctive metallic sounds when the ship's engines brought the vessel back to normal status. When she arrived on the bridge, lights progressed from a dull, weak glow to the normal indoor illumination. Although her monitor didn't show it yet, she knew the ship had entered the exit gate.

She adjusted her navy-blue tunic, noting it had a few wrinkles needing to be pressed out. Although she wanted a shower, it would have to wait until everything was checked, course verified, communications updated, and the usual routine restored. They had a full fifteen hours to the next jump gate at Pelanan, barring any unexpected detours or diversions.

She initiated the various systems' check routines and began the important task of brewing a pot of tea, something all the crew would need after their sleep. While she waited, she poured a cup of plain water to hydrate her body. The jumps always left her thirsty and hungry. If true to his habit, Rory would be the last to arrive. If he followed his usual routine, he would have a quick shower and a cold juice before heading to the bridge. On the voyage to Earth, Brendan had arrived second after each jump, and that was the case now as the tall, gangly teen arrived in a sprint, still pulling on his tunic.

"I'm on the course, Nia. I started the preliminary from my cabin, so we'll see it as soon as we are through the gate."

"Good. So far everything is looking fine."

A crackle of electronics through the communicator served as a pre-warning from engineering as Liam's voice cut through. "Everything is normal down here, Captain. No reds or yellows, only darling greens. Estimate the adjustment in three mites."

"Roger that, Liam."

The next voice was Nansi's. "All secure in the cargo hold."

Grania acknowledged, allowing herself to rela. Then, a timer buzzed, signaling teatime.

She'd barely settled with her cup when Rory hurried onto the bridge, throwing himself into his chair and securing the safety guards. He flicked the communications console to active and popped the receiver pod into his ear as he gave his sister an all's well sign.

The ship lurched a bit as it exited the wormhole, sliding through the Pelanan Gate and back to normal space. Screens displayed the stars ahead and a glimpse of the station at Hermes to the starboard side. Perfect.

"Right where we should be," she said. "Good job, lads."

"No drift at all in the wormhole," Brendan confirmed. "I'm setting the course for Pelanan now."

Up to full power now, the ship's course began the turn toward the station.

"Ready to wake passengers," Rory reported.

"Confirmed and confirmed," Grania answered both reports. She sat back and sipped her tea, confident in the routine. With the lads locked on their tasks, they were fine for the moment. Brendan would sneak an energy bar as soon as she left the bridge, and Rory was good for at least an hour before he stopped for food. Right now, she watched as he busied himself with the backlog of messages that had been waiting for the Mo Chroidhe to clear the gate. Now she needed a shower and food.

Fifteen minutes later, cleaned and pressed, Grania sat in the galley ready to wolf down a plate of bacon, eggs, pancakes, and spuds. As she peeled back the lid on the syrup container, Nansi strode in and gave her plate a once over.

"Looks good. I think I'll have some of the same." She programmed the food server to duplicate the order and poured herself a cup of tea before sitting down to face the captain. "Calm enough wormhole. Everything stayed in its place, it seems. No slips or slides. I did have a few odd readings in the energy checks during the jump, but it may be nothing."

"What kind of readings?" Grania stuffed a forkful of bacon and pancake into her mouth. Somehow, she always seemed to wake from a jump sleep starving. While the pods may slow the body's functions, they didn't seem to stifle the need for food.

"Not too much. 'Twas only an escalation of energy in the hold, showing up as two separate spikes on the recordings. One popped up first and lasted the longest, then a second one showed up. They lasted about fifteen mites, dropping back to a single one before that disappeared as well." The machine beeped, and she rose to get her meal.

"Two separate spikes. That does sound peculiar. Have you ever encountered it following a jump?" Grania asked. With many more years of experience in space travel than she had, the captain often relied on Nansi for information about things she hadn't encountered.

"Not that I can recall. A random burst of energy for a few seconds from a hole—that we've experienced. But this was a sustained spike, almost like ..." Her voice trailed off as if she was reluctant to voice her thoughts and her brow pulled into a frown.

"Like what?" Grania prompted when Nansi didn't continue after a few seconds.

"Oh, I don't know, really. The thing is, the energy sources seemed to move through the hold area as if they were inspecting the cargo. There would be movement, and a pause for a bit, before moving again. The second one came in about five mites after the first, traveled parallel to the first until it vanished about ten mites before the first one left."

Grania frowned. "Show me."

Nansi pulled her tablet from her belt, set it on the table, and tapped the energy screen. She keyed it to run the sequence.

Grania watched the energy grid of the hold and spotted the first spike when it arrived as a bright green line on the grid. Appearing all at once outside the engineering room, it held there for a minute before turning aft and weaving between the crates. A pause for a few seconds and a slight waver of the energy, and it continued for a bit before it repeated the pause. After doing this another time, it retreated toward the engineering room where the second energy line, also green, joined it. Both paused before proceeding.

"What the hell?" she muttered as the energy shifted to the starboard side and passed between the crates. Again, they paused for a few seconds, then continued. They turned down the next aisle, repeating the process. At the last aisle, they moved forward, until one line stopped, and for a moment it dimmed. The first waited for a few seconds before the second energy line disappeared. The remaining one resumed moving, but only for a few more meters. It sputtered for a second or two, seemed to dim, and vanished. "Did you see that? What was that? It looked like interference. Did you check for radiation? Have you run the recordings?"

"Of course. I pulled the recordings right after I saw the spikes on the status check monitors. Nothing. Not a thing. And no sign of radiation of any kind."

Grania nodded. Odd things happened in space. Her granda had said that more than once, and certainly, they had experienced more than one oddity in their travels. Still, they would log the incident and check it out. "Have Liam take a look when he has the time. Maybe he can run a filter or something that might show the spikes on the recording. I'd like to know what scouted through our hold while we traveled through a wormhole and how it did it."

"There is one other thing that is a bit odd," Nansi said, interrupting her. "Do ya ever dream while you're in pod sleep?"

"No," Grania answered, yet reconsidered as she recalled waking from the pod this time. "Although something did pop into my mind as woke up this time." She closed her eyes as she tried to recall the details.

General disorientation often occurred when first waking after a jump, but this seemed different. "When I woke, I saw an image, like a puzzle. At first, I saw Harhiman showing us the Luna jewel at dinner before we jumped, then it changed to some kind of crystal, irregularly shaped with pale blue nodules on it and that image kept multiplying many times. Next, I woke reaching for the oxygen mask, thinking there might be a problem on the ship."

Nansi's dark eyes had grown bigger as Grania spoke. Now she leaned forward, her expression intense. "It could be a warning, Grania. Not a dream; a flash of vision, it would seem. Faith, I've had one, too. I dreamed something. 'Tis all muddled as dreams can be. Like most everyone, I don't dream while in pod-sleep. So, if something breaks through, I have to believe it's a message, a warning."

Nansi was fey. Grania knew it. The whole second-sight thing ran in her bloodline. She often shared her "reads" on people with Grania and her granda. They considered it one benefit of having her in the crew, as it could give them insight into potential problems with shippers and passengers. Nansi hadn't met either of their passengers, Grania realized with a start. Her mouth felt dry again. "So, what is the message?"

"I saw a dragon, a red dragon, with its forearm raised and claws extended. Fearsome and floating in the black of space with only a single star visible behind it. Then flashing for an instant, I saw a skull and crossbones flag, like the ones in the histories of old sailing ships. And I saw the universal symbol for a man and there was a scratch mark across the middle. The last thing in the dream was a small horse that turned to look at me with eyes that looked human, yet alien, all at once."

She sat back, shaking her head gently, as she contemplated the meaning. "'Tis the first time I've given voice to it, and I waited until after breakfast to speak. The dragon is red, representing danger and likely 'tis a dragon because it has something to do with us or our home star system. I interpreted the claws are extended to ward off a threat. Finally, I believe the single star could represent our destination or the Dragon Star itself. As to the man, that would suggest a human."

"Or just humanity. It could be a woman as well. Would the scratch indicate this person is the danger?"

"Possibly." Nansi sipped her coffee. "But nothing identifies him or her."

"What about the horse? How does it play into this?"

"That piece puzzles me, but it could be revealed later in our journey. Between what you sensed this morning and my dream, I think we're being warned, and one of our passengers is in danger or is the danger. We need to be staying alert for whatever this is."

"Whatever what is?" Brendan asked as he entered the galley.

"We're comparing notes, little brother," Grania answered. "Nansi thinks there might be a discrepancy with one of the crates we've got in the cargo bay." She rolled her eyes at Nansi, shifting them to her brother, a sign to follow her lead.

"'Tis a minor item on the manifest," Nansi said, picking up on it. "I'm sure it's nothing. Probably an entry error."

Brendan poured tea and added two tablespoons of sweetener before programming in breakfast. "You're probably right. There was such a rush on Zabrowski that they were likely scrambling to get everything keyed in." He pulled out a plate full of bacon and fried eggs plus a stack of toast and sat down to eat.

"Anyway, the course is set to Pelanan. Everything looks clear ahead and we should dock on time at the station."

Grania nodded. "With luck, we'll only be a couple of hours there to unload twelve crates. Rory will be looking for replacement cargo to go on, so it may be a little more time to load it on and we can be on our way again. Have you checked the status of Pelanan Gate?"

He swallowed a piece of toast with a gulp of tea before answering. "Rory doesn't have an update yet from there. It should be coming soon. I think he may have something for you from Zabrowski."

"For me?" The last news from there wasn't good. Would Vilnius have an update for her already? "I'll be heading back to the bridge then. Thank you for the status report, Nansi. Let me know if there is anything else."

GRANIA STRODE STRAIGHT BACK to the bridge, where Rory still received all the communications coming in from the station. "Is everything checking out?"

"So far. I still have another fifty or so updates to go through, but it all seems normal. There's a message for you. I routed it to your console."

"Brendan told me. Thank you. Take a break and get some food. The rest of the messages can wait."

He swiveled to watch her as she took her seat in front of the command console. "Sure, I can do that. First, let me pick out the rest of the ones from Pelanan. I'm not starving yet."

"Right." She called up the file as she positioned her earpiece to listen. Vilnius' voice poured through with a brief, although cryptic, message. Still, a tender smile lit her face as she heard it.

"Ahoy, Grania." A personal message, not an official one directed to the ship; expensive to send. "Something came up today, which is the same day your ship jumped at Einstein. It's station business that necessitates me traveling to Pelanan. I'm leaving shortly on a sprint ship and should arrive shortly before you're due to dock. Perhaps we can spend some time together. See you soon, sweetheart."

"Good news?" Rory asked when he saw her smile.

"The best. Vilnius is on a sprinter to Pelanan for station business. He'll be getting there before we do. That might make up for the little bit of time we had at Zabrowski."

"Well, you have to love those fast ships, don't you? Wish this old girl could make that kind of speed."

"Watch it, boy-o! Don't be saying unkind words about this grand old lady."

"Not a bit unkind." He rubbed the console reverently. "She's a darlin' ship, for sure. Just a wee bit slow next to those power-gobbling sprinters."

"That she is. Still, I wouldn't trade her for anything."

"Uh huh," he agreed readily. "Looks like there's a big solar flare from Pelanan's sun. They're warning of possible communications interruptions, although it should be clear by the time we arrive." He removed the earpiece and stood. "That's it for now. I'm off for food. I won't be long, and you know where to find me."

Grania acknowledged with a wave of her hand, then replayed Vilnius' message. What kind of business required him to travel on such short notice? Possibly it had to do with the computer virus. Whatever the reason, the trip meant she'd get another chance to see him.

Shaking off the dreamy mood that the prospect of seeing her man created, Grania flicked open the cargo manifest file that listed everything in the cargo bay. She ran her stylus down the list until she found Harhiman's record of crates and items. When she'd awakened from the jump sleep, she'd had a nagging feeling about the cargo he'd brought on the ship. Although she couldn't explain why, at least telling Nansi about her dream jogged her memory. She wanted to see specifically what he'd loaded.

The inventory opened, showing four large crates and their contents. As she scanned it, she noted nothing irregular or different from what he'd told them. The cargo seemed safe, not banned, or dangerous. One thousand boxed, jewelry grade Luna jewels, valued at six hundred and fifty thousand credits, plus the padding to protect the gems were in the first crate. A lot of value there, yet nothing unusual given their current popularity in most of the colonies.

Another crate, also padded, contained Rigelian dinnerware sets, high quality, and valued at fifty-two thousand credits. The third crate held winter clothing, primarily coats, caps, and scarves, from Eiselaun and included fifty bolts of sheep's wool. The last crate listed an assortment of miscellaneous items for cooking, cleaning, gardening, and several other domestic tasks, something many of the outlander worlds couldn't produce themselves.

Of all the items, the Luna jewels were undoubtedly the most valuable. Perhaps her sleep-dreaming mind speculated on the value of the shipment versus the safety of the ship in an emergency.

Still, something didn't feel quite right. She'd sensed a danger on awakening and had feared it affected the ship's systems. But that wasn't it. If it wasn't in the cargo, what was it? One of their two passengers? Not likely the old woman with that travel trunk. That left Harhiman, yet he seemed to be legitimate. Was she imagining threats that weren't there?

On a whim, she opened the ship's reference library and searched for Luna jewel. Seconds later, an image popped up showing a closeup of a gem almost identical to the one Harhiman had shown them. The accompanying article said they were created in the Berigo Sea of Partha, formed from lionite, calcium carbonate, and salt in the underwater sand, much like a pearl on Earth. Then, they washed ashore at high tide when the full moon gave them light to ignite the unique glow in the lionite stone. Only a few hundred stones made it to shore and remain after the water receded each moon tide, so they were a rare and precious gem.

She glanced back at the manifest. While Harhiman might have undervalued them a little, it wasn't by much and could represent his wholesale price rather than the market price. On the other hand, hadn't he said he only possessed a few? The amount he listed on the manifest indicated a lot more. Perhaps he merely didn't want to reveal how many he'd brought on board.

She closed her eyes and pictured the images she'd seen again. Not quite round, the crystal appeared to be a light purple color and had irregular spikes jutting off it. While it seemed familiar, she couldn't connect it. Opening her eyes, she called up a graphic search program and began a rough sketch of the odd-looking crystal.

Just as she put the last touch on it, Brendan came onto the bridge. He glanced at the screen in front of Grania, then came over to look closer at the sketch. "What's that?"

"I saw it in a dream. I don't know exactly what it is. Some kind of crystal with those little spikes coming out of it, I'm thinking." She hit the search button.

Brendan leaned forward to get a better view. "It looks like an unprocessed power crystal. Those uneven spikes would be smoothed out in the refining."

"I think you're right. I should have recognized that. Now if I knew why I was dreaming about them, I might have a clue to what my brain is trying to tell me." The computer found a match and displayed the information. The photo image looked almost identical to the object in Grania's dream.

"Unrefined targassium crystal," Brendan read aloud. "'Found on Partha and on Hope Asteroid. In this state, it is stable although still volatile. A hard collision, such as a crash, could cause a reaction.'"

"In other words, they're saying it could explode. Is that right?"

He nodded.

She frowned and returned to the cargo list, looking for any of the crystals used to process energy cells. Nothing. She wasn't sure if she was relieved or not, and that troubled her.

CHAPTER TEN

Sheilan

"DO YA THINK SHE got the message?" Dari asked when Sheilan materialized in the cabin.

"I cannot say. All I could do was send her symbols and images. I think she is a bright lass so she might make the connection."

Barely visible, the banshee's image hovered just a little beyond her pure energy state. She looked more like a ghost. Dari, on the other hand, appeared in his more solid young lad form as he sipped tea and nibbled at a biscuit. While he needed the liquid, the food had become a simple habit.

"I would like to know what that trader fellow is up to with these crystals. He is likely smuggling them, what with that false bottom on that crate," she said.

Dari's gaze snapped to her trunk with its false bottom filled with undeclared Irish dirt. She followed his eyes.

"Yes, I know I am a smuggler also, but a bit of soil is not the same and you know it, Dari."

"True, I suppose. Those crystals drain our energy, so they are not good for us. I wonder what effect they might have on the humans."

"The youngest lad, Brendan, said they were power crystals. Somehow, they must tap into the energy in them to power the ship and everything on it and even other things back on Earth. So complex everything has gotten in this age of space travel. It feels like the natural laws are being violated. People are going where they do not belong. And yet..." Her voice faded as she rested above the closed trunk and considered the situation.

"And yet what?" Dari prompted, settling himself beside her.

"And yet, here we are, two shape-shifting elementals on a vessel constructed by humans, and other races, traveling across the stars to a place we do not belong."

"That is a fact. Still, we can return easily if we use the soil." His voice carried a cheery tone, unconcerned with Sheilan's worries.

"In theory, anyway." At his questioning eyes, she explained. "Well, it has not been tried from a spaceship, has it? Or even from another planet. The rule has always been that the soil knows its own soil and our kind can shift from plot to plot. But there is naught to say if that will work off the Earth."

His eyes grew wide. "And just now you are telling me this? Are you saying we may have to take a bleedin' ship back to Earth if it does not work?"

"Aye, that would be the case. It is not like either of us has anything pressing if we must travel back that way. But it is my desire that I will have a new home and a renewed purpose on Erinnua. For your sake, I hope the soil travel works and you can return easily to Ireland's green hills."

"Could you not return to the sidhe and make your home there if you are released from your obligation to the O'Ceagan family? It seems to me that if your family has vanished from Earth, whether by death or moving to a different planet, then it should put an end to the arrangement with the family. You should be free of any more responsibility."

She shifted to her old woman aspect as she felt the age of her many centuries of existence weighing on her. "This life is all I have known. I was created for the family, tied to them, and being unbound is something I have no idea how to do. If my purpose all this time has been to warn the family of danger and death and it will no longer be, then what am I to do? Fritter around my time with no design? I do not have your nature, puca. Perhaps I would cease to exist."

He frowned. "'Tis making my head hurt, you are. That ancient crone form suits you for these are wearying, serious thoughts you are troubling with today."

She smiled, a human response that conveyed her fondness for the puca, even as a wave of affection from her true nature touched him. Although they needed no human forms to communicate or express emotions, their hundreds of years of living amongst people had made it second nature to them now.

"Tell the truth now, puca. What prompted you to join me on this trip to the stars? And do not say it was just to have my fine company."

"But that is true," he protested immediately. "'Tis always a joy to be with you, Sheilan. Is it the only reason? No. Not at all. It is the adventure. The chance to see something different from that green island I've spent all me existence traversing, never even venturing to other lands on Earth. And now, to have an opportunity to go to another whole world and explore it is just too much of a temptation. When a group of my kind gathers around and each boasts of what he has done, no other pucas can say they have been to a different planet."

"Well, that sounds a fair reason. To be able to brag."

He nodded vigorously. "Aye. That and to possibly cause just a little mischief in a world that needs distraction. You know, show a foolish human just how much of a folly what he does is. They need to be reminded."

"Ah, and there is the puca I know. Always looking for a bit of amusement."

"Of course. 'Tis my nature. Getting back to your concern about the trader in the nearby cabin, why not do a little spying or perhaps we could rattle him a little with a bit of unexplainable phenomena?"

"Perhaps, my friend. For now, we will wait and see what develops before we create any odd happenings on this ship.

Grania

NIA, I'M RELAYING A message from your man," Rory said as he worked his way through the messages coming in from Pelanan.

The ship approached the docking bay almost thirty mites ahead of the projected arrival time, a result of the smooth trip through the wormhole. Pleased, Grania tapped her earpiece to private and opened the video message, noting that Vilnius' sprint ship had arrived a hundred mites ahead of them. Cor, they are fast ships, even through the gates.

"I have a meeting in a few mites with Pelanan's stationmaster," he said in the message. "I expect to be free about eighteen hundred hours, station time. Tag me when you get in and let me know if we can meet at Rancil's. Can't wait to see you, my girl."

Joy and eagerness filled her heart before she settled down to the business at hand. She watched the final approach and confirmed Brendan's readings as the ship eased into the dock. "Good job, everyone. Let's get off-loaded as soon as possible and—"

"Pick up more," Rory said. "I'm already looking for cargo. Looks like there's a couple for Winthrop's Star and one at least for Tara Station. There's more to go through."

"Excellent. There's extra time for a break here. Let me know when you have a load and if anything changes our planned departure time. You can go ashore once you're done. I'm going to visit the stationmaster."

"Don't you mean the assistant stationmaster?" Rory asked, a wicked grin on his face.

She shot her practiced withering glance at him with no effect except for a bark of laughter. As she swatted a hand through the air in dismissal, she sprang to her feet, eager to get into the station. Nansi already had the off-loading started and as much as she wanted to stay on schedule, this one time she hoped the loading process might run a little slower to give her more time with Vilnius. For now, she had about eighty minutes to meet with the master, stop by the station spa, and meet Vilnius at Rancil's Lounge, a quieter spot than most on the station.

She hurried down the exit ramp from the ship heading toward the station core and glimpsed the brownish blond hair of the man not far in front of her, recognizing their passenger. Harhiman set a quick pace toward the merchant's lounge, a likely place to meet other traders with goods to buy or sell. He carried a rectangular case in one hand, so Grania assumed it contained samples of his merchandise. She wondered if he had included the Luna jewel and what other items he might peddle here.

Although smaller than Zabrowski, Pelanan Station bustled with activity as spacers hurried to conduct business, grab food, or stop at a bar to catch a drink and the latest gossip. A brief formality that most captains skipped, her visit to the stationmaster took less than ten minutes. Brendan had volunteered to check the boards so that Grania would have more time to prepare for her date with Vilnius, which relieved her of that task.

Luckily, she'd procured an appointment at the Stardust Spa where she could get a real scrub shower, clean hair, and fresh face done in less than an hour. For once, she wanted to look beautiful for Vilnius, more like a vid queen than a spacer. Even though she'd seen him off and on for close to five Earth years, about three times each year, the closest they'd been to something resembling a proper date had been the night he'd taken her to a vid showing on Zabrowski.

With the latest showers and dryers, the spa personnel managed their time to service their rush clients, who had only a little time before they needed to be off to a meeting or on a departing ship.

Grania lingered in the hot spray of a shower for a full ten minutes, a rare luxury when traveling through space, and hummed a cheery tune as she scrubbed with a driga, a sponge-like skin scraper. It left her skin feeling revitalized while the bath oil afterward softened it and left a scent of a floral essence.

The technician who washed and dried her hair chatted in a broken form of Anglobasic, the standard language used on most stations. From her first words, Grania could tell it wasn't similar to the girl's native tongue.

"I be Dela. You hair I up put?" she asked, lifting the long strands from the back and swirling them a little.

"Yes," Grania answered as she thumbed through a few images on her mobi-com until she found the one that showed hair swept up from the back and rolled into neat finger-length curls that were pinned from the apex of the sweep. She held the image up for the girl to see. "Like this."

"Oh, see I. Can do." Dela's pale green, almond-shaped eyes sparkled as she smiled and began separating Grania's long auburn hair, pinning sections to one side while she worked. While she chattered as she began shaping the curls and securing them, Grania didn't follow most of what she said. Then she asked, "What way head you?"

"What?" Grania didn't catch that and thought Dela wanted her to turn her head.

"You ship. What way go it?"

"Oh, you mean direction. My ship is going to Dragon Hold."

"Is good. You be okay, I think. Was trouble in Riga. Ship attacked."

"Attacked? By another ship?" Grania hadn't heard anything about an incident, and Rory didn't mention it from any of the reports coming in.

The girl shrugged. "I guess. I overhear someone tell Sinji about it two shifts past." She tilted her head toward a male technician who worked on another client's hair.

"Thank you for telling me. I'll check on it," Grania said, not too concerned. It could be nothing. Then again, if there had been a raider ship, the stationmaster should have known about it and sent a warning.

Dela finished up with her hair, then turned her over to another technician, who applied a light cream foundation to her face and added subtle color and highlighting to her eyes and cheeks. As she gazed at her reflection, her eyes widened at the more sophisticated and older appearance that the hair and make-up created. She'd twisted her hair up before, although not in such an elegant style as she now wore, and the make-up made her eyes appear wider. Shoving any lingering doubts aside, she hoped Vilnius approved of this upgrade.

Grania moved on to one of the boutique shops in the station. Although the store offered limited choices for pretty dresses, she found a classic navy blue sheath that accented all her curves and showed off her long neck. A new pair of shoes completed the makeover, and she still had several minutes before her appointed time at the lounge.

A few appreciative eyes followed her as she passed spacers. She'd sometimes gotten a wink or a nod, along with a smile when she walked around a station; however, they usually didn't continue to stare. Her spirits rose. She couldn't remember how long it had been since she'd dressed in anything other than the slacks and tunics the crew wore on the ship.

"Grania?"

A man's voice pulled her out of her thoughts and when he repeated her name, she turned.

"I wasn't sure it was you." A muscular-looking man, just about her height, with dark blond hair and a short beard, grinned at her.

"Mac! Oh, my heavens ... I must have walked right by you with my head in the stars. How are you?" She greeted him with a friendly hug. A family friend for many years, Maclin Dennison had worked on the Mo Chroidhe a few years before Liam had joined the crew.

"Ah, I'm great, girl. I'm on a merchant ship out of Helgard now, still working engines, and it's excellent. How 'bout you? Is old Paddy at the ship?"

She shook her head. "No, Granda wasn't feeling well and skipped this trip. Just me, Nansi, and my brothers."

"Sorry to hear that. I hope he's recovered by now. Give him my best when you get back home, okay?" He looked her up and down. "By the by, you look fabulous. What's with the dress-up?"

"Oh, it's just a dinner thing here on the station. I'm going to be meeting someone." She didn't want to say anything about Vilnius, and she faltered when she tried to find a way to explain her fancier than normal appearance. With two upscale restaurants and some posh people from other vessels at the station, it wasn't like she was over-dressed for dinner.

Mac simply nodded. "Right. Oh, did you get the word yet? I just saw a bulletin saying the hole is fluctuating, so there may be a delay if you're heading to Dragon Gate."

"Really? No, I haven't been informed. Bad luck, that. Sure, we were delayed at Zabrowski with a computer problem on the station and now this. Ah well, that's just the way it goes sometimes, isn't it?" She flashed a smile. "I must be going now, Mac. But it was grand to see you."

"And you. Of course. Take care and be sure to give my regards to all." He pulled her into a quick hug, then released her to resume her progress.

As she walked, she tagged Rory and relayed what she'd heard about the wormhole. "Have you seen anything on it yet?"

"I just got the notice. The monitoring station is reporting a disturbance in the wormhole, possibly a solar storm along the path affecting its stability. Looks like we may need to wait it out. No time estimate yet. I'll update you when we get more information."

"Right. Thanks, Rory." Her face broke into a huge smile. For once, a delay might be welcome. It meant a little more time with Vilnius.

CHAPTER ELEVEN

Liam

LIAM TOUCHED A SCREEN control, adjusting the image ever so slightly for the umpteenth time as he intently watched the recording of the cargo hold. The intruders were nothing more than specks of sparkling energy, almost, yet not quite, forming shapes. He slowed the images down as the sparkles stopped just outside the engine room, where he had been sound asleep during the jump. Hairs rose on the back of his neck at the realization that those things were outside his door while he was forced to sleep and unaware.

The images crawled by, no clearer than they'd been the last dozen or so times he'd adjusted the settings. He saw enough to know that something had invaded their cargo hold, abruptly appearing, then moving through the area as if they were looking for something. For over thirty-eight mites, they'd explored, paused, even seemed to dart toward a container, then grown smaller for a few minutes before getting larger again.

His scrutiny showed him the transgressors were two or more entities judging by the two clusters of energy. Still, each sparkle might be an individual or even a hive entity, moving in unison, but he didn't think so. For sure, there were two. The larger cluster had arrived first, appearing near the engine room, then scanning the fore section of the hold, and disappearing three times after sudden darts toward containers as if it searched for something. While he suspected the energy went inside the box, he couldn't prove it.

The first cluster had started back, when the second appeared, a smaller grouping just outside the engine room. Then, they joined, moving side by side for a while until they split at the aft end of the hold with the smaller one moving starboard while the larger continued straight on.

Yes, he decided; two entities, and he believed they were sentient. Could they have been probes of some type? Did someone have the technology to create this kind of invader? He didn't find anything in the reference material available to suggest it could be possible, let alone developed.

He sat back and scrubbed his hands across his face, weary with the effort. How long had he been staring at this snippet of video and making little progress? His eyes felt parched and burned from the extended viewing. Time for a break, he decided, stood and stretched his muscles, releasing the tension knotting his neck.

As he rubbed the sore spot, he gazed at the cargo floor, seeing a few empty spots where crates had already been off-loaded to Pelanan Station. Soon, they would have more to replace them; Rory sent the updated manifest not long after docking. They'd depart with a full load and it would make his sister and his granda happy.

Now, wouldn't you know? She had a date, having a grand time at the station while he was stuck down here trying to solve a problem. Yet Granda made her the captain on this trip just because she was older. It rankled him. Time for a cuppa.

A quick glance at the tea station reminded him he needed to refill the unit. He could use a break to the galley anyway, so he grabbed the empty two-liter bottle and the small trash container, then headed up the steps.

He found Nansi in the galley, drinking a cup herself and staring at her tablet. She barely acknowledged Liam's arrival, giving him just a nod as he greeted her.

"How is the loading going?" he asked as he dumped the used tea leaves and papers in the recycle bin.

"'Tis going well. We'll be ready long before we are given the departure clearance judging by the look of this snake of a wormhole.

"That'll give Grania a little more time, won't it? Works to her advantage."

His sarcastic tone brought Nansi's head up and she glanced at him, catching his tight, thin-lipped expression and lowered brows. He didn't care. His frustration with the puzzle magnified his annoyance with Grania, and his conviction Granda favored her.

Nansi changed the subject, and her eyes reverted to her tablet. "Are you finding anything interesting on that recording?"

He leaned over to get a look at the activity on her unit, then grimaced as he watched the wiggle of the wormhole. "That looks nasty. I can see why nobody is going through. As to the video, no, I don't have much yet. It's clearer now with still two sets of sparkles. For sure, something meandered around the hold. It gives me the willies just knowing it was outside my engine room." He got a fresh cup of tea while the machine refilled the bottle, then sat across from Nansi and told her what he'd done so far.

"Have you ever heard of anything like this before? I know strange things can happen in wormholes, but I can't find anything like this in the ship's research module."

"Oh, sure. I've heard stories about bogies in the between spaces and I've met a couple of spacers who claimed to have seen them. But the recorded proof is missing. It's all just stories, in 'nit Still, my granny used to say 'where there's smoke, there's a burning coal.' Truth, though, I've never seen anything like these energy signatures, lad."

While her response wasn't helpful, it confirmed this was likely an unknown situation. He nodded. "I just can't figure it out. I have a few more things I can try though."

Nansi rose, put her cup in the washer, then pressed a hand onto his shoulder and squeezed. "If it's possible to do, then you'll do it, Liam. You're skilled with those computers, so they can't hold back any secrets, can they?" She flashed a grin at him before leaving.

His own smile faded as he considered what other adjustments and filters he might try. He wanted to do everything possible to clear up the image and maybe get an outline or something of the thing. He needed to prove himself, again, to his sister. She was always testing him, checking his knowledge. Like at dinner before the Einstein Gate, when she made him explain how the gate worked for that old lady.

Sure, he loved Grania, but he had high dreams himself. It was almost a done deal she would inherit the Mo Chroidhe when Granda retired from the space lanes. For his own plans, he eventually wanted to get his own ship or at least become second on his father's ship. The third family ship was now captained by Uncle Colm, and his cousin Feoras would eventually advance to her captain.

Plus, he still had to beat Rory and Brendan for a chance at his own ship. And they were both as smart as he was. As for Grania, she wasn't just brainy; she had experience and training.

Back at his computer station, Liam ran the recording again after another tweak to the filters. At first, it didn't seem like anything had changed, then a haze caught his eye. He sat forward, backed the recording up, adjusted the filter one more level, and ran it again in slow motion.

There, where the energy group came to a stop by a container, for just a heartbeat or two, a shape formed like a mist within the sparkling dots. He played it back again, freezing the playback where the image appeared.

Energized, he enlarged it and printed the image. As he studied it, he a form emerged in the mist. He grabbed a stylus and tracked the outline, following the energy's sparks. At first, it looked like a blob until he realized it resembled a dress. A full dress, at that. Moving up, he could see where it narrowed at the waist, then angled up and spread a little to form a torso and arms with another blob that could be a head. A woman, he believed. He'd seen long, full dresses in old movies from Earth.

"Fecking hell," he whispered. "It's possible we have a ghost on the ship." Starting the video again, he watched the image fade as it drifted into the container. A few seconds later, just a trace of the mist remained as it returned to the energy pattern. After that, the haze faded from the video, leaving only the sparkling dots.

He sat back, surprised at what he'd discovered. He saved a copy of the video before trying another setting, then another and yet another. In the end, he lost the ghostly image on the other tries, so only the one filter revealed this image. Taking another approach, he studied the containers where the energy deviated and veered toward them. The first one, he realized as he looked at the cargo bay floor through the window, had already been off-loaded at Pelanan. The second and third containers were still on the floor.

He marked the locations and went into the bay to look at them. Position F14 sat empty. Beyond it, the entity had stopped at F37. Liam made a note of the container's owner number and looked it over, not seeing anything unusual in the standard issue box. Its contents were unlisted, and he made a note to check the manifest. The third unit was at F48, a large standard shipping container, and a cold crate at that; one designed especially for long distance shipping of perishable produce. In this instance, a ton of cheese products filled the box as noted on the container and were destined for the markets of Erinnua. The recipient was likely one of the three major distributors who would disburse the various products to the cities and towns on the planet.

Nothing too likely to interest ghosts if that was what their visitors were. Liam felt something must be in the cargo to draw the creatures here. All this speculation was interesting. But where did they originate, and how did they gain access to the ship?

CHAPTER TWELVE

Grania

GRANIA ARRIVED AT THE club right on time, but Vilnius didn't. He'd made a reservation though, so the meister seated her and brought a glass of Pelaner white wine to sip while she waited. It gave her a chance to gaze around the oddly elegant restaurant, one of the poshest places on the space station.

While Rancil's structure boasted the sleek lines and curved edges of most station businesses, the restaurant displayed a sophisticated character evident in the blue and light tan wall coverings, the golden metal-like sconces, and overhead hanging chandeliers. Earth-style paintings of idyllic scenes adorned the walls while the service stations nestled in concealment behind gold-colored screens. Her table, large for a station establishment, provided ample room for two people to dine without feeling squeezed together.

Rancils catered more to the high-powered businessmen, who frequently met clients and made deals in the elegant and somewhat private surroundings, than to spacers. Positioned into little alcoves, separated by three-quarter high walls, two and four person-sized tables allowed dinner guests more privacy.

The alcove where Grania waited shared its seclusion with another of the same-sized table, which was separated by tall planters with native green and gray plants to complete the illusion. That Vilnius chose it to meet surprised her. Perhaps he wanted more privacy than other eating establishments afforded.

Yes, dinner was likely to be a bit dear ... And late, she speculated as she glanced at the time again. Vilnius was already twenty minutes late. She signaled the waiter for another glass of wine, then checked for the ship's status. Nothing showed on her com, so she sent a quick message. "Just checking in. I'm still waiting here for my lad. Tag me if anything changes."

As the time ticked past, she grew more anxious and hungrier, signaling the waiter for a bread roll to help absorb the wine and ease her hunger. At last, Vilnius appeared at the Rancil's front entry. He smiled as he approached, and she couldn't suppress her own grin.

Gawd, he looks smashingly handsome in his formal station uniform, she conceded, feeling short of breath as she watched him approach. The blue-gray material highlighted his dark hair and olive skin and brought out the deep cerulean blue of his eyes.

As he entered the semi-private area, he opened his arms for her, and springing to her feet, she flew to him.

"My lord, you are gorgeous tonight," he murmured as he pressed a discreet kiss on her lips. Afterward, he pushed her back to get a proper view. His smile grew broader as his eyes devoured her from hair to toe. He motioned to the padded dinner chair. "Please, sit."

Grania sank onto the cushion; her own gaze locked on him as he eased down into the chair and leaned across the table to take her hand.

"Sorry I'm late, love. The meeting ran longer than I had anticipated it would."

"I was starting to wonder if you would be standing me up." Her eyes twinkled as she spoke.

"Never. Not ever would I do that. Ah, Nia, I was actually glad for this little jaunt because of the prospect of seeing you again."

A patient waiter arrived and hovered as Vilnius kissed the back of her hand, waiting to deliver a glass of wine for the "gentleman." Next, he explained the dinner specials and how their service worked.

"Appetizers will be delivered shortly, a chef's selection tonight, then a salad, made with garden-grown greens from the bio-dome. The wine is from the house selection of the evening." He handed them menus with the entrée selections. "I shall return soon for your order." He gave a half bow and departed.

Vilnius raised an eyebrow as he barely contained a laugh. "Well, that was quite formal, wasn't it?"

"Indeed. Have you been here before?"

He shook his head. "I've traveled to this station a few times, but not to this restaurant. It came highly recommended by the stationmaster." He sipped the wine, nodding his head a bit as he swallowed. "That's all right, I guess. I don't suppose they have ale or stout."

She laughed. "What are we doing here, Vilnius? The pub would have been more like us."

"Probably. But I wanted to give you a special evening that wasn't simply meat and chips in a crowded bar. Something that would be an unfamiliar experience for both of us."

"Well, I must say you've succeeded. This is undeniably a novel experience." She paused to open her menu, lowering it a bit so her eyes peeked over the top of it at her date. "What was this meeting that required your personal appearance?"

"I can't tell you much about it. Security, you know. I can say it was connected to the bug we had on Zabrowski. We—the folks I met with and I--think there's more to it than a bid to disrupt station business. That alone doesn't make sense."

"I see. So, they needed your expertise here."

"Something like that." He looked away, opening his menu before their waiter came back. He scanned the short list of entrees, settled on one, and closed it. Grania had already chosen the Fenicob Pheasant, named after the big plump bird that was native to Pelanan. She'd never tried one, and they were rumored to be delicious.

As soon as they lowered their menus, the waiter returned with house appetizers of a breaded and fried shellfish neither of them had ever encountered before, yet they imparted a delightful scent, and an assortment of little cheese balls. He requested their entrée choices before he left them to the "first remove".

"First remove ... Who talks like that?" Vilnius asked.

"Obviously, the waiters in this place. Is this a posh joint or not?" She speared a cheese ball with one of the little two-pronged forks on the plate and popped it into her mouth. It had an odd taste, not bad, and not like any cheese she'd tried before. This promised to be a quite different dining experience.

Nansi

WITH THE NEW CARGO loaded, Nansi made sure the recent crates were locked down and logged in. She now sat on a stool behind Liam as he ran the footage from the second camera showing the starboard section of the forward bay. The smaller visiting entity had gone that way, and unlike the other one Liam now called a ghost, it didn't seem to pause or explore, but made its uninterrupted way down the aisle between the cargo containers.

No matter how much he tweaked the video, Liam couldn't get a better representation of the visitor or manage a ghostly mist as he had with the first one.

Nansi studied the print that he'd outlined. "Are ya sure this isn't a bit of fog or reflection on the camera lens? It's not like you can actually see a person."

"No, it's neither of those. It only showed up with the one filter setting, and it was there for eighteen secs. I just can't get the other cluster of energy to show anything similar. Look at it! The energy points are constantly in motion. No, something happened for a short time to cause that image to show up when I set the UV filter."

She turned the image around to see if it looked different from a new perspective. "I don't know. It could be a spirit or something else. Whatever these things were, they seem to be gone now. A least, they are not roaming through the cargo hold."

"Something in the between space, do you reckon?"

"Could be." Nansi turned to check the latest update from Pelanan. Below, the cargo bay vibrated with the rumble of the ship's docking generator, the air thick with the stale odor of fuel. Space ships weren't meant to be docked with crew on board for long periods. "Looks like we'll be here at least another two hundred mites from the images of the hole's wriggling out there. What do you say we go find a pub for a pint?"

In all her years on spaceships, she hadn't encountered a wormhole as unsatable as this one. She hoped it settled down and remained that way. Although she wouldn't admit it to the Mo Chroidhe's young crew, the prospect of going through it didn't sit well with her.

"Why not? There's nothing more to be done until we can undock. If the Captain can have time off, why not us?" Liam grinned and locked down the workstation, trimming the generator's output to half and cutting the lighting in the cargo bay.

"Excellent, lad. I'll let Rory know we're going ashore. He won't be leaving the ship for the next few hours with all the messages and updates comin' in." Nansi pulled out her com to advise Rory.

"It's not lookin' good," Rory said before she could say anything. "That worm is highly unstable and not settlin' down at all."

"So, no change in the status, eh, boy-o?" she replied.

Nansi knew Rory and Liam quite well, having seen them grow up, although not on the ship like their sister. Paddy had taken Grania on board early when her mother wanted to return to the ship after Brendan was born. She brought her daughter with her while the boys remained with their grandmother and aunts on Erinnua. Still, she'd seen how the boys worked and evaluated their skills as they progressed. Fine boys, and so smart. Their Granda would be proud of them all.

"Not a bit, Nansi. It's turning into a long stay." His voice lacked some of his usual sparkle, but the lad had been on the com ever since they arrived.

"Tell ya what. Liam and I are going for a pint at the pub. When we come back, I'll spell you for a bit, so you can get a break. Is that a deal?"

After a brief pause, he replied, "It sounds fine to me. I'll need a break by that time. Bren's keeping me company, but he's about to nod off."

"No stamina," Nansi chuckled. "See you in about sixty-five mites."

Liam stood at the stairs to the main deck, waiting for her to finish. "You ready?"

"That I am, lad. Let's do it." She followed him up the stairs, eager to get off the ship for a spell herself. As she climbed, she spared a thought for Grania, wondering how she and her handsome man were getting on and if she'd be back soon. She knew what she'd do with a handsome fellow like Vilnius.

Alas, she was way too old for the young fella she was going out with on this night, but if she were younger, Liam O'Ceagan would be quite a catch.

CHAPTER THIRTEEN

Grania

ONE DELIGHT OF PELANAN Station centered on the small, yet spectacular, garden dome in the middle of the hub. Laid out like a park with soft bio-lights providing twilight illumination, the area bathed in the glow from the planet. Looking up through the dome, the nearby sphere seemed to hang like a green and gray moon off to one side. Behind it, densely clustered stars formed a glittering backdrop.

Grania snuggled next to Vilnius on a bench while they admired the view and the fresh air that was common around station parks. A sweet fragrance from a violet dreamshade blossom lingered in the recycled air, adding a sense of enchantment. The deep purple flowers surrounded the tree roots and climbed a luminaire tree to wind around the glowing pods.

His right arm draped around her shoulders, pulling her close so her head rested against his chest. His fingers played with a lock of her copper-toned hair, careful not to pull it loose. She sighed, content with the feel of his touch and the intimacy between them. Too little of this graced their lives and at times, she questioned the wisdom of continuing. They each followed different journeys, rarely crossing paths, so she attempted to keep her feelings for him in check. At this moment, moderation was becoming more challenging.

"I need to ask you something, love," Vilnius asked, his husky voice low and sexy.

"Uh huh, and what would that be?" She anticipated an amorous query she would have to ponder for a few moments.

"I'm aware you've got two passengers this trip, but would there be a way that you might squeeze in one more?"

She straightened up, the romantic moment aborted. "Another one? No. Rory's already given up his cabin and the spare one is more like a storage room."

"Perhaps you could share your cabin? I don't take up a lot of room and I could use the jump pod in the storage cabin or – "

"You?! You're wanting to travel with us to Dragon Gate?"

He nodded. "Yep. Some business on the station, and the sprint ship I came in on has already departed in the other direction. So, what do you say?"

"Oh, feck, you scamp. So, you wine, dine, and charm the lass to get a free ride, is that it?" Grania's outrage was only half-feigned. Was he simply playing with her for a ride? No, he wouldn't ... He'd always been sincere in his affections.

"No, no, not at all! You wound me! I can pay for my passage, Captain. I have government-issued credits, and it's official business." He flashed his most charming smile.

She drew back a little, a cross look wrinkling her brow, then she threw her arms around him. "We'll have more time together. I don't believe it!"

"So, is that a yes?" he asked as he squeezed her closer before he planted a breath-sucking kiss on her parted lips.

WHILE VILNIUS AND BRENDAN retired to the spare cabin to check the jump pod, ensuring it was charged and safe to use for the jump from Pelanan to Dragon Gate, Liam called Grania down to engineering to show her what he'd found.

"I also checked out the crates the ghost seemed interested in. I didn't find anything unusual." Liam slowed the video down for her to view again.

Grania studied the printed image he'd outlined and glanced back at the video, where the image still looked like a misty blur on the screen. She wasn't sure the blob was a ghost, but she agreed that whatever it might be, the thing showed a definite interest in their cargo. "It's looking for something. Did you find anything peculiar in the logged contents?"

"No, only the usual stuff; the cold container is filled with cheese. And all the ones the ghost checked are from shippers that we've handled cargo for before. I don't think the thing knows what container it's trying to find. If it found one, the crate would be in the aft bay. I don't have a camera on the port side and the other entity didn't stop or seem to investigate at all on the starboard side."

"What in blazes are these things?" Grania asked as her dream came to her mind again, the suggestion of a man and a container. She'd checked Harhiman's cargo list and hadn't found anything dangerous on it. Now she wondered if it tied to something else in the cargo. "Did you look at the manifest for everything we loaded?"

"No, I only tracked the ones the ghost showed an interest in. Like I said, I didn't have a working camera on the port aisle, so I can't say if it found anything."

"What happened to the port camera?" She knew they had one. She'd reviewed recordings from it more than once in the past.

"Corrupted memory chip. A power surge or something might have zapped the memory chip. The recording's not readable." Liam looked down, his dejected face reflecting his disappointment at having to admit the failure.

Grania realized how much pride he took in his work zone. "These things happen, Liam. Is the camera repaired now?"

"Aye. It is."

"Great. If anything like this happens during the next jump, we'll see if any of the crates on that side interest the thing. In the meantime, review every manifest for the boxes on that side. Advise me if you see anything unusual."

"I noticed one other thing," Liam started, but hesitated. At her attentive nod, he continued. "When we arrived, I checked the power levels in the jump pods in all the cabins to make sure they performed as expected and would recharge before the next jump. Most of them were down about twenty-five percent, which is about right, and they're fully charged again. But one of them was only down less than two percent."

"You weren't looking at the one in the spare cabin, were you? That one's not been working. Vilnius and Brendan are checking the pod out now."

He shook his head. "No, that one is at fifty percent already since they've brought it back online. The one in question is in Rory's cabin."

"That can't be right, Liam. That's where Miz O'Cairn is, and she came through the gate fine. She couldn't have with only a two percent drop in the pod. It sounds like the pod wasn't used at all. And that can't be. Could anybody go through the wormhole without the stasis sleep?"

"Not to my knowledge. At least, not anything human."

An involuntary shiver ran up her spine. Not a human? What did they have in that cabin if not an old woman? Fated fairies, this wasn't possible.

She swallowed down her uneasiness, not putting too much weight on this possibility. "As I said, check the manifests and tag me is something seems off. We may want to consider scanning all the crates to make sure nothing is concealed in them."

"Scan them? Are you suspecting something amiss?"

"I don't know, brother. Something doesn't feel right, and this 'thing', whatever it is, seems to be looking for something on our ship. I want to know what the form is and how in all the fates it got here."

The bridge com interrupted anything else she was about to say as Rory's voice cut through. "Pelanan is giving us clearance to head through the gate in forty-five mites. Hole's stable for the moment and looks like it's holding. They've been monitoring the movement and confirm the path has been steady for the past sixty mites. We've got a window for the jump."

"Copy that. Alert Brendan and Vilnius. I hope that jump pod is working. Are our passengers back?"

"Aye, they are. Harhiman came on about twenty mites ago. Miz O'Cairn never left her cabin."

"Good. On my way. Get us ready to go, Liam. We'll hope nothing weird happens in this jump, and try to figure this all out when we get to Dragon Gate."

She climbed the narrow stairwell to the middle level and stopped at the spare cabin where Vilnius and Brendan still had the cover removed from the pod. "Is it ready yet?"

Vilnius raised his chin, a glint of assurance lighting up his eyes. "Last check is going now. We need a little longer to be sure the oxygen and sleep mist are all set. While we're not quite to full power, it will be enough for the jump."

"Are ye sure?" She hated the idea of Vilnius using a pod that wasn't absolutely safe. If anything went wrong ... She couldn't bear to even think about the possibility.

"It's good," Brendan said. "'T'was only a minor problem. We had to replace a board is all."

"All right, boys. Get back to the bridge as soon as you can, Brendan. And Vilnius, you get ready for the jump. We're going soon."

CHAPTER FOURTEEN

Sheilan

IN THEIR CABIN, SHEILAN closed and sealed the jump pod soon after the alert was communicated. She thanked the deities governing her kind for the insight to listen in on Grania and Liam talking about the use of the pod, so she learned that if she activated it, the pod would appear to be in use. She should have considered the energy monitoring with the first jump.

More concerning, she heard the conversation about what Liam had learned of her excursion with Dari during the last jump. The lass could be putting two and two together, as the folk often said, and she might come up with the right answer. For now, the crew had no idea what she and Dari were, but with their resources, they might learn more than she wanted them to know.

"That's just dandy," Dari griped. "You are leaving clues behind like leaves falling from trees. Do ye want them to learn what you are?"

"I suspect they will, sooner or later. I would prefer not to be dumped into space. If it looks like they will take such an action, we retreat to the soil and hope we can transport from space."

"Oh well, then, that's a fine plan. Is it not a pity that we do not know if it will work or not? And if we are tossed out like trash into space and it does not work, how might we return to Earth?"

"Well, puca, perhaps we can just reduce to our pure energy form, hide in the venting system, and let them toss the trunk. They will still take us to Erinnua."

Dari crossed his arms and glared at her. "And then 'tis stuck on a distant world we will be, is it not? A fine plan, I say again. How did I let you talk me into this?"

"Oh, no, puca. Do not put this on me. 'Tis you who convinced yourself that you wished to travel with me. Besides, it does no good to worry about the spoiled fruit until it happens, does it? Come have tea and cakes with me, then we can explore." She sat at the little table again and poured a cup for each of them. Sometimes, she genuinely enjoyed her human form.

"Explore what this time? I am not going near that energy-sapping crate below again."

"Nor will I. Instead, let us see if there is any more to be learned about the trader. To my regret, I did not follow him on the station. He exited before I realized he was gone."

They sat in silence with their tea for a few minutes before Sheilan noticed something and spoke again. "Have you noticed the tea is sloshing around the cup, not at all even?"

Dari watched his cup as the liquid rolled back and forth and they felt a shudder in the ship like it hit something. "What do ye suppose it means?"

Setting the cup down, she rose, dematerialized, and drifted through the ceiling to the bridge where the views outside the ship streamed onto the screens. On the main screen, which displayed the forward view, the image jerked and blurred, streaks of various colors cutting through the image. Even though she couldn't feel it when the ship tilted, she saw the angle change through the fractal vision she utilized in her energy state.

What is happening? The previous jump wasn't like this. Even in this state, she detected the ship shuddering like a toy being buffeted by hurricane-force winds. It appeared to slide from one side of the wormhole to the other, with waves below lifting and dropping it again and again. Surely, this isn't normal.

As she materialized to her human form, the piercing shriek of an alarm filled the bridge and yellow lights flashed on and off in warning as the ship lurched forward, missing the outside wall to the right by a hand's width. Almost thrown from her feet, Sheilan levitated a few centimeters from the floor.

Over the next few minutes, the ship shook with violent lurches, bouncing around as though heading into a horrible windstorm, then the shaking eased as the ship stabilized again. Once the turbulence settled, the alarm cut off. The yellow lights continued to flash for a minute before it, too, ceased.

Sheilan settled her feet on the floor, looked up at the bridge camera, returned to her energy form, and zapped into it to blast the electronics. Best to leave no trace of her presence. Last visit, the crew hadn't looked at the bridge footage; this time, she might not be so lucky.

Back in the cabin with Dari, she told him what she'd seen. "It appears the wormhole thing is not as stable as they expected it to be. But it seems to have settled down now. An alarm was making a terrible racket on the bridge, so I suppose we will see what that means when we reach the other end of this tunnel. It was fluctuating like a blessed fishing worm on a hook."

"Everything not tied down in here bleeding bounced all over the place," the puca complained. "Just look at your trunk. 'Tis all askew."

She sat down to mop up the spilled tea that had sloshed in all directions before the cup had overturned and cast a glance at the chest that had moved about a half-meter from where it had been and now turned at an angle. "Not so bad, Dari. At least the cover was closed so nothing was dumped out. Let us see what we can find out, shall we?"

In the end, she explored alone as Dari, still shaken by the unusual event, opted out of the excursion, and retreated to the dirt to recover, or so he said.

Sheilan entered Harhiman's cabin in her energy form, intent on leaving no trace at all to be seen. The problem with this form was that while she viewed everything in fractal form, she couldn't physically touch any of it. Still, she could investigate enough to show her where the energy sources were in the room, and where Harhiman still kept the Luna jewel secure. None of the power levels she'd experienced from the crystals in the cargo bay appeared in the cabin.

Oddly, the trader left his tablet active, its power light blinking in a rhythmic pattern. Sheilan peered at it, recognizing the image displayed resembled the pattern of the crystals she'd seen in the crate below.

As she studied the tablet's screen, she realized it looked like a message he was sending or had sent. She was unable to make out what he'd written or who the recipient was. Again, she wondered why the man would leave the device active when they passed through the gate.

The signals wouldn't get through the wormhole, so Liam had said. What if there was another ship in the wormhole? Would the signal be able to transmit or receive if they were close? While she knew very little about this technology stuff running everything these days, she was astute enough to know when something was peculiar and this qualified.

Abruptly, she was plucked from Harhiman's cabin and next appeared in the solid, young maiden form in the middle of the cargo hold, in full view of the recording device there. Neither could she control the form nor her actions now. This was her calling, her function.

With the sinking feeling of dismay, she knew anyone who saw her, and the camera recording this visit, would see a quaintly dressed peasant girl from centuries long past, kneeling on the floor and weeping. A wooden bucket was at her side while she dipped a shirt in an illusionary stream and scrubbed it, over and over, as if she washed blood from them. With a sniff, she detected the iron scent of blood in the air and the odor of an electronic burn, like a connector shorted out.

Unable to speak except to wail, nor take any action, but the one she now performed, she flowed through the motions. The banshee was bringing a warning, a first-time premonition of danger to the family. A disaster was certain to happen, and the ship's crew must heed her warning. Danger waited ahead, threatening terrible harm or death to the one or more of the O'Ceaghans.

CHAPTER FIFTEEN

Grania

GRANIA JOLTED OUT OF her pod sleep to the shrill sound of the ship's warning buzz alerting her to a problem. She shoved against the lid on her pod and automatically reached for the oxygen mask attached to the side, but took a shallow breath to test the air before putting it on. It seemed fine, so the ship had adjusted her cabin environment before alerting her. She could rule out an environmental failure. After she swung her legs out of the pod, she stumbled as the ship rocked to reach the cabin's auxiliary command station. Red lights pulsed in a series of dots on the screen, indicating a course irregularity. A yellow box under it displayed the message advising a wormhole flux.

"Oh, blast it all! Where the hell are we?" She verbalized the question to the computer and waited, shaking her head and stretching her neck to get the kinks worked out. The rest of her crew would wake soon, and she wanted to tell them where they were. The verbal response that came back sent a chill through her.

"Location unknown. Coordinates corrupted."

"How much time has passed since the ship entered the wormhole?" she asked.

"Exact time unknown, estimated at seven Erinnua hours."

Seven?! Her mind screamed and her stomach lurched. The jump should have taken two. A flux could have thrown them light years away from their destination. "Crew status, report!" she ordered.

"All pods adequate and cycling awake except 2C that shows 1 percent remaining power and conserving," the ship's computer responded.

Vilnius!

Grania's heart skipped a beat. "Override controls! Cycle awake now." She slipped on her deck shoes as she spoke and hurried out the door, running down the hall, and taking the stairs down a level to 2C.

"Computer, open cabin 2C now." Worried, she waited until the door lock released with a click. Seeing the pod hadn't opened, she dashed to it and hit the manual override, forcing it up. The escaping air tasted stale to her, and she grew more fearful. As she leaned toward Vilnius, she noted he appeared pale, but his chest rose and fell with shallow breaths.

She grabbed the oxygen mask from the side of the pod and held it to his face, giving him fresh air to breathe. She waited, watching the steady rhythm of his chest as his breathing grew stronger until his eyes blinked open and fluttered a few times as he returned to consciousness. He drew in a deep breath, followed by another before his hand reached to cover hers on the mask.

"Are you all right?" she asked, her voice sounding hoarse. In response, his hand squeezed hers as he continued to inhale. Fecking hell. Too close, she acknowledged and dropped her head against his chest.

"Grania? What's happened?" Brendan's voice quivered.

She raised her head and turned to gaze at her wide-eyed, scared-looking youngest brother, who stood framed in the door opening. "We're off course, Bren."

"I – I didn't –"

"No, you didn't." She cut him off. "The bleedin' wormhole hadn't stabilized yet. We experienced a fluctuation, and we're not where we were supposed to be. I don't know where we are. Get to the bridge and see if you can figure it out. The computer appears to have lost data and can't get the coordinates. Grab Rory on the way so he can try to contact any station in range."

Vilnius' hand tapped hers as he pushed the mask away.

"Are you all right now?"

"I am, thanks to you." He pushed himself up, reaching to touch her cheek where a tear had started down her face. "It's okay, Nia. I'll be all right. Go take care of the bridge. I'll be along in a few mites."

She nodded and gave him a quick kiss before she headed out the door in a run.

"What do we know?" Grania asked as she hurried onto the bridge. "Where are we?"

Rory glanced up, his brow crinkled by a perplexed frown. "Not very much. Communications are down, nothing but static. The ship can't display coordinates and doesn't have a clue where we are. Either the cameras are all broken or we are in a very dark part of space." He pointed to the forward monitor and Grania's eyes followed.

The screen, almost all black, showed only a thin intermittent flash of white or red, as if something seemed to streak past. No stars, no planets, or any other objects appeared in the view. She turned her head to look at the starboard screen, shifted to the port, seeing the same thing on all of them.

"What do you have, Brendan?" she asked, her voice raspy with dryness and concern.

"I'm running a full system check on the nav computers now. The readout we had as we entered the wormhole looked fine, until forty-five mites into it, the readings went sideways. It looks like the ship took a shaking and the wormhole deviated. The ship couldn't pinpoint the trajectory before the hole dumped us here. Last known solid coordinates put us twenty-eight degrees south and fourteen below our planned route." Although his voice sounded strained, he held up like an experienced spacer.

Scared, Grania noted. His first trip into deep space and this happened. Hell, it frightened her, too. 'Twas an uncommon occurrence, and she'd never been on a ship that exited far off the planned jump coordinates. The odds were against it. If the station had suspected even a chance of the wormhole destabilizing, they wouldn't have cleared the ship to go through. And this—

This, she couldn't even fathom. She stared at the forward screen again while her mind tried to grasp the situation.

"Okay," she said, forcing herself to think through the process. "Reboot the communications system, Rory, and reload any protocols and routers into it to try to contact anyone. At least, our onboard systems appear to be working, and that's a blessing."

She turned back to Brendan. "Try to project our destination based on where we were and the direction of the ship's heading at the last solid reading. If the wormhole fluxed and popped us out at that point and we propelled forward, it should be a straight-line course based on the time from the last communication until we arrived here."

The automatic door swished open, and Nansi stepped onto the bridge, her eyes locked straight on the monitor screens. "Well, this is shite, isn't it? Liam has an engine down, and it looks like we're off the map completely."

"Yep," Grania agreed. "Have you ever seen anything like this?"

"Seen it? No. If it's what I'm thinking it is, then I've heard tales and it's not good."

Grania stepped close and lowered her voice. She didn't want to alarm her brothers until she knew more about the situation and their options. "Tell me quietly."

"The stories say there are areas in space that are empty—"

"Black holes?" Grania asked in a low breath, fearful of the answer.

"No, not that. But stretches of space where there are no stars, no planets, just nothing. They're difficult to navigate and com signals don't penetrate through them."

"And that's where you think we are? In one of these empty spaces?"

"Aye, that I do. The Sea of Darkness, it's called by the old storytellers."

"So, tell me, what is the bad news?"

"Well, the storytellers say that once something goes into the sea, it doesn't come out again." Nansi's voice rasped with strain as she whispered this.

"Nonsense! If nothing ever came out, how would anyone know anything about it? If that is what this is, there is a way out and we will find it. I will not lose my granda's ship in this Black Sea." Grania's heart sank a little, although she would not show it to her crew. They would figure this out, and they would get back on track to home.

Nansi simply nodded, a hint of hope showing in her eyes. For all her second's years as a spacer, Grania realized the old tales still frightened her. Although fearful herself, as captain, she had to show strength and confidence, not only for Nansi but for the rest of the crew as well.

Vilnius strode in, stopped mid-step, and gazed around the bridge, his eyes locking on the forward screen before gradually shifting to each of the other ones. Those big, black, empty-looking images of nothing were an immediate draw, she admitted. Only she had entered the bridge without looking at them. What did that say about her?

"Are the screens down?" Vilnius asked.

Grania shook her head while Rory swiveled in his seat to face them. "No. The wormhole booted us out."

Vilnius' eyes shot back to the screen, and she could see his Adam's apple bob as he swallowed hard. "Well, damnation. What can I do?"

His computer expertise and station experience might prove handy, she reckoned. "Give Rory a hand with the reboot at communications. Let's see if we can find out where we are and try to contact someone. If we disappeared out of the wormhole, then someone should be looking for us. Maybe someone at Pelanan tracked which way the wormhole shifted. Even Dragon Station might have picked it up. Either way, the Mo Chroidhe logged through the gate and didn't exit the other end. They should be trying to find us."

She sank down at her station, tapped to the ship's reference library, and requested information on the Sea of Darkness. Until she learned more, she cut the sound and routed the results to her headset. The available information related various stories and reports spacers told over the years, and those tales corroborated what Nansi said. Over the past three centuries, six ships had vanished from wormholes and were believed to be in the Sea of Darkness or Dark Sea, which were names given to any of the alleged dark spaces. Those were the facts. One report related that one ship had returned to normal space, and it was the only account they had to describe the dark space.

Space charts showed the gates where the losses occurred. Pelanan Station Gate jumped out at her, and it noted one ship had vanished from there. She needed more information on the surviving ship and requested the search to expand. There had to be a way out. She couldn't accept any less.

She jerked a bit when Liam's voice cut through her headset, breaking her concentration. "Grania, I need you down here as soon as you can. Bring Nansi."

WHEN THEY ARRIVED IN ENGINEERING, Grania found Liam halfway through the floor where he'd opened the well to the engines below the ship. He wore an undershirt and glistened with sweat. His hair clung to his face and neck. The oppressive heat enveloped her like a thick blanket and her breath caught in shallow a gasp while beads of perspiration dampened her brow. "What's happened?"

"Number two engine overheated. It's still cooling down."

"I thought there were safeguards—"

"Don't ya be blaming me! I didn't route the ship on a longer jaunt than expected. If Brendan made a mistake—"

"He didn't!" she snapped back at him. "The fecking wormhole fluxed, and it looks like it was more than a little burp. We arrived way overdue in the wrong place. Can you fix the engine?"

He shot an annoyed look at her. "Of course, I can. Do you think I'm an eejit?"

"No. I didn't know if you had what you needed to do it. Is this what you wanted me to come down here to see?"

He climbed to the deck. His clothes, covered with smudges and slick fluid, stank with mixed chemical odors. Then the rest of what she'd said clicked. "Fairy shite! We were booted from the wormhole?"

The engine must have leaked quite a bit, Grania concluded, stepping back to give her brother room. "Aye. We're in a dark sector of space, it seems."

Frowning, he shook his head and led the way to his engineering console. "We have more damages than the engine. The jolting must have jarred the dorsal sail free from its well. It won't be doing us any good until it's repaired."

With a flip of a switch, he turned on the image from the top camera, pointing backward from the prow. A mounted spotlight illuminated the sail half-twisted out of its secure well. The hatch door that normally shut after the sail lowered into the well, tilted to one side. The problem was compounded by the solar cloth twisting partway around the door and looping back to the frame.

"Well, that's dandy. It just goes from bad to worse," she said. "Anything else?"

"Aye. One more thing for you and Nansi to see. We had another invasion incident during the jump."

"The same energy things?" Grania asked, her concern growing.

"Not exactly." Liam started the video at a point during the ship's shaking. "I wanted to see if I could get any clues to what happened during the jump, then I saw this."

On the screen, the ghost-like image of a young woman, dressed in what appeared to be a long, loose-fitting dress, knelt on the cargo bay floor. Her dark hair lifted away from her face with a triangular cloth holding it back. She cried out, making a high-pitched, borderline shrill wailing. Her hands scrubbed at a shirt she held up like she washed it as she cried. Her face, pretty, but very pale, showed grief and anguish. She cried out words over and over in what sounded like Old Gaelic, but Grania could only understand one word, "O'Ceaghan". A shiver of fear raced along her spine as if she'd been touched by fairies. Just as quickly as she'd arrived on the bay floor, the young woman vanished.

"Nansi, what in the name of all that's holy was that?"

Nansi still stared wide-eyed at the screen as if she couldn't believe what she'd seen. "Something that is surely not holy," she uttered. "'Tis a *b'ean sidhe*, I think. At least, it looks like what the old legends said they could look like. I never thought they were real."

"A banshee?" Liam echoed, picking up the phonetic pronunciation. "Now could you explain what that is? All I saw was a ghostly young woman suddenly appears, crying and wailing like she's lost all she loved, and just as abruptly disappears. Is this our ghostly visitor again?" His handsome face screwed into a puzzled frown and under it sat the tension of not knowing what had happened. "Could this thing be responsible for what's happened here?"

Nansi shook her head, uncertainty on her face. "I don't know. I only know that a bean sidhe is a death or doom messenger."

"What?!" Grania's voice rose in shock. "Death? Whose death?"

Nansi grabbed her arm. "No, don't be panicking. 'Tis a warning, I think. They manifest to give warnings to their family. But I never heard any stories about them being away from Ireland or even England or America. They were bound to the Earth, my grandmother said."

"Clearly not."

"She spoke out our family name," Liam said in a muted, worried voice. "Does that mean she is warning us about a death in our family? Or did she come to tell me I'm going to die?"

"Now, how have you managed to come to that conclusion, Liam?" Grania asked.

He swallowed hard, looking at his sister with fear behind his eyes. "She materialized down here, right outside where I was in pod sleep, didn't she? Doesn't that mean the message was meant for me?"

Grania looked away, feeling overwhelmed. "I can't say, Liam. I don't know. We don't have enough information about this. You can bet that I will be finding out as much as I can. You said it was a warning, Nansi. Could you understand what she said? Does it always mean death?"

Nansi shrugged, her face revealing nothing. "It sounds like the old language, and I don't speak it. I've told you all that I can, Grania. They were simply stories or so I thought. Faith, I've never talked to anyone who has actually encountered one."

Grania dropped into a chair, rested her head against her hands, and tried to think. They couldn't do anything about the b'ean sidhe's appearance on the ship. If her appearance related to the energy spikes from the last jump, they might have two on board. She needed to learn more about them, and what it meant to see one. Meanwhile, she had other problems to solve and a crew to calm down. Everyone needed their wits if they were to get out of this mess alive.

Taking a deep breath, she met her brother's eyes, seeing the worry in them. "Liam, we don't know exactly what the banshee's appearance means. If it's a warning, we need to be careful about what we're doing to make sure we don't take unnecessary risks. Now, the engine still needs fixing, and we're not going anywhere until we figure out which direction to point the ship, so for now, take a break. Let's go have food and think about all this logically. And I need to tell our passengers we have a problem because by now, they're likely wondering what has happened. We will make it out of here, all of us, alive. You got that?"

Liam nodded, and his spirit rose with her words. "Yes, you're right. A tea break might do us some good." Just as he said it, the groaning of stressed metal rumbled through the bay and three sets of eyebrows rose in concern.

CHAPTER SIXTEEN

Grania

ON HER WAY TO the galley, Grania stopped by both passenger cabins to offer her apologies for the delay. For now, she didn't want to alarm them. Seeing Miz O'Cairn first, she told her they had exited the gate off course and advised her to please remain in her cabin until further notice. The old lady accepted the information well, saying, "'Tis sure I am that the captain has the situation well in hand."

On the other hand, Harhiman's face reddened, and he sputtered and swore as he expressed his concerns about missed schedules and meetings, as well as the state of his cargo.

"Your cargo is fine," she assured him. "Nothing in the cargo bay was disturbed. That being said, we do have an engine problem that needs repairing before we can get underway again. While I understand your concerns, no one anticipated this type of situation."

"I don't have a signal out on my tablet," he complained. "When can I expect to be able to use it? I need to contact my clients and adjust arrangements."

"I'll inform you when we have access again," she answered, trying to calm the merchant down. As she walked away, she doubted she succeeded in mollifying him, but she had more worries than Harhiman at the moment.

The crew and Vilnius waited for her in the galley and heads swiveled her way as she came in. After grabbing a cup of much needed tea, she leaned back against the counter and filled them in on the situation.

"So, what do we do next, Grania?" Rory asked.

While tea and biscuits had gone a long way toward restoring their spirits, she realized they had many more unanswered questions.

Now, she looked at the anxious faces of her brothers, Nansi, and Vilnius, and outlined the immediate plan. "First, we need to establish communications with some point, a station, or a ship, or anything broadcasting a signal. If can find any way to boost the signal, Rory, we need to do it.

"Liam, concentrate on the engine repair. We can't go anywhere until that's done. Brendan, where are you on the coordinates? Do you have any idea where we might be in relation to Dragon Gate or Pelanan?"

He cleared his throat with a nervous cough. "I'm still extrapolating the changes and trying to backtrack them as well. I should have something for you soon. Some charts I found show the Dark Sea although it's labeled 'empty space'."

"All right. It's a start, then. Now, all we need to figure out is where we are in this empty space and which direction to go to locate the wormhole or a gate."

"What about the sail?" Liam asked. "We won't be able to make decent time with the sail twisted the way it is. Even without using it, we'll risk more damage to it."

"It's not a top priority right now, but I'll study the problem. Perhaps we can fix it, or if not, we can at least get it out of the hatch and back into storage.

"It will take someone going outside the ship to do it," Vilnius added. "I can help out with that."

She shot him a sharp look. "We'll discuss that later. Right now, we have enough to do to get the ship functional enough to find our way out."

"And the bean sidhe?" Nansi tossed that question out.

"For now, there's nothing to be done about it. It appears I have some research to do and several questions to answer, don't I? Everyone, just be careful and take all precautions while you're doing your jobs. It's not a sure thing this creature is only warning us. We all need to take care not to make it a self-fulfilling prophecy. Now, let's get back to work and see what we can do about finding our way home."

As the others left, Vilnius lingered behind. Grania shot him a hard look. "No, Vilnius, I will not have you going out into space to do our work. Don't you even be considering it."

"Who would you have do it? Brendan? He's just a lad and this is his first trip. Has he ever been on the outside? Rory isn't much older, and I'll bet he hasn't ever done a spacewalk either. What about Liam? You?"

"I did it once. I can do it again," she said, but her voice wavered with uncertainty.

"You're the captain. You can't take that kind of a risk. And I wouldn't let you."

"Let me? You couldn't stop me. It's my ship! My rules!"

He caught her arm. "And the crew needs you. If we're going to get out of this dark space, we need every ounce of expertise and experience that you've gained from your grandfather."

"Nansi is second. She could— "

"She's not you! You're the one that Paddy O'Ceaghan trained. Not Nansi. Be reasonable, Nia. I have experience in space. Many times, I've worked outside the space station, made repairs, and fixed sections that make this seem like child's play. I'm here, so let me contribute."

She pursed her lips, worry combined with anger. "We'll talk about it later. I need to evaluate it, and now I have other things I must do." She pulled away from him.

He resisted letting go, his eyes seeming to plead with her to see reason. She glared back, determined to maintain her authority. With a deep sigh of resignation, he dropped his hand from her arm and stepped back.

Conflicted, she hurried away. While Vilnius was experienced in free space work, she couldn't allow him to do the task. Blast it all, he wasn't crew. He was a paying passenger, a government official, and ... She paused, leaning against the corridor wall as the crux of it hit her. She couldn't bear the possibility of losing him. Of it being her decision if something went wrong out there.

Grania retreated to her cabin rather than the bridge to do research. She jotted quick notes into her tablet, listing what she needed more information about by priority. First, she wanted to examine what charts they could access of the Sea of Darkness near Pelanan Gate. Then she hoped to find the account from the previous ship that had escaped. The report she'd found related the incident in such sparse detail that she feared nothing was recorded. She only had limited records in the ship's research archive and, without access to any of the station libraries, it might not have what she needed. Saying a silent prayer, she hoped it would be included.

Second, she needed to review the Mo Chroidhe's data logs from the start of entry into the wormhole until they emerged here. They may reveal where they deviated and what caused such a major disruption to their journey. Brendan had the trajectory readings, and he was working on those. Now, she hoped the logs themselves would give her more information.

She check-marked the third problem, their disabled engine. No worries there; Liam covered it. He understood how those engines worked and how to repair them, as well as anybody might. Her brother had inherited their dad's knack with engines. While the stressed metal concerned her, Liam was less worried about it. The engine was cooling and contracting a bit, he'd said, and she trusted him about this. She was confident he would check for any cracks or tears in the metal.

Restoring communications ranked number four on her list, although it stood equal with the others, and Rory worked on that problem. Perhaps she might aid Rory's search for signals or boosters, but their distance within this dark space may prevent them from connecting. Without signals, they would be in total darkness, both visual and auditory, which would hinder their efforts to determine where they were and which direction to go.

The solar sail was the fifth point and that would need to be addressed before they could go anywhere. Vilnius was right; damn him. None of them were that experienced at spacewalks, and going out into the blackness of this space was an unknown to all of them. Somehow, she needed to get a closer look at the damage to see what needed to be done before anyone went out. With luck, they could enlarge the image from the foresail camera.

Last on the list was their intruder, the so-called banshee. Nansi's knowledge of folklore, space oddities, and general things that go bump in the night added insight and background, both positive things. However, this time, her second officer showed genuine fear with both being in this space and having the appearance of this impossible creature from Earth. While curious about the spirit and what her warning meant, she needed to address the more serious problems before the one they possibly couldn't resolve.

She contemplated for a couple of moments before she added another item. The dream from their previous jump still bothered her, and the actions of the two entities, whether they were banshees or not, seemed to imply a search for something in the cargo bay, which brought her back to wondering if they related to either of their passengers. Rory had checked the travel clearance for them; the old woman's came from London and Harhiman's relayed through Zabrowski. Maybe their travel packets might give her more information, but other priorities had precedence.

Her work laid out, Grania started with the research program, speaking the search parameters to the computer. "Dark Sea, Pelanan Station, survivors."

"Searching," came the machine's audio reply. Within a few minutes, fourteen entries were displayed on her screen. None of them appeared to be specific, so she would need to go through each to find any information. Resigned, she tapped the first and began reading.

Sheilan

"YOU ARE TELLING ME that you were pulled to the cargo bay without any warning? Just whisked there?" Dari asked with clear disbelief in his voice and concern etched on his face as his eyebrows slanted down and his mouth dropped open.

Sheilan paced the floor in her young woman form, not the young peasant lass that had appeared in the bay, but in her preferred form. Dari had materialized to a semi-transparent state again to talk to her. Even though their telepathic communication employed images and symbols rather than words, sometimes speaking was easier.

"I was. From the trader's cabin right down there without so much as a blink of my eye. 'Tis not often such a thing happens to one of us without some indication of what the purpose is. The whole incident is puzzling."

"Was it a death warning, then, for one of the family, do ya think? Did ya feel any pull to one?"

"That is the thing, you see. I did not. I was close to the engineer, but I did not feel any particular pull toward him. Nor did I have a choice of the form I appeared in or my actions. It was the wailing lass, wringing her hands like they were soiled rags. Most often, that is a death warning. There's grave danger here, and I do not believe it is from only those crystals in the cargo. We have been set adrift in space, even though Grania did not tell me as much when she came to the door. I saw the ship tossing in the wormhole, and I believe the wiggly worm threw it right out. It is possible the danger is to the entire ship and everyone on board."

"Are ya thinking that maybe the ship is stranded here in this section of space?" Fear didn't touch the sidhe in the same way it did mortals, but they could still be concerned about their fate. Eternal exile on a dead ship or drifting in empty space would be a nightmare worse than the death that awaited the crew to creatures used to the earth, light, and water. Even now, the puca was far away from his prime element and the soil alone would not provide for him if a disaster were to happen.

"It is possible. Destruction of the ship is always a possibility with travel. We do not know yet if the soil will work to transport us across space. It seems logical given that it will transport us to a different dimension." She referred to the alternate world that shared Earth's space where the sidhe resided. It was the place their kind retreated to when the humans came. Their homeland.

"I can tell you it does not work from here," Dari said.

She stared hard at him. "You tried it?"

"Aye. I did. When the ship began clattering like it was pulling apart, I tried to transport back to Ireland. I feared we were doomed."

"I see. That is why you were in the trunk when I returned to the cabin and did not come out for a long while. You were a frightened pony."

"I was not! I was simply trying to get to safety in case the ship failed." His indignant objection was accompanied by a telling whinny.

She laughed aloud then, something she didn't do often. "Your horse instincts won out. Admit it. You do realize that if you had succeeded, you would not have been able to get back to this pile of dirt until the link is established between the dirt on the planet and Earth, do you not?"

He looked surprised. "I thought it just linked from dirt to related dirt, and it would take me back. Would it not work the other way?"

"It would if it were closer to the source, I think. I cannot say for sure. If I were to take a pouch of dirt and go out into the space out there, then I would be close enough for the dirt in the pouch to be drawn to the dirt in the trunk. For a very long distance, I believe the dirt must be set in the new location and the location recognized by the original source for it to become a two-way transport."

"And how might you be so well informed about it?" He looked piqued at the suggestion of how soil transport might work. It remained one of the mysteries of the sidhe world, magic at its finest.

"I spoke to one of the wise ones; one who had quite a bit of knowledge about how the mysteries work. He had studied and considered the long-distance use often as he knew the soil transport worked from one country to another. He even had details about some Irish dirt transported to Mars with the first settlement there, saying a sidhe made the journey both ways, with it being initiated from Earth. Did you think I had not done some research on this?"

Dari shook his head and admitted, "I did not think about it at all."

"Indeed, you did not. For now, there are bigger concerns, Dari. If these young people do not figure out how to get back to normal space or into the wormhole, then the prophecy of doom will be fulfilled. I can only come to them two more times in warning before one or all of them die."

"Can you not guide them somehow? You have already broken the rules to get here. What would be the harm if you assisted them?"

Even though Sheilan knew the puca wasn't concerned about the humans, he recognized his fate, and hers, rested on their actions.

"Perhaps it is possible. I will see what Grania does and if there is a way to help her." And thought made deed; she vanished into energy and out of the cabin.

CHAPTER SEVENTEEN

Grania

WITH A RLL OF her shoulders, Grania stood and stretched to ease the tension knotting her muscles. She massaged the back of her neck, then rubbed her fingers around her eyes. They burned from staring at the screen for so long. Even her head ached from digesting the pieces of information in the reports. Most accounts on the ship missing in the Pelanan sector of the Dark Sea amounted to rehashes of one report done by a researcher approximately two hundred Earth years earlier. Although the report covered all the known instances, not simply Pelanan, the only one to have gone missing from this sector was almost twenty years before the report's date. That had been a cadet ship with fifty students from the Academy at Sterngard on Pelanan.

Reading about the disappearances didn't give her much hope for their success in escaping from the situation, which left her discouraged and worried. Some way, one ship had returned. She needed to learn how.

She tagged Rory on the bridge for a status update to learn nothing had changed so far as locating, yet alone initiating, any sort of communications.

"It's not the equipment," he said. "No signals are going in or out of this place. We can communicate with anyone anywhere on the ship, but that's all. I can't think of anything else I can do to make this work."

"How's Brendan doing? Any luck with the trajectory?'

Her youngest brother answered himself. "I have something pieced together, though I can't swear the data is accurate. We had some data loss along the way, so the degree of change may not be correct."

"At least you've got a start, Brendan. I might have something from the logs at the time we popped out of the wormhole. I'll brief you on the bridge in about thirty mites. I just want to pull my notes together and we'll see if we can find anything of value."

Next, she checked in with Liam to find that he and Nansi almost had the engine repair complete, giving her a bit of positive news. Liam had studied the sail problem again, trying to piece together what needed to be done to untangle them and get the solar quilt back into the well. At the worst case, they could jettison the whole sail, framework and all. While dumping would be a costly action, if they failed to refold it back into its compartment, they had no other option.

Feeling a bit more hopeful, and knowing Brendan's skill with the navigation computer, she hoped they might find a way out of this. At the back of her mind, the apparition in the bay and what the warning meant for them worried her. She got another cup of tea and sat down again in front of the computer screen, staring at the notes she'd made on her tablet.

A knock on the doorframe announced her visitor only seconds before Vilnius spoke. "A penny for your thoughts, Captain."

He paused in the opening, waiting for her permission to enter her cabin. She waved him in. "Now there's a curious expression. Old Earth, I suppose."

He smiled. "It is. A penny was a small piece of currency. A coin, I believe. Apparently, despite once being valuable, the copper, as it was sometimes called, was deemed worthless and production stopped. But let's pretend the value is at the higher level and your thoughts are worth a great deal to me."

"Well, then, sir, they are some somewhat dire ones right now. We are in a very serious situation, and I don't have a lot of information on how to get out of this dark space. The last ship to disappear from a wormhole never returned and searchers had no way to determine where to look for it. In fact, only one ship has ever returned from the Dark Sea. Unfortunately, the captain's report on that didn't tell me much. I think they accidentally escaped from the sound of it. He believed that when they were deposited in it, they were quite near to the wormhole, and they were swept along until they were pulled back into normal space.

Vilnius frowned. "Not encouraging at all. Was it the ship that returned from the Pelanan gate?"

"No. But, a bit of useful news, the other ship that had gone missing from Pelanan was being monitored from the station. They had four ships in the hole, then something along the path caused the hole to flux mid-way through and one vanished. It was never seen again. With only a rough idea of where it was and no way to search the Dark Sea for it, the ship was presumed lost."

"Four ships and one 'vanished', you said?" He mulled it over, his eyes seeming to focus in the distance. "That's an odd way to describe it."

"It is, but that's what the report stated. They were tracking it up to the point where it disappeared from their equipment. The ships passed through the gate, at least, thirty to fifty mites apart, it said. So, they were in different sectors of the hole when the disruption to it occurred and ..."

"... only one was caught in it," he concluded. "It's more likely the ship was somehow ejected from the hole and this dark space either parallels or surrounds the gate."

"Exactly what I've been thinking. I don't know if that helps us to figure a way back though. Yet, I believe that somehow, we have to piece together all the bits of knowledge we have and find a solution."

She saw the worry in his eyes and realized he recognized the treacherous position they were in. For herself, fear touched her more than she dared to voice. She had to be strong for the crew, for her brothers. Her grandfather trusted her with his ship, and she couldn't let him down. Yet that is what she would do if they couldn't find a way out.

"All right, love. This is a tight spot we're in, but we're not done for yet."

She realized then that Vilnius perceived her fears, and he was not a man to panic or give in without a fight.

"You said that Pelanan tracked the ship until it vanished. Did they record the coordinates where it went off their tracking?"

"Yes! I have them in my notes and I have our ship's log of positions until we were ejected into this place. We've been dead and not drifting since we've been out of the hole. The computers lost a lot of information, but the ship estimated the wake-up sequence began seven hours from the time we entered the gate, so we'd been here anywhere from seven to five hours depending on when we were bumped out. The ship quit logging time about forty-two mites into the jump." They were both on the same page here. The position might help them figure out if both ships exited the wormhole near the same point in it.

Vilnius pulled her into his arms into one of his tight, reassuring hugs. "It's a start, my girl. Your brothers are all smart arses, and I'm a genius, so let's see what else we can cobble together to figure this out."

As she squeezed him back, savoring his comforting presence, he kissed the top of her head before lowering his lips to her forehead, next her nose, and, at last, they found her mouth for a long kiss. As he pulled away, he whispered, "We'll find our way back. Believe that."

Vilnius accompanied her to the bridge, as much a part of the team as her crew. They were in this together, and she admitted he had expertise they could use.

Grania had summoned Liam and Nansi to the bridge, which made it more crowded than usual. Vilnius leaned against the wall while she yielded her chair to Nansi and now stood in front of her entire team to fill them in on what she'd learned from her research. As she spoke about the coordinates from the report, Brendan plotted them into the computer, subsequently converting and adding their position information as she gave it out. On the screen, a representation of the wormhole appeared, with the positions marked. They were very close, almost on top of each other.

"How close, Brendan?" she asked.

"It looks like less than ... yes, it's exactly 21.2 klicks. We were only a little farther into the hole than the cadet ship at the last recorded point.

"So, we popped out at about the same point, which might mean the wormhole fluxes at the same point. That could mean a nearby star affects it," Rory said. "If we could check solar activity from the stars near the wormhole, we might figure how close the exit point was from the star."

"It might help correlate the position," she agreed. "Liam, do you know when the engine broke down? Did the other one cut out concurrently?"

"I don't have the exact time when it failed. At a guess, I'm thinking that whatever flung us out of the hole caused the damage. Once we landed in this dead space, nothing could have done it. As for the other engine, it looks like it overheated and shut itself down. So, I would guess it ran alone for some time after we arrived here."

"Okay. That's a bit of good news and bad news there. If we take your trajectory and plug it in, Brendan, and extend it out at about half speed, we might be getting an idea of how far we are into the Dark Sea." Grania tried to piece it together as she talked. Would any of this make any sense to provide a position, or were they making too many assumptions? "Did the operating engine log a shutdown time?"

"I didn't check it, Grania," Liam replied. "I'm sorry. I'll review it and let you know."

"The jump pods might also give you an indication of how much time had passed from the jump," Vilnius added.

"Right you are," Liam shot back. "Let's see if we can work it out, mate." He shot a quick glance at Grania for permission to go.

"Do it." She jerked her head toward the door.

"We still have a problem," Brendan offered tentatively.

"We have several, but what's on your mind?"

"With communications down and dead space surrounding us, we don't have a way to compute direction. I can't tell which way we're going, toward the wormhole or Dragon Station or even farther away from it all." His voice showed his nervousness as it shook a little.

"Yeah, that's another problem on the list. There must be a way to figure it out. I don't know what it is yet, but we'll find something." She prayed she was telling them the truth,

"Take a break," she told Brendan and Rory. They'd been working on this ever since they came out of the pods, so they could use some downtime to relax and refresh themselves. After they left, Grania crossed her arms and stared out into the black void surrounding her ship.

Nothing was out there. Nothing at all. Yet somewhere in it, the wormhole meandered through and locating it provided their best hope of escape. How do you find a needle in a haystack when you can't see either the stack or the needle?

CHAPTER EIGHTEEN

Grania

"IT'S ALL LEGENDS AND folk tales about this banshee," Grania complained to Nansi over tea and biscuits in the galley. The refreshments offered comfort and a sense of normalcy they needed. The taste of strawberries sat on her tongue, reminding her of home. At least they were thankful the ship had the power to keep their systems running.

After her research, she wanted to talk to her second about what she'd found on their visitor and how much of it was unverified. "There are stories people tell in which they swear they've seen the creature, but they don't have any proof. While the archive has a few blurred photos and videos over the centuries since the camera was invented, as near as I can tell, there's nothing resembling what we have on the recording from the cargo bay."

Lines creasing her forehead, Nansi's face looked drawn and solemn, far more affected by the situation than Grania expected her to be. She had known the older woman even before she, herself, had come on the Mo Chroidhe as a teenager. She'd never seen Nansi appear so downcast or worried as she did now. They were in a tight spot, true enough, but they couldn't give up hope, and Nansi acted as if they were doomed.

"'T'was a bean sidhe," Nansi repeated, like the name explained everything. "They aren't like people, and they take on different appearances. They're spirits, shape changers. Is that not what all the tales are telling you? They have only one purpose and that's to bring warnings of impending death."

"Yes, I understood as much from my reading. Still, we have no proof of any of it except for the recording. Why would this creature allow us to record it so clearly when it appears to have avoided any concrete recordings for centuries?" She opened her tablet, keying in a sequence. "Look at this old video from an Irish family in Donegal. Does that resemble anything like what we are seeing on our recording?"

A video from the databank played, showing something like a fog rising from the floor of a house and whirling around like a twister. "The people who took this called it a banshee and said the night it was seen, an elderly cousin passed beyond the veil. They claim the appearance announced the death."

"I don't know why it is allowing us to record it. Maybe it is because we were in pod sleep at the time, and it needed to get the message to us. I don't know. I just know that the young woman scrubbing her hands is an aspect of the creature, and it is foretelling death." She shook her head in misery. "Maybe we're all going to die, and it already knows the ship will never be found, so no one can ever bear witness to her appearance."

"We're not going to die, Nansi. We are going to get out of this mess. I need you to pull yourself together and begin to think through the situation. We've been together for over a decade now, and we've been through some rough times. You were at my mam's side when the pirates boarded, and you were with us when she died. You never gave up hope or quit fighting. I need you to take a stance now. No spirit is going to end our lives, and a foolish superstition might lead to a self-filling prophecy more than the act of a hand-wringing ghost."

Tears formed at the edges of Nansi's eyes and her mouth turned down while she slumped in her seat. "I'm sorry, Grania. I've failed you and your brothers. Somehow, I should have seen this coming or felt that the jump through the gate wasn't safe yet." She folded her hands, fingers tense, on the table, staring down at them like they had committed a crime.

"No, you haven't failed us. Not yet. You couldn't have known. Fey or no, you can't know everything that's going to happen." She laid her hand over Nansi's and the other woman lifted her eyes up to meet Grania's. "It is going to be all right. Believe that."

Nansi nodded, the dullness in her eyes telling Grania that even though she wanted to believe, she didn't. She rose, shoving her half-drunk tea aside. "I'll just go down and see what Liam needs me to do."

After she left, Grania leaned back, her eyelids closing out the world for the moment as weariness settled on her. A long ten hours had passed since the ship had awakened her. Ten hours of tension, worry, and research. Her eyes ached, burning from the excessive reading, and her body wanted to stretch out and sleep.

Still, they'd made progress. The engines were repaired, Brendan had a reasonable idea of their trajectory from the exit point, and Liam and Vilnius were studying the sail problem. Soon, she would have to decide who would do the spacewalk to untangle them, and she didn't want it to be Vilnius.

Faith, she'd only walked in space once, about four years earlier in a sector of space bright with starlight. She'd only done a minor repair. Go out of the ship on the tether, weld a new piece of metal to support the aft camera, then right back into the ship. Easy and it only took her forty minutes to do it. While the view stunned with its vastness, it was frightening. Despite the safety procedures and all the caution, you had to remember that even a slight mistake might send you drifting into space, unreachable, and doomed when the suit exhausted the air supply.

Now, looking at this dead-looking part of space, it added to the fear. The blackness was like looking into nothing. They saw no life in it except their ship and some streaks of light in the distance, passing now and then. It would be incredibly dark outside. Even with every spotlight on the ship turned on, it wouldn't be enough.

To jettison the sail, someone would have to go out and cut the fabric free of the hatch to lock it down again. If the mechanism sustained damage, then more repairs would be necessary before the ship could get underway again. Giving up the dorsal sail would not only be expensive, but it would also slow them down more when they returned to normal space. Besides being a booster and navigation aid, the huge surface was a major collector of energy for the systems on the ship, from the bridge equipment to life support. No, they needed to untangle the sail and repair it. More than just saving face with her granda, it meant survival.

Yet the only person she would, in good conscience, send out there to do it boiled down to herself. How could she risk anyone else on the ship? Still, a quiet voice in her mind whispered, Vilnius' qualifications are far better. What would her granda do in this situation? "Use your resources, lass," he'd often told her. "Whatever or whoever they may be."

She heard the galley door swoosh open, and her head popped up in time to see Vilnius saunter in. She must have drifted off for a bit.

Like all of them, he looked tired and ready for some downtime. "Is there any coffee in this place?" he asked, heading for the counter cabinets.

"Of course. I can't guarantee how good the quality is, but we stocked some. Just request it."

He spoke the order to the unit, drew a breath to say something more, then turned to Grania. "How are the food supplies?"

"Good. So long as we're not stuck here for more than a couple of weeks." Her mouth quirked into a twisted smile. "On the other hand, we have a ton of cheese in cold storage in the hold and at least twenty cases of Rigan brandy that we might raid. I think some canned food is in some of the other crates."

He laughed. "Sound like the makings of a party. Okay if I get a meat pie then?"

"Sure. You paid for meals. So, how's everything going in engineering?"

He added the pie request and leaned back against the counter as he spoke. "It's in decent shape. Liam is a top-notch engineer, very smart fellow. He had the engine repair well under control when I went down there and all he needed was an extra pair of hands. Nansi seems a bit shaken."

"Ah, well, she is worrying about this whole situation like she should have prevented it somehow."

The machine dinged, offering his coffee and pie, and he took them to the table, sitting across from her. The aroma of the cooked meat filled the small galley and made her stomach rumble. "And you?" he asked. "Are you thinking you might have done something to avoid it?"

"No, I know there was nothing I could have done. We trusted the station knew the wormhole was stable, but sometimes these things happen when ships are traveling through folded space. Now my only worries are on how to find the wormhole and get back into the fecking thing." Her voice carried a touch of anger at the situation. "I wish you hadn't chosen to take this ship to Dragon Gate. You're missing your meeting there and ..." She paused to swallow a threatening lump in her throat. "... we may not get back at all. I am so sorry for it, Vilnius. If we can't get back ..."

He reached over and pressed a hand to her cheek. "Then I will live the final days left of my life with you and that's all right, love. However, I am not planning on dying here, so we're going to figure this out."

She forced a smile. "Of course, we will. The strain is just showing a bit."

Rising a little from his seat, he stretched across the table and kissed her, a gentle reassuring press of his lips against hers. "Go and get some sleep. I'll join Rory on watch."

Rory

WHILE VILNIUS REVIEWED THE specs on the solar sail
with an eye to what it would take to get the unit untangled,
Rory continued to monitor the ship, checking the cameras on
the various key points, both externally and internally. Apart from
Vilnius and himself, everyone else appeared to be sleeping, or at
least in their rooms. Liam had even abandoned the engineering
area for the pod in his cabin. Still, with the incidents in the cargo
bay, Rory checked that section often.

Outside the ship, nothing changed. The same blackness loomed
everywhere, no matter which way he looked. Except for those
occasional streaks of light interrupting the view. In a strange
way, he found them a comfort, the only indication of something
besides their ship in the void. The top, aft-facing cameras on the
ship also showed the same thing they'd seen since they arrived;
the sail twisted and looped around the hatch door. At least, with
no movement from the ship, nothing made it any worse.

An unexpected creaking sound from the ship made him jerk,
and he glanced toward Vilnius, who lifted a quizzical eyebrow.
With the engines idling rather than thrusting the ship forward,
every stray sound seemed louder and more worrying than normal.
"It's just the metal breathing," Vilnius said, his voice soft as if he
might disturb the sleeping vessel.

Still jumpy, Rory switched to the security view on and cycled
through the cameras, stopping when he spotted movement in
the cargo bay; a person, he thought. Not an apparition this time.
When the figure moved again, he recognized Harhiman, moving
from the back section of the cargo bay forward to the middle
section, where the engine room and deck steps were located.
Perhaps he was checking his cargo, Rory guessed. A plausible

excuse for his presence in the crew-only area, especially with their abrupt exit from the jump.

Harhiman stopped outside the engine room, looked around in all directions as if to assure himself no one was around before he pressed the panel to open the door to the room. Liam hadn't locked it, Rory realized. Although they seldom put security seals on these doors, this action made it apparent they should have.

"Vilnius, look at this," he said, calling the other man over.

"That's your passenger and see where he's heading," Vilnius said as he leaned forward, peering over Rory's shoulder.

"The main computer station."

"Can you slave that computer to us to see what he's doing?"

Rory nodded, keyed in a few commands. Harhiman peered at the main screen and attempted to enter something, frowning as he got an error response.

Rory wore a satisfied smile. "Liam's got it password locked, so he won't be able to access any files. It looks like he attempted to get into a couple of them. What's he doing now?"

Harhiman gave up on accessing the computer, instead turning his focus to all the manual control switches on the main engines panel.

"I don't know, but it doesn't appear good. I'm going down." Vilnius straightened and was out the door before he formed a reply.

Rory continued to watch as Harhiman seemed to examine most of their control equipment until the man heard the noise from footsteps descending the stairs. Harhiman scuttled away from the equipment, slipping out into the cargo bay and back behind some crates.

Vilnius stepped into the engine room and swept his gaze to confirm it was empty before he searched. He turned toward the forward bay and started up it, his gaze traveling up, down, and ahead. As he reached the end, he turned to starboard and disappeared for a couple of minutes, then came back into the picture with Harhiman in tow, his left hand gripping the trader's arm as he pulled him along. With an apologetic face showing, Harhiman talked to Vilnius, offering an explanation, no doubt, then Vilnius displayed his station-master-stern expression as he spoke and released the man's arm. Harhiman left, scrambling up the stairs.

Rory watched Vilnius go into the engine room and check it over to make sure everything was secure. He flicked the com switch. "Rory, I can see no damage or anything amiss. Lock this room and the cargo hold after I leave."

Rory acknowledged, then flicked to a camera to watch Harhiman return to his cabin. He switched back in time to see Vilnius start up the steps. After sending the code to secure the engineering door, he transmitted the lock signal for the bottom deck once Vilnius entered the walkway.

He expected to catch hell from Grania for this. Since he'd booked Harhiman, he'd no doubt get the blame for it. Face scrunched in annoyance, he swore under his breath.

CHAPTER NINETEEN

Grania

THE INSISTENT BEEPING OF her mobi-com pulled Grania out of a sound sleep. As she sat up blearily, a sharp knock on her cabin door drew her attention. She pulled a robe around her and said, "Enter." She reached for the mobi, seeing the message from Rory.

"We've encountered a slight problem, Grania. Not urgent. We'll discuss it when you're up here. Take your time."

She turned to see Vilnius in the doorway. "Are you part of the problem?"

Despite the slight smile on his face, he sounded quite serious. "Not directly, no. The problem is with a passenger, the merchant fellow. Rory spotted him snooping around in the engine room and the cargo bay."

That woke her up. "What?"

"Rory caught him on camera, and I went down to confront him. No damage or anything to the equipment. Liam had locked the computers down so he couldn't access it."

"But he tried? Feck ... Tell Rory to secure everything, even the galley. I don't want anyone to gain access that isn't authorized.

Give me a few mites to get ready then you and Rory can fill me in." She lunged toward the shower.

"Right." Vilnius acknowledged as he stepped back out, presumably to return to the bridge.

Could this situation get any worse? She turned the weak spray of hot water on, immersing herself in it, section by section. She'd managed to allay her passengers' fears about their situation with a bit of smooth talking and downplaying the gravity of it; now she had this to add to her concerns. She finished her shower with a cold spray, then yanked on her jumpsuit and dashed to the bridge.

Rory started his update as soon as she arrived, even before she'd made it to her chair. In terse words, he described what he'd seen with Harhiman coming from the aft cargo bay, then he played the recorded feed from just outside the engine room.

She watched the whole thing in tense silence, her jaw tightening as he attempted to access the computers and studied the engine controls. After she watched the soundless segment with Vilnius confronting Harhiman, she asked, "What did he say? What excuse?"

"He said he was just checking on his cargo as it was quite valuable. He claimed he didn't see one container, and he wanted to get onto the computer to see where it was placed in the cargo bay. Of course, he apologized for coming into the area with no one around, claiming he did look around for someone to ask," Vilnius replied.

"I checked the placement of his cargo crates, and they were all together in the same section, Aft G-Port side. He would have seen them all there," Rory informed her.

"So, he's lying. Did he say anything about studying our controls?"

"No. I didn't ask him specifically. He was calm, although he knew he was in the wrong. He asked when we might be getting back underway, concerned about reaching his destination. I told him we were still making repairs, and he had best stay in his cabin until you advised him otherwise." Vilnius reclined with his long legs stretched out in front of him, leaning back in the chair. He steepled his fingers and tapped them against each other. "For what it's worth, I think there may be a grain of truth in checking on his cargo, but I also think he searched for more than that. The missing crate was an excuse, and he had it prepared in case he was caught."

"I agree." Grania turned to her computer and did the last thing on her list; something she should have done much sooner. She called up the passenger information on their two guests.

Ansel L. Harhiman, she read, was a citizen of Bellamar, coming from a mining town in the Stolt region. The area, once settled by Russian immigrants, more recently housed poorer Earthlings. With work options and a chance at a decent life, many settlers were lured to the area. Harhiman now listed Bindorf as his home city, and his occupation was a merchant trader.

"Looking at his last six trips, he checks out. Here's the odd thing, he never pre-books passage to anywhere and he doesn't appear to go planet-side. He conducts his business on the space stations, then books passage to his next destination when he's ready to leave."

"It's not unusual to conduct trade from the station, Nia," Vilnius told her. "The cargo is right there and it's easy to transfer it from the ship or the dock to another ship bound for a planet or another station. It's what the trade hubs were designed to handle. So far as not booking the next destination, it is a little peculiar. Maybe he doesn't follow an actual trade route but varies his trip according to what he manages to buy on the station or on a future deal he's made."

"I did see him go to the Traders' Lounge on Pelanan," she admitted, so that might be the case. "Still, it almost looks like he's trying to avoid the full inspection that a planet landing would bring. His clearance is grade three, not the highest, yet passable."

"Well, it could mean he's had some shady dealings in the past or has been disciplined for failing to properly report cargo or to provide proper transport containers," Vilnius said. "If it's a solid clearance, with no restrictions, then he's cleared whatever the issue was."

"So, he's a little suspect, but nothing that's really jumping out, is it?" Rory added. He yawned, stood, and stretched. "Brendan will be coming along shortly, and I'm due for a sleep period. If there's nothing else, I'm heading to bed."

"Go ahead," Grania replied. She shifted her gaze to Vilnius, observing the tiredness in his eyes and the dark circles under them. "You, too. You look totally flogged."

He nodded as he tapped his fingers on the console. "I need to tell you something because I wasn't completely honest with you."

She gave him her full attention, trepidation darkening her eyes. "About what?"

"This trip. I didn't come on this trip for a meeting at Dragon Station. I came because I wanted to be with you, just in case ..." His voice trailed off.

She waited for him to say something more, then when he didn't continue, nudged him. "In case of what?"

"Three pirate raids occurred around Dragon and Pelanan in the past three cycles. The Mo Chroidhe, no offense, is not one of the faster ships on the merchant lanes and you're carrying a full load. I was worried there might be an attempt to board you."

"Freebooters?" She used the common term on her world for space pirates. "And you're being serious about this? You chose to finagle your way onto my ship to do what? Protect me from the thieves?" She would have laughed if he didn't look so offended. "You are serious! And instead of a fine 'booter battle, you got yourself lost in space here with the rest of us wondering if we'll even survive let alone fend off pirates."

"Well, that wasn't the plan," he replied sharply, sitting up and leaning forward. "I chose to be here to help. Damn, Grania, I care about you."

"And Pelanan Station, was that just an excuse to see me or what?"

"No, I had to go there. I needed to discuss the coding problem with them. Zabrowski was the third station that had experienced a problem with the loading 'bots. Incidentally, your man Harhiman had been on all three stations when the problems occurred. Coincidence? Maybe, but I don't believe in that much coincidence. Now we catch him sneaking around and eyeing your computers."

"So, you think—"

Mid-sentence, her voice stopped as a young woman appeared on the bridge, a repeat of the cargo bay incident. No ghostly image this time, she appeared solid and real. She was dressed in simple clothes, a dirty linen blouse tied in front, and a ragged-looking brown skirt. A brown scarf caught her long blonde hair away from her face as she knelt on the bridge floor while her hands scrubbed with urgent moves at barely visible clothes. Tears streaked down her cheeks as she made a wailing noise of such terrible sorrow that Grania shivered while icy fingers of fear pinched her spine.

The banshee brought a warning of death. She was the "washer at the ford" who foretold the death of those who were about to die in battle by scrubbing the blood from their garments. The words popped into Grania's head, gleaned from her reading.

"For whom?" Grania cried out. "Who are you warning? Is it me?"

The solid-looking spirit didn't reply but continued to wash and wail for another few mites.

"Tell me!" Grania insisted, trying to get the spirit's attention. "Say something?" she screamed.

For a second, the banshee seemed to stare straight at her, then she vanished as expeditiously as she'd arrived.

"Did you see it?" Grania asked, her voice a shade higher than usual and her fear-filled eyes wide with the vision of something that was impossible.

"Who or what was that?" Vilnius sounded shaken, and a glance at him revealed the ashen paleness in his face. He'd risen from his seat, his hands clutching the armrests, but had moved no closer to either Grania or the banshee, like he'd been in frozen in place.

She swallowed hard and reached for her bottle of water, wishing for something more potent. "Nansi called it a banshee, a spirit from Ireland, who warns people of an impending death. It's the second time it's made an appearance on this ship." Her voice was uneven, her emotions warring with her need for logic. "'Tis said it appears three times and on the third time, the person dies."

"I've heard rumors of this type of creature, but ..." Vilnius moved to her and wrapped his arms around her from behind, pulling her into a comforting embrace. "We'll find the way, love. Keep the faith."

* * *

EVERYONE ON THE SHIP gathered in the galley for the meal and a brief meeting. Grania included their two passengers because they were entitled to know the gravity of their situation. To conserve the ship's power, they'd cut the lighting to only essential areas, with those at half-light. In the dim lighting, she gazed from face to face, reading the anxiety and fear as they stared at her.

"As I told all of you, the Mo Chroidhe was ejected from the wormhole, and we are now in a section of space referred to as the Dark Sea. While we are still addressing some damage from the sudden exit, most issues are repaired. The dorsal solar sail is tangled, and we're going to attempt to repair it. Once that is resolved, we will try to find our way back to normal space. In order to conserve as much power as possible, our lighting has been cut back to half-light in essential areas of the ship and the reduction extends to the cabin lighting. When it is not needed, please shut it off completely.

"Miz O'Cairn and Mr. Harhiman, I do apologize for this terrible interruption in your travel. And I also apologize for having to tell you that returning to normal space is not a given or a simple task. Our instruments do not function in dark space, no signals for communications work. We are going to do the best we can to navigate our way out of here."

"Are you saying that we may not get out of this 'sea'?" Harhiman asked, the tone in his voice on the edge of anger. "Are we all going to die here?"

She glanced down to steel herself, then met his eyes. "I sincerely hope that isn't the case. But yes, that is what I am saying. There is a distinct possibility we can't escape. We are, none of us, eager to end our lives here, so we will be doing everything we can to get the ship out. That, sir, is the only assurance I can give you."

Now, he looked and sounded angry. "How the hell did you let this happen? Did someone make a navigation error?"

Brendan drew a breath and opened his mouth to reply before Grania cut him off. "No, sir, no one made any errors that resulted in this. 'Tis a risk of using the wormholes and a rare occurrence. As a seasoned traveler, I expected you would be aware of this risk, but like most of us, I suspect that you never gave it a second thought because it does occur so infrequently. There were no errors, and we did not 'let it happen'."

Harhiman grew more red-faced while she talked and looked like he was ready to explode. Instead of the angry verbal outburst she was expecting, he jumped to his feet and stormed from the room, with a string of curses muttered under his breath while he exited.

Grania let out a breath she hadn't realized she'd been holding, then turned her attention to the old lady. Moira was still calm, seemingly unfazed by the announcement. "Are you all right, Miz O'Cairn?"

She nodded twice, then pushed herself to her feet, and her lips curved into a sad little smile. "I am, thank you. 'Tis a difficult situation, for sure, Captain. I have faith in you and your crew. Whatever the outcome, it will be as it was meant to be. Trust in yourselves, all of you, and in your instincts. Follow your lights." She shuffled toward the doorway and out.

As the scent of freshly made coffee filled the room, Grania turned to see Vilnius with a large cup for himself and a cup of tea for her. Right now, that coffee smelled pretty inviting. Tea had a more delicate aroma, not the kind that fills your senses the way the coffee did. Still, she took the tea with gratitude, sat, and waited while the others grabbed their own drinks and settled again.

"That felt a bit like a pep talk from our lady there. I guess she was reminding us to maintain our faith at the end. We've had a second visit from the banshee a few hours ago." She heard Nansi's sudden gasp, then continued. "Vilnius and I saw her on the bridge at almost a full twenty-four hours since her last visit. If there are three warnings that she gives, then it means we only have one more before disaster strikes."

She hadn't noticed that she'd ceased to think of the banshee as an "it" and was now calling the spirit by gender terms. "So, I think we need to decide on a plan and get to it. We're wasting our resources and energy sitting here. Brendan, let's go over your information and decide which way is most likely to lead us safely out of here."

"And don't forget the pixie in the oatmeal," Liam said, using their father's term for a minor problem. "We need to take care of the sail. It's got to be the next step."

"Right, you are," Rory quickly agreed. "So, who gets to space-walk?" He sounded eager, as if he might be the one to go.

Grania shot a dour glance his way. "Only two people on this ship have actually done a walk in space under real conditions." She held up her hand before anyone could object. "I know you've all trained to do it and been through the simulators. Going out there and doing it is different. I've done it, and Vilnius has done it. He is a passenger on this ship, so that leaves me. I will do it."

Everyone tried to speak at once until Vilnius' voice cut through them all. "You will not! I told you before; you're the captain, and you can't risk it! It would be devastating if something happened, and you were lost."

"Listen to him, Grania," Nansi added. "He's right. There can't be even a slim chance of losing you if the ship is to find its way home." Rory and Brendan added their voices, echoing Nansi, although Liam did chime in.

Grania held up her hand, waiting for the voices to calm down. "I can't ask Vilnius to do it, and I can't ask any of the rest of you either."

"You don't need to ask," Vilnius cut in. "I volunteered. I've been outside many times at the station, and this vessel is calmer. Though I may not be as experienced on a spaceship, this much I do know. Liam and I studied the sail and what we need to do to fix it."

Liam jumped in then. "The only drawback is that it does need two people for the job. Logically, I think the second one should be me."

"No, Liam! We can't afford to lose you either. Your expertise with the engines is the best we there is. I'm good, but not as good as you when it comes to those babies." Grania's eyes pleaded with him to see her point of view, her will battling with his.

Out of the pause in the conversation, Nansi spoke up. "You omitted my name when you mentioned those who had experience. I have been outside a few times myself. I'll do it. 'Tis volunteering, I am."

As Grania sucked in a breath, ready to argue against it, Nansi said, "Grania, think. What would your granda tell you to do? Use your resources, girl."

The room fell silent and Grania stared at the older woman. She admitted Nansi had done a few spacewalks in the past and heaven knows; she was qualified to do the job. Grania had intentionally omitted her, not feeling she could ask Nansi any more than she could ask any of her crew to take the risk. She chewed on her lower lip, more to keep herself steady before she spoke. Granda would say it was the best chance for them all.

"I have two volunteers, and I accept their service. Liam, you'll give them full support from engineering. If it looks like we can't easily untangle the sail, or if it appears to be unsalvageable, then we cut it loose.

"Rory, I want the fore and aft cameras trained on that sail so we can see everything out there. If we can add any additional lights to the area, do it. It's blacker than a well. We'll do this in one-hundred-eighty mites from now if that is acceptable to Nansi and Vilnius."

Her gaze moved from one to the other as they each nodded. "Vilnius, when you've checked out the suit and gotten everything prepped, I want to see you in my cabin."

"Of course, Captain," he acknowledged on the way out.

As Liam passed her, he met her eyes, and his jaw clenched. "I could have done it, Captain. But you always underrate me."

"No, I don't, Liam. I said you're essential to the ship and I mean it. I cannot risk losing you, too."

"Then, why are you always testing me? Questioning my ability?"

"I'm pushing you, brother. Just like Granda has done with me. Making sure you're thinking of everything. At the end of the day, this ship and the crew are my responsibility. If it fails, I fail."

She gazed deep into his eyes, seeing the acknowledgment dawning in them, and he nodded before he stepped through the door.

CHAPTER TWENTY

Grania

OVER THE NEXT HOUR, Grania repeatedly questioned her decision regarding the spacewalk, fearful she was leading everyone into disaster. She had experience and learned from her granda, yes, but that didn't make her an expert at being a captain or even an elite spacer. Just because she grew up in a family that lived and breathed space travel and shipping didn't make her a natural at it. Because she was the eldest of her father's offspring, everyone assumed she would inherit the Mo Chroidhe. Now it looked more likely that she would be the ship's last captain.

Despite her positive words to Harhiman and her crew—her brothers—she wondered if she could have done something differently to prevent this from happening. Could she have refused to be in the first wave through the gate at Pelanan, opting to wait until they were completely certain that the hole was stable? Someone at Pelanan could have rushed the decision to open the gate again or it could have just been an unexpected flare up from their star. No matter what caused it, the problem belonged to her now and, if she was honest, it looked bleak. Only one ship had ever gotten out of the Dark Seas. One out of fourteen ... Those were not good odds.

She paced the room as she considered, too keyed up to sit. Soon now, Vilnius and Nansi would be going onto the ship's hull, another call she wasn't comfortable making, to fix the sail, one way or the other. She prayed she didn't lose one or both of them.

After that, they would fire the engines up and begin limping toward what they hoped was either the wormhole or normal space. So, what direction was that? They had no idea where anything was or even what was up or down. Despite Brendan's projections on how far they might be from the wormhole, they didn't know which way was back or if the ship had drifted above or below it. And next, she would have to decide on the direction they would go.

She stopped pacing and gazed at the forward screen. Ahead of them was the same blackness that surrounded them, except off to the edge, occasional streaks of reddish, goldish, or bluish colors pierced the black. What caused those? A phenomenon in the dark space itself? Perhaps it was some kind of energy.

"Stop beating yourself up," Vilnius said as he loitered in the doorway. "You weren't in your cabin, so I figured you'd be here."

Turning, she nodded and took a couple of steps toward him. Brendan had gone below to confer with Liam, and she shot a glance at Rory as she jerked her head toward the exit. Taking the cue, he flipped a switch on the console and quickly stood.

"I'll be grabbing a bite to eat before we get started if that's all right?"

"Aye, 'tis will be a good thing to do, Rory. Take thirty."

Vilnius sauntered over and sat on the edge of the console, at ease and seemingly unworried. "What were you frowning about?"

"I wasn't. I was thinking; that's my thinking face, mister." She leaned against the console, almost touching him. "And I was thinking about those streaks of color we keep seeing off the starboard edge. They don't show up on the aft or the port screens and only slightly on the starboard one. What do you suppose they are?"

"I dunno. Reflection of a starburst maybe or something may generate some energy in this dark hole. I'll take a good look when I'm outside. Maybe the full picture will tell us more."

"I don't like you going outside. I didn't like you over-riding my decision." She looked away from him, not angry, merely unhappy with the outcome.

"I know. But I am the best, and only choice and you know it's true. I really am quite competent at repairs on exterior hulls."

"Oh, feck, Vilnius, I don't think I can do this." Her voice cracked, and he reached for her, sliding a reassuring arm around her shoulders.

"Do what, love?"

"Save the ship. Save us all. The odds are against us making it. I have no idea which way to point us."

He pressed a gentle kiss to her lips, a light brushing in tenderness for comfort. "When the time comes, you'll know, Nia. You have good instincts, always have, and your grandfather trained you well. Just listen to your intuition because somewhere inside, you already have the answer. You're just afraid to trust it."

She brought her hands to cup his face, staring into the depths of his eyes and seeing the confidence in them. "You better not fecking screw up out there. I want you back."

Then she kissed him hard, her mouth crushing against his, while she hoped it wasn't the last time.

ON THE BRIDGE, THE tension was palpable as Grania, Brendan, and Rory watched the forward camera image showing the two suited figures climbing onto the top of the ship to reach the dorsal sail. Despite the sleek look of the suits, they were still cumbersome when it came to climbing in the vacuum of space. Magnetized to help hold the wearer to the ship, the boot soles were weighted and clunky, so moving required pulling free of the grip with the correct amount of force to not inadvertently push the other foot off at the same time. They moved with caution, making steady progress toward the sail. Rory had shifted the lights, so they illuminated the top of the ship enough to see. If anything viewed them from the black depths, the Mo Chroidhe would be a virtual beacon in space.

Vilnius took the lead with Nansi trailing a little behind, connected to him by a tether line. They picked up the pace as they gained more comfort and made good speed across the length of the vessel.

With a flick of a switch, Rory pulled up the view from Vilnius' suit camera and the bridge crew could see him approach the halfway-opened hatch cover for the sail. A thirty-meter-long piece of metal jutted out with the thin, metallic fabric of the sail wrapped around it like cooking foil.

As Grania watched Vilnius kneel to tug a little at the edge of the fabric, she leaned toward the screen, her hands clasped together, and forefingers pressed against her chin. Strained nerves bit at her while she fought to appear calm. She'd still rather be the one on the hull than sitting, watching, and praying that nothing went wrong.

"It looks like the sail twisted a couple of times around the aft end of the hatch." Vilnius' voice came clearly through the com. "We're going down. It's a clear night for a walk out here. Too bad there aren't any stars to see." As he looked behind him toward Nansi, he turned slightly to the starboard side and gazed toward the area where they'd seen streaks of light. "Nothing anywhere at the moment."

Nansi pulled even with him, and they moved on, carefully stepping alongside the open sail bay. He paused midway along to lean down for a good look at the inside as Nansi leaned forward to point out a couple of things to him.

Then she said, "It's looking good, Captain. There doesn't appear to be any damage to the inside of the bay or the sail's frame. It partially deployed before the sail tangled. The good news is it hasn't broken. If we can get the sail loose, we should be able to manually deploy it, then crank it back into the bay normally."

A small sigh of relief escaped from Grania's lips. At least one thing looked promising. "Ah, you're bringing me good news, Nansi."

The duo moved on, paused twice more to look at the twists in the sail. When they got to the end, Vilnius jumped from the hull's surface to the top of the bay door, about two and a half meters, catching the edge of the sail to pull himself onto it. Grania let out the breath she'd held when he started the jump as she watched the tether line, verifying its secure attachment to the ship. He stretched out along the top of the hatch and ran his hands against the folds of the sail as he looked for the double-back creases that had trapped it.

Nansi moved inside the well, working her way toward the inside fold to follow it from the mast. Although slow progress, the team seemed to be loosening the twists as they worked them free. Vilnius managed to shove one section of cloth away from the end of the hatch and it floated down in a slow, weightless drift toward Nansi, who caught it and pulled it in. As he started back up the edge, he looked up toward the starboard side.

In the faceplate of his helmet, Grania spotted the reflection of the vivid streak of blue-white light that shot across space for a few heartbeats. It looked like something moving, a burst of energy. "Do you see that, Brendan?"

"I do. If we were on land, I'd be calling it lightning. Out here ... I don't know."

"Do we get any kind of reading on it? Is it showing any power?"

"Not now. But I wasn't watching the instruments at the time it shot past."

"Keep an eye out. It might repeat. Let me know if there's any energy signature with it."

"I have it on the helmet camera," Vilnius told her. "It's more intense out here than on the screens."

"Back to work, laddie," Nansi reminded him. "Let's be getting this done and get ourselves back inside. This place is creepy."

He dutifully reached down for another fold of the fabric, followed it down to the twist, and began working it free. In another ten minutes, the second tangle fell off the hatch and flowed down to Nansi's waiting hands.

"I think there's only one more," Vilnius informed them as he slid further off the hatch to get down to the twist. Rolling into the cloth, he swung it around with his legs to get it worked to the end. Then it slipped off and, still clinging to it, he floated down with it.

"That's it!" Using the sail to propel her, Nansi bounced up into view and gave them a visual thumbs up.

Vilnius pulled himself back up to the top of the bay. "We've got a lot of loose cloth in here, so we may need to help it to deploy without tangling again. Liam, can you give us a little leeway with the mast?"

"Aye," the engineer's voice came through. "I'll be giving it a tap. Tell me if it's enough."

Through the com, the bridge crew could hear the whine of the mast starting to move, then a quick stop. They watched as the sail bounced a little, but didn't blossom outward.

"I'm thinking we need to stretch this big loop outward to get it out of the pole's way," Nansi said, tugging at the edge of the fabric.

"Good thinking," Vilnius replied. "I'll do it."

"No, I've got it. You be the solid anchor for me." With that, she grabbed near the middle edge of the pile of cloth and shoved off toward space above her. As she rose, the sail pulled out of the bay and flew outward, propelled by her momentum. Vilnius grasped her tether line and set himself to hang on.

Without warning, the pole mast shifted, lifting, and finding freedom, snapped out of the bay, rising to pull the sail, and Nansi along with it, to its full position. At the same time, the tether jerked, dragging Vilnius across the hull, then upward.

"Oh, fecking hell!" Nansi yelled while the pole locked into position with a snap.

For a moment, Grania couldn't see what happened then her heart jumped when she spotted Nansi tumbling backward and out of sight. "Nansi! No!"

She sprang to her feet, eyes riveted on the main screen. Her shipmate had gone over the edge of the ship, below the curve of the hull. Feeling helpless, she watched the tether tightening, pulling Vilnius toward the edge, then he, too, was over, no longer on screen. "Talk to me! Are you all right? Vilnius? Nansi?"

Oh, shite! Her nightmare was coming true. In a heartbeat, her mind leaped to the worst outcome. "Rory, do we have a camera on that side?"

"Yes, but no light." He keyed the feed to the aft portside camera that showed an image on the screen so dark you couldn't see anything.

"Switch it back," she ordered, her voice tight with pent-up emotion.

Grania strained to see the tether line, at last locking on it again. Was it holding? The line seemed looser, not as much tension and she held her breath. It seemed forever before a gloved hand appeared, followed by another as Vilnius pulled back up on the tether. He dragged his body, hand over hand along the rope, to the flat of the ship, just barely above the curve. If she stood near the aft end of the corridor in her cabin, he would be right over her head. And still as far away.

Vilnius turned, then reached down to grab Nansi's wrist where her hand was wrapped around his bootstrap. He pulled her up and they both sprawled prone on the ship's surface.

Grania breathed again as Rory mumbled, "Thanks be."

"Buíochas le Dia," she echoed. "Are you two all right?"

Vilnius raised a gloved hand and waved, then lay back and looked up at the sail as it hung in the dead space, unfurled, yet still in place on the mast. After a couple of minutes, Nansi climbed to her knees, still grasping the tether in a firm hold, then set her boot on the metal surface to lock it before positioning the other one.

Following Nansi's lead, Vilnius clambered back to his feet, then they checked their tether lines for damage.

They moved well away from the bay before the bridge crew heard Nansi say, "Aye, we denied the devil, though that was a bit of a wild ride. Now, Liam, will you please be lowering that sail back into the bay and we'll see if this baby will go into the cradle smoothly?"

With a one-word acknowledgment from Liam, they watched as the sail pole eased down. It slid in without a problem, the cloth folding somewhat neatly over the pole. Once it locked down, the bay door began to close, then stuck on something.

"Hold, Liam," Vilnius instructed. "We still need to fix the bent hatch cover."

Vilnius looked at the hatch and reported it wasn't as bad as they'd feared. The arm that pushed the hatch out of the path of the sail appeared crooked, but it turned out to be a damaged bolt, and he easily replaced it.

Grania's eyes followed along via the helmet camera images as Nansi slid into the bay and pulled herself along, inspecting the hinges on the hatch. A little over two meters down, she found a small problem, pulled out her utility knife from the external suit pocket, and dug out the piece of torn sail cloth lodged in the hinge.

After Vilnius gave her a hand up, he signaled Liam to resume closing it. The hatch locked into place setting off a round of cheers on the bridge.

Relieved, Grania said, "Good work, you two. Now get back in here." She felt a celebration was in order.

Rory shouted and whistled with enthusiasm and a few moments later Brendan joined in.

Through the com, Liam added his two cents along with, "I told you we could do it. Now, which way do we go?"

Grania took a deep breath. She had an idea about that. "I'll tell you in a bit. Right now, the celebration is in the galley."

Rory whooped, ready to head down as Brendan came to her side. "I caught a burst of those lights again, just as the hatch stuck. We showed a slight energy reading from it. Not enough to determine much about it. Whatever it is, it's either generating or using power."

Encouraged by this, Grania grinned, her spirits rising. "Thanks for that. Good job. I'll be down in a few mites. Get out a bottle of the Lowland Whiskey, all right?"

CHAPTER TWENTY-ONE

Grania

TWO THINGS HAD BEEN running through Grania's mind for the past few hours and now they were firming up. Those streaks of light were the only things to be seen in the dark space. Either they were from bursts of light from a nearby star or another light-emitting body, or they were from the wormhole. More than that, she recalled something else.

To confirm it, she played back the video of the banshee in the engine room and on the bridge. Feeling confident about her conclusions, she met with her crew in the galley. With the celebration well underway, the conquering heroes were out of their spacesuits, seated, and accepting toasts.

With a big smile on her face, Grania added hers. "To two fine and brave people, who I am so grateful to have in this predicament with me. I salute you both and say job well done!"

After everyone had, at least, a first sip, the captain looked around at each of them and said, "That toast extends to all of you. As a team, we've come this far. And ..." She paused to suck in a breath, building anticipation. "... I know where we need to go. Let me fill you in on my thinking. First, we've been seeing those lights on the starboard side ever since we arrived here. Brendan caught a slight energy surge from them this last time. So, it's something with power out there. And nothing else anywhere in this vicinity seems to be giving off power."

Follow your instincts, Vilnius said. Well, here she went with that. "I think we received another clue from an unlikely ally. I watched the videos of our banshee again. Although she appeared to be doing the same actions each time, the first time, in the cargo bay, she was wringing her hands and scrubbing, nothing more. When she appeared on the bridge, she scrubbed, twisted the imaginary clothes, then reached to hang them on a non-existent line or tree branch. However, the interesting part was that when she reached to hang them, she turned her torso toward the starboard side. As if she was trying to draw our attention to something there. She even repeated it."

"'Are ye saying that the bean sidhe is trying to help us?" Nansi's eyes widened and her brow wrinkled at the suggestion.

"I believe she is. Her appearance here is a warning to us. If she is hinting, doesn't that imply we still have a chance to avoid the fate she is predicting? And if she can warn us of disaster, can she not give us a clue of how to avoid it? If we pay attention to her actions, we can save ourselves."

"It's a bit of a stretch," Liam said. "If this spirit, or whatever it is, has come to call us to our demise, maybe she's trying to send a subconscious message to achieve that goal. It would not be to save us."

"She's a messenger, that's all," Grania argued. "The legends say that those who heed her warnings may be saved. I have considered all the information I have, and I feel this is the right answer. We need to go toward the lights."

"I agree with Nia," Brendan spoke up. "For one thing, it's the only thing in this whole area giving any indication of energy. If we travel any other direction, we have no beacons, nothing to follow. We could go in circles and never know it."

"That, at least, makes some sense," Liam agreed. "And when we get to the lights, if we do, then which way, starboard or port? Did your banshee give you advice on that, too?"

Grania frowned. It depended on what the lights were as to which direction might take them out of the Dark Sea before their resources gave out.

Follow your lights, a voice whispered in Grania's mind. Moira O'Cairn had said it. Grania had believed it was a spiritual message. What if she meant it literally? Which way were the lights going?' Grania took a deep breath. "Fair question. When we get there, I think I can answer it. For now, we will prepare the engines for movement in forty mites and start on a visual heading starboard toward the lights. We need to keep an eye on them, so we don't lose our direction; therefore, we sleep in shifts; two on duty at all times."

As the crew started to disperse, Nansi came close to Grania and indicated she wanted a private word with her. Probably concerned about the banshee still, Grania concluded as they waited until everyone had left. "What is it, Nansi?"

Her first mate shifted her shoulders uncomfortably and glanced around the room as if to assure herself they were alone before she said in a low voice, "Something is out there, Grania. When I lost the grip on the sail, it wasn't just a slip. Something brushed against me, shoving at me. It knocked me off the sail."

"What? I didn't see anything moving around you. It was just the sail. Granted, the light was dim, but it was clear enough to see you hanging there."

Nansi pursed her lips and shook her head once. "I know what I felt. It wasn't the sail. It had weight and substance to it, yet I couldn't see any kind of figure. Perhaps it's a spirit creature or something that blends into the blackness, and it moved quickly."

"But it didn't attack you? It wasn't trying to kill you?" Grania pointed out the obvious. "Maybe it was an unexpected jerk from the pole, enough to feel like something hit you." Or maybe it was your own imagination and fear.

Nansi crossed her arms over her chest and shrugged. "I have proof. Come with me."

Grania followed her out and down to the docking bay on the third deck. The ready room for their spacesuits was a two-meter square area with the single-door pressurized exit on the back wall. Four suits dangled off hangers opposite the entry door from the cargo bay. Nansi reached for the one she'd used for the spacewalk and turned it to show to Grania. There, on the back and just below the shoulder, were three uneven scrape marks.

Grania grabbed the suit and studied them. While they were not deep enough to penetrate the outer material of the suit, they looked like something with thick claws had scraped against the suit. A pole bouncing against the suit wouldn't produce that kind of damage.

As her eyes met Nansi's, she gave her head a shake and said, "I have no idea. We all assumed there was nothing in this dead space. We haven't gotten any readings from anything outside the ship. Maybe there's something alive there. Could it have been a spirit? Did Vilnius see anything?"

"I don't know. I didn't talk to him about it. I haven't said anything to anyone excepting yourself. 'Tis a bad omen, I'm thinking. Perhaps those other ships never even had a chance to return if there's an unseen predator in the void."

"All the more reason to get out of here as soon as possible," Grania said as she replaced the suit on the rack. "Keep this quiet for now. We'll keep an eye out for any other strange incidents."

PROGRESS ACROSS THE VOID proved to be slow and boring with little for the crew to do. To most eyes, it was dead space, quite literally, and the only things with any energy, other than the Mo Chroidhe, were the streaks of light beckoning them onward.

As Grania started into the galley, she caught Rory and Brendan playing a two-handed game of Gallivia pokuh, a card game similar to Earth poker's Deuces Wild with space monkeys being the wild cards. She paused in the doorframe, watching for a few moments until the door beeped, insisting she exit from the path.

Brendan glanced up at the sound, took a moment or two to assess her demeanor before returning his attention to the game. "Everything okay, Nia?" he asked.

She crossed to the food dispenser, ordered a half-sized portion of cheese pie, then turned to watch her brothers. "Yes. No change in the course; nothing to threaten the ship out there. Who's on the bridge?"

"Vilnius and Nansi," Rory answered as he dropped a three of comets in the discard pile.

Brendan contemplated the discard for about three seconds, then called Rory out, raising their juicy beans bet thirty more beans. Rory frowned, studied his cards for a moment more, then folded. Grinning, Brendan spread his hand to show three space monkeys.

"You were lucky this time, little brother. I'll get you the next time. Count on it." He handed his cards across, then clambered to his feet. "I'm going for a jog through the ship before going back to the bridge. See you up top."

Grania's lips hitched into a small smile as Rory jogged out, already getting into the run. His course would amount to two or three rounds of the ship's corridors, the vertical stair climbs, and a full circle of the cargo bay aisles. Then he would be revved up to resume trying to locate a non-existent signal. She'd witnessed his frustration with not being able to get anything on the com. His curses under his breath, tossing the code manual across the way as number after number yielded nothing, and his defeated slump when no response returned. But bless him, he kept working on it.

She sat across from Brendan, who now put the cards and stale juicy beans back into their game box. The beans were so old and hard that they were good for little more than gaming wagers. "How are you holding up, Bren?"

"I'm fine, Nia," he replied, set the box in a drawer, then added, "No, not entirely. We don't talk about it, but I am scared. I mean, this is never what I expected. Are we going to make it back?" His voice wavered a bit.

She saw the fear in her brother's face, the light bruises under his eyes hinting he wasn't sleeping well and darkness in his eyes like the light had dimmed. It echoed the anxiety in her soul that she struggled to keep from reaching her eyes. Even though logic told her this situation wasn't her fault, she still felt the guilt that somehow, she'd let her ship slip into the Dark Sea and possibly—probably—doomed them all. She'd failed them.

Her voice wobbled a little as she answered. "Truth? I don't know. We have so little information about this and wormholes in general. What I do know is I have the best, smartest crew in the universe, and if it can be done, we'll do it."

He nodded although he didn't look more assured with that answer. His voice sounded hoarse with bridled emotion. "I don't want to die. Not yet."

"We're not giving up." She rose and circled the table to hug her brother, wrapping her arms around his shoulders from behind. Her voice softened as she added, "I don't want to die either, little brother. None of us do, which is why we'll do everything we can to get back into that bleedin' wormhole. I can't explain it, Bren, but I feel like something is looking out for us."

"I pray you're right." He laid a hand on top of hers as if to draw strength from her. Wiping a bit of emotion from his eye, he pushed her away and rose to go back to the bridge.

Grania watched him step through the door, then whispered, "So do I."

CHAPTER TWENTY-TWO

Grania

WITH NO LIGHT TO feed them, raising the solar sails would be useless, so the ship traveled on the basic engine power. At least both appeared to be working well, and the ship closed the distance toward the light streaks. After almost forty hours, the flashes, when they passed, were becoming wider bars of blended colors and were giving Brendan stronger readings.

Best of all, after so much worry about freeing the sails, their banshee had not yet returned. So, either they had made the right choice, and the spirit no longer needed to warn them, or they had only delayed it, and she would return when danger was once again imminent. When she thought about it, Grania questioned whether she wanted to have an entity around who would appear with dire warnings whenever danger threatened her or her family. It could prove too distracting and drastically change her way of thinking.

She turned her attention back to the light streaks, watching the patterns and feeling more and more certain she knew what they were approaching. At their travel rate, Brendan estimated they would be on top of it in about thirty hours.

"You know, Brendan, I'm convinced we're heading directly for the wormhole," she said.

"Is that what you think that is? I always pictured it as a sort of tunnel through space, and it seems it would have a more cylindrical shape." He stared at it again. The entire crew had spent more time watching the phenomenon as it grew on the screen.

"It might," she agreed. "I don't believe we're seeing much of it yet. The lights are probably energy generated by movement through the hole. Ships going through it maybe. When we get closer, the shape of it will probably become more apparent."

"Then what will we do?"

"I don't know yet. When we see what's ahead, we'll figure that out."

Follow the lights.

Why had Moira O'Cairn told her that? Grania turned to the ship's computer and opened the passenger information files. Although she'd checked on Harhiman, she hadn't gotten to Moira, and now her curiosity prodded her to learn more about the old woman. She keyed in "Moira O'Cairn" under the passenger database for London Spaceport and waited. In a short time, the program returned a "No Results" message. She frowned, checked her spelling, then tried it again without the apostrophe. Still nothing.

She changed to the ship information list and entered the Mo Chroidhe and the request passenger list option along with the departure date. In a heartbeat, the computer returned two results: Harhiman, A. and Sheehan, M.

"What the heck?" she muttered under her breath, then clicked the Sheehan entry open.

The folder displayed her passport information, a photo, and details of her travel voucher. The photo certainly looked like their passenger, a wrinkled old lady with almost white hair. She thought many old Irish ladies looked very similar. She scanned down the document. Place of origin showed County Wicklow, Ireland, Earth. That checked out. It all seemed good until she got to the passport and saw the 'Cancelled" watermark across it. Clicking on it, the expiration date showed voided and time-stamped less than twenty-four minutes after they'd left London Spaceport. The expiry date was still valid, so why was it withdrawn? And why weren't they notified?

Delving in a little more, she found a "more information" link and tapped it. Another picture popped up along with a blurb below it, saying Moira O'Ceagan Sheehan was presumed deceased in a fire at her home in the Wicklow Hills. Grania's stomach contracted like she'd been gut-punched. O'Ceagan? That was her great-great Aunt Moira, who had just died. So, who was this woman in Rory's cabin and how did she have her aunt's passport? Or was this her aunt? She was "presumed" to have died in the fire. What if she hadn't? Had she made her way to London?

No! It pushed the likelihood too far. Grania refused to believe in the possibility. She needed to have a conversation with their passenger to learn the truth. But it had to be later, she noted, as Liam's voice came through the com.

"Grania, I just ran some calculations on the energy output we're getting from the direction we're heading. It has tripled in the past six hours. Before, it was a slow build; now we've hit a point where it seems to be reaching us faster. We should be able to benefit from it soon. Once we're close enough, I believe we can raise the sails, and we should get some power through them."

"That's encouraging news. So, you estimate the lights are producing enough luminescence for the sails to convert to energy? Is it possible?"

"Hypothetically, yes," Liam replied. "The tests run by the manufacturer said artificial light works with the sail receptors, but it's not as powerful as a star's output. Still, it will give us a boost."

"Sounds great. At this point, I'll take any help we can get. Are the jump pods getting charged up? If we need them, I want them ready to go."

"No, they've been offline since we woke up the last time. Most of them are between 55 and 70 percent charged, except for the one Vilnius used. His is almost drained. I'll bring it online now. I don't want to put too much demand on the power we have until we're confident we can get more."

"Agreed. I'm going for a sleep period. If anything happens, wake me." Signing off, she stood, ready to head to her cabin where Vilnius was already sleeping. "Got that, Brendan? If anything out of the ordinary happens, tag me at once. And pass that along to Rory when he comes on."

IN HER QUARTERS, GRANIA shed her slacks and tunic and crawled over Vilnius to lie wedged between him and the edge of the sleep pod. Designed for a single person, the unit proved a tight fit for even the slim woman and the equally trim man. As she settled next to him, he shifted in his sleep, turning to give her more room. She tucked in snugly and wrapped an arm around him.

Sighing, she considered the near perfection of the situation if not for the fact they still faced a dangerous situation. But to have him here by her? That gave her more happiness, bittersweet though it might be, than she'd ever dreamed.

Their relationship went back several years to when she, a gangly fifteen-year-old, first met the handsome young station assistant when the ship docked at Zabrowski for her first Earth visit. Already taller than most girls her age and skinny as a rail, she appeared awkward and clumsy.

A recent graduate from the university at Greenwich, Vilnius possessed a fair bit of knowledge, but little experience on a space station. Still, he was charming and funny and, most of all, he seemed to enjoy being around her. He teased her the way he would a little sister, and she hung around him like the smitten little girl she was. Her granda had called it a crush and laughed about it. By the time the Mo Chroidhe had returned to Zabrowski Station again, Grania had blossomed into a shapely and beautiful young woman and their fledgling friendship evolved into something more.

It warmed her soul with his admission he joined them because he'd been worried enough about her to undertake the trip to protect her. Although he ended up stuck with them, he bore it well and acted like part of the crew. She adored him for doing it, even though she also feared the outcome of this disaster.

Realistically, their romance would never be more than a "catch you when I'm in port" affair, especially if she became a ship's captain. As a career stationer, he expected to move up the line to stationmaster on Zabrowski, although he joked sometimes about one day transferring to Red Dragon Station, the endpoint to Erin-nua's star.

At this moment, she wished it could be more. Even though she wanted to deny it, she realized she was plunging into the deep waters of hopeless love with Vilnius Majeck. With a light and lazy touch, she traced her finger over the dark blue stationer tattoo on his left shoulder.

Like Zabrowski, the ink displayed a wagon wheel station with the perfect circle of the central hub etched in his skin. From it, thin, elegant lines arched outward like the spokes of an ancient wheel, connecting to an outer ring shaded to evoke the metal texture and tiny etchings suggesting docking bays, windows, and antenna arrays. When she first saw it, he revealed he got it the night before he graduated. On an impulse, she pressed her lips onto the center of the stylized design in a gentle kiss. Resting her head against his broad back, she drifted to sleep.

AS GRANIA PRESSED THE button to open the galley door, she contemplated how she would approach Moira O'Cairn about the passport discrepancy. She drew up in surprise when she found the woman seated at the table sipping a cup of tea. After a polite greeting, Grania turned to get her own cup. The old woman greeted her warmly, adding an invitation to sit with her. As if there were any other seats in the galley, but Grania understood the gesture.

While this wasn't quite the approach to the conversation she had intended, perhaps it would be a suitable opener. They were alone and not likely to be interrupted. She sat down and took a sip of her tea. "Allow me to apologize again for the unexpected delay in our trip. Accidents are a slight possibility when traversing wormholes. Such things are rare, and we were unlucky this time."

"I accept that," she replied in a calm voice. "Being perfectly frank, as you have not been in discussing this with myself and Mr. Harhiman, there is considerable uncertainty in our being able to resume the trip and survive, is there not?"

That was direct, Grania thought. The lady saw and understood more than she had credited. "You're right. I didn't want to worry you both, but the situation is uncertain. My crew and I are doing our very best to get this ship, and all of us, back to normal space."

"I see on the screen in here that we are getting closer to the light streaks, much closer. Do you expect to find normal space there?"

"Perhaps. I hope so." She paused for another sip of tea, then took the lead. "Speaking of not being entirely frank, there is an irregularity in your transport papers. I confess I hadn't checked them sooner, relying on your honesty. When I did a routine check recently, I learned your passport is issued to a 'Moira O'Ceagan Sheehan' not 'Moira O'Cairn'. Is that you?"

The old woman gazed at her with a gentle look in her gray-blue eyes. "No, 'tis not. I knew Moira Sheehan all her life and was often with her. When it became necessary for me to leave Ireland to get to family on Erinnua, I needed a passport. Since Moira had no need for hers any longer, I used it. 'Twas a bit of deception, that is true. Faith, 'twas not for any wicked reason. My regrets for not being honest. I simply needed to get to Erinnua quickly and the whole passport process is so complex."

Could she believe her? Uncertain of the veracity, Grania still felt she seemed sincere with her answer. Perhaps Moira had willingly given her passport to an old friend. She cleared her throat with a slight cough. "Moira Sheehan was my great grandfather's sister, my twice-great aunt. News reached me, after we were underway, that she was believed to have perished in a fire at her cottage. Do you know anything about that?"

"I realized Moira's health was failing, and her days were growing short." The old woman's face wore a sad expression with her eyes tearing up as she spoke. "Tis likely that her death was natural and not from the fire. Although the cottage had a fireplace in it, you know."

"I hope 'twas the case. So, who are you?"

"Just a tired old woman on a quest to find her family, who bears the name Moira O'Cairn."

They sat in silence for a few minutes, each mulling over their own thoughts. Moira spoke first. "Will you be turning me in if we survive this excursion?"

"I haven't decided." Grania rose, took her cup to the cleaner, then turned back. "Whether I do or not, you will still have problems at Dragon Station. The passport has been canceled, so you won't be cleared when you try to go to the planet."

"Ah, thanks to ye, then for the concern." The woman gave her a simple nod at this news, seeming unworried about it.

Although puzzled by Moira's mild reaction, Grania excused herself to start her shift on the bridge.

CHAPTER
TWENTY-THREE

Grania

"OKAY, LIAM. DEPLOY THE lateral sails when you're ready." Grania leaned forward watching the reddish glow of what surely must be the wormhole in front of them. color streaks fluctuated with energy, shifting in tone to blue to white and back to red. Rory registered bursts of static on the external com, but no actual transmissions. After ninety-six hours of travel to get this close, the energy reading had increased a hundredfold.

"Copy that, Captain. The starboard one is unfolding now."

Grania glanced at the monitor for the starboard aft camera and watched the triangular-shaped sail move into position and lock.

"Port is deploying."

Rory toggled the port camera feed to the same screen, and the action repeated on that side. They looked good; the operation had gone without a hitch.

"We're picking up speed now and the sails are charging up. Once they reach capacity, we should be getting the excess into our power cells." Liam sounded happier than he'd been since they'd been flung into the dark.

Rory let out a celebratory cheer. "Fates be with us. Now if we can just get a com signal, we could work our way back."

They still had a long way to go to reach normal space and the next gate, wherever that might be. At least they weren't dead in space. The endeavor to get to this potential energy point had cost them most of their reserve power. Without the sails to help maneuver and collect radiant power for the ship, they had relied on the engines and the ship's rudder to move in the correct direction. With the amount of light and energy feed they were getting now, the reserves would be restored within a short time.

"Have you figured out which way we need to go when we get to this barrier ahead?" Liam asked. Although her brother still declined to call the phenomenon a wormhole, Grania accepted his opinion that it could be an energy field separating the dark space from normal space. On one issue, they agreed; taking the ship through wasn't the wisest plan.

"I think I have."

Follow the lights.

Not just go to the lights; follow them.

The streaks of light they'd been observing all moved in one direction, following a flow through space. "We'll turn to port to parallel it when we're two hundred meters from the field unless we get an indication before then that the range is unsafe."

"I agree with that," Vilnius chimed in from the engine room. He volunteered to work with Liam and Nansi during this phase in case they needed an extra pair of hands.

"No argument from me," Rory added. "I'd have tossed a coin."

"Ah ha, the traditional scientific method." Brendan shook his head in mock disgust. "For what it's worth, I think you've got the right idea. I'm seeing an energy flow pattern, and it's all going to our port side."

She watched the flicker of lights playing on the sails and felt an odd reassurance that they would get through this. While the trip may take them a long time if they weren't near normal space, at least they were moving.

FOURTEEN HOURS LATER, THE com in Grania's cabin woke her from a blissful sleep. Groggy, she reached across Vilnius to get to the mobi unit and her hand jerked away from its destination while the ship appeared to lurch. Either she was unsteady, or the vessel was. Her fingers connected with her target, and she flicked the button. "What is it?"

"I've slowed us, Grania," Liam said without preamble. "I think we're as close as we dare to get to this thing. The ship is beginning to shudder."

"I noticed it." Once she noticed the movement, the more intense shakes and jolts declared an unstable ride. "On my way, Liam."

"What's happening?" Vilnius asked as she rolled over him to get out of the pod.

"Trouble, maybe. We may have gotten as close as we dare to the lights."

She pulled on her slacks and tunic in record time and tore out, running toward the bridge. When she dashed through the door onto the deck, the glow filled the bridge with light. "Filters! Show me the sails, Nansi."

Her second pressed the command to filter the light coming through the overhead window and switched the screen to the port side sail. Light reflected from the fluctuating metallic fabric, and it shuddered more than normal. Grania pressed her com button. "Full stop, Liam, then take her to port."

Vilnius burst onto the bridge then and froze as he encountered the wall of lights ahead of them. Sparkling and brilliant, it shone with colorful rays and energy. It looked enormous. Grania gaped at it, adding two and two and not pleased at the result.

"It's the outside of the wormhole, isn't it?" Though her mouth was dry, she moistened her lips with her tongue before speaking again. "The Dark Sea is the space between where the worm-hole tunnels across space."

Vilnius put his arms around her, pulling her close and rubbing her shoulders. "I think you're right. Jay-sus, it's huge. It's a helluva discovery we've made on this trip."

"Now what?" Nansi asked. Gripped by overwhelming fear, her face paled and her eyes bulged.

"I'm not sure. For now, we stick to the plan and run parallel to the hole while we try to figure the situation out." The ship seemed to settle down, even though the sails still trembled in the power bursts. She pressed the com button again. "Liam, are those sails going to be all right?"

"I've been watching them. I think they're just whipping a bit in the energy storm this thing is creating. Don't worry; I'm on them. We may need to back off some"

"Is the back draft dangerous? Are we getting any radiation readings?"

"I'm seeing a bit, yes. For now, the ship's shields are protecting us. They're not that high."

She let out a sigh of relief. "Monitor that, too. Let's pull back another hundred meters and see if the ship settles down." On her words, the Mo Chroidhe lurched a bit, and Vilnius held Grania a little tighter with one arm as he grabbed for a rail with the other. Stable again, she lunged for her seat and belted in. She motioned him to Brendan's seat.

Her stomach tipped with the subtle shift as Liam eased the ship to a shallow angle away from the tunnel, then evened it out again.

For now, they could do nothing more than watch and study this thing. She hoped they would find an answer in it. She glanced again at Nansi's frightened face. "Nansi, you're off watch for now. I'm here and Rory will be along in a few mites."

At first, it looked like Nansi might refuse. "I can stay, Grania. It's just a bit overwhelming."

"Hey! We've made it this far. We'll figure it out, you know. I still need to get this ship back to Granda." That brought a bit of a smile, although underneath the bravado, she felt almost the same way.

GRANIA ENTERED DATA INTO the computer, recording everything that had happened to the Mo Chroidhe since it had been ejected from the wormhole. If they returned to normal space, it might be valuable to anyone else who had the misfortune to end up in one of the Dark Seas. If they didn't succeed, well then, perhaps someday someone would find them or the slipstream from the tunnel might pull the ship along until ultimately spitting it out into normal space somewhere.

For now, she hoped all the information would tie something together enough to show them the way back. The ship responded to the effect of paralleling the tunnel as its speed was increasing, yet the power reserves were barely climbing.

When he wasn't watching the two sails to be sure they weren't taking damage from the buffeting caused by the back draft, Rory fiddled with his com frequencies, trying to find one that would connect them with the station or even another ship.

"If a ship is in the hole, we should be able to talk to them," he complained. Static was the only answer he was getting so far.

"Nothing's getting through that wall of electro-static energy," Vilnius informed him. "That's likely why nothing works well out here and you can't use any com in the wormholes. You can't get readings on anything."

"Well, thank you for telling me something I already know," Rory growled.

Grania cocked an eyebrow. Good-natured Rory seemed to be getting a mite testy. The strain pressed down on all of them.

Chuckling a bit at Rory's frustration, Liam waved a hand at Grania and turned to head back to his engines. He'd stopped after a few hours of sleep to tell Grania he wanted to see the bridge view of the wormhole.

"Ah ha! So, you admit it's a wormhole!" she crowed.

"It's difficult to deny it when you're staring at it. You win," he conceded in a flat tone.

"It wasn't a contest," she said, wanting to ease his disappointment.

"I left a program running that's recording and correlating any readings we're getting from the wormhole," he said, shrugging. "There may be a way into it. The sails are pulling in plenty of energy to power us, but we're not really accumulating any extra. I think we need the dorsal sail for that."

"I don't want to have to use it," Grania answered. "With this much turbulence and the tear already in the sail, I doubt the fabric would hold up long. Are the jump pods getting charged?"

He consulted his tablet, which was tracking the computer. "Slowly. They've only gone up a little. Huh? Here's an oddity; the pod in Rory's cabin is almost fully charged while the rest are around seventy-five percent. The spare one is registering at nine percent. I'm thinking it needs to be fully refurbished."

"That's going to be a problem." She glanced at Vilnius with a worried frown. "Can you go check on it, Vilnius? See if you can figure a way to boost the power. How about the one in the captain's cabin? Is the pod up to full?"

A pause as Liam looked, then he said, "Oh, shite, no. That one's not even online. Since you decided not to use Granda's cabin, I took it off."

"Can you bring the unit on now and begin charging? If we can get back in either the slipstream or the tunnel, we're going to need it."

"I'll see if what I can do with the pod in the spare cabin. Do you have a tester?" Vilnius asked.

She pointed to a cabinet below the desk next to the navigation console.

As he went to grab the tool, Liam said, "I can't get that pod to stay online. A cold start from the unit may be necessary."

"You go on down to the engine room. I'll do the cold start," Grania replied, motioning Vilnius to get going. "I'll be back shortly, Rory. Tag me if anything urgent shows up."

"Urgent? What would be urgent? We're being dragged alongside an energy slipstream!" Rory shouted, his nerves fraying faster than the sails.

On the same level as the bridge, the captain's cabin occupied the prow of the ship, close in case of emergencies. She keyed in the code for the door and entered. While somewhat larger than the crew cabins, she wouldn't call place spacious. Room enough for a small desk, the computer link, and remote consoles in addition to the oversized sleep pod.

Built-in next to the desk, a bookcase held an assortment of real, hardbound books. Most of them ranked as family heirlooms, treasures her granda had read several times in his life. Some were ancient and had traveled from Earth with Gramps. She touched the spine of one, tipped it out a little to read the title, The Once and Future King. She knew that one and dozens of other ones on the shelf and an inexplicable wave of fear that she would lose all these with the ship rolled over her.

Of all things to worry about ... Shaking off her negative feelings, she turned to the business at hand.

The jump pod, a unit that was twenty percent larger than the rest on the ship to accommodate her grandfather's substantial frame, sat on the starboard side. No power lights showed on it. On the entry wall, a file cabinet stored the ship's archives. While data pods had most of the history, Granda kept a few things on paper.

On top of the cabinet, a holographic photo of her mother and herself seemed to gaze at her. She recalled the day it was taken. She had just turned fourteen, and they'd been on Pelanan Station prior to the jump to Dragon Station on their way home. For them, the day had been quite special, a rare mother and daughter shopping spree. A fond smile touched her lips at the memory before she turned her attention to the pod.

At first, the unit didn't respond to her attempts to reboot it; the lights refusing to come on or give so much as a blink. She fell back to checking the connections and found a loose wire in the base that fed the main board. She found the tools she needed and secured the connection. The pod powered up, then ran through the startup sequence.

"Do you see it, Liam?" she asked after she'd tagged him.

"Aye,I do. The power is showing almost non-existent on that unit, give it a while to charge."

"Acknowledged. I'm starting back to the bridge now." She glanced around the cabin again. Technically, she could have used the space this trip; however, she didn't feel that comfortable in her granda's cabin amongst his things. One day, this might be hers, although not until she had earned the right and her granda was ready to remain planet-side. Before any of that, she had to get the ship home again.

After Brendan came on duty, Grania met Liam and Vilnius in the galley for a sandwich. While Liam had been studying all the information they had, he still didn't have any answers.

"Can you see any way that we can get back into the hole?" she asked flat out.

She took a bite of her sandwich, thinking it looked a little lean on the processed meat filling. How long would they be able to keep the food coming? Not long before their stores would be depleted. The ship wasn't stocked for more than two months for the crew, not counting their three extras on this excursion. Their food stores, only marginally replenished at Zabrowski and not at all at Pelanan, left them with around ten days' worth, she reckoned.

"Not really. We'd need to get into the slipstream and try to punch through into the wormhole. The action would take a huge amount of power."

"Getting into the slipstream would bring the ship to light speed," Vilnius commented. "It would be a rough ride and conceivably more than we can withstand."

"If we move a little closer, would we get more power?" she asked.

"Maybe, but it is riskier and presents more danger to the ship."

She ran a hand through her hair, pushing a lock back from her face and twisting the end as she spoke. "If we think we have a chance to get into the hole, we may have to risk it. For right now, let's keep looking for a way to do this without getting us all killed. How long do we have before we run out of resources?"

Liam's lips tightened into a grim line. "Under a week, I'd estimate, before the effects begin to affect us. Life support is stable provided we can reuse the oxygen, but the air will soon become musty. The food is going to give out before then."

"Ok, so we'll need to make a decision and pray we choose the right one before that happens. For now, let's cut back rations twenty percent." She looked at Vilnius and said wryly, "Still glad you hitched a ride with us?"

"Maybe not. On the other hand, I wouldn't choose to be back at Zabrowski hearing this kind of news and not being able to do anything about it."

Her mouth shaped into a sweet, sad smile as she reached across and pressed her hand on top of his.

Liam rolled his eyes, stood up, and headed for the exit.

CHAPTER TWENTY-FOUR

Grania

A DAY LATER, GRANIA called another meeting with everyone, passengers included, in the galley. She gazed around the
room, her view slipping from one anxious face to another, one
by one, while she gathered her thoughts. She didn't consider this
solely the captain's decision, for it affected them all. They had
run out of options and the time had come to make a final run at
getting home, if that was the choice. For the past few hours, she'd
debated how to approach this, but when you came right down to
it, you just presented the facts and said it.

"I've asked you all to this meeting because we have a difficult
decision to make. We're traveling just outside the slipstream of the
wormhole, which has been pulling us along faster than we could
have traveled on our own." She paused and pointed at the screen
along the starboard wall where the view from the bridge showed
the broad, colored bands and the slight curvature of the wormhole
behind it. All eyes shifted to the live image. "However, the speed
isn't enough for us to continue this way. Here's what the situation
is right now.

"We are running low on supplies. At best, we only have a few
days left before we will run out of food." That had Harhiman's

attention, and his eyes snapped to her, which hadn't been the case until now. She continued, "The wormhole barrier isn't solid. We've analyzed the data we've picked up over the past few days and believe we understand more about how the ER-bridge works. The energy field surrounding it keeps it in the tunnel form and generally prevents anything from exiting or entering it. A disruption to this field created an exit point and ejected our ship. We hypothesize we can reenter the wormhole by pressing into the slipstream to break through the energy field. Our problem is the ship's energy, like its supplies, is greatly reduced. We have deployed our port and starboard solar sails, and they are providing the power for us now, though they can only add a a slight amount to our reserves."

She paused as Liam brought up an image on the screen of the dorsal sail before they collapsed it. Plainly visible, the two-point-three-meter rip in the lower edge formed a statement. "The dorsal sail, which is our mainsail, suffered some damage when we were evicted from the hole. If we deploy it, there is a high chance it might be torn further or ripped from the ship. Yet, if we elect to punch through the energy field, we will need all the power we can get to succeed."

"Is it even possible?" Nansi asked. Like the rest of the crew, she knew the situation well, yet she voiced the question their passengers might want to know.

"That's entirely an unknown," Grania replied. "This is hypothetical based on what we've learned. No instructions exist for escaping from a dark space. Only one other ship returned and that was because it was close to the endpoint when it was ejected. They managed to limp to normal space. We have no idea how far away normal space is. We could reach it tomorrow or we might never make it."

Harhiman sat forward, a frown on his face. "So, you're offering us a chance to die now or die later. Does that sum it up?"

"It does, Mr. Harhiman. Except that it also offers a slim chance that we might punch back into the wormhole and survive. Make no mistake, it is a small possibility we're talking about." She let that sink in before adding, "Nonetheless, it offers a chance. We can hold off until the last minute, try to conserve on our food usage and go a few more days hoping to emerge in normal space near a space station or other ship that could rescue us."

No doubts hid in her mind that every person in the room understood precisely what the risk was and realized they most likely would die in the attempt. Liam, more than most, knew the very low odds of this working, especially without enough power. He'd worked out the theory, done the math, and projected the probability they could do it. Even with the dorsal sail active, he didn't calculate they could accomplish the task, and he'd told her that. Still, with the poor prognosis for their survival anyway, he supported the decision to try. Would the rest of them?

Grania's view moved across the grave-looking faces while each absorbed the information, before she concluded. "This gives us the chance of survival or a quick death. We don't have to decide now and even if some prefer to wait until we're down to the last day of food, we can do hold on. Then the ultimate decision will need to be made."

Harhiman's brow furrowed, the corners of his mouth tightening as he stared at the screen. The set of his jaw hinted at frustration, while a glimmer of panic flickered in his gaze, as if he hadn't considered they wouldn't be able to proceed to the next station. He rubbed a hand over his jawline as he appeared to deliberate the options she presented.

The youngest of them, Brendan, spoke up. "I know the odds aren't good, but another day or two to see if we can find our way out wouldn't be harmful."

She couldn't blame him for that view; he reached for hope. They had all been hopeful at some point. She turned her gaze to Moira O'Cairn. "Do you have any questions, Miz O'Cairn?"

Serene-looking, hands folded on her lap, she appeared calm, although a touch of sadness darkened her eyes. "I am an old woman. My life has been long, and if it is to end, then it does not matter if it is today or ten years from today. 'Tis a decision for young people to make, and I will abide by whatever you all choose."

"I have one more question," Harhiman said, leaning back in his chair while his gaze traveled from face to face of the young crew. "If you had additional power, do you honestly believe you can insert the ship back into the wormhole, and we would have a chance at surviving it?"

"I do," Liam answered before Grania could speak. "I've done the calculations, and I've studied the hole for the past few days. It isn't solid and there are small periodic gaps. With additional power, we can utilize a gap and slip back into it. It will be vital that everyone be in his or her jump pod before we attempt it. I can program it up to a full thirty secs ahead, which gives me time to get to my pod."

"And you don't feel the dorsal sail will add enough additional power to do it, do you?"

Liam met Harhiman's eyes straight on and answered with honesty. "I expect it will take more than that to improve our odds. Still, if the sail holds and we give it, at least, one more day to gather energy, there is a slight chance."

The room fell silent after Liam spoke while Harhiman shifted his eyes to the floor, saying nothing more.

Grania took charge again. "We have at least one request for a delay in any action for up to forty-eight hours. During that time, if you have any more questions or would like to talk more about it, please see me. I'll ask for the final vote to wait or to try it within twenty-four hours. That's all for now."

* * *

Sheilan

MIZ O'CAIRN WAITED WHILE everyone else exited the room, using the excuse of getting a cup of tea to delay. After they'd all left, she slipped out of view of the galley camera, and Sheilan changed back to her energy form. In this invisible state, she followed Harhiman to his cabin. He was annoyed with the situation; that much was obvious by the scowl on his face as he snatched his tablet.

"Communications out," he muttered, anger oozing in his voice. "Can't send any messages, and I'm about to die with the mother lode. Damn it all!" Dropping onto the pod bed, he slid his finger across the tablet several times to a specific page on his tablet and stared at it, his tense brows and rigid jawline indicating he was doing some serious thinking. In her present form, the banshee couldn't make out the displayed page, though he pondered over it for several mites.

Decision made, he went to the lock box he'd brought with him, keyed in a code, pressed his finger to the identification pad, and opened it. Even before he pulled the small, glowing sphere out, Sheilan felt its power and recognized the pattern. She didn't hesitate, disappearing at once.

Dari's eyebrows shot up, his eyes widened in shock, pupils dilating as the banshee materialized as a ghostly young woman in their cabin. His mouth fell open as he gulped a quick intake of breath. "Mawa! Ye startled me, Sheilan!"

"The trader has one of the crystals in his room," she blurted out.

"I thought I felt something just now," Dari said. "It's not like the ones in the hold. It's not as draining."

"Draining enough! It is a different shape, though, rounded and polished, I would guess."

"What do you suppose he is going to do with it?" The puca looked worried. Those crystals were the only thing to threaten their existence that they'd encountered in their long lives, so any time they were in play, it made them nervous.

"I do not know," she answered. "Maybe he will blow up the ship."

"Now, that would not make any sense, would it? The man is inherently not up to anything good, that is true. Still, he would be looking at a way to save himself, would he not?"

"I would think," she agreed. "Maybe 'tis something to help the ship. He was asking questions about more energy improving the chances of the ship's survival."

Dari scratched at his shoulders with his hands, feeling the itch from the crystal's proximity. "Is the ship in that much danger?"

"It is. The captain presented a bleak view of the future with a slim chance of survival."

Dari's voice was a horsey whinny. "Doom awaits! Would there be anything in your sidhe bag of tricks that might help the situation?"

"I am a banshee, not an idol-praised god! I don't think wailing at that wall of energy is going to have any effect on it."

She sat on the trunk, comforted by the feel of the soil below her. Calmer now, she filled Dari in on the situation and the plan.

"If we retreat to the soil when they begin to take the ship into the wormhole, we might make the transition to Earth if the ship blows up. If not, then we will be stuck in either the wormhole or the so-called slipstream outside the hole. Eventually, it should deposit us somewhere, although getting back to Earth or any planet would take some work. I regret that you agreed to accompany me on this journey, old friend.

He shrugged. "What better company for eternity than each other? 'Tis much like it has always been."

"True, puca. That is valid. But I will have failed in my quest to reach my family, and four of the youngest will be gone forever. I like them quite a lot." Her eyes shadowed with sadness as she considered losing the young ones and never delivering the rosary to the youngest. While she'd lost many young ones over the centuries and these were just four more, it still bothered her.

Then she thought of something, and her expression brightened. "Dari, there will be a warning. If they are to die in this endeavor, I will know before they do, for I will be called to announce their deaths. Perhaps there is hope."

Liam

FINGERS TAPPING WITH RHYTHMIC speed on the keys at his computer, Liam worked the numbers again, trying to factor in as many scenarios as possible for survival. While most were total failures, three presented possibilities. The best option needed triple the power they could generate with the sails, even using the dorsal one. If they turned everything else off on the ship, including the jump pods, they still couldn't accumulate that much power.

The buzz from the above deck door startled him, and he glanced at the screen image from the camera positioned above it. Harhiman waited at the entry, gazing up at the camera.

"What is it?" Liam asked.

"I have something that might help us out in this situation. If you will allow me down to show you and explain, I think it would be to your benefit, as to all of us."

Although wary of the merchant, Liam keyed in the unlock code and the door slid open. Harhiman stepped through and clambered down the stairs, the thud of his boots on the steps echoing in the cargo bay.

Liam greeted him at the bottom. "What is it that you have on your mind, Mr. Harhiman?"

Harhiman reached his left hand into his bulging pocket and withdrew a large pouch about twenty centimeters across. He opened it and rolled out a glowing crystal onto the palm of his hand.

"Is that what I think it is?" Liam asked, his mouth suddenly dry.

"It's targassium. I represent a company that mines it on Hope. This is a polished sample, ready to use. It's quite valuable. If it can save us and the ship, then it's yours to use."

Liam didn't trust the trader, and it rankled him to accept the offer. Yet the power from the crystal could mean their lives. That, of course, had to be Harhiman's motivation in offering it up, to save his own life. Liam held out his hand to receive the precious rock. "If our converter can use this, it might make all the difference," he conceded. "Thank you, Mr. Harhiman."

With a brief nod, Harhiman said no more, turned, and climbed to the deck above. Stunned, Liam caressed the crystal and returned to his computer to look up the specs for using it in their converter.

CHAPTER TWENTY-FIVE

Grania

"I STILL CAN'T BELIEVE he handed it to you without trying to make a deal or anything," Grania said while she watched Liam working to adapt the receptacle to hold the crystal in place. For a small object, it held a lot of potential energy and could power the ship for years by itself. "It's worth a bleedin' lot of credits. We could never have afforded one this large."

"Maybe he considers saving his life worth the cost," Liam answered as he turned the contact brace another notch. "That should do it. The crystal is pushing the size range the converter's cradle is designed to hold. It's a snug fit, but it should work." Holding the crystal in his fingers, he slid it into place, making certain it settled before he released it, pressed the contact into position, and closed the door to the unit.

"Let's fire it up and see what happens." He pressed the start button for the converter and watched the readings as it came to life. The crystal glowed brighter, progressing in output as it took almost a mite before the power readings registered.

"It's working," Grania said, her voice barely hiding her excitement. The energy bars kept increasing. "Fated fairies and benevolent saints, it looks like we have a real chance if we have enough power to cross the slipstream."

Liam nodded, then pulled up a diagram of a trajectory he'd been working on. "Look here, Nia. The slipstream is racing at a velocity that nearly matches the wormhole's, which means the ride will be just as turbulent as venturing directly into the hole. If we attempt a straight traversal, the back draft generated will exert significant force against us. My thought is to approach at an angle and allow it to pull us across. This way, we can utilize the slipstream's momentum to our advantage and reduce the pressure on the ship. This should help us get closer to our target. I'll be searching for a fissure in the energy tunnel to breach into the wormhole and will set the ship on autopilot prior to engaging with the slipstream. It's critical that everyone secures themselves in the jump pods before we initiate this maneuver."

"You're saying we'll be relying on the autopilot being able to get us to the target without any intervention?"

"Yes. It's a risk we must take."

She sighed. "I don't much care for that. What kind of variables are there?"

He shrugged. "So far, it's been consistent once I've located a fissure. If we can match the speed of it for a short time, then I can instruct the autopilot to angle in, expand it, and force the ship through it. If we can't match it, then it won't execute the insert command."

A small part of her wanted to tell him to have Brendan check his calculations, but she stopped herself. No, Liam ranked as one of Erinnua's best engineers; he knew the ship, and he knew the engines. She trusted him and needed to show it. Her lips formed a tender smile as she gazed at him, aware of the number of hours and lack of sleep he'd put into finding this option. "I think you've given us a real chance to do this. Do you think we can sell everyone else on it?"

"I imagine so. What's the alternative? This offers hope and that's better than anything else we have. And if it fails, we won't know anything about it, will we?"

Grania

OVER THE NEXT DAY, Grania spoke to everyone in the crew personally about the improved chances of success with the new power crystal. Ever the pessimist, Nansi pointed out that the crystal would give them many more days of travel to attempt an escape without risking the ship and their lives.

"True," Grania replied. "But it does not have the capability of providing more food for us. Even though we can recycle the water, our waste system is still garbage and not reusable. Do you have a solution to that problem?"

Nansi's shoulders drooped, as if the weight of their ordeal pressed harder on her than on anyone else, each sigh seeming to echo the fatigue that clung to her like a heavy fog. This situation appeared to stress her more than the younger crew members. Perhaps she was still haunted by the unseen phantom she thought attacked her during the spacewalk.

She shook her head. "No, Grania. I do not. You know, lass, when I chose to be a spacer, to sign onto a cargo ship, it was with the understanding that the risk of dying on the job was higher than a planet-side job. I always thought it would be from a sudden accident, like an explosion, or from freebooters overtaking the ship. This is a drawn-out death, one I have been having far too much time to think about."

"Oh, Nansi, I understand how you feel," Grania said, her own fears and worries realized in Nansi's confession. "We all feel it. We pretend it isn't real and underneath that, we hope our brilliant Liam can really pull this off, that the physics behind what we're attempting are sound. And when the time comes to make our move, we're going to lie down in our pods, close the lids, and pray to our God that we will wake up at a jump gate." On an impulse, she pulled the older woman into a hug. Nansi had comforted her often enough through her own fears and her grief after her mother's death; it seemed only right to return the favor.

As Nansi hugged her back, she whispered, "Ah, my lass, it is not for myself so much that I worry, but for you and your brothers and that fine man from the station. You have your lives still to live and my Lord; you're a whole generation of your family! Your granda will never recover from it if you're lost in a space accident."

"He would grieve for you, too, Nansi. You're like another daughter to him, you know. By now, the family have doubtless resigned themselves to the loss of the ship and all of us. Word will have reached them that the Mo Chroidhe disappeared from the wormhole. They'll assume there is little hope of us returning. So, let us keep our hope alive until the very end and see how this plays out. With a little leprechaun luck, we can beat the odds and not only bring ourselves home but provide some direction for any other ships who find themselves in the same predicament."

"Aye. Hope, Liam, and leprechauns are the best we have. And a whole lot of prayer." She graced Grania with a half-hearted smile.

As the captain left Nansi's cabin, she turned next to old Moira's cabin and knocked on the door. She heard nothing on the other side, and she considered that perhaps the old woman slept until a loud thud reached her and Moira called out, "Come in."

Grania stepped through the automatic door, glancing around Rory's cabin. Apart from the trunk in the middle of the floor, which Moira perched on like a nesting bird, it looked undisturbed. Appearance suggested she hadn't touched anything, except the food server. Even that was spotless and well-arranged.

"Captain, what brings me the honor of your visit here?"

Grania flashed a quick, warm smile before she grew serious. "I am sorry to disturb you. I wanted to personally provide you with an update on our situation."

Moira motioned for her to sit. "That is very kind of you. Is there news then?"

The captain sat on the bench at the table and replied, "There is. Mr. Harhiman gave us a power crystal, his sales sample, to use. It will give us the additional energy we need to transition back into the wormhole. Of course, the mechanics are all theoretical at this point. It's not been done before, so we can only rely on the math for it to work."

"I see. And I suppose you are asking me if I am in favor of the plan you outlined yesterday? As I said before, I do not need to be part of the vote. Old, I am, and my life shall be as it is destined. Would you care for tea?"

Very gracious. A woman who observes the old customs and hospitality. Grania knew her grandfather would have approved of her.

"No, thank you. I only stopped to bring the update and talk to you for a bit. Tell me a little about my great-aunt Moira, if you will. I never met her, although my great-grandfather talked about her now and then. She had been older; married and moved away before he was ten."

Moira's face lit up with a smile of remembrance. "Ah, she was a lovely person, although also cantankerous, opinionated, and stubborn. A fine Irish lady! In spite of that, she did well and lived a good, long life." She paused, her eyes lifting as she seemed to search for a memory for a few seconds, then she stood and lifted the lid on the trunk, reaching into it. "I have something of hers that I believe should be passed to you. Tradition held this should be handed down to the youngest daughter in the family when the current owner was ready to pass it on. Unless you have a younger sister, I believe the recipient would be you, Grania O'Ceagan. Am I correct?"

"She had no family of her own?"

"She had two boys; both were killed in wars before they had any children. She had no girls." Moira lifted the Connemara marble rosary the real Moira had clung to so fiercely. "It is time now to pass this to its proper owner."

Grania's breath caught as she gazed at the exquisite artifact. The green stones, polished smooth by countless fingers over the ages, shimmered with a timeless luster, while the silver Celtic cross gleamed in intricate detail, its tarnish delicately worked into the pattern to enhance its beauty. Every facet of the piece spoke of its ancient origins, its history almost tangible in her hands. She accepted it with reverence, holding it up to examine it, as the fine craftsmanship captivated her. "Mine?" she asked, her voice soft with wonder. "Are you certain this should be mine?"

"Yes. I am quite sure. Someday, fate willing, I will tell you the history of the rosary. Keep it and pass it on to your granddaughter one day."

As if I am going to even have any children, Grania mused. Perhaps 'tis a positive omen for their success. "I will treasure it. Thank you. My aunt must have trusted you a great deal."

A crooked smile bloomed on the old woman's face, though Moira said nothing more when Grania tucked the rosary away in her tunic pocket and started for the door. She paused. "I will make an announcement prior to the maneuvers to take the ship into the wormhole. At that time, I'll ask you and any of my crew who aren't essential to retire to their jump pods for safety reasons. Then, we'll sound the alert, the pods will close, and I will expect to see you when we arrive at Dragon Station."

"Keep faith and safe travels to us all," Grania heard Moira say as the automatic door swished closed behind her.

Grania

BY THE TIME GRANIA called the crew and passengers together, the vote seemed a certainty. Fearful though they may be, the chance for life against the prolonged certainty of death resulted with the whole crew voting to proceed, as did Harhiman. Miz O'Cairn only nodded her head in acknowledgment.

Sensing they all wanted this over as soon as possible, Grania set a deadline to insert the ship into the slipstream with the punch to the wormhole coming as soon as a solid opportunity presented itself.

"The ride once we enter the slipstream will be fast and, most likely, rough. For safety's sake, I will ask our guests to strap into your pods and the crew will use the safety restraints on the chairs."

She declined to mention the possibility the ship couldn't handle either the increased sped or the added pressure on the hull. She suspected all her crew knew it.

Liam

LESS THAN TWELVE HOURS from the deadline Grania had set for the slipstream insertion, Liam ran a check on the jump pods again. The one in the spare room still wasn't charging enough. Power on it had increased to only twenty-five percent. Worse, the pod in the captain's cabin had gone offline again. His voice reflected his worry as he told his sister the bad news.

"I don't know when it dropped," he replied when she asked. "Can you get it back online and I'll see if it charged at all?"

Before she replied, Vilnius' voice said, "I'll go. Key the cabin open for me, will you, Nia?"

About fifteen mites later, the pod came online for about 20 seconds before it shut down again. It gave Liam enough time to see that it hadn't charged in the slightest.

"It must have gone down shortly after Grania brought it on," Liam said. "I suspect that one's unuseable."

"Let me check it a little more. I might figure out what's wrong with it." Vilnius' voice said over the com as he went back to work on it.

Liam turned his attention back to the data he'd been gathering. He told Grania the timing of the lesions in the energy tunnel appeared to be consistent. "One seems to pass every ninety to ninety-five mites, suggesting they are a natural occurrence in the wormhole and not what kicked us out. Our best chance to reenter is to go through it. Once we get into the slipstream, I can calculate when the next one will arrive." Like the rest of the crew, he tried not to think of the possibility of failure, even though he knew their chance was minuscule. Even a safe entry into the slipstream posed a massive risk.

Within twenty mites, Vilnius came on the com again. "It looks like the secondary circuit board is fried. Do you have another?"

"No. We used the last one trying to fix the spare pod and that's a failure."

"So, do we wait?" Grania cut in. She had been monitoring the conversation. "What do we do for Vilnius?"

"I can share yours," Vilnius replied without hesitation. "Is Nia's up to full power?"

"It is. We can boost the oxygen and sleep mist to handle the two of you. If we don't have a long way to go when we hit the wormhole, it should be enough."

"It'll be cramped," Grania warned.

"We won't notice," he quipped back.

Liam groaned loud enough for them to hear. "Fated fairies, if we have a long way yet to transit, the pod may not handle both of you. The automatic should wake you up before it cuts off completely. The only problem is that you'd both be in wormhole space and who knows how your brains would handle it. But I can make the adjustments."

"Maybe not," Vilnius said, growing serious. "What about the spare pod? Can I take the secondary board from it and put it in the captain's pod? I don't want to do anything that would risk Nia's life any more than this plan already is."

"It isn't working in the spare one," Liam replied. "The connector in the spare might be bad while the board is functional, so give it a try."

"On it," he replied and ended the communication.

"I hope he gets it working, Grania said to Liam. "If not, I'll willingly share my pod. If we are going to die, at least we'll together."

"Oh, don't go all Romeo and Juliet on me," Liam said, disdain clear in his voice. "Even if Vilnius can repair the pod, it will still take it a while to recharge. Meanwhile, we can position ourselves as close as we dare to take advantage of the energy and increased speed. So, I'm going to start bringing the Mo Chroidhe closer to the wormhole, Nia."

"So long as the ship can handle it, *buachaill*. Let's not push it too much."

Grania

ON THE BRIDGE, GRANIA monitored the screens as the ship began moving back toward the wormhole. The two sails shook and waved in the battering from the slipstream, but they were holding. Closer in, it would be worse. Right now, they were going along the edge of the flow, and she could feel the ship moving quicker.

"Liam, I think we're going to need to pull the sails in before we enter the stream. It's hitting them hard right now."

"Copy that. I figured that might be the case. Let's get as much extra energy from them as possible until we start to move. If we get too close to it, the stream might pull us on in. If that happens, I'll retract them as quickly as possible."

She turned when Vilnius came back on the bridge. "Were you able to repair it?"

He shook his head. "No, too much damage. It looks like we're back to the first plan."

"Doubling up in the pod, eh? Clever plan that, mister. You'll be tired of my weight when we get where we're going."

He smirked, "It will be fine, love. I'll just snug you like a blanket."

From the navigation station, Brendan coughed and said, "Eewww."

They laughed; a light moment shared before it got serious again.

"I'm going to check your pod out once Liam makes the changes to be sure it will give us enough oxygen. See you soon." Vilnius squeezed her shoulder as he left.

Grania watched him go, then figured she'd take the chance to get a cup of tea and a sandwich and slipped down to the galley.

While she waited for the tea, she pulled out the rosary to look at it again. She fingered the stones, unconsciously running through the prayers she hadn't said since her mother's death. "Please, God," she whispered, "guide us to safety or bring us home. Amen."

She returned to the bridge, feeling the shimmy in the ship as she went. As expected, the ride grew rougher. At almost the moment she stepped onto the bridge, the unexpected occurred.

Materializing on the bridge, just above the step leading down to navigation, the banshee appeared—not in her previous guise, but as a strikingly beautiful woman with cascading white-blonde hair. She clutched a coarse, homespun shawl snugly around her shoulders, her glowing eyes darting toward the forward screen as the ship drifted perilously close to the tunnel. Her long, spectral fingers trembled in agitation, and then she let out a piercing wail—a keening cry so unearthly it sent icy chills racing up Grania's arms.

"Liam! Sails! We're going in," Grania shouted into the com. "Rory, sound the alarm and get to your pod. We don't have much time." Out of the corner of her eye, she saw a wide-eyed and fearful Brendan already running for the door.

Grania watched the sails begin to fold in, then the starboard one, closest to the stream, was wrenched loose. The ship jolted, bouncing even more.

Liam's voice came back. "I've got a lock programmed in, Grania. Port sail is in, starboard is cut loose. Get to your pod now. I'm starting it in thirty secs."

"Copy!" She glanced at Rory, who'd already flashed the warning and was moving toward the door. She glanced back to see the banshee wave her arms wildly toward the wormhole, then she vanished.

Just for a moment, as her eyes passed the port display screen, she glimpsed an image of something big and dark at the edge of the light stream. Something that moved on its own power and disappeared rapidly. Was it Nansi's phantom monster? Gasping, she turned and dashed to the exit.

Running right behind her brother, she watched him slide down the stairs to the next deck as she raced to the end of the corridor. Somehow, she kept her footing as the ship shook and rocked, then her hand slammed on the door controls outside her cabin. Where was Vilnius? Anxiously, her eyes darted around her quarters. No sign of him, so she tagged him on her com.

"Get in your pod," he shouted back. "I'm on my way."

She climbed in and the lid lowered partway. She could feel the ship being yanked into the slipstream, beginning to angle across it. The speed increased and the pressure on the ship continued to build. Not much time left. Either they had to go in or the ship would likely be pulled apart.

"Lock it!" Vilnius' voice through her com commanded.

No time. An aching emptiness stabbed her stomach. He was beyond her reach, a ghost slipping through her fingers, and she was powerless to pull him back. He was as good as dead. Tears welled in her eyes while her trembling fingers locked the pod. She pulled the rosary from her pocket and her hand clenched around the smooth beads, each one a desperate prayer whispered into the silence.

Before sleep took her, the banshee's return occupied her thoughts. The sidhe had given her third warning. *We're not going to make it.*

CHAPTER TWENTY-SIX

Sheilan

SHEILAN MATERIALIZED AS MOIRA in the middle of the corridor outside her cabin. This time, she hadn't been conscripted to appear as the banshee as she had the last two times, so she chose her form and willingly served the warning, knowing she could communicate her message. Lights along the corridor flashed red and yellow and the alarm to go to the pods sounded all over the ship.

Rory stumbled down the corridor in an unsteady run while the ship shuddered and rocked. He slowed when he saw her and shouted, "Get to your pod quickly, ma'am. There's very little time."

She nodded and stepped towards her door, hitting the open button while she watched him duck into Liam's cabin, since she'd been assigned his. Again, she stepped back into the corridor and waited for the one yet to come. From the hatch to the lowest deck, the thuds of feet climbing steps echoed closer. The door opened and Vilnius jumped through into the walkway. Mobi held to his mouth, he talked as he ran toward her. She stepped into his path to block him.

"Quickly, Miz O'Cairn. Get to your pod," he shouted, the urgent tone making it a command.

She grabbed his arm. "Take my pod, lad. I am an old soul, and you have more need of it than I."

He sputtered out, "I can't do that—"

She cut him off, dragging him into the cabin with powerful hands and arms. "There's no time for arguing. This is your best chance to survive. Use it."

She gestured toward the waiting pod, urging him forward with a firm push. His eyes sparked with defiance, determination glinting in their depths. He opened his mouth to protest, but the words died on his lips as she locked her gaze on him.. "Take it. Now!" she commanded, her voice filled with her will.

As if in a trance, he did, climbing into it, fully clothed—shoes and all—and the bubble lid lowered over him. Sheilan locked it, stepped out of his vision's range, and disappeared into energy particles.

She arrived inside the engineering room a moment later and glanced over to see Liam secured in his pod. The ship was accelerating and shaking as if it would pull apart. On the screen, she watched the fractal patterns of the energy field from the wormhole as the vessel sped toward a thin break that would allow them to enter. For a few moments, it looked as if they would miss it; however, the autopilot corrected at the last moment. It skidded forward, edging into the opening and pushing through as the energy stream spread wider. The craft bounced and shook like it would fly apart at any moment.

While Sheilan couldn't feel the motion in her non-corporeal form, she could see the patterns shaking on the bridge and the yellow and red warning lights that flashed from the computers and other electronics. Alarms sounded throughout the ship, screaming of dire consequences. For a moment, she considered a return to the dirt in the cabin, but she reasoned she had not been summoned to attend a death, so she remained.

With a hard jolt, the ship was through into the wormhole, angled to resume the course. The autopilot corrected to straighten their position and, as the ship settled into the relative calm of the wormhole, alarms ceased, although the warning lights continued to flash.

Dari arrived beside her, a transparent youth. "So, we are back on our course to the next station, I take it."

She partially materialized. "I believe we are, Dari."

"And you have done things today that some among your folk might call foolish and not in the character of a sidhe."

"Possibly," she agreed as she watched his amused face. "Perhaps I have fallen under the influence of a chaotic spirit and the fey creature has changed my view."

He laughed, a sound like a whinny, and turned into his pony shape as he danced in the open aisle of the cargo bay.

We have been confined to this ship too long. Sheilan sent her thoughts to him. Let us return to the dirt until we are at the station. Even for a spirit, I am beginning to grow weary.

Grania

ONCE AGAIN, GRANIA EMERGED from pod sleep to a cacophony of alarms and flashing red warning lights in her cabin. Her mind felt foggy, heavy with the remnants of the deep slumber meds. She struggled to lift the pod's dome and pull herself upright, then a jolt of realization surged through her: She, her ship, and her crew had survived the harrowing jump. Swinging her legs over the edge of the pod, her left knee buckled beneath her, and a sharp pain shot through it like a lightning strike. With a grunt, she sank back, rubbing the aching joint while a dull throb in her shoulder made her wince. Every part of her ached. No doubt, the ride had been brutal, but this level of pain was new.

She hobbled to the auxiliary station in her cabin and began checking the alarms. Nothing indicated critical, although some dire warnings flashed. Assured that life support was fully functional, she keyed the command for the ship to wake the crew if it hadn't already started. With that many warning lights, the protocol might have keyed the secondary alarm system that cut in if the captain or the designated captain, in this case, had not responded within set parameters.

Had everyone come through alive? Vilnius? He hadn't made it to her cabin. What had happened? Was he dead? She recalled her tears of despair when the pod lid had closed. He didn't have another pod to use, so was he lying dead somewhere down below? Dread settled on her with fear of confirming it.

She tagged Rory, relieved to hear his voice. "We made it. Are you okay?"

"A little bruised up. Nothing serious," he replied, sounding upbeat and alert.

"That's good, then. Try to establish communication with Dragon Station as soon as you can, assuming that's where we're heading. Let them know we're alive and limping our way in. I'm not sure how quickly that will be. I'm seeing alarm lights all over the place. Meet you on the bridge."

Next, she contacted Liam, hearing the drowsiness in his voice as he came out of the drugged sleep. "It appears we made it back, Ace. Fecking fantastic job! Are you all right?"

"Yeah, I think so. A little worse for the wear. Give me a mite or two to wake up and I'll get you a status on the ship. At least, it appears to have arrived in one piece, but I've got enough lights blazing down here to light downtown Duntara."

"Did you see Vilnius before we moved into the stream? He didn't make it back to my cabin." Her voice strained with the emotion she tried not to show.

"He came down here when the jump alert sounded to see if he could help. He got the shattered mast on the starboard sail released and the hatch locked in while I was dealing with the port one. Then he started back up to the cabins. Possibly he took a chance with the partially charged pod since time was short."

"Right, maybe he did that." The prospect gave her hope. "I'm heading for the bridge now."

As she started for the door, she tagged Brendan, who informed her he would be on deck within a couple of mites. She resumed the path to the bridge, still favoring her injured knee with a lopsided gait. At times, her knee caused her to wince from the pain, though she was moving, and she considered it a blessing.

She could see Nansi through the clear door to the bridge. Her second looked a bit worse for the wear, Grania noted as she pressed the door open.

"I think I broke my elbow," Nansi complained as soon as she stepped through. "At least, I'm alive to endure it. Thanks be to God."

"Aye, thanks be to God and to all the blessed saints." Her grandmother said that often enough that Grania's response was automatic. "Wake our passengers and follow up on their status, will you? See if you can find Vilnius. I hope they all made it safely. And take care of your elbow. Perhaps it's only a bruise."

Brendan slipped in just before Nansi started out. Dashing straight to the navigation computer, he began addressing the alarms. Grania turned her attention to the alerts on the bridge and, as she acknowledged each, the flashing lights shut down one by one. Most resolved themselves since they'd returned to normal space. Rory came on deck while she tackled the last few and addressed the communications console, adjusting the frequencies and shutting off warning lights there.

"Nothing serious here, Nia," Brendan announced. "The unit rebooted and tried to recover our last course. I'm getting an update to our current position now. I think we have a lock on Dragon Gate, so it can find our position." When he looked at her, his bright grin reflected the joy all of them felt to have made it. Banged, bruised, and bedraggled, it didn't matter. They were alive and the ship still functioned. It was a miracle and a credit to the crew, not to mention the power crystal.

The com crackled and Rory opened the feed from the gate to the bridge broadcast so the others could listen to the contact. "We're getting a hail from Dragon Gate to confirm our ship's identity."

"Send it. We've been lost for at least eight days. They'll have a lot of questions. Advise them we are bound for Dragon Station and will discuss everything with the authorities there."

She gazed up at the main screen, seeing the expanse of populated space ahead of her, and her heart lifted. Stars showed all around and a large glowing blue-white moon hovered near the closest planet to the gate. Dragon Station lay just a short distance from that moon.

The starboard screen showed only static. No signal to it. Most likely a dead camera on that side, if it hadn't been ripped off along with the sail. Lots of damage to the ship, she acknowledged with regret. For all that, they were alive, and they'd come back from a place few had visited and returned.

"Grania ... We made it."

She heard Vilnius' voice behind her and turned, afraid to believe. But he stood there. Although he looked somewhat worse for the wear and with a bump swelling on the right side of his head, but alive.

"Thanks be." Truly, she gave thanks to whatever deity looked over them as she flung her arms around him in a tight hug. "Did you use the spare pod?"

"I'll tell you later. You have plenty to do now." His gaze shifted to the new action lights demanding her attention. As tears threatened to spill from her eyes, she turned back to the messages Rory relayed to her and began addressing anything requiring her response. She wondered what Vilnius had to tell her later.

Vilnius made himself useful by fetching tea for each of them before sitting down next to Brendan. She glanced over at him now and then, reassuring herself.

Nansi reported their passengers were accounted for, alive and well, and that was a relief. Although when she cast a happy look back at Brendan and Vilnius, she noticed a puzzled look on her man's face.

Once everything was under control, Grania sent Rory and Brendan to get food and take care of any injuries. Vilnius stood as well. "I'll go relieve Liam so he can grab something."

"Wait just a bit. What happened? I was afraid you hadn't made it to a jump pod before we hit the wormhole." Her voice revealed more concern than she liked.

A half-smile softened his face. "I went to help Liam when the alert sounded. I figured he might need another set of hands. It took a bit longer than I thought it would, and I had a little trouble with the starboard release. I was on my way when the O'Cairn lady stopped me and told me to take her jump pod. Of course, I told her no, then she yanked me into her cabin and somehow talked me into it. I don't know how. I can't explain how she got me to consent, but I woke up in it." At the alarmed expression on Grania's face, he added, "She said she would take the partly charged one, and it would be enough. Like she knew. That's all I remember about it."

"Well, she was right that it was enough. She's fine. And so are you, for that matter, I am grateful to her."

He pressed his hand to her cheek, running a caressing finger down it. "I would have told you if I'd had time. I wasn't sure I'd ever see you again. I think the old lady may be an angel." He leaned forward to kiss her, and she melted into it, her lips pressing fiercely against his.

With reluctance, they separated, each wanting more than they could do right now. Grania took a deep breath. "Go on down and send Liam up for food. If Nansi is there, tell her to go as well."

He nodded, leaving her to deal with the bridge alone. She saw the signal at the com console and tapped her headpiece to respond. It was Dragon Station, acknowledging their ship's identification and requesting their ETA at the station.

"Unknown at this time. We're working on an estimate and will send it as soon as we have it. Our ship has been damaged, so we'll need emergency repairs once we're there."

"Copy that, Mo Chroidhe. We are most anxious to learn what happened in the hole and where you have been. Are there any injuries?"

"We have a few banged arms, legs, and bruises. 'Twas a rough ride."

"Once you arrive and are rested, the space agency has requested a meeting. Fair warning, news media are already picking up on a ship that was presumed missing suddenly returning."

She grimaced. "Is there any way you can patch me through to Erinnua or, at least, get a message through to our family? Mo Chroidhe is a family ship, and I'd prefer my family not hear it through the media."

"We'll see what we can do. Out."

She hoped they could send a message to Tara Station; if nothing else, it could be relayed to her grandparents before the news media identified their ship. She feared they would have given them up for lost when they were so overdue, with no word from them. Now, this would come as another shock.

The ship made a subtle shift in direction and surged forward toward the moon ahead. It appeared Brendan had programmed the course correction, and the Mo Chroidhe now responded. Presumably, the last thing Liam did before he headed up to eat was to engage the autopilot. At least, she hoped he'd come up to eat. Her stomach told her she needed food soon herself.

She felt a surge of pride for her brother, and how he'd handled this situation. Sometimes he could be a little hot-tempered, yet in this crisis, he came through like a champion. What did folks call that quick temper? Having your Irish up? It suited him.

She checked the log to see what the ship had recorded during the transition back to the wormhole. From the entries, it had lost direction twice when the slipstream tugged it across, and the autopilot had corrected it within a millisecond. If they'd missed the open slot in the tunnel, they would have exploded in the energy field. That sent a shiver down her spine. The timing was everything. If the banshee hadn't called her attention to the ship veering toward the energy field, they most likely would have disintegrated when they entered the slipstream.

Once they returned to the hole, the ship's programming became inactive, yielding all control to the hole. Standard protocol. As they approached the gate, the ship had received the auto-signal from the portal computer and came back online to prepare for the exit. All in all, it looked like they'd covered the rest of the jump in a little over ninety-six mites. Amazing, she thought. Even though distances seemed so close when you had a wormhole, how many light years of bumbling through the dark space would the ship have taken if they hadn't escaped?

Just then, Rory and Brendan swept onto the bridge, laughing at some shared joke as they came in.

"Life is good," Rory said. "We're alive and we're fed. The station isn't far away, and it looks like the crystal is working fine to provide all the power we need."

"Good thing it is," Brendan added. "We'd be getting precious little help from the one decent sail we still have. I'll wager we have some pricey repairs ahead."

"Our insurance should cover a quite a bit of it," Grania said. "We'll get the absolutely necessary work done at Dragon then finish it up when we get to Tara. Things will be a less expensive there. I just hope Granda isn't too upset with the damage to the ship."

"Are you kidding?" Rory looked at her as if she'd lost her mind. "After what we just went through, he'll be so proud of us just surviving. Do you realize we'll have a whopper of a story to tell from now on? I can't wait to tell the lasses at Riley's."

Grania laughed despite her own misgivings. The lad had the right of it. They had a spectacular story, and it would be told over and over until they were turned into heroes, maybe. Perhaps even a spacer legend. "Maybe you should write a book, Rory. You're full of enough blarney to make it a tale for the ages."

"Perhaps I should," he agreed. "By the by, your man is waiting for you in the galley. We've got it, Nia. Go on down."

"Why didn't you say?" she replied. "Let Dragon know our ETA when Liam gets it to you." Then she hobbled with as much speed as she could out the door.

Grania paused at the galley door and leaned against the doorframe, keeping it from closing as she watched Vilnius reading his tablet. He'd grown a light beard over the last few days, and it made him look more attractive than ever. Just seeing him here and alive made her heart swell with love and appreciation of how much she cared for him.

"We've contacted Dragon Station and are heading toward it," she said as an opener.

His eyes came up from the tablet, an amused twinkle in them. "I heard. We are either very lucky or amazingly good."

"Some of both, I think." She sat down next to him and leaned against him. "Lucky Harhiman had a crystal we could use. Lucky Liam is the best engineer in this quadrant. Lucky—"

"Hey! What am I?" He frowned as he objected.

"The second best, but only by a hair." She reached her right hand up to touch his beard, expecting it to feel coarse, and finding it soft instead.

"Ah, well, thank you for that, love. It's good to know where I rank."

"I'm only talking about engineering. There are other areas where you definitely rank at the top." She leaned toward his mouth and his met hers midway in a deep kiss that spoke more of their emotions than words ever could.

Grania's stomach rumbled, telling her she needed food, though, at that moment, it ranked the furthest from her mind. What she needed most stood right beside her, holding her close.

CHAPTER
TWENTY-SEVEN

Grania

LATER, AFTER THE CREW completed their checks on the bridge controls, Grania stepped off the bottom stair in the cargo hold, turned, and surveyed the large open space, expecting to see damage or at least a jumble with the cargo caused during the turbulence, but it appeared the locks had held. The crates remained firmly secured, as near as she could tell. However, a peculiar, pungent odor hung in the air, a kind of sour smell.

She strode across to the engine room where Liam bent over his console, making notes and flicking through views from the cameras outside the ship.

"Ho, Liam. Outstanding job getting us here. You really are a genius!"

He looked up, grinned, and his face almost glowed under her praise.

"It doesn't look like the cargo was disturbed much. How badly are we damaged?" she asked

He shrugged. "We have a pile of pots and pans aft that are mingling with some canned food where a crate broke loose and crashed into another one. At least, it's not messy. The only other problem is a cold crate loaded with various cheeses seemed to have been bumped by the crate next to it hard enough that it damaged the controls and it's no longer cooling. It's a good thing that we'll be arriving at a station soon or that could get smelly."

He turned back to his console and changed the screen view. "We have some minor exterior damage, except for this ..." The screen displayed the starboard side of the ship where an uneven bump of metal protruded from the ship's hull. "This is from the aft camera. The starboard camera ripped off, as did the aft-facing one at the front of the ship."

"What is that bulge?" Grania asked as she leaned closer to the screen as if that would improve her view.

"The ship's sensors are reporting a hull breach on the starboard side. When it broke the pressure seal, this section ruptured outward. It's on the external shell only, the internal one is undamaged, as near as I can determine from the readings. It's at cabin level, so it might have happened when we had the sail problem. This must be repaired before we go through the gate to home."

"Agreed. We can't be taking any chances with it. What else is on the list for repair?"

"Besides replacing the starboard mast and sails, repairing the dorsal sail, replacing the cameras, acquiring a new refrigerated crate, if possible, and transferring the cheese to it, you mean?"

"Aye, besides all that. Is there anything else critical?"

"I don't know. We need an inspection of the entire ship's hull, and I want to run a full check of all the sensors before we take her out again. We also need to replace the circuit boards in both pods that aren't working properly."

She straightened. "Fair enough. We can do that at Dragon. I expect we'll be delayed there with reports, meetings and a debriefing of everything that happened."

"One thing puzzles me, Nia. I checked the power on all our pods a short time ago and most of them, the ones that were fully charged, show the power down about twenty-two percent. The one in the spare cabin had been up to about twenty-five percent when we headed back into the hole. It's showing at twenty-seven percent right now. The one in the captain's cabin is still offline. Where did the old lady go during the jump? If she wasn't in one of the pods, she should be dead."

Grania looked thoughtful. "Good question. There are a few things troubling me about that woman. I have something to ask of you, and I will ask it of the whole crew also. I am pretty sure that the space agency is going to ask for duplicates of all our logs, recordings, and records from the time we entered the wormhole at Pelanan. They will likely want to interview all of us. I would prefer that they not hear or see anything about a banshee on the ship."

"You want me to erase any recordings of the creature?" He arched an eyebrow at her as if questioning her request.

"I want our copy to remain. Can you prepare another copy to give to them that doesn't include any of the incidents? If the recordings of the creature get out, I'm worried we'll have more of a media frenzy around the ship and the crew than we already have. It has little to do with what happened in the dark sea and contributes nothing to the investigation. Will you do it?"

"Aye. I see your point. I don't have a lot of time before we arrive at the station, just about ninety mites now. Can you stall them before we have to send it?" His fingers already moved to call up the recordings.

"Pretty sure. They're going to set an appointment to meet with the Space Agency after we've had a chance to take care of our immediate needs and rest. They shouldn't be looking for it before that, so that will give us several hours."

"All right. You've got it. Apart from the press getting wind of it, why don't you want anyone to see it? It's an odd phenomenon, but it happened, and we have it recorded."

Grania played with a small green, gold, and lavender sphere of Erinnua that Liam kept on his console, a little reminder of home.

"I can't really explain it; it's just a feeling I have that this should be kept among us, not told to anyone. At least, not now."

"Okay. Do you want to look at the damage in the cargo area?"

She shook her head. "No, you've already checked it out, and it seems like the damage is pretty minor. I'll get Nansi to stuff the loose cargo back into the crates as best she can. We can get new ones once we dock. By the by, what is that odd smell out there?"

"'Tis awful, isn't it? One of those big cans of something called sauerkraut broke open and spilled all over. Quite a stinky mess."

As she started back to the stairs, she paused to glance toward the aft section where she spotted a couple of metal pans lying loose. Minor damage down here, it appeared. The hull breach had only pierced the outside hull. Faith, but they may have used up all their Irish luck on this trip.

She spoke to Brendan and Rory next about keeping the banshee visitations a secret for now. Again, she tried to explain that her intuition suggested it shouldn't be something shared outside the crew, at least, for now. Their passengers didn't know about it, and Vilnius only knew of the appearance he'd witnessed. She'd convinced him not to say anything about it.

"Sure, you know, it would be a great pub story," Rory objected.

"You mean escaping the Dark Sea isn't enough, Rory?" she replied. "Besides, if you tell anyone you saw a banshee, they'd think you were daft or drunk, wouldn't they? And don't tell Granda or Da, either. I'll tell them about it at the right time."

"We'll keep it quiet," Brendan said, "Although you may have a problem with Nansi. She knows what she saw and she's superstitious enough. Don't think she won't bring it up if they interview her."

Grania had considered that and agreed with Brendan's assessment. She might not be able to convince Nansi to leave the banshee out of her report. Despite that, she had to try.

Grania

""No, Grania O'Ceagan! No! I will not be telling any fibs for you!" Her face skewed into an angry scowl, and Nansi shook with emotion as she responded to Grania's request.

"I'm not asking you to lie, Nansi. I'm just asking you not to say anything about seeing a spirit on the ship. If we did see such a creature, her appearance didn't change anything about what happened or how we got back to the wormhole. It has no relevance to what the Space Agency will want to know about this situation."

"If we did see it? Now, are you trying to tell me that we didn't witness a b'ean sidhe with our own eyes? Are you trying to make out that I'm daft?"

"Of course not. But the Space Agency might think you are if you go babbling about seeing a wailing spirit on the ship. We were stranded in uncharted and non-functional space, and maybe we were all seeing spooks. We don't see any reason to put it in the report."

Nansi crossed her arms in defiance. "'Twas no hallucination. And neither was the thing outside the ship. I know what I saw and felt. We have proof. Are you afraid to admit it?"

Grania took a deep breath. She'd hoped to convince Nansi to go along with her plan without having to resort to emotional bribery. "I'm not afraid. At least, not for me. Except you consider this. Everything I read about this creature says that she's attached to an ancient family of Ireland or Scotland. If that's so, isn't it reasonable to assume that she's attached to the O'Ceagan family, and she somehow came aboard from Earth on this trip? And if that's the case, isn't it likely it's because she has a death message to bring to someone in the family? If it's my gramps or gram, or even Granda, would you want them to hear some report of a banshee on our ship from anyone other than one of us?"

That hit home as Nansi's hand went to her mouth. "Oh, Lord, what if we have been misreading the message? Maybe the warning was about Paddy. Have you talked to your grandparents yet? Are they both safe?"

"Calm down, Nansi. I haven't had any news from Erinnua, and I haven't gotten a link to the station yet. They said they would try to contact them before any media coverage got out. As to the message, perhaps it's a delayed report about Gramps' sister, Moira. You know, a death in the family and the spirit came to announce it. Or maybe it was just what we thought, and she appeared to warn us. No matter which option, I would prefer that my grandparents not be finding out about it until I can tell them in person. This affects our family, not the Space Agency. Can I count on you, Nansi? You don't have to lie. You just don't have to bring it up unless you're specifically asked."

Nansi's shoulders slumped in defeat. "Aye. I'll not be telling them ... for old Paddy's sake."

Grania felt bad for having to take this tact with her, yet her instincts told her to keep this quiet. She had just voiced something that had been in her mind for the last several hours. The banshee came from Earth, and Moira O'Cairn, and her trunk, also came from Earth. She considered it possible that the spirit had somehow stowed away in the trunk. Something more niggled at her thoughts, although she couldn't quite put a finger on it.

After she thanked Nansi, she left her to continue the inventory of gathered pots from the spilled box. She had no doubts Nansi would soon be telling her banshee story in a pub at Duntara, and then it would come across as the whiskey talking or a fanciful take on an old legend. For now, she was sure Nansi wouldn't say a word until after she'd talked to her family

Grania

BEFORE THEY REACHED DRAGON Station, Liam called Grania down to review the modified recordings he'd created. She leaned against the back workstation and watched the images on the monitor.

"This is the first appearance during the jump when it appeared in the cargo hold. This turned out to be easier to modify than I thought it would. You can see a bit of fogginess where the image was, but it's nothing you could point at and say something had been there."

The recording did look clear except for what Liam had noted. It would pass inspection and could probably be written off as a fluke of the light if anyone even noticed it.

"That looks good. Next one."

He quickly cued up the second appearance on the bridge. Again, it showed a bit of haze, although nothing resembling a woman on her knees scrubbing something. The cameras did capture the shocked expression on Grania's face and Rory's wide-eyed look as they watched the banshee. Surely, they could explain that away as being stunned by the view of the wormhole. The cameras captured the tunnel look of that rather well from a different angle.

"Apart from me looking spooked, that looks good. There's another one on the bridge, isn't there?" She glanced at Liam, who cued up another clip.

"Yes, I have this one as well. Luckily, only the two bridge recorders were pointed in the direction to catch the banshee." He played the clip; however, the view coincided with the wormhole's energy field in the background. The Space Agency would be far more interested in that image than in the barely discernible wisp of light on the bridge.

"That looks great. That view will keep the officials buzzing for days."

"It will," Liam agreed. "We have several days' worth of it from this recorder alone, from a distance and close. We have a really sketchy recording as we punched through that can probably be enhanced to show more detail once their experts get their hands on it. But these three clips will not reveal the bean sidhe's image in it." He grinned up at her.

"You are truly amazing. What about the third appearance?" Grania smiled, pleased with the deception they were cooking up.

"What third appearance?" Liam looked puzzled.

"On the bridge, right before we were pulled into the slipstream. When I yelled to retract the sails. Did we not get a bridge recording at that time?"

He quickly keyed in the sequence for the last bridge footage before they went into the hole. "Aye, we have it. Except I'm not seeing a banshee on it."

The first bridge camera showed the scene as Grania had stood watching the screens with the starboard and port sails. Then it showed a shocked look on her face, and she stared intently at the starboard screen for almost a whole mite before she yelled down to Liam. The clip showed her seeing the sail rip-away on the screen and dashing for the console, shouting orders to Brendan and Rory. But they could see no sign of the spirit in the recording.

Throat feeling a little dry, she said, "Play the other camera for the same time frame."

The back camera had caught the subtle shift into the slipstream and Grania's voice barking orders, yet nothing at all on the bridge in front of the main screen. She swallowed hard as it hit her that the banshee had not recorded this time. Had Rory and Brendan seen her or was this a special performance for her alone?

"Are you all right?" Liam's voice cut into her thoughts.

She dipped her head once.

"You saw it on the bridge then, didn't you? Did it give you a warning?"

"She did. She called my attention to the dip into the slip-stream. I think she saved our lives, Liam. If I hadn't seen that shift when I did ..."

"Then we might have lost both sails and missed the slot completely. And the ship might have ...." He looked bewildered as his voice trailed off. "What is that thing, Grania?"

With a bit of wonder in her voice, she replied, "I think she's our family banshee. According to the stories, these spirits only bring warnings or announcements of death in the family. This one seems to be intent on protecting us. From everything I've read, that's not in their nature. There is a reason for it, and I am fearful it will still be sad news for us." Her thoughts went to her granda and the lingering illness that prevented him from making this run. He might have taken a turn for the worse; even now might be dying or already dead. They had no word yet from the station on whether they had contacted her family.

Liam made the connection also. "Granda?"

She put a hand on his shoulder and squeezed affectionately. "It could be. Say nothing to your brothers until I can find out more. When we get to the station, I'll get through to home."

When Grania reached the stairs to the mid-deck, she looked back and saw that Liam had called up the original bridge recording again, studying the banshee with a new perspective. She stopped and turned to watch him as he played it twice more, before he tapped something into the computer, no doubt to learn more about this phenomenon that seemed attached to their family. She could almost read his mind on this.

By the time she stepped back on the bridge, a head-on view of Dragon Station almost filling the forward screen greeted her. Unlike Zabrowski and Pelanan, Dragon was a two-pronged V-shaped structure with a central ball linking the two arms together.

"We're docking at A-sixteen," Rory informed her. "Estimated in thirty-three mites."

"At last. Thanks, Rory. Is the docking sequence set, Brendan?"

"Affirmative. Everything is good to go."

She took her seat and glanced at the numbers on her screen. "Has the station sent me any kind of a message confirming communication with Erinnua?"

"No, I don't have anything. Were you expecting it?"

"I was hoping," she answered. "Just to get this clear, how many times did you two see the banshee?"

"Not at all," Brendan said without hesitation. "I don't know what you're talking about."

She chuckled. "This isn't a test. I really want to know how many times you actually saw it."

"Oh, once then. Except for the recording from the cargo bay, of course."

"Same here," Rory replied.

"Okay. Looks like we're all on the same page and now we've seen nothing of it at all. Alert everyone that we're docking." She settled back to wait for the ship to glide in. The lack of evidence confirmed the spirit's last appearance had been for her eyes only. Now, if the authorities didn't wish to speak to everyone on the ship, they should be able to avoid any mention of a mythical spirit on board.

CHAPTER TWENTY-EIGHT

Grania

ONCE THE SHIP DOCKED, Grania checked in with the station communications to get any updates and to see if they had contacted their family yet. No messages were waiting for her, so she repeated her request for a comlink to Tara Station. The technician informed her he couldn't connect them through at the moment. What the heck? Under normal circumstances, she could link from her mobi through the station network to another station, who would then relay the signal to the planet. However, her mobi showed a blocked marker for anything off the station.

She turned to Rory, keying in Liam to the bridge's com, then filled them in on what little she had. "I'm going to the stationmaster. Get started on the repairs and replace the damaged crates. Leave the sails until we get back to Tara. Tag me if anything needs my attention."

She started to leave the bridge when Vilnius met her at the door. "Want some company?"

"Sure. Maybe you can help me get a link to home."

On the way, they ran into Harhiman in the mid-level corridor, who approached her with his mobi pulled out and his finger pointed at it. "I can't seem to get a com signal out. Is there a problem?"

"It appears so, Mr. Harhiman. Our communications are blocked as well. I'm going to see if I can get it cleared. You might try going onto the station to see if it's limited to the ship docks."

"Well, it's just one thing after another on this trip, isn't it?" he said, an annoyed expression making his sentiments clear, even though Grania could do nothing about it except apologize for the inconvenience.

As the trader strode off in a huff, Vilnius muttered in her ear. "You'd expect the man would be grateful to be alive, wouldn't you?"

Grania frowned. "I don't presume he's happy unless he has something to complain about."

They disembarked to the more sterile environment of Dragon Station. Like many city spaceports, Dragon restricted entry beyond its boarding gates to only passengers and cargo, meaning no shops or food vendors serviced the meta-steel corridors—just the gates themselves, each featuring around 100 seats in their docking areas. Auto-bots traversed the walkways, ensuring everything remained clean and well-polished. The corridor resonated with the sounds of footsteps and the chatter of various voices in different languages. In front of Grania and Vilnius, a loader transported a full pallet of shipping crates to the ship docked alongside the Mo Chroidhe.

They continued toward the station's core with its many shops, offices, and lounges. It resembled a bustling small town. Except for the stationmaster's personal decorations, his office was identical to any other human-run space station, a small workspace with a desk, a computer, and a pair of visitor's chairs. A man of average build, Master Grindorf had been in charge on this station for the past six Earth years. Of Dutch heritage, Grindorf's walls displayed symbols of the Earth's nation on the deep yellow walls.

Grania had spoken with him several times over those years. His piercing blue eyes greeted her cordially when she strolled in, introducing Vilnius.

Pleasantries exchanged, Grindorf asked, "What can I do for you, Captain?"

"The Mo Chroidhe requires a few repairs that can't wait for our home station, so anything you can do to expedite those would be appreciated."

"Of course. What else?"

"I need a comlink to Tara Station to contact my family there. They must be worried about us. It appears our communications are blocked. Is there anything you can do to clear that up?"

Grindorf's brow lowered into a small frown, and his hand stroked his short, groomed beard. "I'm afraid not. The Space Agency has us in a communications lockdown."

"Is there an emergency situation?" Vilnius asked.

"Evidently, they suspect something. Only official communications are going in or out right now. While it's been tight for the past few days, they locked it down completely from almost the moment your ship exited the gate."

"Our ship?" Grania echoed, surprise clear in her voice. Had their arrival caused that much concern?

"Yep. I can't tell you anything more than that because I don't know any details. There's more going on than just your ship arriving after being missing for almost ten days. Perhaps you'll learn more when you talk to them."

"What about a com to Zabrowski Station? I'd like to report on my status," Vilnius asked.

Grindorf shook his head. "Sorry. My station can't put it through. You can talk to the Space Agency liaison to see if they can patch you in. They're on the other side of the dome, just about opposite us."

Frustrated, Grania's eyes narrowed, furrowing her brow while she crossed her arms across her chest, and drew a breath to argue her position. This delay was absurd. She needed to talk to her granda.

"Thanks, we'll do that," Vilnius replied, catching Grania's arm to pull her out with him.

"You can't argue with him about it," he told her as they started across the central dome. "The man's hands are tied and all we can do is negotiate with the Agency. There must be a lot of concern over what happened to your ship for them to lock down communications this tightly. Given that, I'm surprised they didn't meet when we docked."

"It's crazy, Vilnius. Why would they be so interested in the Mo Chroidhe?" She glanced back toward to the master's office, spotted a pair of average-looking men loitering outside it, and caught the movement of one turning his face away from her. "I think someone may be watching us. Don't look around, but we appear to have a couple of fellows back there keeping an eye on us."

"Okay, then we are officially suspect. I guess from their point of view, the ship disappeared from the wormhole on a routine jump and suddenly appeared again several days later. What happened? Was it hijacked or lost or did something else happen? They are being somewhat gracious in waiting to interview the crew, so I guess it may be natural for the Agency to have someone watching us." He slowed, pulled her into his arms, and gave her a big, reassuring hug, which allowed him to glance back over her shoulder to see the two men loitering behind them.

"They've moved away from the station master's and are keeping a fair distance behind us," he told her. "Let's go on to the Agency and see what we can do to clear this up."

From the outside, the Space Agency office looked plain, a simple door with the agency logo stenciled on it and about a six-foot entry area where a counter separated visitors from the young woman who worked at a computer behind it. The nameplate on the counter identified her as Ms. Rafella Bendle, Liaison Agent.

When Grania explained her situation again, the liaison couldn't help them with the communications issue either. This time, Vilnius got pushy and insisted they must talk to someone with authority. With a plastered smile, she asked them to wait and summoned her superior.

A few mites later, another woman marched in, introducing herself as Senior Agent Chatura Palla and offering a more sincere smile while she guided them into her office next door. The small room was cramped with a gray metal desk, her computer, three black cushioned guest chairs, and a row of four media cabinets. Of medium height and build, Palla appeared trim and, no doubt, fit under the tailored jumpsuit, Grania deduced. Her hair was almost black, while her features and skin tone were influenced by her East India heritage.

"It is an honor to meet you, Captain O'Ceagan and Second Master Majeck. Please sit. What can I do for you?"

Gracious and to the point, Grania conceded as she sat in the chair and paused while Vilnius followed suit. "Thank you. As I am sure you are aware, our ship has been considered missing for the past several days. I am certain this information was relayed to my family back on Erinnua when we disappeared. I am anxious to contact them to let them know that we—my brothers and I—and the ship are safe and mostly unharmed. What can we do to establish communication with them for at least a short time?"

Before Agent Palla replied, Vilnius added his piece. "I also need to get a communication through to my home station at Zabrowski. I am long overdue to report in and my stationmaster is, no doubt, deeply concerned."

Palla gave them each a nod of acknowledgment. "I understand your desires to relieve the anxieties of your loved ones and associates. The lockdown on the station is precautionary until after a debriefing meeting. Please understand this is an unusual situation and whatever happened to your ship is of the utmost concern to our agency.

"Our protocol doesn't allow me to provide a com channel at this time, although I can send a coded message through our agency on Tara Station and they can relay it to your family, Captain. I can send a direct message to Zabrowski station on a cleared channel. Regrettably, I cannot authorize voice or video com until after the debriefing is done. Will that help you for now?"

"It's less than desirable," Grania said drily. "At least, they will know that we're alive."

"Ditto," Vilnius replied.

Palla flashed another brief smile, then pushed electronic pads toward each of them. "Please write out your messages, and I'll send them."

Grania grabbed the stylus and scribbled her message: Had an incident in the Pelanan wormhole. All safe. Home soon. Hope all is well, Love, Nia.

She pressed it back to Palla. Vilnius had also finished his brief note.

"Excellent." Palla transferred the notes to her computer and keyed in the codes to send the messages.

"If I may ask, why the lockdown and security for a missing ship arriving? It's a little unusual, I admit, although not a threat," Grania said.

"It's just protocol in this situation," Palla answered, that reassuring look still on her face. "Your ship's arrival is only one of three incidents in recent days that we're investigating."

"Other missing ships?" Vilnius asked.

Palla shook her head. "Not missing, no. More like encountering trouble coming out of a wormhole. I can't give you any details. A big reason for the lockdown is to contain any news reports going out that might create additional problems."

Very cryptic, Grania thought. "And those two men following us since we came on the station?"

"Just precautionary. It's for your safety as much as for us to monitor your whereabouts. There are many news agencies on the station at the moment."

"When can we get the debriefing done so we can clear this up and restore our communications? I have a passenger who is giving me grief over it." She exaggerated a little, but if it helped her case ...

"Of course. We wanted to allow you time to rest and clean up after your experience before scheduling the debriefing. It is tentatively set for seventeen hundred today if that suits you. I believe the message was sent to your ship a short time ago."

That placed the meeting several hours away while Grania preferred to get it done sooner. "Can you move it forward? We are cleaned up, repairs are underway, and we'll sleep better once we can get this settled."

Palla sent a quick message and gave them a reassuring smile. "I'm checking if the other two participants are available sooner. Ah, there's one and the second one. It looks like we can move it to thirteen-hundred, just after lunch. Is that better?"

"Yes. Will it be here? Do you want all the crew?"

"For now, we just need you and your engineer. That would be Liam O'Ceagan, correct?"

Grania nodded.

"Good. Yes, meet us here and we will go into the conference room next door. You can expedite it a little by sending us a copy of your ship's report and any video from the bridge."

"Would my voice carry any weight in this?" Vilnius asked. "I am a passenger, even though I was involved in the situation, and I am an agency employee."

The agent regarded him for a moment, considering. "Yes, perhaps it would be valuable to have your observations."

Grania stood to go. "Then we will be seeing you again in a few hours. Out of curiosity, do you have any idea what happened to our ship?"

Palla gave her a puzzled look. "None at all. That's why we are so concerned. A ship disappears for days, then reappears. We are anxious to know what happened."

Vilnius leaned forward. "Here's some food for thought then. Dark Sea."

Palla's eyes grew wider as they left the office.

Grania

AFTER TELLING THE REST of the crew they would meet them later at Finnegan's Wake, a pub on the station that most of the Celtic heritage folks preferred, Grania, Liam, and Vilnius headed off to the meeting at the Space Agency. As they walked, Vilnius remarked the two men remained on their tail.

"I guess they don't trust us," Grania replied. "You'd think we were criminals or something by the way these people are acting."

"I wonder if they've even looked at the recordings and records yet," Liam added. "I sent them as soon as you relayed the request. While they provide quite a lot of data to go through, if the agents started at the beginning, they should have a pretty good idea of what happened by now."

"We'll know soon enough," Grania answered, as they arrived at the office.

Palla waited for them out front, then guided them to the conference room next to the office. Rather than having several meeting rooms for businesses taking up valuable space, designs for most stations included two or three that any of the business owners could reserve for meetings, training sessions, or even parties. Big enough for twenty people, the spacious room provided a large conference table and comfortable, padded chairs in a neutral beige shade. With the color-selective walls set to a soothing pale blue, the light tone to warm, afternoon light, and a delicate floral scent, the room professed to be relaxing and non-threatening.

Besides Palla, two other agents, whom she introduced as Brian Shiua and Jagur Franc, joined them, although Palla took the lead.

"We have reviewed some of the material that you sent over. Although it is quite a lot to go through, it seems obvious from the first part that something occurred in the wormhole to eject you from it. Do you have any idea what that event might have been?"

Liam answered this question before Grania had a chance. "There were fluctuations from the star in the Pelanan system before we were allowed through their gate. When the solar flares appeared to settle down, the station gave several ships clearance to go proceed. Our systems didn't record any details regarding the incident that ejected us from the hole. Later observation of the wormhole tunnel suggests rips or gaps occur in the wormhole that a ship could be punched through. We used a gap to reenter the hole."

Palla made notes, even though she recorded the whole interview, then backtracked to ask another question about whether Liam considered the station had cleared ships to go through too soon. As he answered her, she continued to write, and it became clear to Grania they had a long afternoon ahead of them. Vilnius, who sat next to her, caught her hand under the table and gave it a reassuring squeeze.

She backed up Liam's assessment of the station not being too hasty to release the ships through, but, of course, flares can happen at any time. Then Palla asked about positioning in the Dark Sea, which they had referred to several times as "dark space" in their reports. Grania answered that one, explaining their theories about the space next to all wormholes having this dark zone where no communications signals would work. Vilnius added his opinion. And the session dragged on.

When they got down to more detailed parts of the events, Pala instructed Grania to follow her into her office while Liam left with Shiua to a different office. Vilnius remained with Franc. Once they were in the office, Palla said, "I believe the general statements you made are a satisfactory account of the events. Now, I would like to ask you a few specific questions about what happened and the activities of your crew, as well as your own thoughts about the situation. We are, of course, quite concerned about the ship being ejected from the wormhole. Your brother indicated that it could have been a solar flare that caused it. Do you agree and is there any other possibility?"

Grania sat back and took her time, reflecting again on coming out of the wormhole into the Dark Sea. "I assume he is speculating on the most likely cause. Unfortunately, we were all in jump pods, so we don't have any actual knowledge about what caused it to happen. As captain, I was the first person the ship awakened, and I woke up a little groggy. Alarms were flashing and I checked them out. There wasn't anything advising me about what had caused the situation. I reviewed the logs, as did Liam, looking for any clue as to what happened."

"So, it might not have been a solar flare. Could it have been a ship problem? A navigation failure, for instance?"

"If we'd had a mechanical or an electronic malfunction, we should have seen something recorded in the logs. Everything checked out and we didn't appear to have any damage other than to the engine that Liam told you about. Our inspections gave no indication of failure prior to the ejection in our logs. Our navigator programmed the course, and I double-checked it. In fact, we checked it manually as well. Once the ship is in the wormhole, navigation just keeps it steady on the course, no changes," Grania answered, finding it a curious question since they could do nothing once the ship entered the jump.

Palla continued to ask more questions, gathering Grania's impressions of the situation, why the ship hadn't drifted farther into the Dark Sea, what had led them to find the way back, and others. Grania grew weary of answering questions that seemed to be variations of the ones the agent had already asked. If they were grilling Liam like this, she hoped he kept a tight rein on his temper.

At last, Palla put her stylus down and keyed off the recorder. Almost four hours had passed since they'd started. Rubbing her neck to ease the tension, Grania asked, "Is that it now?"

"This is an amazing story," Palla said as she closed her file. "To escape from the Dark Sea is like a miracle. It has only happened once before, as you mentioned. We will be scrutinizing everything we might find capable of knocking your ship out of the wormhole, as well as your actions to get the ship back in again. As you can imagine, this information could be invaluable toward dealing with this type of event."

She opened the door to escort Grania back to the conference room, where Vilnius and Liam waited. They each had a pint and looked relaxed. They chatted about a soccer match with Franc. A file folder sat on the table in front of Franc, and the other agent had gone. Grania got the impression the boys had gotten off easier than she had.

Palla addressed them all. "Let me thank you for your time in answering our questions. While this is an extraordinary event, I am requesting you not divulge any of it to the media, or anyone else for now. We have statements for you to sign affirming you will not discuss this until we give you permission. We want to have time to really study it and prepare an official statement before the media begins reporting any of it."

"Of course," Grania agreed. "We are not all that eager to discuss it now either. Although I would like to tell my grandfather what happened to his ship at some point."

"It won't be long," Palla assured her.

"What about the comlink?" Vilnius asked. "Will we be able to contact Erinnua and Zabrowski? I'd like to make sure I still have a job." The engaging smile he flashed at her stopped just short of flirting.

She responded to it. "I am certain I can clear communications for your ship for about an hour to allow you to make contact. Until we are ready to present an official press release, we prefer to keep the media under a communication lockdown."

Grania's thanks were heartfelt. Finally, she could speak with her family and make sure everyone there was fine.

As they rose to leave, Palla held up her hand. "I have one more thing. One of your passengers, Mr. Harhiman, has filed a complaint, alleging that you were ..." She paused, touched her computer screen, and read, "... 'negligent in your duties as ship's captain and failed to protect the passengers and cargo by allowing the ship to veer off course into a dangerous sector of space.' It's a harassment complaint, I suspect, after hearing your stories. Nevertheless, we will need to investigate. It may delay your departure a couple of days."

CHAPTER TWENTY-NINE

Grania

"CAN YOU BELIEVE THAT man?!" Grania said as they left the office, her anger flaring. "After everything we all just went through to try to save our lives, he files a complaint?!"

"Why do you suppose he did it?" Liam asked. "He seemed to be all right, what with giving us the power crystal to help us get out. Of course, it was saving his own neck, too. Still, he gave it to us."

Grania had a thought. "Did he say anything about us paying for the crystal or give any indication that there might be compensation attached?"

"No, nothing at all. He just said that he had the sample, and it might help us out. Do you think he is trying to get us to pay for it by filing the complaint?"

"No, though I am speculating he has a scheme in mind."

"And I can guess what you're thinking," Vilnius cut in. "If he files a complaint and there's some doubt as to whether you or the station at Pelanan are at fault for the accident, then he can file for insurance compensation for the cost of the crystal, plus damages for late deliveries and possible damage to his cargo."

"And in order to do that, he needed to file the complaint," Grania finished. "That shyster. He can take his cargo and get it off my ship! You know, I was going to tell him that we have a signal. Now, I'll just be a tad forgetful in mentioning it to him."

Liam laughed outright as they headed for the pub to meet the others. "He has it coming. He'll be ticked off enough when he learns we aren't leaving right away."

Grania rolled her eyes. "Too bad. Like I said, he can take his cargo and go. His complaint won't hold up. Let's pick up the pace. I want to contact Granda before we lose our window."

Grania

FINNEGAN'S WAKE CONVEYED THE ambiance of someone's large living and dining rooms rather than a pub. The long bar filled the back third of the main room, with a smaller dining room off to the right as customers came through the door. To the left, a lounge area with link stations for reading or viewing and a display bookcase with actual books occupied another side room. In front of the bar, a dozen or so small cocktail tables outlined a three-meter-square dance floor. An old oak burial casket, finely polished, rested against the right wall, next to the open archway to the dining room. In homage to the song that gave the pub the name and the spirit of the wake, the casket's top lid stood open to reveal the satin-lined interior. It stood empty. After all, Tim Finnegan had recovered.

Despite the meeting with the Space Agency taking so long and adding in the trip back to the Mo Chroidhe to contact her family, Grania and Vilnius arrived at the pub before Brendan and Rory had finished their second round of beer. Rory called out to her almost as soon as she'd stepped through the entrance and came at a brisk pace from the dining section.

"Hey! We've been holding a table over here for all of us. Where are Nansi and Liam?" He pushed a lock of reddish blond hair back from his forehead and grinned.

Grania inhaled the distinct spicy scent of Kilmarin Gold stout, a brand produced in their hometown on Erinnua. Her taste buds begged to indulge in a pint, and she followed her brother to the table he and Brendan had commandeered. She motioned to the bartender on the way, pointing at Rory's glass, then answered his query. "They'll be along shortly. Liam wanted to check on the repairs and make sure work was progressing. Nansi is about done transferring the cheese into the new cold box."

She settled and gazed around the room. Near to the entry arch, their table had a perfect view of the pub's entrance, so she could watch for Liam and Nansi. With the ambiance of a home dining room, antique plates, cups, and saucers rested on a ledge along the walls. A large mural of Duntara Harbor at dusk, with the glowing lights of the city in the background, hung in the center of the back wall. The three-dee mural glimmered with tiny glow-dot lights, giving it an eerie look. Grania had seen similar murals at the pubs on the stations at Tara and Cardyff.

Although eager to tell the lads everything and especially to let them know she'd talked to their grandfather, she wanted to wait until Liam and Nansi joined them. Nonetheless, she quietly told them that the Agency had asked them not to speak to anyone about what had occurred during the jump until after they had made an official press release on it and cleared the hold on communications.

"I knew it would be quite a story that we managed to get back," she told them when Rory asked why. "I just didn't realize it would attract so much media interest. I take it there are quite a few news hounds on the station wanting to get an interview with any of us and break the stories back at their respective outlets as soon as possible. As I talk about it, I'm surprised they haven't tried to accost us already."

Brendan ran a hand through his dark hair and produced a sheepish half smile.

"What?" she asked, her tone a little sharp.

"'Ah ... Tis nothing. Just a woman approached me when I came out of the gate arm and asked if I was from the Mo Chroidhe. I didn't tell her anything, though, I promise. I just shrugged her off." He sipped his brew, looking uneasy.

"You said nothing?"

"No. I didn't even confirm that I was."

"Good for you, then. Well done, Brendan. We just need to keep a low profile for a couple of days."

Vilnius gave up waiting for a server and stood to go get drinks. "Kilmarin all around?" Each confirmed with a nod or an "aye" and he strolled off.

"You two are getting awfully close," Rory said, watching her eyes follow Vilnius to the archway. "Are you going to marry him, Sister?"

Her head snapped back to her brothers. "What?! Are you silly? We're not even considering it."

"Why not? I like him," Brendan added his approval.

"Aye, he is a great fella," she agreed. "He is also a career stationer, and I don't plan to live my life on a space station. So how would that work out? We'd see each other once or twice a year. That wouldn't be fair to either of us."

"Isn't that what you're doing now?" Rory's mouth split into an infuriating grin.

"It is. But we're neither of us committed to the other so we can both see other people if we choose."

"And have you?"

"Just never you mind, Rory! 'Tis none of your business anyway." Maybe it wouldn't have been such an annoying question if she hadn't been reflecting about Vilnius returning to Zabrowski and feeling the loss already.

Just then, Liam and Nansi came through the door and joined them, settling at the table. Vilnius arrived a mite later with a serving lass in tow, who carried a tray filled with half-pints of ale for them all. He settled next to Grania, then placed an arm around her shoulder and squeezing like he owned her. The server promised a waiter would be along to take their food orders soon. Once she left, Liam raised his glass in a toast to their safe arrival, and the rest of them echoed it as they clinked glasses for continued good luck.

They perused the menu, made their selections, and settled back with their ale. After a few relaxed moments, Grania leaned forward, which caused all of them to lean in like a group of conspirators. "We can't talk about anything with the media right now and really, I would like to keep all of our 'adventure' as quiet as possible for now. The official record will tell the story for those who need to know, so there's no point in getting sensational coverage, is there?"

"We can keep quiet, Grania," Liam said. "But what about our passengers? Harhiman is out for making a credit wherever he can, so it wouldn't surprise me if he isn't out trying to sell the whole story, true or not, to the highest bidder."

"He may be. Except it won't be the entire story because he wasn't actually involved in it. It would also be dumb of him to do since he filed a complaint against me, and it would surely influence the agency's review of it."

"What?" Brendan interrupted before she'd even finished the sentence.

"Aye, he's trying to say we, and more specifically me, were negligent and the ship ended up diverting because of it. We think it's a tactic to try to collect insurance."

"I really do not like that man," Nansi grumbled. "You did poorly to bring him aboard, Rory."

"Don't blame Rory," Grania said quickly. "It seemed like a favorable deal and the man paid well. I don't know that any of us would have done any better. In other news, I talked to Granda, and all is well at home. They had been terribly worried, of course, and are singing praises to God that we're all safe." Muted little "hoorays" rounded the table as each relaxed with this news.

She'd almost broken out into tears telling her grandfather about the damage to his ship, although he'd been not at all concerned so long as they were all alive and safe. She couldn't tell him everything that had happened, although she promised him a grand story when they got home. Whatever the banshee had intended on their ship, it hadn't touched the family at home as Granda had sounded well and sworn his health was restored.

Vilnius took a moment to say, "I also have a little news. I am still employed. I'd been worried that they might have replaced me on Zabrowski already."

The glasses went up again in a salute to his positive news. Grania knew Master Hartman would have been severely concerned about his assistant not making it back as scheduled. Hartman knew he had been on the Mo Chroidhe and could surmise the ship had come to an ill end. Now that everything had settled down, Vilnius' mood notched higher.

The conversation drifted to other things, ranging from how odorous cheese smelled even when it wasn't spoiled to how much Rory planned to see a certain young lady back home during their break there. It felt good to be back to normal, Grania decided and wondered if a hotel room might be available on the space station.

Grania

AFTER DINNER AND A few more drinks, the crew began drifting back to the ship, some more quickly than others, as Rory and Brendan decided to see a show before they headed back. Vilnius wrapped both his hands around Grania's hand as they came out of the pub and led her toward the central pillar staircase in the dome that fronted the entrance to the Starlight Hotel.

He'd had the same idea as Grania, only sooner, and had done something about it. A bellman escorted them to a beautiful and spacious room with an over-sized bed, a full-sized bath with a hot tub, and all the luxuries a weary traveler could want.

She grinned at him. "How did you know I was thinking of this?"

"Because I was thinking of this. We don't have much time left before I need to go back to Zabrowski. Once the Agency clears me to leave, I'll be heading back on the next ship going that way."

Her grin disappeared. "I know. For all the time we've had together this past week, it isn't enough, and we were both stressed on the ship. I want more time with you."

Without hesitation, he gathered her into his embrace, their eyes locking in a moment that seemed both fleeting and infinite, a silent acknowledgment of the love shimmering between them. His first kiss settled gently on her forehead, a feather-light touch that sent delicate shivers coursing through her. He followed with gentle brushes of his lips against her cheeks, savoring the warmth of her skin beneath him. As he traveled lower, his mouth found her throat, trailing along her neck, causing her to arch back, a spark igniting deep within her.

Finally, he captured her lips in a tender kiss that lingered, leaving her breathless as she drew him closer, an insatiable longing sparking between them. The nearby bed whispered promises of warmth, but the allure of the hot tub, only a bit farther away, also called out to them. Eager for contact, they tugged at each other's clothes, the discarded garments piling carelessly on the floor as Vilnius led her toward the bed. Cradling her face in his hands, he kissed his way down her neck, allowing his fingers to wander, teasingly trailing to her breasts. Scarcely clothed, they lay on the bed, awash in a moment that felt both newfound and profoundly familiar.

"You are so beautiful," Vilnius murmured, the reverence in his voice echoing the awe in his gaze as his hands explored the gentle curves of her athletic form.

"No, you are," she replied, her voice a soft melody of admiration, her eyes drinking him in as if seeing him anew. Their stolen moments aboard the station had never granted them the leisure to fully appreciate one another, and this opportunity felt like a treasure.

Vilnius, his body a tapestry of strength and definition, invited her touch. She traced the light mat of dark brown hair that adorned his chest, her fingers grazing over the rugged texture, relishing the way his breathing deepened with her every caress. As his hand molded around her breast, he offered gentle squeezes, teasing her nipple with an exquisite touch that left her breath catching in her throat. In response, her fingers explored the contours of his chest, delighting in the soft moan that escaped his lips when she captured the sensitive peak between her own.

Their bodies entwined, an exquisite tapestry of skin and desire, as he slid her panties away and positioned himself above her. She could feel the urgency, the deep-seated need that mirrored her own, pulling them together in a shared rhythm. When he entered her, a gasp escaped her lips, followed by a cry that echoed in the space between them. Her legs wrapped snugly around him, pulling him deeper while their bodies rolled in a primal dance, momentum building around them.

With each thrust, waves of pleasure cascaded over her, an exhilarating tide that stole her breath and filled her with desire. As the crescendo of their passion built, his own gasp broke the air, a shudder coursing through him just before a wave of warmth surged within her, a blissful culmination of their union. It was a moment suspended in time, an intimacy that enveloped them, blazing trails of ecstasy and connection that would linger long after the waves had ebbed.

At last, he collapsed next to her, wrapping his arms around her, and pulling her as close as he could to his glistening, perspiration-drenched body. Her senses filled with his musky, sweet scent as her own mingled in a heady mix of desire and passion.

When they cooled down, Vilnius kissed her throat and gradually worked his way to her lips, where he planted a deep, lingering kiss, then murmured against her face. "I want this to be forever, love. My darling, wonderful Nia—you're my amazing Erinnuach firebrand. You're everything I've ever dreamed you'd be—smart, fearless, and so sexy I can't get enough."

To her chagrin, she giggled like a young girl instead of the captain of a spaceship. He made her feel so beautiful and special. Her heart swelled like a well overflowing with her love! Can he genuinely be experiencing these emotions towards me?

Aloud, she played it down, saying in a low, sexy whisper, "It's the drink talking, my man. You're besotted tonight and tomorrow everything will look different."

He pressed his index finger against her lower lip in a silencing touch. "Mmmm, I think not."

Almost skittish, Grania pulled herself away from his embrace and sat up, looking at the dreamy gaze he steadied on her. "I'm for that hot tub, my love. How about you?"

She twisted out of his reach and scampered, half-hiding her naked body with a towel she'd snatched up from the end of the bed to the waiting tub of water. As she slid into it, she heard his feet thudding off the bed and the sound of his footsteps, not running, but heading to the bathroom. Then she looked up, and he stood framed in the doorway, a gloriously handsome man with every attribute a girl could want. Her eyes issued the invitation, so he stepped with careful, confident slowness into the tub beside her, allowing her to fully appreciate him. She sighed and slid under his arm. If this one night was all they had, she wanted no regrets and only wonderful memories.

Grania

GRANIA WOKE THE NEXT morning to a knock on the door. Already up and dressed, Vilnius hurried to answer it and accepted the breakfast tray he'd ordered. As he set it on the table, he smiled at her and shrugged. "Sorry, love. I didn't mean to wake you."

She pulled the sheet around her and sat up. The delicious aroma of fresh coffee wafted across to her. "No, it's okay. Time for me to be up anyway. Pour me a coffee. I'm just going to get a quick shower and dress." She hopped off the bed, dragging the sheet, and grabbed her clothes before retreating to the bathroom. She knew he was watching her with a quirky little smile on his face all the way.

A short time later, she joined him at the little table. With her copper-colored hair still damp, she had pulled it back and ringlets of curls escaped, dropping down to frame her face.

The breakfast tray held freshly baked rolls, cheese, a variety of meats, and fresh fruit. She dug in, her stomach awake at the delicious scents and demanding feeding. The coffee was divine; the genuine stuff, not the blended variety that lacked substance, but all coffee beans. "Blessed coffee. If it tasted like that all the time, I might be drinking it more than tea," she said as she held out her cup for a refill.

He obliged and refilled his own. "Nia, I have something to say. Last night was extraordinary. More thrilling and fulfilling than I ever imagined it would be. I can't envision waiting months to see you again for a brief encounter the next time you dock at Zabrowski."

Here it comes, she worried, the smile freezing on her face. The letdown afterward. We both knew this wouldn't work, so why did we do it?

"So, here's what I've decided, love. There is an opening for an assistant stationmaster at Tara Station, and I am putting in for it. I have enough experience, so I assume I have an excellent chance. If I can get on there, we can see each other more often and even have off time together. What do you say?"

Stunned, she stared at him with her mouth open, no words coming out for a few seconds, then she found her voice. "But you're in line for promotion at Zabrowski. Hartman will be retiring in a few years and you're the likely candidate to move into the job."

He rubbed a hand across his lips, wiping a bit of jelly off, and his eyes widened in surprise. "It's not the only promotion to be had, Nia. The stationmaster at Tara is not a young man either. It might be a little longer before I get the job and even Zabrowski isn't a given. I thought you'd be happy at the prospect ..."

"I am happy. It's just didn't want you to give up something I know meant a lot to you. You've talked about it so often. Faith, love, it would be wonderful!"

"I'll do it then. Today, in fact. I love you, Grania ... and I've never said that to anyone before."

As her heart soared with overflowing emotion, she sputtered out, "Not even your mother?"

"Well, not in the same way." His smile grew devastatingly wicked.

A buzz from her mobi interrupted the retort she'd readied, and she tapped it on, listening as Liam gave her an unwelcome update. She sighed. "I must return to the ship. Harhiman is giving Liam grief about his cargo. I'll see you back there later?"

"You will. I'll take care of the hotel and see if I can get my transfer put in today. I'll also check for our status at the Agency."

She kissed him, a promise of things to come, then exited into the real world to deal with a problem.

CHAPTER THIRTY

Grania

WHEN GRANIA ARRIVED AT the cargo bay, she found Harhiman steadfastly facing off Nansi and Liam. The trader crossed his arms in a defiant stance while Nansi presented her equally insolent glare. Behind them, a loader 'bot bearing two crates idled, but wouldn't advance any farther.

"What's the trouble here?" Grania asked as she stepped up to them.

"We're trying to unload this man's cargo, Captain," Nansi said, her eyes blazing. "Excepting he's telling us no."

"Mr. Harhiman? Is there a problem with this?" Grania contained her own annoyance with the man.

"Yes, there's a problem, as I told these two. I don't want my cargo unloaded here." His voice reflected his anger. "I contracted to have it delivered to Tara Station and that's what I expected. Bad enough we'll be getting there several days late, but now you want to renege on your agreement and dump my cargo, and myself, here?"

"Forgive me; however, I was under the impression you were unhappy with the service my ship and crew have provided. Despite her dislike of Harhiman, Grania kept her voice calm. "I gave the order to have your cargo removed to the station so you could reload it on another ship. I will, of course, refund the portion of your fee that would cover the transport from here to Tara Station."

He took a step back, his arms dropping from the crossed position and flinging outward as if asking a question. His expression changed from anger to confusion. "You took the complaint to mean I wanted to leave the ship with my cargo? That is just business, Captain. You can't deny your excursion into the Dark Sea, or whatever you called it, inconvenienced me and caused me to miss a business connection I had scheduled here on Dragon Station."

She took a moment to gather her thoughts, her eyes going to the floor of the bay to reveal nothing of her emotion. Just business, was it? Behind her, she heard Liam's low growl and the slap of his hand against the engine room wall.

"I guess you are correct that you were inconvenienced by our unexpected exit from the wormhole into a situation that was likely to kill us all before we could resolve it. In fact, you should modify your complaint to include endangering your life. We did not make an error to cause the ship to leave the wormhole. Under the circumstances, it seems you would prefer another ship for your transport. Especially since the complaint you filed has likely extended our stay on the station while it is investigated."

"Clearly, you're over-reacting to the complaint. You must know I needed to do it in order to cover my losses, both in time and potential sales, with your shipping insurance company. At the very least, I would like to get back the value of the targassium crystal I provided. You must see I did miss the business opportunities I had expected to have here before going on to Tara. Captain, I do not wish to change ships with our endpoint only one jump away. Can we just deal with this on a professional level?"

She took a few moments to reflect, then turned to Nansi. "Put the cargo back in place, Nansi. We will deliver it, and Mr. Harhiman, to Tara, as promised."

Liam sucked in an annoyed breath of air, then stomped back toward the engine room. Nansi said nothing, twisting away to direct the 'bot loader to replace the crates.

"If that's all, sir. Please leave the cargo bay."

His head bobbed down in a brief acknowledgment before he turned to take the ramp to the mid-deck.

"Grania." Nansi hissed her name when the 'bot started to roll back to the forward section.

"I know, Nansi. Truth, it would have made matters worse if I'd kicked him off. One more jump, and he'll be gone."

Grania ambled to the engine room, stood just inside the door, and watched Liam working at his console. He peered at a diagram of the ship's hull with the damaged area marked. On another screen, the station's video feed showed the repair crew working on the rip in the starboard side.

"How long until it's repaired?" she asked.

"Another day, I think. The crew here is skilled and the work is going smoothly. You know it always takes more time when you must work in space. We'll need to test their patch to make sure it's airtight." He spun his chair around to face her.

"That man's arrogance makes me so angry. To make those accusations against us and then say it's just business. I wanted to punch him." His voice conveyed all the anger he felt at the situation.

"I know, Liam. I feel the same way, but you can't let your anger overrule your logic when dealing with people. While I don't like what Harhiman did, nor the accusations made in the complaint, I do understand why he did it. Admittedly, it surprised me he wants to continue aboard our ship. A few others docked at the station now are bound for Tara, I'm sure, and will be leaving before we can get clearance or our repairs complete."

"I know. It doesn't make any sense, does it? I expect the man will be billing us for the crystal before he's done as well as trying to collect from insurance."

"Maybe. Are the other repairs progressing okay?"

"They are. I repaired Granda's jump pod and the spare one as well. Both just needed a new circuit board. The pods are all charged up full now, so we're set for the jump as soon as we get clearance to leave."

"Speaking of the pods, I think I need to have a little chat with Miz O'Cairn about how she managed to make the last jump without a pod. It's the one thing that could cause a problem if Agent Palla tumbles to it in the report. I hope she has a satisfactory answer."

On an impulse, Grania wrapped her arms around her brother's shoulders and hugged him as they once did as children. She felt him tense with surprise, then he relaxed into it. They hadn't shared this closeness in a long time, and it reassured her now.

A little later, she knocked at Moira's cabin door and waited while the woman took almost a full mite to key it open.

Moira O'Cairn greeted her cordially, offering tea, as tradition demanded. While Grania thanked her and refused, she did take a seat at the little table to talk. She started by bringing her up to date on the ship's status and their delay at the station. "I'm hoping it won't be long before everything is cleared up and we can resume our trip. An incident did occur during the mad scramble to get back to the wormhole. You gave up your jump pod to Vilnius, and we're grateful for it, but where did you go?"

Moira sipped her tea then a small smile touched her face for a moment. "I used the spare one in the empty cabin. 'Twas enough for me."

"Here's the thing. Our ship tracks the oxygen use and that jump pod showed sparse use. So, it's difficult to see how you survived the jump. Folded space, or hyperspace as it's sometimes called, has a negative impact on organic bodies, especially when we've lowered the environmental factors, such as oxygen and temperature for the transition."

"Oh, I understand that. Here is the thing, my dear, I use a meditation technique that can put the body into an altered state so that it does not require as much to survive. The pod maintains the environment, but I have little need for the resources."

While Grania had heard about a hypnosis technique capable of slowing the body's functions to almost stasis, she doubted the truth of this. She suspected the possibility of her alternate explanation more and more, yet she didn't want to confront the woman with it now. The question to answer remained, would O'Cairn's account satisfy the Space Agency? "Well, it's a clever trick. I've not heard of anything like it being used for jumps. I might like to learn how to do it."

"It does take time to master," Moira replied.

They spoke a little more before Grania excused herself to return to her duties. Moira O'Cairn was a puzzle, one she wasn't quite ready to admit to herself or to anyone else.

Grania

AS IT TURNED OUT, Grania worried about the explanations and delays for nothing. The Space Agency issued a statement concerning their ship's diversion into the Dark Sea and subsequent return to normal space. They assured everyone that the details would be thoroughly analyzed to gain more knowledge about the space surrounding the wormholes, and how more ships that might be pulled into it could survive. Their message stressed that the odds of it occurring were quite low and using the wormholes were still considered extremely safe. For now, more details remained classified as confidential. They asked the media and others not to violate the privacy of the Mo Chroidhe's crew.

"Typical bureaucratic statement," Vilnius commented as they listened to the announcement on the bridge. The Agency sent a private message granting them clearance. As for Harhiman's complaint, they dismissed it, as it had "no substance". The Mo Chroidhe was free to depart as soon as repairs were complete.

"Communications are fully restored," Rory reported.

"Excellent," Graina replied. "Check the status of the jump gate and inquire about a slot."

Before she could say anything else, Vilnius pulled her into the corridor for a few private moments. "I've requested the transfer. It'll be at least ten days before I'll have an answer, although I think it's a strong possibility. If I get it, then possibly another thirty days before I'll be on Tara Station, so fingers crossed, eh?"

"Finger crossed," she repeated. "Are you sure this is what you want?" She still didn't believe he planned to forfeit an almost sure thing at Zabrowski for her.

"Totally. Now for the bad news; I have passage back to Zabrowski arranged on a ship scheduled to depart in another forty mites, so this is goodbye for now." He pushed a hand into her hair, tenderly twisting the long curls and pushing it back as he leaned forward for a goodbye kiss.

Her heart ached with the pain of this imminent departure yet rejoiced with the hope he'd given her for their future. "Be safe, my love," she said, her voice low and strained with emotion. "You'll be in my heart and thoughts until we meet again."

"And the same for me," he replied. "Contact me when you get to Tara." He planted one last quick kiss on her lips, then left to get his travel case before heading to the other ship.

"We can get a slot in two hours, Grania," Rory informed her when she returned to the bridge.

"I'll confirm it." Things are looking up, she thought. One more jump to Tara Station and home. She had a decision to make about Miz O'Cairn, but the rest of this trip should be easy. If the insurance came through on the repairs and all continued well, they still might show a profit.

CHAPTER THIRTY–ONE

Grania

RED DRAGON GATE, THE outward bound one to Tara Gate, loomed just ahead of the Mo Chroidhe as they stopped and waited for clearance to enter. Following standard procedure, the gate control requested their cargo manifest to file, and the ship automatically responded, sending a notification to Rory that it had done so. Ships entering the Dragon Hold's space needed to declare their cargo and, most often, clearance only took five mites or so.

As time dragged on, Grania grew anxious with the delay. "Everything on our manifest is allowed," she said, expressing her concerns to Rory. "We didn't offload or add any cargo at Dragon Station, so it should be a simple routine check. What's holding it up?"

Rory shrugged. "I dunno. Maybe it's a—wait! There's a message now." He listened for a few moments before he turned his face to her, his eyebrows pinched together in puzzlement. "They're sending an inspector."

Concern turned to alarm as she said, "An inspector? Why? Did they say anything else?"

"Only that he'll be arriving within ten mites."

What now? They never send an inspector unless they found a problem or illegal goods in the manifest.

Grania hurried below to the cargo bay to stand outside the boarding dock's air lock to greet their guest. She heard the thud as the small transport ship locked onto Mo Chroidhe's side. Liam stood beside her while they listened to the sounds coming through the chamber where the inspector entered and stopped until the air cycled into the chamber. After what seemed a long time to Grania, the inner door slid open and a small man in a pressure suit stepped through. He'd already removed his helmet and now reached a gloved hand out to greet them.

"Inspector Maddox," he said by way of introduction. "Sorry for the delay and intrusion. Just a formality, really. A few of your containers aren't matching their digital signature numbers with your manifest. I need to double check the items."

"Of course. Perhaps we keyed a number in wrong. We had to swap out a few containers at Dragon Station."

"That might explain it. One is a cold box, and the number transmitted appears to be a completely different one from what shows on the manifest."

Liam began pulling up the invoice from the Bretice Company at Dragon Station, who'd sold them the cold box. In only a few moments, he brought the tablet with the display over and led the Inspector to the new cheese box. "This is the replacement one."

Maddox consulted his notes, peered at the tablet, and used an electronic gun to read the digital signature. "Ok. It looks like this one didn't get the update into the manifest. Nevertheless, your invoice and the digital signature match, so it should be fine."

Next, he asked about Harhiman's crates. A quick check of those revealed the crates had been switched in position when they were moved back. A simple switch error, Maddox appeared satisfied once he'd confirmed both. He made a note on his tablet, turned to her, and said, "According to the manifest, Mr. Harhiman is transporting one thousand high-value Luna jewels. I need to warn you there have been two marauder attacks in Dragon Hold system, one near Glamour and one just inside Rhiannon's Gate."

"Marauders? That close to Cymraic?" Grania's voice scaled up some. Marauders, freebooters, pirates—they were all the same in the universe. Her people called them freebooters, though the plain line translated to thieves and murderers. They seldom operated close to a planet—chances of a quick response from law enforcement increased quite a bit more if they were too close—but Glamour was Cymraic's moon.

A rare star system with three habitable, Earth-like planets within the greenhouse zone for life, Dragon Hold lured the Irish, Welsh, and Scottish people of Earth to homestead in this sector of space for that very reason. They could each establish their own, yet similar, culture within reach of each other.

"It is unprecedented," Maddox agreed. "Before you pass through the gate, we're advising ships to block the auto manifest transmission signals in case the marauders have managed to hack into the signal to identify cargo. You have quite a bit of merchandise and other valuable cargo like those jewels and even that cheese could make you a target. Be prepared in case there's an attack before you reach Tara Station."

"Are the planets taking any precautions?" Liam asked. Grania noticed his eyes flick to his tablet a few times, and she assumed he was checking for any reports.

"There are guard ships patrolling around the planets, except they don't have too many out. While it's not enough to prevent an attack, if they are in the right place, they can aid an attacked ship and capture the culprits. The Mo Chroidhe does have operational weapons, doesn't she?"

Liam answered before Grania could speak. "Yes, our weapons are in superb condition and loaded."

"Good. I'll be heading back now. Be alert, and I wish you a safe journey home." With that, he returned to the airlock, reseated the helmet on his suit, waved a farewell, and activated the door to seal the chamber.

"That media blackout makes a little more sense now," Liam said. "They were concerned with more than our ship. The reports of any marauder activity in Dragon Hold are sketchy. It looks like it's been thievery, not fatalities. The thieves were working on the other side around Winthrop's Star prior to entering our space. And they've been hitting often."

Both Vilnius and the beauty tech on Pelanan Station had mentioned freebooter activity, so it now seemed more substantial than a suggestion of it. "It appears we would be a likely target for them. Can we exit into the system in silent mode and run that way for most of the trip until we're almost to Tara Station?" she asked.

If the ship could traverse the space without any transmitted signals, then they couldn't be tracked. Unless the thieves got a visual on them, they would be undetectable. "Of course, that would mean no garda ships would be aware of us and if spotted, they might suspect us of being a freebooter ship," she added after a few moments of thought.

"Aye. We can run silent. We can set the com to notify us if it picks up a garda signal so we can transmit a quick identification back."

She nodded her agreement. "Let's do it. I'd best tell everyone we could encounter some trouble before we get to Tara Station. Yet another pixie in the blooming oatmeal, isn't it?"

Grania

WANTING EVERYONE ON THE ship to be aware of the potential danger, Grania included their two passengers in the briefing on the situation ahead. By now, she anticipated Moira O'Cairn's calm acceptance of every untoward event with little to say, as if she had scant concern about the outcome.

Harhiman's eyes almost bulged out while his face reddened at the news, then he reacted with sharp, angry words. "Now we must protect ourselves against marauding thieves?! I thought you people could travel safely between planets."

"What do you mean by 'you people'? Are you suggesting that we, in any way, planned this? Are you suggesting the people of my planet are not capable?" Grania's eyes narrowed in anger.

He backed down at once. "No, no ... of course not. It's just that it seems to be one thing after another. Is your travel always like this?"

"No, it is not. While we have had some peculiar occurrences on this trip and more than our fair share of bad luck, we've also had some good luck. As to freebooters and thieves, it has happened in the past, but only twice since the time my granda took command of this ship. However, the Mo Chroidhe is armed, and our crew is well trained in using weapons. We will protect our ship, cargo, and passengers; you can be counting on that.

"Now, if there's nothing urgent, we need to prepare for the last jump to Dragon Hold. Please return to your cabins and get ready."

Both their passengers left without another word, although Miz O'Cairn cast a glance that caught Grania's eye, and she winked at her as if to give her approval of how she'd handled the trader.

"That man is the testiest fellow I've ever encountered," Nansi said after they had left. "He tries to make it seem like all of this is our fault!"

"Aye, he'll no doubt file another complaint at Tara Station for this inconvenience. For a man who has done years of space travel, he seems somewhat naïve about it."

Grania had other thoughts as well. Most likely, Harhiman's concern centered on his valuable cargo. Maybe the need to keep it private because of thievery explained why he booked passage at the stations rather than pre-booking and clearing his cargo. He dealt with customers on the stations, not going planet-side, so he might do it to keep the cargo content as quiet as he conceivably could.

"Double check all weapons and make sure you have them close to you before locking down your pods. I hope we don't need them but be prepared. Liam?"

"I've checked out the ship's guns and they're ready for anything. They're fully charged, and we have plenty of power for them. They'll be online as soon as we emerge in Dragon Hold."

"Grania, we have clearance for the jump from the gate tower." Rory's voice came through her mobi.

"Copy that. Okay, everyone, let's make this jump to home."

CHAPTER THIRTY-TWO

Sheilan

"I TRUST YOU ARE getting enough adventure on this trip," Sheilan said to Dari as the puca ambled beside her down the corridor. Today he'd chosen to go with half-horse and half-youth, the lower half being the horse so the clomp of his hooves thudded on the metal floor of the ship.

"While it certainly has proven to be exciting, not being allowed to materialize and interact has been disappointing. Now, it seems we might meet some pirates! I always imagined it would be fun to go with some of them for a while. I once worked on a sailing ship as a cabin boy, expecting it would be a grand adventure."

"And what happened?"

"I got bored after a few days and they expected me to work all the time. 'Twas not the fun I was hoping to have. So, I turned into a horse right there on the deck, which gave those sailors a fright, kicked two who lunged for me, broke a hole in the side of the ship, then I jumped over the side, changed to me water horse form and swam for the shore. I could hear them shouting behind me and one or two even fired their pistols, as if they could hit me with a bullet." He chuckled at the memory.

Sheilan responded with a merry chuckle. "You certainly showed them. So typical of human not to acknowledge the magical thing they see, but to attack it."

Her long silvery-white hair draped across her shoulders and down the front of her dress, giving her a serene look. While she had concerns about what lie on the other side of the gate, her own issues to solve revolved around getting her chest to the planet and finding a proper place for it to reside. If the captain decided to turn "Moira" over to the authorities, she would change to her energy form and disappear long before they arrived. But the chest was another issue.

She suspected Grania had deduced she was not human, but she didn't seem to have made the connection to the bean sidhe, which she'd seen twice now. To her credit, the girl didn't perceive the spirit as a threat, so Sheilan considered that a positive sign.

She turned to watch Dari eyeing the closed galley doors. "If all goes well, this jump, which our captain has said is a short one, will bring us into the Dragon Hold system very close to Erinnua. Our journey is nearly done, puca."

"Have you any intuition on what might happen when we come out of the gate here? Will there be pirates ahead and is this ship and crew in danger?" Dari asked questions like a school kid, with an eagerness in his voice for the very thing he asked to happen.

"Will I suddenly be whisked away to serve a warning without any foreknowledge of it, you mean? It is possible, but at this time, I do not know if we will encounter deadly danger or if it will threaten these people."

"I suppose that is proper then."

"On the other hand, I do not always have the chance for a warning when people go into battle. Sometimes it is just a death announcement to the relatives after the deed."

She paused, looked around the empty corridors of the deck as if trying to detect something. "I am still troubled by this trader. I can see why he was upset about the pirates although he directs his worries and anger at people who are not responsible for it. His cargo is valuable and, as you and I know, even more valuable than anyone on this ship or those stations suspects. Me old instincts tell me there is something more to it than just smuggling."

Grania

"EVERYTHING'S LOOKING GOOD, GRANIA," Brendan reported after he'd run their position. "We're right where we're supposed to be, and it looks clear ahead on our screen."

They exited from the Red Dragon Gate without complications; no trouble alarms or klaxons ringing this time. They arrived where expected, and without signs of any impending trouble. A tension around Grania's heart loosened, and she drew a deep breath.

"I've been listening for any signals other than the remote tower on this side of the hole and it's quiet out there. I sent a low range signal to the tower with our identification number and status, so they realize we are here. Even if another ship waited nearby, they couldn't intercept the message," Rory said, adding his status report.

"If marauders are near, they won't be waiting at the gate, so to speak," she answered. "But good job, Rory."

Their ship had exited the wormhole about two hundred forty mites from Tara Station, and Grania hoped to make it the rest of the way with nothing to delay their travel. She gave the okay for the ship to wake their passengers and invite them to breakfast in the galley.

Once his task was done, Rory proceeded to the galley to get his food before anyone else started arriving. He would cover while the rest of the crew ate their breakfast and tea, a homecoming ritual for them.

Nansi settled in next to Grania and confirmed everything looked okay. "The cargo hold is secure. It's been locked down ever since Liam caught that scoundrel in the engine room."

"I need to be apologizing to you," Nansi spoke a little nervously. "I have not been acting logically for most of the last few days. I realize I started falling apart when the b'ean sidhe appeared. It was a childhood tale come to life, and I recalled what all the stories said about the creature. I assumed we were all doomed. Then you add in we were stuck in some place where hardly anyone escaped. It all seemed surreal. The truth is I failed you when you needed me. I am sorry for that."

"We were all under a lot of strain. Still, we survived. Stressed or not, you did your job, and I am grateful for that." Grania covered Nansi's hand with hers in a reassuring gesture. "I'm not sure I could have been as strong if I didn't have you there to back me up. And I knew you would, no matter what happened."

"Your granda will be so proud of you. You and the boys have handled the ship well under extraordinary conditions. No one should be forgetting that. Now, let's hope there are no more trials coming up."

"Freebooters." Grania's eyes grew dark just thinking about them. "Now that prospect scares me. I've trained on the weapons, and I've fired them in training runs, but never at anyone. I'm not sure I can actually kill someone."

"I understand what you mean. It is no easy thing to kill a person, yet people do it all the time. From experience, I will tell you that when the threat is on your life or a friend's life, then the killing is driven by an uncommon emotion, and you can do it. I've done it."

Grania nodded, her voice slowing as a memory unfolded. "Back before, when freebooters boarded the ship. Then with my mum ... I saw her fire." She paused and swallowed hard. "Granda told me about all of it."

"It was the only time I've killed anyone," Nansi said, lifting her right arm like it held a weapon. "But when that man pointed a laser rifle at me, I didn't hesitate." She mimicked firing at her enemy.

"You won't either if it reaches that point. If we are boarded, remember the ship's protocols and stick to them."

Grania's lips twerked into a feeble smile. "Thanks for the pep talk. I have something to confess to you also."

Nansi lifted an eyebrow, her eyes reflecting an unspoken question.

"Back when we left the Dark Sea, I saw something near the rear of the Mo Chroidhe. Something huge and moving in the blackness. It was like a shadowy giant mohrgant beast." She likened the thing to a sea creature on Erinnua, although she'd never seen one in reality, only in images. "I thought it was going to ram the ship, but it turned away or stopped when we were whipped into the slipstream. I think it might be like what knocked you free during the sail repair."

Nansi's eyes grew larger, and her mouth parted as she sucked in a deep breath. "I told you. And I showed you the scratched suit!"

"You did," Grania agreed. "But I only half-believed you. I realized something had damaged the suit, but I didn't fully credit your story. I am sorry for that. If not this same creature I saw, other things might inhabit the dead space that we couldn't detect. I'll add it to the official report."

Nansi's shoulders relaxed and a smile crept onto her face, lighting her eyes with a mix of joy and triumph. "Thank you, captain."

Grania

A SHORT TIME LATER, EVERYONE except Rory gathered in the galley, pushing the room to its full capacity to enjoy a celebratory breakfast.

To some extent, despite the invitation, Grania was surprised to see both Harhiman and O'Cairn at the table in the galley. They, and the rest of her crew, already enjoyed cups of tea along with the fresh sausage rolls piled on plates on the table when she joined them, more than ready for food. The delightful odor of the pastry-clad meat made her stomach growl in anticipation.

Harhiman cleared his throat, then said, "Well, that jump went well, and I must say I felt relieved to wake and find everything normal."

"As were we all," Liam replied with noticeable sarcasm as he ripped a sausage roll apart and dipped it in a creamy mustard sauce.

Harhiman ignored him. "Do we have a clear run now to Tara Station, captain? Is there still a concern with the marauders?"

"If we don't encounter any more delays, we should be arriving in about two hundred mites. Yes, we are still concerned and are monitoring constantly for any indication of trouble."

"Might I inquire what kind of security this ship has? I recall you mentioned weapons."

A frown creased Liam's face as his head shot up, eyes turning to the trader.

Before he spoke, Grania responded, "We are adequately armed." Like her brother, she found Harhiman's sudden interest in their security odd, and it made her uneasy. Ship's protocol stated her response, though. They didn't talk to any non-crew about the weapons or security measures on the ship. "As I stated before the jump, we are prepared to defend the ship, our cargo, and our passengers. You needn't worry about that."

Harhiman wiped his mouth with a napkin and leaned over the table, shiting toward her. "What about personal weapons for passengers? In case we need to defend ourselves?"

"The best thing you can do, sir, is to remain in your cabin with the door locked. Freebooters are after the cargo, items of value. They won't bother passengers, and breaking into sealed cabins is more trouble than it's worth for them."

"But I have cargo to defend," Harhiman objected, his eye narrowing.

"That will be our responsibility to secure," Grania replied. "If we fail to do so, then your claim to our insurer may be valid."

He frowned, and his eyes darkened with his anger. Springing to his feet, he muttered, "You'd best do an excellent job then, captain. He stormed out of the galley, heavy footing it down the corridor.

"Ah, he is never happy, that one," Miz O'Cairn said. Then she, too, rose to her feet. "Thank you kindly for the most excellent breakfast. Now, I will be heading back to my borrowed cabin to prepare for the debarking. That is what you call it, is it not?"

With a grin, Grania answered. "Debarkation is the proper term, but you have the general idea."

After the old woman left, Liam stood, snatching up his plate and utensils, and turned an unsmiling face to Grania. "I don't like that fella at all. He's butting his nose into things he doesn't need to know about. I don't trust him, Nia."

"Neither do I," she replied. "I'll be glad to wave goodbye to him at Tara."

"I wouldn't even do that much," Brendan commented. While he'd been silent, the scowl on his face expressed his dislike for the man adequately.

Grania

NINETY MITES AWAY FROM TARA Station, the ship approached the large asteroid orbiting Erinnua, called Boru's Relic. An oblong, phallic-looking rock, the shape prompted the name assigned to it, which came from an old risqué song referencing the great Brian Boru's sexual member. For herself, Grania didn't see it so much as anything more than an irregular, although very large, hunk of space rock with a rugged surface.

"What the heck?" Rory said, a note of alarm in his voice. He spun around in his chair, concern etched on his face, motioning for her to come closer. "Look at this, Grania."

Rising, she stepped to see the screen where he pointed and saw at once what had caught his attention. The galley area filled the screen showing the remote console the crew used to monitor the ship if needed from there. Harhiman stood in front of the console and keyed strokes into it, trying to log onto it. While it didn't have the full capability of the bridge consoles, with the right password, you could access quite a bit. Even from the here, they could see the "denied" screen appear each time he hit the enter key.

"What is he doing? I'm going down there. Zoom in on the screen. I want to know what he's trying to access."

Grania scurried out, hit the stairs two at a time, slid the last few down, then ran to the galley. She surprised Harhiman, coming in with little sound and finding him still trying to get into the system.

"Is there something you're looking for?" she asked without preamble.

He straightened, stuttered a little with his reply. "I – I just ... I was looking for a map of Tara Station. I thought you might have one stored I could call up easily."

"I believe you'll find one on the com unit in your cabin."

"Of course. I didn't think to check there. Silly of me, wasn't it?" He moved away from the console, with a chagrined look on his face.

"Just request 'map' and 'Tara', and it will come right up. I will ask you not to use the computer in this room as it is for the crew's use." She moved protectively towards it.

"Right. I didn't realize that. It won't happen again." He slipped out and headed back to his cabin.

She watched him leave, then crossed to the computer, keyed in a command and said, "Grania O'Ceagan, acting captain, put this computer terminal on voice lock. Accept only crew-identified voices for access. Execute."

Whatever the trader sought, he wouldn't get it from the ship's computers, Grania thought. She would put them all on voice, crew-only lockdown. Thank goodness they were almost at the end of this trip, and she could get Harhiman and his cargo off her vessel.

She didn't believe for even a moment he sought the layout of Tara Station. At least two attempts to access the ship's computers suggested the man had another agenda, and she wanted to know what it was.

CHAPTER THIRTY-THREE

Grania

BORU'S RELIC EXPANDED ON their forward screen, the crater-like detail of the rock becoming more pronounced with each mite. For the most part, it appeared as a dull, gray-black rock, but just barely discernible in the gray were streaks of silvery color, a hint of what might be rich veins of platinum ore in the rock. Thus far, the planetary governing board had resisted the urge to mine the rock, although it loomed out there as a temptation.

Grania leaned back into the captain's seat, relishing it one last time. Next trip out, her granda would be back in it. She reckoned it would be some time before she might claim it again, if at all. Once they passed Boru's Relic, Tara Station would be in sight. Erinnua was already visible behind the rock and, farther in the distance, the reddish glow of the Dragon Star provided a beacon with the system. Their trajectory would bring them in a shallow curve to the station docking within seventy mites. Home again.

"I'm getting a static reading, Captain!" Rory's voice carried the urgency. "It could be a ship's engine coming from behind the Relic."

"Can you identify? She sprang to her feet, moved closer to the main screen, and scrutinized the rough edges of the rock for any indication of a ship.

"No. No identifying transmissions. She's running silent, like us."

"I don't like it. Go to high alert. This could be the freebooters. Advise our passengers to lock themselves in their cabins and stay there," Grania ordered as she continued to stare at the screen. Her mind worked frantically to evaluate the possibilities.

"Brendan, are there any hiding places we can get to fast?"

"I'm looking, Grania."

She glanced over to see his screen flipping through the system maps near Tara.

"The moon is not too far away, but I'm not seeing any obvious hiding places. Possibly a crater. Or maybe something on the Relic itself ..." Brendan said.

She turned back to her own monitor screens. "Rory, message Tara on low frequency. Let them know— Feck! There it is!" The unidentified ship had just cleared the edge. "Magnify the forward screen to twenty-ex, position lower right quadrant," she commanded.

In a heartbeat, the image grew much bigger and focused on the lower right section, where she could see more detail on the sleek-looking vessel, maneuvering toward them. Larger than the Mo Chroidhe, it also had bigger engines, which translated to more speed. It bore no visible identification on the hull, no name, or any numbers.

"Let Tara know we've encountered the freebooters and are requesting immediate assistance. Keep a channel open to them. Liam, trouble is coming. Lock us down!"

"I see them, Captain. Locking now. Ship's weapons are coming online in five secs." Liam sounded all business. He had it handled. No worries there.

Her gaze shifted to the indicators on the bridge, and she watched as the six ion and two laser cannons indicators blinked from red to green as they became operative.

"We're getting hailed, Grania," Rory announced.

"Let's hear it."

"Ho, Mo Chroidhe." A rough-sounding, deep voice spoke in a casual, almost friendly manner, although he mispronounced the name of the ship. Not from around here, then, Grania surmised as he continued. "Cut your engines and unlock your cargo bay dock, and this will be quick and painless. You know we can take your ship, so don't make it hard on yourselves."

Grania drew in a sharp breath. She turned to face Brendan. "Anything close?"

"The nearest things are the Relic and the moon, just beyond it. It would take us half the time to the moon as to the station. I see a few craters on the rock that might be workable. There is Lanigan's Peak at the other end of the Relic. Info says it's a dead volcano, and it has a deep, tunneled crater through it where we might hide."

Lanigan's Peak ... Grania pictured the landmark in her mind. She'd seen it a few times in passing, and she knew about the tunnel system in it. Although deep, the path risked trapping them if the freebooters followed inside. If she surrendered the cargo, the 'booters might leave them without any other trouble. So far, the reports implied they had killed no one in their attacks.

At that moment, an old, locked-down memory broke free, springing into her thoughts. Dread filled her, threatening to turn to panic as she remembered the incident.

HEAVY FOOTSTEPS POUNDED OUTSIDE *the cabin door and Grania crouched down behind the folding bench of the small dining table in her mother's cabin. Though slim, the thir-*

teen-year-old girl struggled to fit, her long legs a hindrance as she tried to tuck them out of sight.

Her mother tossed a cushion in front to help conceal her hiding place. Grania yanked it into position, trying to peer over the top without revealing herself. Her mother moved in front of her to provide protection. Although barely able to see out, Grania managed a peephole between the pillow and the table leg. She could see her mother well enough to recall every detail.

A tall woman with cropped chestnut brown hair, Alais O'Ceagan sported an attitude as cocky as any man on the ship. She had traveled the space lanes even before she met Sean O'Ceagan. Undaunted, she pulled her gun from the drawer when the first warning of the freebooters sounded and now braced herself with the weapon aimed at the door.

A blast from outside forced the locking mechanism to release and strong, thick fingers closed around the edge to shove it aside. Her mother waited for a better target, letting the freebooter push the door better than halfway open before she fired. The invader fell back, wounded, then returning gunfire from a second man struck her before she could get an aim at the new target.

That fast, Alais was gone. Helpless, Grania saw it all, clapping her hand over her mouth to stifle her outraged and shocked cry.

The freebooter stormed into the room, shoving her mother's body aside without a second thought, his eyes searching the room for any valuables to pillage. He looked like many other spacers she'd seen except for the black ball cap hat perched on his head bearing the pirate symbol and the matching tattoo on his left forearm. Hot tears leaked down Grania's cheeks as she stifled the sob threating to break from her throat.

"Bastards!"

She heard her granda's yell and more gunfire, with pings of energy weapons erupting from the corridor. The man turned just as her father appeared in the doorway and fired, dropping the freebooter as easily as the man had killed her mother. A few more *shots echoed from the corridor, then silence, and the fight was over.*

SHAKING AND SOBBING NOW, Grania crawled out to where her father sat on the floor, holding his wife's body and caressing her face as tears ran down his cheeks.

Grania bit down on her lip and shook the memories away. A piece of her soul had died that day, along with her mother. Innocence was gone and a fear of freebooters and other marauders was born. Stories of Grania O'Malley, the Pirate Queen she'd idolized from childhood, ceased to be romantic imaginings, and the horror of a real pirate attack dominated her nightmares for several years.

Jaw tightening and a fire lighting her eyes, Grania shouted instructions to Brendan. "Answer them with a jolt from number two gun, flash screen, and break for Lanigan's Peak."

She dashed for her chair to strap in, expecting the return fire from the ship. But she swore her ship would not be an easy mark for these marauders.

While the laser cannon fired, an accompanying flash blinded the other ship's screens, giving them a few seconds of cover, and Brendan executed the course change. The ship shifted its direction in a second and dropped fifty meters down. Missing them by a meter, the return fire might have connected if they hadn't made the downward shift.

"Evasive," Grania ordered.

Brendan had already programmed a movement pattern in the navigation computer, and it began an erratic run toward the end of the Relic, dropping farther down to go under it. From here, it was a dodge and guess game for the two ships. If the freebooters got a hit on them, it would slow them down, and they might not make it.

"Don't be foolish, Captain." The 'booter's voice came through again, the sound now filtered with static. "Is someone else's cargo worth the loss of your ship and possibly your lives?"

Grania signaled Rory to open the return communications. "How do I know you won't kill us all and take our ship anyway?"

"Well. Hello, Lady Captain." The voice changed to sound smarmy as he addressed her. The tone set Grania on edge and she gritted her teeth, wishing she could slap the man. "Be a smart girl now and cooperate."

She motioned to Rory to cut their side of the comm. She gazed from one of her brothers to the other, then tagged Liam and Nansi. Her voice reflected her fury as she asked, "What do you all say? Do we let them have our cargo and hope that's all they want?"

Liam answered first. "I'm not keen to letting thieves get away with anything, let alone our cargo. Our reputation is built on our ability to deliver what we're entrusted with, so I say we fight them. But I will back whatever decision you make."

"Aye, we do not like giving into robbery. Although we need to consider we have passengers." Nansi voiced her opinion.

"That's true," Grania replied. "Except I don't think these 'booters are a threat to our passengers. Brendan?"

He seemed a little hesitant, then their logical Brendan spoke up. "We only need to stall them, Nia. Help is on its way from the station, isn't it, Rory?"

"It is. They got our message, and they'll want to stop these thieves as much as we do. If we don't try to delay them, then they'll get away and keep on raiding other ships. Maybe even us again on another run."

She took a quiet moment to consider, then said, "I agree with you all. Let's try to stall as long as possible. I hope your dodge program is a top notch one, Brendan."

"It is," he answered, grinning before he turned back to his station to monitor the ship's progress. "They may be bigger and fast, but our smaller ship can maneuver better and fit in places they can't go."

Another shot from the freebooters went past them to let them know they would not wait much longer. Grania shivered a bit and hoped Bren was right.

"Get me some speed, Liam. We're running!"

CHAPTER THIRTY-FOUR

Sheilan

WHEN THE ORDER CAME over the ship's com for the passengers to stay in their cabins, Sheilan and Dari did what any self-respecting sidhe would do and changed to their energy forms to see what was causing the brouhaha. They both expected the long-awaited freebooters, as the captain called these pirates, were the reason.

They picked up Harhiman's fractal pattern as soon as they exited the cabin. He headed toward the cargo bay, glancing over his shoulder now and then. While difficult to ascertain how, the trader's coverall-type suit with a hood gave off a muted pattern that seemed to blend into the pattern of the ship's walls. The security cameras at each end of the corridor should see him. Suspicious, Sheilan's energy form popped to the bridge, where she edged to a corner at the ship's curve and switched to her young woman form long enough to get a quick peek at the security monitors. No sign of the man in the images, confirming the suit, and the hood concealed him from the cameras.

She returned to her previous form and rejoined Dari, sending a thought-picture-speak message to him. He's blockin' the signal with that outfit he's wearing. The crew has no idea he's roamin' about.

Nor us, Dari sent back.

Whatever the man was up to, Sheilan vowed to find out. Even though this activity extended beyond her duties as a banshee, she'd come too far with these people to have this conniving shyster take advantage of them.

Outside the cargo bay door, Harhiman stopped and turned his back to the corridor to conceal his actions, then fiddled with something he carried in his hand at the door. Sheilan couldn't see the object in this form, only the fractal pattern, although she could tell he used something with energy. Whatever he did, it resulted in the cargo bay door sliding open and Harhiman stepped through.

Go below, she indicated to Dari and made the dive through the floor. Once in the cargo hold, they found an observation spot behind a crate, and Sheilan changed to her semi-transparent form. In this state, she could see as a human did. Dari followed her lead and emerged as his not-quite-solid youth form.

Harhiman made it halfway down the steps when the ship lurched and dropped downward. His eyes jerked wide, while his forehead scrunched into deep creases, and his mouth fell open in alarm. He clung to the railing, thrown off balance by the sudden maneuver. He scrambled down the rest of the steps, recovering his balance, and hid behind a huge crate in the hold, flattening himself against it to stay hidden.

The ship continued to move erratically, turning and changing positions from one spot to another, going up, going down, shifting starboard, or port. Even Dari recognized an evasive pattern. "They are trying to escape," he whispered to Sheilan.

In a burst of speed, Liam sprinted out of the engine room and made for the stairs, taking them two at a time to the top. If the door at the next deck remained open, they had no sign as his steps thudded without stopping and grew fainter while he ran down the corridor. Now only Nansi remained in the engine room to handle things.

Liam

LIAM RAN ONTO THE bridge, taking over the weapons console, and firing their port side lasers at the freebooter ship while it attempted to pull alongside. The Mo Chroidhe lurched upward, then shot forward before dropping again.

"Almost to the bottom of the Relic," Brendan called out. "We're going under it in five–four–three—"

Liam switched to the aft cannon and fired an ion blast at the pursuing ship while the Mo Chroidhe made the reverse turn to go under the Relic. The screen showed the bursts of light and a hit on the ship.

"There's a deep gash in the stone about one-third of the way if you can find it, Brendan. We should be able to pull up into it and disappear from sight before they can get to us. It's hard to spot unless you know it's there," Liam said, turning the aft cannon toward where he expected the other ship to make an appearance.

He glimpsed Grania subtle head turns as she scanned between the other screens to look for any movement. "I'd forgotten about that gash, Liam. Grand idea."

"Found it!" Brendan shouted. "Putting coordinates in now and we've got it. Looks like another three mites, then we'll slide right into it."

"Is there room enough to maneuver in it?" Grania asked. "We need to escape if the 'booters find us in it."

"I think so. Depends on how big their ship is. It's a wide gash, even though it doesn't look like it. If we get in and shut down, they won't know where we went."

"No, but they'll be back to look for us when they can't find us ahead of them. Eventually, they'll spot that gash. I think we need to go in, shut down, and let them go past, then we can go back out under low power and run back over the top of the rock, heading for Lanigan's Peak. There are more hiding places inside that cone, so it will be easier to play hide and seek until help arrives."

"Sounds like a plan. Let's do it." Liam turned back to the guns.

"They're still signaling us," Rory said, keeping a firm hand on his seat while switching frequencies.

"Do you have anything from Tara?" Grania asked.

"Nothing new. They said garda ships are on the way."

The crevice in the stone came up, and the ship slid upward and into the opening as smoothly as if it had been designed for their freighter. They coasted in about fifty meters before slowing to a halt and killing their engines. All the exterior lights shut down, so they sat in the dark and silent, which would make it harder for the other ship to detect them. Only their radar remained active to track when the 'booter ship went past.

Sheilan

AFTER THE SHIP WENT QUIET, Sheilan watched Harhiman's expression shift to a determined look as he saw his opportunity and he took it. When Liam had dashed out, the engine room door didn't close completely, leaving a small gap that the trader grasped. Although the cargo bay was pitch black, the engine room had low-level emergency lighting giving off dull illumination.

She watched Harhiman ease a wooden truncheon from inside his overall as he padded on silent steps through the door, coming up behind Nansi, whose attention focused on the console as she monitored their power levels. With one swift swing, he bashed the back of her head. Nansi dropped to the deck floor, unconscious.

Switching back to her energy form, Sheilan moved to follow Harhiman as he stepped over Nansi to access the computers. Like the rest of the electronics, the machines used only limited power. The ship was silent and unmoving, no engines humming.

"Weapons," he muttered. "Need to access and disable them."

Although agitated, Harhiman appeared to know what to do as he poked at the equipment, then he frowned as a computer voice said, "Computer on voice lockdown. Please identify."

He slammed his hand against the console. "Damn! That bitch! Why didn't she just surrender the cargo?"

Turning back to Nansi, who lay prone and unconscious on the floor, Harhiman knelt and slapped her face twice. She didn't respond to his efforts and, from the look of the low energy she radiated, Sheilan thought she might be more severely injured than the man had intended. He shook her like a rag doll before dropping her back to the floor.

Disgusted, he tried a different console with the same result. Even though he tried to get past the voice protocol, he couldn't find another way to access it.

Proper job, Sheilan thought as she observed his actions. Grania had done well to protect the systems. While the banshee understood little about the computers everyone had been using for the past three centuries, she did know security was often an issue, and some humans excelled at breaking past the safeguards. For now, the voice protocol appeared adequate to stymie the trader.

With a slight jerk, the ship moved again, albeit gradually, and the captain's voice came through the com. "Nansi, we're moving back out. Bring the engines up and prepare to give me additional power if we need it."

"Additional power," Harhiman repeated through gritted teeth. "I'll fix that." He grabbed his truncheon and smashed it into the consoles over and over, damaging the screens and smacking the sensors on the keyboards.

CHAPTER THIRTY–FIVE

Grania

ONCE THE 'BOOTER'S SHIP passed them without detecting them in the rock crevice, Grania released a pent-up breath and ordered the ship to reverse engines. "Keep the thrust low so that we don't generate enough noise to be noticed. When we're clear, we can make the swing upward and go over the rock at the fastest speed possible, then run for Lanigan's Peak."

Liam initiated low power using thrusters as Brendan, mindful of any obstacles, navigated them back out of the crevice. Grania called down to warn Nansi they would be making another sprint for safety. Rory relayed another message to their passengers to buckle up in their cabins so no one would be injured by the sudden movement.

"We're clear," Brendan informed them after a few tense mites. "Course change initiated." The ship picked up power as Liam opened the full engine boosters, and it began the climb to the top of Boru's Relic.

Grania frowned, her forehead ceasing as her eyes reflected her uneasiness. "Nansi hasn't replied."

"Maybe she's not at the console. She might be checking something else," Liam answered. Yet she could see the concern in his somber expression. "I'll go down as soon as we get to the top."

"Yeah, you do that. Something doesn't feel right, Liam."

The ship rose over the top of the Relic and veered to port, then picked up more speed over the uneven surface to a barely visible rounded cone that thrust up barely twenty meters above the surrounding rock. The crater went deep into the heart of the rock and branched into tunnels. Most didn't go through to the bottom side, although one or two had very narrow openings that even their small ship couldn't navigate. The crevice they'd just left sliced the bottom side of the lava tube, suggesting Boru's Relic had once been part of something much larger with a molten core.

Although the speed picked up, the additional power didn't meet Grania's expectations. "We're not moving fast enough."

In reaction, Liam jumped to his feet, heading for the door. "Going down now."

Sheilan

SHEILAN WATCHED AS HARHIMAN pull out his mobi to contact someone, and she moved closer to listen. For a moment, Harhiman glanced around him, eyes darting toward the stairs and scanning the area, swallowing visibly before he shrugged and pressed his back against the engine room wall. Sheilan guessed he sensed her presence, even though he had no idea what it might be other than a sensation of someone watching. Then again, he might just be worried Liam would be returning.

He thumbed the send button and spoke with authority. "Burnham, they've hidden from you. Turn around now. And be careful with any shots on the ship. We have valuable cargo down here, and those crystals are more volatile than I like. Aim for the top of the ship, the bridge. Take out that bitch captain if you can!"

He grabbed onto the table's edge as the ship swung around and picked up speed. They were running again. Moving with a sudden decision, Harhiman hunted for the power inputs to the system and knelt to examine them. He pulled out a laser gun from inside his coveralls and fired at the ones to the engine room. The other set was needed to open the docking bay and airlock. "What didn't I think of this sooner?" he muttered to himself as he watched the thick cables melt apart and spark out before dying completely.

He contacted his ship again. "Their weapons are dead. Let's get this done. We're running out of time."

The rhythmic thumps of footsteps descending the stairs drew Harhiman's attention. He moved out of sight, crossing to the back wall and leaning against it near the airlock with his laser gun held hard in his hand.

Liam

LIAM SPOTTED NANSI'S PRONE body on the engine room floor before he got to the door. The distinct scent of burned fluoropolymer insulation assaulted his nose while his eyes confirmed the power to the engine room had failed. With a jerk, he pulled out his laser weapon, armed it, then bending low, hurried to Nansi's side. Her closed eyes and lack of movement told him she was unconscious.

In position to face the entry to the room, he kept his gun pointed toward the door while his other hand checked Nansi for a pulse. As he pressed a finger against her throat, he found the pulse of her heartbeat and nodded his head, then he gingerly touched her head until his fingers met the swollen lump on the side of her head. He tapped his com unit and spoke in a low voice, expecting whoever of their two passengers did this was still in the cargo bay. "Nansi is down. One of our passengers assaulted her and cut the power to the ship."

"We noticed that sudden decrease a mite or two ago. I had hoped it was you doing something to the engines."

"No, it wasn't my fiddling around. I don't imagine our saboteur was an old lady, so I'm going to be looking for that treacherous bastard."

"Be careful, Liam."

Liam crouched low, kept his gun at the ready, and edged his way around to the small opening at the back of the engine room wall. As soon as he got a few feet closer, he could see that the cables had been cut. A swift repair was impossible. He'd have to run new cables to the box here and the one inside the room.

He scanned the area for Harhiman, expecting the man to be nearby. He moved with caution along the aisles of the cargo hold, taking care at the openings between boxes with the assumption the trader could lurk there. Mid-way through, the blast from a hit rocked the ship, and he almost went sprawling.

He guessed the 'booters' ship had found them and opened fire on the Mo Chroidhe. It looked like it would be a firefight, and they were sure to lose. The 'booters would have to enter through the airlock down here, so he figured he needed to position himself to stop them.

He tapped his com and whispered, "Grania! Are you all right? Grania?" Even keeping his voice low, it carried the urgency. He didn't get an answer, so he worried the blast had done major damage on the bridge. "Rory, are you there? What's happening?"

After a crackle on the link, Rory's voice replied, "Bren and I are on our way down to you. Nia's on the bridge alone. She said to lend you support. It's the cargo the 'booters are after and that's down there. She's going to try to slow them down." While he spoke, the sounds of his and Brendan's running footsteps came through the connection.

"Harhiman's loose down here somewhere, so be prepared and cover yourselves. Use caution coming down the steps. He could be armed."

"Got that," Rory replied. "We'll have our weapons ready before we start down."

"Be careful, Liam," Brendan added before Liam clicked off.

Grania

GRANIA CRAWLED TO THE communications station's deck chair and pulled herself off the floor, then gazed at the surrounding damage. The second blast had breached the outer hull with enough force to cause damage to the consoles and knock down the port and aft screens. The scent of shorted out electronics filled the air and a haze from the burned seat cushions made her eyes water and she coughed. Left arm and knee throbbing from the hard slam into the weapons console, she directed her attention to the main screen. Facing them head-on, the 'booter ship filled the giant monitor as they waited for her response to their surrender demand.

She stumbled to the console and keyed the broadcast to the 'booters, the station, and her ship. Everyone was going to hear her response. She spoke through gritted teeth, forcing the words to come out without antagonizing her adversary. "My ship is disabled, thanks to your cohort in the cargo bay. I have no power and no weapons. I have little reason, or ability, to resist your plans for boarding my ship. My only request is you not harm my crew or my other passenger."

"About time you saw reason. Unlock the cargo dock and give the air lock access from the terminal next to it. No one needs to get hurt, so don't do anything stupid, girl." The 'booter said the word "girl" with a sneer, letting her know he didn't regard her with any legitimate authority.

Grania seethed, her jaw twitching with anger and her eyes burning with unshed tears, but she fought to control her temper. "It will be done in a few moments." She cut the transmission, then spoke to the ship's computer. "Open communications to Tara Station Garda and transmit all records from the ship for the past sixty mites. Continue to send until this command is terminated. Advise that the ship is under attack and our passenger, Ansel Harhiman, appears to be a co-conspirator. He has attacked the crew and ship and caused significant damage by his actions. Lock the bridge and seal the outer door. Open only on my command or on Tara Station override. Unlock the cargo bay dock and enable the airlock. Confirm to keywords 'bás a thabhairt duit'."

"Commands confirmed." The computer's voice responded. Grania's mouth shaped a grim semi-smile, knowing even if the freebooters circumvented her voice command, they wouldn't be likely to guess the Gaelic phrase for "death to you" in order to access the bridge. And the phrase itself set a booby trap in the system, one of her granda's precautions after the last time free-booters boarded the ship.

She shoved her hair back from her face, aware of the wetness on her hand, and pulled it down to see the blood on it. She'd cracked her head against the edge of the computer station as she'd fallen. It must have gouged it a bit. She located the first aid kit, which had flown off its bracket on the wall during the attack, and applied an antiseptic-covered bandage to clean it. Limping back to the captain's seat, she lowered herself into it and dropped her head into her hands.

A fine captain I am, she thought, wallowing in misery. I almost lost the ship and crew in the Dark Sea, and now I'm falling prey to a band of conniving thieves. Damn! Every instinct I had warned me not to take passengers on this trip, but I'd allowed the lure of extra money for the trip and doing a good deed for an old woman, who is most likely not what she seems, cloud my judgment. As Nansi often says, what is the point of intuition if you don't listen to it? And Nansi! How was she?

"Unconscious," Liam had said. What if she was severely injured? Grania concluded she had made a total muddle of this entire trip. She'd be lucky to get the Mo Chroidhe back to Tara Station, let alone ever claim it as her captain. Not after this.

On the verge of tears, she reached for a tissue in her pocket and her fingers touched the cool stone of the rosary beads. Her great-great-aunt's. Bequeathed to her. Were they meant to bring luck? The old woman, or whatever Miz O'Cairn was, hadn't been clear about the stones, and despite saying the prayers when she'd first received the beads, she didn't count herself a religious person to use them as intended for prayer.

What the heck? She prayed help would arrive soon, and they would all be safe, even if it meant the loss of her cargo. Harhiman had revealed his hand on this trip, so it meant he might be more inclined to eliminate any witnesses and the ship itself if it meant covering his tracks.

Your granda wouldn't give up, a voice in the back of her mind whispered. It sounded like her mother. In fact, her mother had said as much to her when she had felt defeated over an unusually complicated navigation problem she was learning.

It was the truth. Her granda wouldn't give up and just hope for the best. She had to do something. Her brothers were down in the cargo bay, ready to fight, and would do it if she knew Liam. Even her little brother, whom she should have protected on this trip. Brendan may be scared, yet he put his faith in her. She needed to figure out a plan. She bore the name of a famous ship's captain, a noble bleedin' pirate at that, but that Grania had also been a clan leader. Now, this Grania bore the responsibility for her ship and crew. Her jaw hardened while her eyes turned to steel, and she drew a determined breath.

I am the Mo Chroidhe's captain, and I will not lose my crew or my ship!

CHAPTER THIRTY-SIX

Liam

IN THE CARGO BAY, the freebooters' shuttle rocked the Mo Chroidhe when they docked at the bay's airlock. Harhiman forced the lock on the door to allow the thieves onboard. Liam watched from where he had retreated to the engine room. He'd pulled Nansi to a protected area out of sight where he crouched next to her, laser out and ready. Rory and Brendan had slipped in while Harhiman had gone to the forward section to check his cargo, so he didn't see them arrive.

They located a secure hiding place behind one of the structure support spines almost directly across from the airlock, where they crouched, waiting for his signal. He could see them from his vantage and knew they also had drawn their weapons. Now Harhiman, with his laser still in hand and wary, hovered behind a crate near the airlock, waiting for it to cycle through the open sequence to allow the freebooters to board.

While Liam had a tricky shot, he thought he could target Harhiman, yet he waited for the others to arrive. He wanted them to step onboard and killing Harhiman might spook them. A little antsy to get on with it, his brothers held their fire, waiting for his signal. Liam reassured them through his mobi, telling them to wait a bit. He keyed a code into his mobi to pick up the signal from the comlink at the airlock.

"We need to move quickly, you fools," Harhiman said, watching the three men step out of the airlock.

From his position, Liam listened to the conversation through the com, although he didn't need it. Unaware of the others in the cargo bay, the men shouted to each other, allowing the O'Ceagan brothers to overhear them.

They'd brought a small robot-loader with them to do the heavy lifting, but it couldn't take more than one crate at a time.

"We're doing the best we can here," one man objected.

"Right, Freeman. Whose bright idea was it to begin raiding ships in this zone? You tipped off your hand to the authorities, so it's made this job a whole lot harder. Get these three containers off first." Harhiman handed the man a list with the numbers on it. "These are the ones I had loaded and there's one more to go. It will have to wait for the next trip. That's the one with the crystals in it, so it may take some special handling. There's also a container of valuable wines from Earth that should be worth a respectable amount to some connoisseurs I know. Let's get that off in this first run and that will be about all the shuttle can handle."

As they moved away from the airlock, Liam pressed up against the side of the engine room wall where he could overhear more of the conversation.

Crystals? No crystals showed on the manifest. Then it connected. Harhiman was smuggling crystals in one of his containers. Targassium crystals, to be exact. Add to it that Grania had a dream about it. While he'd thought the container with the Luna jewels seemed a little big, a false bottom explained it. The jewels, if the manifest was correct, weren't lavishly packaged in roomy boxes like the one Harhiman had shown them. No, they were making space for a more valuable smuggled cargo.

That explained why Harhiman didn't pre-book. He prevented close scrutiny of the cargo by moving it through the stations. Take it off one ship and load it onto another. It cut the red tape because it had cleared one ship already. Now he really wanted to stop this bastard and his thieving companions.

Grania wanted him to wait before the attack. He knew she had a plan in mind, but they had the opportunity now. With Brendan and Rory, it positioned the three of them against the four 'booters, and they wouldn't be expecting them. Like his brothers, he was itching to do something soon.

While the 'booters moved to load the crates, Liam slipped back next to Nansi. He crouched down under the console, where he figured they wouldn't notice him unless one of them came inside. With the power out and only the emergency lighting on in the cargo hold, the engine room appeared dark and silent. He settled down, his weapon held ready in case one of the bastards came through the door. How much longer until they could do something, or the Garda arrived?

Sheilan

FROM THEIR HIDING PLACE, Sheilan and Dari, both in semi-transparent forms, watched everything unfolding in the cargo bay.

Dari thought-sent a message to her asking if she felt the urge to materialize in front of the family.

Oddly enough, she did not, which meant that they weren't in any imminent danger or likely to be soon unless something prevented her from warning them. No, trouble was here, to be sure, with the marauders stealing their cargo and disabling the ship, but not death. At least, nothing indicated it yet. She motioned to Dari, pointing to the bridge.

Grania

GRANIA CRAWLED UNDER THE weapons console, looking for the cable that connected the forward cannon to the power source. Although it routed from the engine room, a backup power source for the bridge had cut in for the computers and screens when the engine power failed. Her granda had once shown her how to rewire the cannons to it in case of emergency.

When she remembered this, she'd told Liam to wait to do anything until she could try to get a cannon active. One return volley to the 'booters' ship should buy them enough time for her brothers to get a chance at Harhiman and his raiders.

As she found the cable and located the panel to disconnect it, she could almost see Paddy O'Ceagan kneeling on the floor next to her, showing her what she needed to do. Remove the panel cover, unscrew the circular clamp, and remove the red and blue cables. Done. Next, remove the panel cover on the emergency power, use an empty socket and plug the cables into the appropriate receptors, being careful not to touch any of the live sockets with any of the tools. Next, she needed to replace the circular clamp and secure it, and that could be the tricky part with live power. She employed the hard plastic screwdriver to avoid a shock and, while manipulating the tool in the tight space proved difficult, she persisted until the clamp was secured. With the power back to the gun, all she had to do was position it.

Crawling back out, she pulled to her feet and checked the power level on the cannon. Already up to twenty percent; it would be charged soon.

"Hold tight a little longer, Liam. I've got the main forward cannon rewired, and I'll have enough power soon. All I need now is a brief distraction on the bridge of that ship, so they won't notice the laser blast coming at them."

"The raiders have the shuttle almost loaded. They've put all of Harhiman's crates on it except the last one. I overheard Harhiman say they'd need a second trip, and he wants to take a couple of other crates. There's one filled with rare wine and, oddly enough, he thinks he wants to take the cheese container."

"Let them go with those crates. I won't have the cannon for a few more mites at least. Once they've gone, nail Harhiman. I'll fire at their bridge when I have the enough power." She glanced at the power reading again; up to thirty-five percent charged.

Sheilan

WHEN SHE OVERHEARD GRANIA'S comment about the distraction on the freebooters' ship, Sheilan made a sudden decision. She teleported to her cabin and changed to the solid form of a dark-haired young woman. While still in the garb of a peasant girl, she had opted for long pantaloons with a shorter over-dress than usual so that she could move more easily. Then she grabbed a leather pouch from her trunk and half-filled it with dirt from the lower section. She left the lid open with the inner compartment skewed enough that the dirt was exposed. She tied the pouch to the belt at her waist. So long as she held onto the pouch, she would need to remain in corporeal form.

"What are you doing now?" Dari asked when he popped in a short time later.

"I have a plan to offer a little aid to the crew. Since I am not getting any premonitions about their fate here, I am guessing they are not in mortal danger. Perhaps it is because none of the family is fated to die here and now. I am thinking they can use a little insurance. You stay here and keep watch. You can distract if you need to, but right now, I need you to help get me on the shuttle before it returns to the pirate's ship."

"Oh, no! You do not go over there without me!" His eyes blazed red for a moment. "If you are going to wreak havoc, then I am going with you. I am ready for some excellent fun."

"We may not be able to get back," she warned. "I think this pouch of dirt will work with the ships being so close to each other, but I have not tried it."

He nodded his consent.

"Good, then. Help me get on the shuttle. You need to distract the thieves while I slip onto the ship and hide. Then you can slip in unseen with them. Will you do that?"

"I will. Now we will have some fun." His voice turned to a whinny while he changed into his energy form.

Sheilan had to take the corporeal route down, and it took longer. Climbing down almost vertical stairs was a rare experience, so she took it a little slower. With the urgency to return to the cargo bay before the 'booters returned to the ship, she took a few chances and the possibility of being spotted by the lads down here or even the thieves added a risk she needed to take.

She darted, moving like a wraith in silence from the stairs to the aisle, passing in a blur in front of the engine room's enormous glass walls to the edge of the stacked cargo just before the airlock.

The thieves were loading the last container for this run and preparing to go back themselves. "Cotoli, stay here and we'll start getting the next load lined up. Freeman, get this group unloaded fast and get back here. We don't' have a lot of time to transfer the rest," Harhiman instructed. Cotoli already directed the robot loader back toward the long aisle, where Sheilan pressed herself against the nearest crate.

Without even a glance her way, Cotoli turned away from her. From the starboard side of the cargo bay, opposite the crate that neither of the sidhe wanted to go near, Dari let out a shrill whinny that drew the attention of everyone in the cargo bay. Pleased with the reaction, Sheilan watched Harhiman's head jerked up at the sound and he and Freeman ran forward to investigate, turning down the aisle.

The sidhe moved, a blur of color moving faster than any human, while she dashed into the airlock and flattened herself behind the shipping container in it. The fourth man went across to the shuttle to get it ready to move once Cotoli arrived with the final crate. A moment later, she detected a few sparkles and sensed the puca had joined her, then footsteps told her Freeman was returning.

After a few shouts, Harhiman yelled, "Just get that shuttle moving, Freeman! Be back here in ten mites, and we'll have these other three crates ready to go."

Sheilan found a foothold on the crate and used it to climb to the top, where she lay down spread-eagled on it. These fools wouldn't look at the top of the crate and a sufficient edge along the top helped to hide her if they did. Freeman told Cotoli to return to the hold while he finished loading the crate.

The crate bumped through the airlock onto the shuttle, and she picked up the swishing sound of the lock shutting behind them. Then the crate rolled a little farther from the door, and Freeman shouted to his partner on the crew deck to go.

Sheilan

IN LESS THAN THREE mites, the shuttle reached the 'booter ship and connected with their airlock. While the air cycled, Freeman began pushing their crates into the cargo bay of their ship. His partner came back to help and in no time, the containers were loaded. They started back to the airlock again when Sheilan decided she needed to delay them so the crew would only have two to contend with on the Mo Chroidhe.

Looking around, she saw the perfect opportunity to reveal herself to the freebooters and a wicked smile crossed her lips when she settled on just the guise to gain the attention of the men unloading the ship in the cargo bay. With just a thought, she let Dari know her plan.

From her vantage point on the cargo, she could see a compact decontamination shower, the round platform on a movable rail beneath the spray head. Designed to cleanse people or cargo, the unit included a ramp that made it easy for the men to put a crate on the platform and slide it under the unit's spray. However, Sheilan neither knew nor cared about how it worked or its purpose. She removed the pouch of dirt from her waist, set it down, and transformed into her energy form.

In an instant, she shifted from the crate to the round platform, assuming the appearance of a partially clad, voluptuous, dark-haired young woman, one arm crossed over her naked breasts while the other swayed with suggestive motions of enticement. She had once seen a seductive Celtic warrior woman that she modeled for the illusion. Her arms were adorned with tattoos, much like the ones she had seen on Zabrowski Station. She thought they would appeal to these outlaws.

Swirls of the chemical fog used to decontaminate formed wisps of swirls around her. She tilted her head back, lifting a hand to her throat and a low wail came from deep within her, not the usual shriek she would make in warning, but something far more sensual.

She was correct in her assumption, although her sudden appearance startled and frightened the two. One man pointed at her, his eyes wide, and he asked his partner, "Where did she come from? Is that a projection?"

"I don't know, Berger. How the hell—?" The one they'd called Freeman took a few cautious steps closer to her, squinting like it would reveal if she was solid or not. Sheilan lowered her head and focused dark eyes straight on him. Full, burgundy-colored lips puckered into a seductive promise if he came closer. At the moment he reached out to touch her, she mind-whispered, Fear me.

His eyes widened in shock, and then she transformed to the semi-solid shape of her most hideous aspect, the warrior crone, a shrieking banshee out of legend. With a yell, he pulled out his laser pistol and fired a burst that somehow missed before his shaking hand dropped the weapon. The blast shot past Sheilan and scorched the wall behind the decontamination unit, burning out the power to the control board. After the fog disappeared, the crone remained. Berger jumped back, turning to retreat to the shuttle while Freeman backpedaled from her.

At that moment, Dari materialized in the form of a full-sized white draft horse, capable of taking a man down with his hooves if he came close enough. He galloped back and forth, daring Berger to pass him. He stopped, shrieked a high-pitched scream, and rose on his hind legs, flailing the front ones in warning to the man.

With Dari stopping either man from moving toward the ship, the puca and the banshee began closing on them, forcing them back toward an almost empty container. Dari made a threatening lunge at them, and they scrambled back into the container, looking for something to offer protection. Sheilan took on her corporeal form again and slammed the container closed, setting the lock on it.

"Can they breathe?" Dari asked when he switched forms.

"If someone gets to them soon, they should have enough air," Sheilan answered.

She climbed back to the crate's top and retrieved the pouch of dirt, securing it to her. Still in corporeal form, she started up the stairs and instructed Dari to follow her. The layout looked similar to the one on the Mo Chroidhe, so she continued toward the mid-ship, where a narrow spiral staircase connected to the next deck. When she reached the top, Dari materialized in his fierce, white horse form. Once again, she again set the pouch of Irish soil aside to return to the Celtic warrior manifestation, which had been so effective. This time, she tied the leather bag to her waist.

She grinned at him, and he began a clomping, noisy run down the corridor toward the bridge wall. A high-pitched, elongated whinny accompanied the romp. The 'booter on the bridge rushed to the clear wall and gaped open-mouthed at the huge horse in the corridor. Next, he noticed Sheilan, an attractive, partly unclothed young woman, who gazed at him provocatively. He may have been a thieving freebooter, yet he was also a man, and the vision stunned him for a few moments.

Now, Grania, Sheilan thought. *Here's your moment; fire now!*

Grania

ANXIETY MAKING HER FIDGETY, Grania tapped her fingers while she watched the power build in increments that weren't fast enough. Even though it had risen to almost eight five percent, they were running out of time.

"The shuttle's gone back," Liam's whisper came through her mobi. "We have a chance now. We're going to try to take these two that are left here."

The line went dead before she answered, "Wait for my signal..." They were going to make their move and hadn't heard her. She turned back to the targeting computer and positioned the cannon for the third time. She had it dead on to the bridge area where the pirate vessel had three cannons placed that could do more damage to the Mo Chroidhe's main deck.

So, she waited, gazing around her bridge and glancing back over her shoulder, wondering if something hovered behind her and watched right now. She expected the banshee to show up at any time. Could their situation get more desperate and dangerous than right now? *Our desperation mirrors the Dark Sea's, so where is the sidhe now? Had she confronted Liam and the others instead? Were they in more danger than she was?*

Feck, was she beginning to expect the creature to warn her every time danger threatened?

The power edged up toward ninety percent when Grania heard a voice in her head urging her to fire now. Listen to your intuition, she thought. It's enough power to do significant damage.

She had the target lined up and the button to fire sat under her fingertip. Now ... she felt it. Now! And she tapped the button.

The laser beam shot across the short distance to the 'booter ship and tore into it with a wide spatter blast. Her forward screen showed the damage when it hit. Even without analysis, she could see it took out the top cannon and tore into the nose cone of the vessel. A glance at her cannon showed she still had thirty-eight percent power on the weapon. She needed to cripple the ship if she could. She aimed lower for the ship's engines and tapped the button again. Lights on the bridge dimmed when the cannon drained more power than it had stored, but they flickered back and she watched the laser rip into the rear engines.

That finished it. She'd done all she could do from here. With a jerk, she sat back, pulled her personal weapon, a Lazlo 99—her mother's laser gun—and waited. Elation and pride bolstered her spirit; pride in fighting back the way she did, yet the questions lingered. Did I do enough? What is happening with my brothers? And most of all, what delayed the fecking Garda ship that should have arrived already?

Liam

LIAM MOVED ALONG THE edge of the engine room with silent caution. He reached the end, made the step across the open area along the back wall, and pressed against the cargo containers and worked his way toward the opening for the dock and the airlock. He pressed back, his weapon held ready and gazed across to where his brothers were now easing their way up the center aisle, using the crates for cover while they moved from the narrow spaces between them to the next narrow space.

Almost, he thought. Only a couple more to go and they'll be in position.

He froze when the 'booter's voice carried in the cargo bay. "That's it, Harhiman. There are some other valuable items in the cargo, but I doubt we have time for anymore."

"I agree, Cotoli. We've lost a lot of time, and I expect we'll have to do some fast running once we get this load over. I want you to do something for me. Go to the top deck and blow up their bridge. Kill that bitch up there. She's caused me enough trouble."

Liam sucked in his breath and moved back into a spot between the crates. He needed to get out of sight, despite the cramped space. Muscles tensed and his heart raced with the anger flooding his body at Harhiman's words. While his sister had sealed the bridge, would it be enough to stop an explosive?

Steps came toward him, and he lifted his weapon to fire, except a laser beam burst from the other side where Brendan and Rory were hiding. The laser blast only winged Harhiman, causing him to stagger a little, yet he swiveled to return fire. He heard Rory yell, "Get down!" And his brother opened fire.

Liam sprang out to confront the other booter, the one Harhiman had called "Cotoli", only to have the man plow into him in his attempt to dodge Rory's fire. Knocking Liam to one knee, Cotoli stumbled, turned, and lunged for Liam. He shoved back, scrambling to his feet.

"I'll handle this!" Harhiman shouted. "Get the girl!"

Following orders, Cotoli ran for the stairs to get to the next deck while Liam tried to get a clear shot at him. He fired when Cotoli started up the stairs, then the other man surged ahead, and the shot missed him.

Harhiman ran toward Rory and Brendan, firing his weapon in the general direction. Liam swung around, drawing an aim at Harhiman, who hadn't realized Liam was behind him. Liam fired, and the blast caught Harhiman's shoulder. His gun clattered to the floor, and he cried out and stumbled. Liam dashed ahead, using his fists to knock Harhiman to the ground, while Rory sprinted out to join him.

"How's Brendan?" Liam asked. He knelt on top of Harhiman, shoving his knee into his back, and Rory handed him a cargo strap to secure the trader's hands behind him. Liam pulled the excess strap down to the man's feet and wrapped his ankles, securing the lock on it, leaving Harhiman hogtied in an uncomfortable bow.

"He'll live. The blast burned his shoulder. Hurts like hell, but he's going for the med kit." Rory's voice wavered, but he seemed okay when Liam peeked at him.

Worried a little about Bren, but maybe more about their sister, Liam figured. "The other one's going after Grania. Watch this bastard, and I'll go help her. If he moves, shoot him or knock him out. Your choice."

He clambered to his feet and ran to the stairs after Cotoli. Right hand on the rail, he bounded onto the steps and that's when the Mo Chroidhe rocked, like it a wave had hit the ship. After a moment, he realized Grania must have fired the forward cannon. He grinned and jumped the last few steps up to the second deck. The next round caught him by surprise, and he gripped the rails tighter, riding the ship's sway.

When Liam reached the top deck and started toward the bridge, he saw Ace outside the door, threatening his sister. Through the transparent-steel door, he could see Grania sitting on the floor next to the weapons console with her gun pointed at the man.

"Open this door, girl! If you don't, I'll blow it all apart, including your whole bridge. You've surrendered the ship already, so why be uncooperative?"

"Because of that—" Grania waved her weapon toward the forward screen where there was a clear view of the 'booters' ship with damage to the bridge and engine deck leaving it hanging in space. Behind it, the long-awaited Garda ship approached at a fast clip. Then she looked smug and waved her weapon toward Liam, who had now slipped up behind Cotoli with his blaster almost in the man's back. "And because of him."

Liam shoved the blaster into him and growled, "Don't move. I wouldn't mind shooting you at all. You hurt my brother, and you threatened my sister. I'm sure you would have killed us all if you had the chance. So, make a move, why don't ya?"

"About time," Grania said. "Who's hurt?"

"Brendan has a minor burn. Enough to hurt, but he's okay."

Eyes narrowing, she glared at the freebooter and her voice chilled like ice. "You'll pay for this. Believe me." She addressed the computer to unlock the bridge doors. "What about the others?"

"Harhiman's down and Rory's watching him." Liam finished securing more cords on Cotoli's wrists, then shoved him into a storage room on the bridge and locked it.

"What about the shuttle?" she asked. "Is it coming back soon?"

"Feck!" Liam turned to make the trip down to the cargo bay again. "Tell Rory."

CHAPTER 37

Liam

"**NOT TO WORRY,**" **RORY** answered through the com. "Brendan changed the airlock code. They won't be able to dock."

Relieved, Liam took the time to check on Miz O'Cairn before heading back down to the cargo bay to help his brothers with the raiders, and they would need to open the docking bay for the Garda to board the ship.

He knocked on the cabin door and waited for an answer. When he didn't get one after the second knock and his hail to the old woman, Liam used the override code to enter the cabin. He scanned his surroundings upon entering, not wanting to startle O'Cairn if she was indisposed or just being cautious. Although he soon determined she wasn't in the cabin, he noticed the open trunk. A distinct musty odor like old dirt floated in the air and he saw the skew of the inner compartment. Peering into it, he noted the upper compartment held a few pieces of jewelry, a passport, five small pouches, a scarf, and an old-looking book.

Under the compartment, he found what had produced the distinct scent he'd detected; about half the trunk appeared to be dirt. The soil, a rich-looking dark brown color, felt moist to his touch, though not too wet. Curiosity piqued, he pushed a finger into it, feeling the texture, and noting that it seemed like coarse dirt, nothing more. Puzzled, he hesitated to put more than a finger into it. He searched the cabin for something he could use to probe the soil without risking his hands in case something was living in the dirt.

After a brief search, he found a thin wooden dowel in the model-making kits Rory kept in the cabin and used it to poke the soil in several places. It went in with little effort and came back out clean, except for a few particles of the soil clinging to the wood.

Nothing but dirt, Liam concluded. Why bring a trunk full of dirt onboard? He also noticed no woman's clothing in the cabin. Nothing hung in the closet other than a couple of Rory's shirts.

He thumbed the mobi. "Grania, the O'Cairn lady isn't in her cabin. There is something peculiar though. That trunk of hers is half-filled with musty-smelling dirt. There doesn't seem to be anything in it. Why do you suppose she would bring it with her?"

"Odd, indeed. I have some ideas about that, and I think I'll have to ask her when all this is over. Check the galley to see if she went in there."

In the background, Liam heard the Garda ship hailing Grania on the ship's main com. "Mo Chroidhe, this is Garda Peace. We'll be with you in about ten mites. Are you secure?"

"Aye, we are," his sister replied. She told him they contacted her as soon as they had come into range and already had the status of the fight. "We do need medical attention for some of our crew as soon as possible."

"Copy that, Mo Chroidhe. We're sending a shuttle to the free-booter ship and will dock directly with you."

"Copy that. We're ready for you."

After the Garda transmission ended, Liam said, "I'll look in the galley and send O'Cairn back to her cabin if she's there. After that, I'll hurry down to clean up in the bay."

The check in the galley came up empty as well. Wherever the old woman had gone, she wasn't in plain sight, and he had no more time to search for her. Liam ran back to the lower deck steps and slid most of the way down them. He paused to check on Nansi and found Brendan sitting with her.

"She's still out but seems to be breathing evenly." He'd covered her with a blanket for warmth. Liam popped his thumb up with approval.

Rory perched on a small container and kept his gun trained on Harhiman. The latter lay prone on the floor and had kept quiet until Liam walked in.

"What now, smartass?" he asked, venom oozing in his voice.

"Things are looking up, Mr. Harhiman." Liam squatted down beside him, bouncing on his heels, and his lips curved into a satisfied smirk. "You and your men will soon be the guests of Erinnua's law enforcement. I do believe you'll have an extended visit to one of their fine facilities. As for your ship, it's about to be impounded. I'm afraid my sister made a mess of it. She's always been a wee bit untidy."

He grinned at Rory, who wore a broad smile on his face. "Let's just dump this trash, shall we, Rory?" He crossed to the airlock to greet the authorities.

Sheilan

AT THE SAME TIME Grania and Liam fought off Harhiman and Cotoli, the two sidhe onboard the freebooter ship raised their own brand of ruckus, having a splendid time. Free to have fun, Dari galloped up and down the corridor, kicked at the bridge walls, whinnied, and snorted his heart out, much to the terror of the 'booter left on the bridge. Sheilan contributed some serious wailing and frightening expressions to the mix, which left the man wide-eyed and cowering at the aft section of the bridge. The glowing red eyes on both the horse and Sheilan, no doubt, added more spice to the drama. His gun hand shook with fear as he realized he couldn't shoot them through the walls, not that a laser could do any actual damage to an energy creature.

Sheilan barely glimpsed the incoming cannon's blast before it struck the bridge of the ship with a flash of light and a severe jolt that set it rocking. Although it didn't breach the ship's inner hull, it did significant damage. The impact threw the ship's pilot into the back wall, knocked him to the deck, and caused enough physical injury to leave him struggling to get to his feet.

Lucky man, Sheilan thought, since their distraction might have saved the scoundrel's life. Had he been at the front of the bridge, he might well have perished in the destruction caused by the blast. Parts of the ship's console were destroyed, and ceiling tiles, lights, and cables tumbled.

Eager to show off a little more, the puca raised his forelegs, shifted to his spirit form, and his ghostly appendages came down through the transpari-steel wall. Terrified, the 'booter opened fire on the spirit as soon as Dari entered the bridge. The laser had no effect on the sidhe but hit the wall behind him and burned deep gouges into it. Prancing and whipping his head wildly around, Dari tromped over the rear bridge area, forcing the cowering 'booter into a corner.

With the man crouched and covering his head with his arms in fear, Sheilan turned her attention to the port screen where she spotted the approaching ship. The Garda ship, Grania had called it. The authorities had finally arrived. She signaled Dari, who made one last pass of the bridge. With a smirk on her lips that looked more like a fearful grimace to the terrified man, she relished the sight of her companion romping around the bridge. A spirit in its full element was a delight to behold. However, their intent here wasn't to do damage but to provide a diversion, which they'd now accomplished.

Dari dematerialized, his energy-self arriving next to Sheilan in a blink. She opened the pouch at her waist to expose the soil of Eire, set it on the floor in the corridor, then let her form go back to energy. Diving into it, their tiny sparks merged into the dirt where they, and the soil, vanished, leaving behind an empty leather pouch.

Sidhe soil calls to sidhe soil.

The two travelers returned to the trunk through the ether, along with their travel medium.

"We are back," Sheilan said to Dari as her spirit-self floated out of the trunk in their cabin on the Mo Chroidhe. "Thanks be to the goddess, it works."

Grania

FROM THE TIME THE Garda arrived, everything came under their control. Grania hovered nearby as their medic administered first aid to Brendan and Nansi. A numbing, antiseptic spray took care of the minor shoulder burn, giving Bren instant relief. Nansi's head injury worried the medic, who transported her to the Garda ship where her medical facilities could diagnose and treat her.

The medic turned her attention to the captain, examining the cut on her head. After a couple of tests and a scan from her mobile device, the woman advised Grania she hadn't sustained a concussion. After cleaning and sealing the wound, she turned her attention to the bruises on Grania's leg, knee, and hip. They appeared dark and nasty looking, but the scans revealed no fractures in the bones, although the medic told her she'd be sore for a few days.

As Grania returned to the bridge, Liam relinquished the com to her, saying, "A tow ship's been dispatched to pull us into Tara Station. I think we're looking at some lengthy and expensive repairs ahead, Captain."

"Aye," she agreed and stared at the extensive damage on the bridge. Add in the repairs in the engine room and it would be a while before the ship could go out again. "At least, we got our cargo here and we can complete our deliveries. Insurance will cover a chunk of our repairs. I hear there's a bounty on the 'booters. That will help if we get it." Heck, she thought. We might break even on this run once everything is repaired and the insurance settled.

After the tow ship latched onto the Mo Chroidhe and started pulling them at one-quarter speed toward the station, Grania turned the com over to Rory and retreated to the galley. A dull pain pulsed through her head and her stomach rumbled, reminding her she had not eaten before the attack, and it had been a long, wearying day.

With a cup of tea and a pair of scones, she sat and ate, thinking about everything that had happened. What might she have missed that she could have been detected earlier? Although she'd had clues in her dreams, she didn't understand them until she learned Harhiman was smuggling the targassium crystals. She didn't puzzle them out, connect the dots, or trust her instincts, as Nansi reminded her so often. Despite her reservations, she took on passengers. If she hadn't, perhaps the entire trip would have turned out differently. Then again, perhaps they would never have made it out of the Dark Sea. Fate could be as fickle as the blooming fairies. Speaking of which, it seemed they had a banshee, and conceivably more, on the ship.

Before he left, the Garda investigator had told her the two 'booters, who had taken the shuttle back, had been found locked in a crate, claiming a shape-changing monster and a giant horse had forced them into it. The freebooter ship's pilot had babbled about a white animal out of a nightmare threatening him. The investigator asked if she knew anything about it and all she could do was shake her head.

Alone now, she tapped her tablet and stared at the image displayed on it of an old woodcut drawing of a huge white horse, rearing into the air and by it stood an old woman with a shawl wrapped around her; both looked terrifying. The writing on it read, "The bean sidhe with her companion puca." When she'd looked up O'Cairn in the reference computer, the only thing that came up was in relation to a cairn being a pile of stones under which a body was usually buried. Who, then, was Moira O'Cairn? Or maybe the better question was, what was she?

Sheilan

SHEILAN EXPECTED THE VISIT from Grania, anticipating it since she returned to the ship. With the rumors of what had happened on the freebooters' ship, the lass must have put two and two together and come up with an answer that was likely to be close to the truth. So, when Grania knocked on the cabin door, she was ready for her.

After the courtesies were exchanged, the captain got to the point. "I have been wondering a few things about you. There are things that don't match up and yet the other possibility is crazy. But if the facts don't fit and the improbable does, then maybe it's not so improbable."

Sheilan sat on the lid of the trunk and motioned for Grania to sit as well.

She took the desk chair.

"Go on then, Captain. Ask me what you will, and I shall answer you truthfully."

"I've done some checking on you. First, you don't seem to exist. The name O'Cairn is not on any birth certificates on Earth, and the only reference I can find is to a stone grave or marker. Second, in looking at the cabin usage, it appears you ate very little over these many days that you've been onboard. A few cups of tea and a scone now and then, except for the few times you dined at my table, eating little to keep a body alive. Third,—" She paused and tapped the third finger on her right hand. "--the jump pod usage log shows it was hardly used at all, except when Vilnius was in it. You never used it, did you?"

Sheilan shook her head. "And what does all of this lead you to wonder?"

"Nansi told me about a spirit from Ireland that was a harbinger of death. That spirit appeared on my ship three times to warn me of fatal danger. Yet, it didn't show up when we were in the fight with the freebooters. Instead, there was a frightening pair of spirits on the pirate's ship, just when I needed a distraction before I fired on them. The descriptions led me to believe it might be this..." Grania tapped her tablet's page to the image she'd looked at earlier. Sheilan leaned forward to look.

"Very strange, wouldn't you say? Did you have anything to do with it? And what is this box of dirt that you're guarding?"

"If you are asking if the spirits on the bridge of those thievin' scoundrels were a banshee and a puca, the answer is yes. Did I have something to do with it? Yes. The dirt in this trunk is soil from my homeland. I wish to put it in the ground in my new land as a tie to my birthplace."

An almost smile parted Grania's lips. "It appears I need to ask the right questions to get the whole truth. Are you a banshee?"

"Some call me that," she replied. "I am actually a sidhe and in my language, it is b'ean Sheilan. My name is Sheilan. I was the first, and I am an eternal spirit."

Grania sat silent, a stunned expression on her face reflecting the disbelief this confirmation brought. Even though she'd suspected it, being confronted with it, she wanted to deny it. She wet her lips and asked, "How is this possible?"

"Come now, lass. In all your travels, have you never encountered things that are not like you? Have you not looked at worlds different from your own, so extraordinary that for a moment, you thought they could not exist? Yet the evidence was in front of your eyes. I am an energy form, and I can use my energy to shapeshift and create illusions that appear solid and real."

To offer evidence, Sheilan shifted gradually, within a few seconds, from the old woman to her younger version. The transformation seemed like a cinema trick as her face grew less wrinkled, narrowing and smoothing into the beautiful young woman she preferred to wear. The elderly body became slimmer and straighter, the youth in the form coming through to complete the illusion.

Wide-eyed, Grania watched the shift, a realization dawning in her eyes. "I've seen this woman before! On Zabrowski Station and again on Pelanan. That was you! And you're also the wraith washing off the blood of the dead that appeared on the bridge, aren't you?"

Sheilan lowered her head in a silent acknowledgment.

"You pointed out the danger in the slipstream, making sure that I saw it. Why? I don't understand. If you're the bringer of death, why did you do it?"

As she smiled, the impish look on her face suggested she was explaining something to a child. "I am not the bringer of death. I am a messenger. 'Tis not my task to end life, only to advise it may be coming soon or it has occurred. My appearance was a warning of something which might have occurred if you had not acted quickly and correctly. I simply tried to give you an adequate prediction. It was not yet your time."

"So, you saved me. All of us."

"I pointed out the danger. It was a stretch of what I am allowed to do, and it may cause me trouble down the line, but I will deal with it."

Grania frowned, a wrinkle of consternation making a furrow between her brows. "I don't understand."

"And it is not meant for you to understand everything, Grania O'Ceagan. Only know that you come from a very old line of Irish nobility. It is not only your father's line for your mother's pedigree was very strong on the west coast of Ireland. Not all families were graced with a bean sheilan."

"When you said you needed to get to Erinnua to your family, it was my family you were referring to, wasn't it? You knew my Great Aunt Moira and took her identity to travel. Did you kill her?"

"No, my dear girl. I told you I do not bring death. 'Tis true I was with her when she died, and I sang her life song when she passed. But I was not the cause of her death. She was the last of the bloodline on Earth, so I needed to come to Erinnua to serve my function. 'Twas fate your ship was the only one for a week going there."

Grania stood and paced the narrow width of the cabin, her arms wrapped over her chest. "And yet, you didn't appear to me on the bridge this last time when it seemed like we might be killed so easily. Why not?"

"I did not get a sense of it being deadly. I repeat, it was not your time, although I did ensure you had an advantage with the thieves."

"The spirits on the ship. You and a puca."

"Indeed. Nevertheless, mark my words that the time will come when I do come to you to announce your death or the death of a family member. It is my purpose."

"And the puca? Is it on my ship also."

"Like me, he is an energy sidhe, but of a different nature. Yes, he travels with me."

Grania's heart thudded in her chest as she came to a standstill, her brow furrowed and lips pressed together in a thin line. She leaned forward, the intensity of her stare a warning and a question rolled into one. "I don't know if you're a blessing or a curse to my family," she said, the weight of each word hanging between them. "I hope you won't be appearing on my ship every time you perceive danger."

Unruffled, Sheilan replied, "A fair enough request, Captain. But I will tell you this, you have the strength and the mettle of your sea captain ancestor."

Grania's expression softened, the praise filling her with joy and a sense of worth with the sidhe's pronouncement. In a kinder tone, she said, "Thank you for that. Still, I believe you have a problem. You have traveled on an expired passport and my great-aunt is listed as dead. You won't be able to get off at Tara using it."

Sheilan feigned a sigh. "Ah, well, that is a bit of a hiccup, I guess. If I must be dead, then I will be. You've apparently transported your dead great aunt home to her family. Now, I have a small favor to ask , if you will grant me something for my assistance in these travels?"

EPILOGUE

Epilogue

GRANIA WALKED ALONGSIDE HER great-grandfather through the fields behind their family's elegant, two-story mansion. The house, a testament to their clan's legacy, boasted eight bedrooms, seven bathrooms, and two family rooms—one for visiting, the other for entertainment. The kitchen and dining area occupied one wing, while the living room and parlor filled the opposite end. Seamus O'Ceagan, or "Gramps" as the family affectionately called him, had his own office in a separate building at the far end of the estate.

The O'Ceagan lands stretched wide around them, originally homesteaded by her great-great-grandfather when he first arrived on Erinnua. The planet, reminiscent of Ireland in its wild beauty, thrived under the red sun of Dragon Hold, casting the landscape in shades of bluish-purple rather than green. Though much of the terrain remained untamed and hostile, humanity had carved out a safe haven amidst its dangers.

"So, you brought your Aunt Moira here? Is she in the trunk you had delivered?" Seamus asked.

"Not all of her. She had a proper burial on Earth, I believe, even if no family was there. A friend brought some of her ashes, along with a few keepsakes, so she could rest here with us."

"She needed an entire trunk for that?" Seamus arched a skeptical brow.

"Well, no." Grania hesitated. "There's also some dirt from Ireland in it—so her remains would still be in proper Irish soil."

He grunted, half amused. "Now that sounds like the old lady." He gestured toward the hillside. "And you think this spot, well away from the house, is the right place?"

From the crest of the gentle slope, Grania surveyed the breathtaking panorama. Fields of lavender vegetation rippled across the hillside, their color deepened by the crimson-tinged sunlight. Below, the Chromalight Sea shimmered, shifting hues of blue, pink, and gold in the afternoon light.

She inhaled the heady scent of wild berry blossoms and nodded. "Aye, I do. It reminds me of the Wicklow Hills—well, almost."

Seamus eyed her, as if questioning her sanity, then shrugged. "Very well. We'll prepare the ground and bring her trunk here. Then we'll give her a proper funeral—and a wake after. T'will be a fine occasion."

Relieved, Grania turned her gaze back to the distant hills, where deep purple mountains formed a crescent on the horizon. A nearby fíonmara tree, its thick branches sheltering the land below, bore sweet fruit in the warm season. As a child, she had played beneath that very tree. She hoped Sheilan and her púca would approve of the chosen site.

THREE DAYS LATER, THE family gathered for Moira's funeral. Sheilan assured Grania that some of Moira's remains had mingled with the soil, easing her guilt over the ruse. Convincing Gramps to open the trunk had been trickier; he had grumbled about her being "daft" but eventually relented, muttering that it hardly mattered anyway.

The wake turned into a grand affair, brimming with music and laughter. Tales of Moira—her generosity, her sharp tongue, her undeniable presence—filled the house. Gramps shared stories of his departed sister, painting a vivid picture of the woman whose rosary now rested in Grania's pocket. As she ran her fingers over the smooth stones, she wished she had known her great-aunt in life.

Gramps approached, a twinkle in his eye. "'Tis a fine wake, isn't it?"

Grania smiled, wondering if Sheilan watched in her spirit form.

Then he leaned in and lowered his voice. "What's this about a banshee on the ship?"

"What?" She stiffened. She had asked the crew to keep quiet about that—for now.

"Nansi said there was a banshee, wailing and washing her hands."

Grania forced a chuckle. "Oh, you know Nansi. There was a bit of light, a noise in the engine room—she mistook it for a ghost. It was nothing."

Seamus caught her arm, pulling her closer. "Don't scoff at these things, Nia. The family has a banshee. Always has. I saw her once when I was a child. A terrifying sight, but beautiful, too. They serve their purpose. One day, she'll come for me." He chuckled. "I hope it's the lovely one and not the old hag."

Speechless, Grania watched as he turned away, sweeping Great-Grandma into a lively dance.

Slipping out the back door, she made her way up the moonlit hill. The oblong shadow of Boru's Relic crossed the sky, its orbit faster than the moon's.

She stopped before the newly completed grave. The Irish soil had merged with Erinnua's, and a small white fence framed the site. A temporary wooden cross bore Moira's name, awaiting the engraved perma-stone Celtic cross that would soon replace it.

"Sheilan?" Grania called softly. She wasn't sure if the spirit lingered here. The sidhe were tied to the land, but she still didn't fully understand the nature of their existence.

A faint whinny answered her. A short distance away, a small white horse pranced, its hooves barely touching the earth.

A puca.

A moment later, Sheilan appeared—young, radiant, and eerily real despite her ghostly form.

"Is this suitable, Bean Sheilan?" Grania asked, gesturing to the view.

Sheilan's lips curled into a smile. "It is. Quite splendid, in fact. My thanks. But I have one more request."

Grania's stomach tightened. "What is it?"

"Will you and your brothers always carry a small pouch of this soil with you, wherever you travel? It will allow me instant access to each of you."

Grania blinked. "You want me to carry around a pouch of dirt?"

Sheilan's grin widened. "Just a tiny one. If your twice-great-grandfather had carried some of the Irish homestead soil with him when he left for Erinnua, I wouldn't have had to stow away on your ship."

Grania smirked. "Perhaps it's for the best he didn't. Without you, we might never have escaped the Dark Sea. The freebooters could have taken the Mo Chroidhe—and all of us with it."

"Perhaps." Sheilan inclined her head. "Until next we meet, Grania O'Ceagan."

Then, as easily as they had arrived, she and the puca vanished. When she glanced at the plot, four little pouches filled with soil rested on top.

A sudden chill crept over Grania's skin. She worried how this would play out in the long run but conceded the banshee delivered both positive and negative actions. Even though they worked hard to bring the Mo Chroidhe home this last trip, the whole crew owed both the sidhe a mighty debt. A family debt.

Picking up the pouches, she turned back toward the house.

For better or worse, I have brought the banshee home.

And she prayed she had done the right thing.

The Adventures continue in *Outer RIm*, the second book of the **O'Ceagan Saga** and in a related book *In Strange Waters*

From Lillian: I hope you enjoyed this fanciful tale. If you liked it, please consider leaving a review at whichever marketplace where you acquired a copy. Reviews are manna from Heaven for an independent writer, so it would mean a great deal to me as well as possibly pointing other readers toward it. Thank you.

AFTERWORD

ABOUT THE BOOK

The seeds of the idea for O'Ceagan's Legacy came into my mind many years ago and grew slowly over at least two decades. At one point, I started the story as a screenplay, but didn't progress too far on it. In 2014, I began writing it as a novel and completed it in October, 2014, just before I wrote Funeral Singer: A Song for Marielle, which I edited and published first before turning again to this book.

It's a special book to me as I wanted to capture all the love and magic of the Irish people and the island itself in the characters, who have long been generational expatriates of their homeland, yet still carry so much of the essence of the country. I hope this comes through in the story along with the fanciful creatures.

The bean sidhe or banshee and puca or pooka are part of Celtic folklore, although not exclusive to them. While these creatures of myth may seem only tales, I have talked to several people from the British Isles, who either claim to have seen or heard one or knew people who did. None were threatened directly by the spirit, but all knew that it heralded a death in the family. Is it a case of the suggestion of the spirit creating an illusion that happens to coincide with a death event or is there something more to it?

As with many science fiction and fantasy novels, this book uses several words and terms that are created for the book. Here's a short list of the ones I either created for the story or are already used but not common.

Bean Sheilan is a similar name to the bean sidhe, but presumes a race of spirits in a parallel dimension.

Chrono – chronometer, a watch

Com, mobicom, comlink all refer to the communications devices the crew uses on the ship.

Lev-dolly is a levitation dolly used to transport goods. It rises above the floor on a cushion of air and moves automatically making it easier for people to move large items.

Perma-logs are permanent logs, similar to ceramic logs that can burn fuel to give the illusion of wood burning in a fireplace.

Perma-thatch is a synthetic thatching material for roofing houses that is fire resistant and doesn't need replacing frequently.

Transpari-steel is transparent steel. I am not sure if the term has been used before, but I couldn't find a reference for it although it could have been in a Star Trek film.

Lillian Wolfe, March 2016/2025

AFTERWORD

FROM THE AUTHOR

Thanks for reading my book. I hope you've enjoyed the characters and the story. For me, as an author, the best reward is getting feedback from the readers, whether it is directly to me via email, via my blog, or as an honest review posted to your book source.

Comments from readers are the best incentive to continue writing. While I love writing and telling stories, it encourages me on to the next story when I hear from people that they like my stories or my characters and want to read more about them.

Even a not-so-good review can be beneficial to me as it might point out a weak area in my writing that I can improve on.

So, if you've enjoyed the book, please let me and other readers know by reviewing it or contacting me. Or both!

Email: LillianWolfe.author@gmail.com

You can also go to my web site:

www.LillianWolfe.online

If you want to know more my books and when they will be released, sign up to be notified when a new blog is posted.

Also, it's not a secret that Lillian Wolfe is my pen name for Sci-Fi Fantasy and Urban fantasy, although I think that's becoming Magical Realism now. But if you'd like to read more about all my books and some interesting articles, you can subscribe to my Substack newsletter/blog at

https://reneaverett.substack.com/
and/or follow me on BlueSky Social at:
@renea-author.bsky.social
Thanks and keep reading! Rene/Lily

ABOUT THE AUTHOR

ABOUT LILLIAN I. WOLFE

Lillian I. Wolfe (yes, it's a pen name, although there's a connection) has been writing since she first figured out how to hold a pencil, spinning stories from the age of ten and completing her first novel by seventeen. (That one remains safely hidden in the vault.) Since then, she's written everything from fan fiction to short stories, novels, training manuals, (because even writers need to pay the bills). and newsletters. Basically, if it involves words, she's probably tried it.

Her first published novel, *Funeral Singer: A Song for Marielle*, kicked off a suspenseful supernatural series following Gillian Foster, a musician with the inconvenient ability to communicate with lingering spirits. But before that, she penned *O'Ceagan's Legacy*, a science fiction fantasy adventure that launched her into the stars—though it waited patiently for publication. Lillian adores all kinds of fiction, but fantasy, urban fantasy, and mystery hold a special place in her heart. She's eternally grateful for the invention of the computer—because manual typewriters, while charming in theory, are an absolute nightmare in practice. This revision marks the 10-year anniversary of it being written.

She currently resides in northern Nevada with her best friend of over thirty years, three cats who tolerate her presence, and a dog who pretends not to be under feline rule. When she's not writing, she's either reading, strumming her guitar, daydreaming about her next story, or plotting ways to squeeze extra hours into the day. She is a proud member of the High Sierra Writers Group.

You can connect with Lillian through her web site:
https://www.lillianwolfe.online/
Or email her at:
lillianwolfe.author@gmail.com

Her real identity is on Substack at:
https://reneaverett.substack.com/

ALSO BY

Other Books by Lillian I. Wolfe

In this series, the O'Ceagan Saga:

O'Ceagan's Legacy
In Strange Waters
Outer Rim

Funeral Singer Series:

A Song of Innocence

A Song of Retribution
A Song of Betrayal
A Song of Forgiveness
A Song of Redemption

Time Threads Series

Time Walker
Splintered Time

READ ON FOR TEASERS FROM
In Strange Waters AND *Outer Rim*

IN STRANGE WATERS

IN STRANGE WATERS

CHAPTER 1

A New World to Explore

PEEKING THROUGH A BREAK in the concealing growth of something resembling an Earth shrub, Dari n'a dearga sniffed the off-putting alien order of the plant and concluded it didn't smell like the ones he knew. From what he'd seen and sniffed so far on this new world he was beginning calling home, none of vegetation did.

But for now, he heard girlish giggles growing louder as his marks made their way down the dirt path that ran through the forest toward the town just on the other side. Chattering as they walked, the pair of young voices carried the same conversation he'd heard thousands of girls utter over the centuries. Boys. It was always about boys with the young lasses. Although for a period there, they'd talked about other girls almost as much. In this sense, life with the humans on Erinnua resembled life back in Ireland.

For this encounter, he'd chosen his young lad form, one that he'd taken from a mid-teen boy back in the eighth century. When boy had charmed him with his attitude and bravado against a puca, he'd spared his life, but taken enough of his flesh to record the form. In this guise, he presented a handsome face dusted with a sprinkling of freckles and capped with dark, reddish-brown hair. Those features always proved attractive to young ladies.

As the girls drew near, he stepped out on the pathway and strolled toward them, looking as if he had been approaching all along. Giving them a big grin that made his sea-blue eyes sparkle, he greeted them with charm and enthusiasm. "Bedad, if it isn't two of the loveliest colleens I am having the pleasure to see on this stroll. 'Tis just my good fortune to be on the same path this glorious day."

True to form, the lasses giggled, and the ginger-haired girl blushed, coloring her cheeks a fetching dark pink. The other girl, a saucy-looking blond, maintained her composure a little better but smiled back at him. Just beginning to bud out, the rounded bumps on her chest pushed out against her blouse like an inviting pair of small oranges. Not that Dari cared much about that sort of thing, not even in this form.

"You speak rather oddly," she said, a look of curiosity in her huge gray eyes. "You're not from around here, are you?"

He shook his head. "Nay, I have only just arrived in the past few days, and I am still trying to find me way around the area. My name is Dari."

"Well, welcome to the area then. I'm Katy, and this is Maureen." She indicated the shy redhead, who peered more at the ground that at him. "Do you live near here, Dari?"

"I do. Fairly close."

"Then are you enrolled at the town study hall? We've just come from there." She indicated an electronic tablet that she held in her hand as if it explained the whole thing.

"Study hall? Is that like a school or something?" he asked, perplexed by the question.

"Don't you have them where you came from?" Maureen asked, a look of surprise crossing her face along with another blush.

"Well, there were schools and home education and all that," he replied. "But I didn't go."

"You didn't?" Katy asked. "But why not?"

"Because," he replied with a wicked laugh, "I am already more educated than you will ever be." With that, his laugh grew into a sound that sounded more like a whinny, and he vanished into thin air.

Shocked, the girls shrieked and ran down the path as fast as they could as the now invisible puca's laugh lingered in the air.

Well, those two will have a fine story to tell their friends, he thought, satisfied with his little prank. 'Twas his first encounter with the humans on the planet. To be honest, he wasn't sure if they even knew what he was.

Back in Ireland, everyone still knew about pucas, but here in a world millions of miles from Earth, he wasn't sure the people even knew much about the old legends let alone his kind. He'd come to the planet with the bean sidhe, Sheilan, on a cargo ship, the Mo Croidhe, that happened to be owned by the very family she had been seeking. While the two of them might have the means to return to Ireland using soil travel, they hadn't tried it out yet. Immortal or not, they were both a little hesitant to trust the travel over such a long distance, and neither was keen to end up stuck in the ether between worlds.

But soon, he would like to return to make sure he could get back and to visit some of his puca friends to boast a bit. Then he worried for a moment or two that if he traveled through, would he be able to return again through the soil connection? It was more complicated than his puca brain could handle.

Materializing back into a corporeal form as a white Irish Hobby pony, Dari wandered farther down the path in the direction the girls had fled. While the pony was a splendid form in Ireland, he'd quickly learned that horses were non-existent on Erinnua. Either they didn't survive the new land, or the settlers didn't bring them with them.

From what he'd seen, only a few life forms from Earth seemed to thrive here. He'd seen something that resembled a badger, a fox, a couple of rats, and a whole bunch of odd-looking animals that might have been native to the planet. One, in particular, looked like a boar, only much larger with a bluish coat and a longer snout, plus two wicked-looking horns at the side of its head. Grunting a warning at him, the beast dashed away before Dari could study it for long.

To tell the truth, he didn't think this New Ireland felt much like the old sod even though it flourished with lush vegetation enough to remind him of the green hills. Little by little, even the purplish tinted colors on the planet looked more normal to him. But the smell and the taste lacked a great deal of the fresh, sweetness of home.

As he drew near the town, he left the path and made his way to the edge of the forest where he could get a good view. A decent-sized place with dozens of buildings and streets, the town was larger than many of the villages back home but much smaller than a city. He wondered what people called it and how friendly and Irish-like these immigrants might be. Would they be good storytellers or drinking companions? Would they gather at the pub for an evening of song? Along with missing his companions, he also missed the way of life. Maybe later he'd change back to his youth visage and explore, but for now, he wanted to go somewhere else.

The swimming-pool-sized, roughly oval, pond had attracted his attention a couple of days earlier, which brought him back to study it some more. So far, he'd found the water to be different from Earth's, a little bitter to his taste, and it felt heavier and harder to move in. He'd only waded in once, so he thought he'd try again in his horse form. While he had a water-horse-body option as well, he felt the pond wasn't deep enough for him to use it.

Dari stepped into the water, feeling the cool liquid around his legs as his hooves sank into the gritty sand at the bottom. This much felt familiar although still a bit sluggish as he moved through it. He waded out as the water got deeper until he was submerged to almost the top of his back and the liquid sloshed against him. Apart from the color being more purple than blue, the heaviness, and that bitter taste, the liquid surrounding him resembled Earth's lakes. For all that, he observed that the pond seemed to have no life in it apart from a few types of odd-looking vegetation that he couldn't identify as anything that resembled water weeds back home.

He ducked his head below the water, seeing a yellow and red plant with paddles on the end that almost looked like a cactus, but lacking any mouth-injuring thorns. He nudged it with his nose then took a tentative bite and spat it out almost immediately. Extremely bitter and nasty. The horse side did not approve. A fern-looking plant waved at him as the water rolled against it, and he tried a bite of one of the tips.

Popping his head back out, he sputtered and dropped the clump of mushy, icky stuff back into the pond. No wonder no fish swam in the water here. Everything in it tasted terrible.

Wait. What was that?

Out of his horsey eye, he spotted a dart of movement near the fern things and ducked his head back underneath. A little cluster of small triangular fish darted around the ferns, then scurried back into them. Barely larger than tadpoles, they seemed to have only one eye in the middle of their bodies. Peculiar, but at least, indicative of some kind of life.

Wading back out, he trod his way to the top of the rise and gazed out toward the sea. Just below him, the O'Ceagan estate, a large farm where Sheilan's family lived, spread out for miles. For their help on the ship when space pirates with the intent of stealing the cargo nearly destroyed it, the O'Ceagan had given the bean sidhe a small parcel of land near the place where Dari now stood.

IN STRANGE WATERS is **available on Amazon** and other book sites.

OUTER RIM

O'Ceagan Saga Book Two

Follow Grania O'Ceagan and her crew on their next BIG adventure in *Outer Rim*!

A routine cargo run takes an unexpected turn when Captain Grania O'Ceagan is tasked with delivering a young, unwilling bride-to-be to Earth—and Ireland—for an arranged marriage. Her familiar run turns into a high-stakes mission when the crew of *Mo Chroíde* is strong-armed into making a perilous delivery to Desolation, a remote planet on the galaxy's edge. The cargo? Highly classified. The risks? Astronomical. With a Planetary Provisional Government agent watching their every move, rivals closing in, and their tight deadline slipping away, Grania must push her ship—and her crew—to the limit. But on the Outer Rim, trust is a rare commodity, and survival is never guaranteed.

OUTER RIM

PART ONE

An Errand to Earth

CHAPTER ONE

GRANIA STOPPED AT A transparisteel window facing her ship, which was docked at Tara Station. She gazed at the blow-fish-like shape of the long-haul freighter and noted the new patches on the starboard side. Workmen had completed the repairs to it the day before, replacing panels on the exterior and remodeling part of the interior that had taken quite a bit of damage in the freebooter attack she and her crew had faced thirty-eight days earlier. She was itching to get back onboard and back into space.

She turned to go to the entry ramp, pausing a moment to observe a conveyor belt pushing several large crates along the loading dock to the ship's cargo hold. She knew her brothers, Liam and Rory, were already down there settling the containers.

Things are going to be all right. She repeated that a couple of times as she boarded the ship and took the circular stairs to the bridge level. Pulling a deep breath, she keyed the door open and stepped inside. Her eyes moved from the navigation console to the communications station, continuing to the captain's chair. Her place now. Captain Grania O'Ceagan of the Mo Chroidhe out of Erinnua.

Her granda had officially handed the ship over to her, putting her in charge of this aspect of the family business. Frankly, she questioned her own competence. She'd been badly shaken by the events, and her confidence had taken a hard blow. Yet, Granda thought she was ready to handle it. Then again, he'd also sent an old mate of his on this trip, ostensibly for a final jaunt before the man retired to his farm life on the planet. Teghan O'Toole would be acting as her first officer, replacing Nansi. Her friend and long-time ship's mate had decided to remain grounded for a while longer. She, too, had been badly shaken by the previous trip.

GRANIA'S THROAT TIGHTENED AS she swallowed her nerves and checked out the new captain's console. The upgrades would be significant, not that she'd found anything wrong with the old one. She sank into the cushioned seat and flipped on the cameras, lifting her eyes to the screens on the back and side walls where the activity in and around the ship was displayed. As she flipped through the cameras, the images looked clear and well-defined. Her computer came up at her command, so she started a confirmation run to ensure everything checked out.

"Permission to come aboard, Captain?"

Grania turned her head to the familiar voice and smiled. "Granted. Glad you're here, Brendan."

Her youngest brother grinned as he stepped onto the bridge and gazed around. "Ya wouldn't know it had been blasted so badly, would ya?"

"The workers did a good job. Check out your station."

He nodded, a dark lock of his hair falling onto his forehead, and settled in at navigation, pressing buttons and bringing the system online. Her brother began charting the course for their planned stops on this trading trip. They'd be heading to Cardyff first, then out to Valhalla before heading toward Earth.

Grania spotted a light flashing on the communications console and hurried over to answer. She hoped for news from Vilnius about his pending transfer, but the call came from Tara Station control. "You are cleared to depart in one-hundred-twenty mites," the crisp voice of the station computer informed her.

"Acknowledged," she replied. Not much longer before they'd be taking their shakedown run. She glanced at the camera feed from the entry ramp and saw O'Toole starting to board. His wiry frame made him look taller than he actually was, but his step bounced with energy as he took the steps up.

Granda had told her the man had gotten engaged to a Bantry woman, so he planned this voyage as his last. Within two more mites, O'Toole was at the bridge entry, asking to come aboard. His pack was slung over his back as he greeted her.

"Tis kind of ye to allow me this trip, Cap'n. It means a lot to me." Wrinkles around his eyes and mouth revealed his age as he smiled, but he looked fit.

"Ah, you're doing me a favor, Mister O'Toole. My granda said you're one of the best second officers he knew, and since I am short mine this trip, it's glad I am to have you aboard."

"And where might I stow me things?" He shifted his pack part-way off his back.

"I'll show you to the first officer's cabin. It's on this same deck, so you're close to the bridge." He followed her as she led him to her old cabin mid-way to the aft of the ship and just past the stairwell. She'd cleaned her things out of it a few days earlier, but it still felt odd to be handing it over to someone else.

She opened the sliding door and ushered him inside the small but comfortable space. As ship quarters went, it was a decent size and had a well-maintained jump pod that doubled as a bed.

O'Toole gazed around it and nodded. "'Tis nice enough. T'will do fine, thank ye. I'll just get settled then and meet you back on the bridge if that's all right."

"It is. Let me know if you need anything." Grania stepped out and headed back down the corridor toward the bridge. She'd relocated her own things into the captain's cabin at the nose of the ship, a much larger space.

By the time she got back, Rory had come in and was checking out the communication system, flipping switches and turning dials to pull in different messages across the ship.

"How's the cargo looking, Rory?" Grania took her place and turned her chair to face her middle brother.

"Good. We have almost a full load with only two big crates leaving at Cardyff, and I show four coming onboard there. I hear we have passengers on this trip."

"You heard right. We should have a young lady showing up anytime now, and we're picking up two fellows on Cardyff. All are heading to Earth." She glanced at the entry monitor as she spoke, wondering where their passenger might be.

"I'm hoping they aren't like our last ones." Rory lifted his eyebrows as he peeked at her.

"I don't think they will be." Their last passengers had been a banshee and a puca, along with a trader who turned out to be one of the freebooters, setting up the attack on them. For all that, the man had given them a targassium crystal for power, saving both the ship and their lives when they'd been thrown into the Dark Sea. That was an experience she hoped to never repeat.

"Ah, I think Dari is coming on this trip." Brendan looked up from his console.

"Dari? He didn't say anything to me about it."

"He's feeling lonely since Sheilan hasn't returned yet and thought he might want the chance to see other places."

Surprised, Grania strolled over to Brendan's console. "Is he on board?"

Brendan shrugged. "I don't know. He's a puca. How can you tell when an energy being is around?"

"When did he tell you this?" Grania's suspicions rose. Ever since the puca had acquired Brendan's genetic pattern, she wasn't sure if she actually spoke to Brendan or Dari.

"Yesterday," he answered. "I don't know for sure if he means it. But if he did, would it be a problem? I mean, he doesn't eat or need a cabin."

"Who said he doesn't eat?" Rory asked, a big grin on his face. "I recall him finishing off a tray of cakes at the house."

"No matter," Grania stepped between them, heading back to her console. "If he wants to come along, he needs to talk to me. Although, he might provide an extra pair of hands if we need them. We can make him work for his passage."

"I'd like to see—" Rory cut off mid-sentence as he pressed his headset to his ear and listened intently. "Call coming in from Zabrowski Station for you, Nia."

Zabrowski? Vilnius. She nodded and went to her station to pick it up.

"Hello, love," the deep baritone voice said as soon as she answered. "I hear you're taking your ship out soon."

"Indeed, I am. And what about you? I was expecting some news before this." She held her breath, anxious for the reply.

"Well, that's what I'm calling about. My transfer request has been delayed, Nia. Master Hartman has suffered health problems and won't be able to return to work for a while, if at all."

"Oh, no. What happened?" Her heart sank. Hartman was a good friend of her granda. He'd been station master at Zabrowski even before she'd started working the space routes.

"Heart attack. A bad one. The surgeon on the station barely got to him in time, but he may require a replacement. Even then, it could be a long time before he can return."

"So, what does this mean for your transfer?"

"For now, I can't leave the station since I was next in line; the agency wants me to stay until they know for sure if they will retire Hartman. This has been a big shock for me. He's a good friend, and I'm just grateful he didn't die on the spot."

"Oh, Vilnius. I'm sorry. I wasn't thinking about how close you were to him. Of course, it's a shock to me, too. I'll have to tell Granda. I'm just..." Her voice died. What could she say? She was disappointed, but he'd nearly lost a friend. Besides, she was getting ready to pull out and would be heading to Earth's station within a few days anyway.

"I know it's a letdown for you, but I'll see you when you get to the station. Maybe I'll have news by then. I just want to say safe travels, and I love you."

"Love you as well." Her voice caught a little as she ended the call.

"Bad news?" Rory asked.

Her face must have shown her disappointment. Grania straightened her back. "Yeah, the station master had a heart attack. Vilnius isn't transferring here yet."

"Sorry, Nia," Brendan said quietly.

She shrugged. "It's okay. Meanwhile, we have a ship to get ready to pull out in about fifty-two mites. Where is our passenger?"

"I think I see her coming if that reluctant girl being escorted toward our ramp is the one." He pointed to the screen showing the entry where a young woman was practically dragged by a middle-aged man and a woman. Each held an arm, pulling the girl along, and she clearly didn't want to come.

"Oh, tarnation. We have a recalcitrant passenger for this trip. I'm going down to meet them." Grania sprang to her feet and hurried down the steps to the entry ramp, arriving just as the couple with their rebellious offspring reached the boarding ramp.

"I'm Captain O'Ceagan. Is this Ms. Hennessy? We've been expecting you."

Dark blue eyes shot up to meet Grania's, a glare radiating from them and a scowl on her lips. The girl jerked her arms in her parents, she presumed, grip.

"It is," the man answered. "Our daughter is less than pleased to be making this trip, but she is betrothed to a man in Ireland on Earth."

"I don't want to marry some farmer I never met," the girl wailed. "This is barbaric."

"Nonsense." The woman tried to smile at Grania while attempting to calm her daughter. "It's a good match, and Callum is not a farmer, Orla."

"Shall we just bring her on board?" Mr. Hennessy asked.

"Ah, yes. Follow me to her cabin so she can get settled in." Grania turned and started up the ramp as Hennessy caught up with her and, under his breath, asked, "Is there a lock on the door?"

Grania held her shock in, but she seethed inside. *What are they doing to this poor girl? Have they sold her to someone on Earth? And they expect me to deliver her? Holy Father, what am I to do now?*

Get your copy of Outer Rim at Amazon.com